“Bradley creates a [illegible] she weaves fascinating details of the lives of park rangers. With several plot lines involving different mysteries, *Crosshairs* will surprise readers until the very end.”

Booklist

“You absolutely have to read this! It’s an absolute can’t-put-down book, and your head will spin as you try to solve this murder mystery. I highly recommend this book!”

Interviews & Reviews

“Bradley continues her Natchez Trace Park Rangers series with a layered second-chance romance. Bradley unwraps a mystery of the past through a modern investigation that mends relationships, strengthens faith, and offers a couple a renewed chance at love. There’s much to dig in to for fans of crime fiction tinged with faith.”

Publishers Weekly

Praise for *Obsession*

“A fantastic suspense read with tension at all the right spots! Fans of Patricia Bradley will not want to miss this one.”

Write-Read-Life

“Patricia Bradley remains one of my favorite authors in the romantic suspense genre. I loved this story! I loved the characters, and I also loved the setting. This book has it all—it is full of suspense and mystery, has lots of twists and turns, and more!”

Life Is Story

“Suspense writer Patricia Bradley’s second installment of the Natchez Trace Park Rangers series weaves plot twists and thrills that her followers have come to know and love.”

Mississippi Magazine

"A skillfully written thrill ride set on the Natchez Trace in Mississippi."

Interviews & Reviews

Praise for *Standoff*

"Bradley has done it again with her unique brand of mystery and intrigue, penning another gripping tale of greed and betrayal, as well as redemption and hope. Brimming with action, romance, and page-turning thrills, *Standoff* will hook readers. What a fantastic start to a brand-new series!"

Elizabeth Goddard, award-winning author of the Uncommon Justice series

"An explosive start to a brand-new series by Patricia Bradley that suspense lovers won't want to miss. Full of family secrets, a mysterious old flame, and murder."

Lisa Harris, bestselling author of the Nikki Boyd series

"With a plot as twisting as the villain's schemes, Patricia Bradley's *Standoff* spins a tale that will keep the reader racing through the pages and wondering 'Who is the killer?' until the thrilling conclusion."

Lynn H. Blackburn, author of the Dive Team Investigations series

"My first ever Bradley book, and I very much enjoyed it! I really wish that I could give it more than 5 stars. Her style of writing is astounding! I'm a fan for life."

Interviews & Reviews

"Patricia Bradley knocks it out of the park with the first installment of her new series! Twists and turns, romance, action and suspense galore keep readers glued to the edge of their seat until the very last page."

Write-Read-Life

DECEPTION

Books by Patricia Bradley

Logan Point Series

Shadows of the Past

A Promise to Protect

Gone without a Trace

Silence in the Dark

Memphis Cold Case Novels

Justice Delayed

Justice Buried

Justice Betrayed

Justice Delivered

Natchez Trace Park Rangers

Standoff

Obsession

Crosshairs

Deception

NATCHEZ TRACE 4 PARK RANGERS

DECEPTION

PATRICIA BRADLEY

Revell
a division of Baker Publishing Group
Grand Rapids, Michigan

Published by Revell
a division of Baker Publishing Group
PO Box 6287, Grand Rapids, MI 49516-6287
www.revellbooks.com

Printed in the United States of America

Library of Congress Cataloging-in-Publication Data
Names: Bradley, Patricia, 1945- author.
Title: Deception / Patricia Bradley.
Description: Grand Rapids, MI : Revell, a division of Baker Publishing Group, [2022] | Series: Natchez Trace Park Rangers ; #4
Identifiers: LCCN 2021050613 | ISBN 9780800735760 (paperback) | ISBN 9780800741464 (casebound) | ISBN 9781493436187 (ebook)
Classification: LCC PS3602.R34275 D43 2022 | DDC 813/.6—dc23
LC record available at https://lccn.loc.gov/2021050613

This book is a work of fiction. Names, characters, places, and incidents are the product of the author's imagination or are used fictitiously. Any resemblance to actual events, locales, or persons, living or dead, is coincidental.

Baker Publishing Group publications use paper produced from sustainable forestry practices and post-consumer waste whenever possible.

22 23 24 25 26 27 28   7 6 5 4 3 2 1

In memory of my daughter, Elisa Renee Sides.
You will be in our hearts forever.
August 22, 1962–September 25, 2021

1

Today was not a good day to die. Her Sig P229 ready, National Park Service Ranger Madison Thorn pressed her sticky back against the hangar as another bullet kicked up dirt three feet away. The shooter's aim was getting better.

The Brewster County sheriff and his deputies were at least thirty minutes out. And an FBI response team based in Dallas was more than an hour away.

The hangar provided little shade from the Texas sun, and Madison backhanded sweat from her face. Sometimes being one of the elite Investigative Services Branch special agents tested her endurance—this case in particular. For the past six months, Madison had been part of the team investigating the human traffickers using Big Bend National Park for their smuggling operation.

She'd texted the FBI agent she was partnering with to meet her at the airstrip after getting a tip from a confidential informant. The human traffickers were flying in a load tonight. No word on what their cargo was.

Where are you, Chad?

After finding Chad's vehicle hidden behind an outbuilding at the entrance, Madison expected him to be at their rendezvous point, but there was no sign of him. Her stomach churned. What if the cartel had lured them both here and Chad had been captured? No. The Chad Turner she'd fallen in love with was too smart to have been captured, so where in the world was he?

Madison hadn't meant to fall in love with him, but he'd been so wounded when they met. His wife had left him, and he only saw his boy once a month. She was able to make him laugh again, and in turn he made her feel loved.

Movement in the rocks to her right caught her attention, followed by rapid gunfire. Madison zeroed in on the location, recognizing the shooter's sandy hair. Chad. He was all right. She breathed a little easier and gave him cover as he dashed from the outcropping to the hangar.

"Where have you been?" she asked.

"Scouting."

"When you weren't here, I was afraid you didn't get my message. Could you tell who the shooters were? Or see where they went?"

Chad shook his head and turned away from her. Madison slipped another clip in her Sig and studied him. His fingers tapped the side of his leg. A sure sign he was nervous.

Something was off. She glanced toward the thicket where the shots had come from. No one was firing at them now . . . Had it been him all along?

No. He loved her. In the months she'd known Chad, she'd trusted him with her life, her heart. But Chad had changed in the last two months—ever since his ex-wife left town with their four-year-old son.

"You okay?"

They'd spent enough time together for Chad to read her. Pushing aside her thoughts, she managed a wry grin. "Are you kidding? People are shooting at us. A Dr Pepper would be good about now."

"You and your Dr Peppers." His chuckle sounded forced to Madison's ears. "You've already had your one for the week."

"Desperate circumstances call for desperate measures. At this point, it can only get better." She glanced toward the thicket again. "I texted the sheriff. He's on his way."

Seconds passed.

"He's not coming."

Her breath stilled. "What do you mean?"

"Just what I said. I called him, told him it was a false alarm."

Slowly she turned toward Chad, her heart almost stopping at the sight of his service revolver leveled at her.

"I'm sorry, Madison." Regret filled his eyes.

She forced air into her lungs. This couldn't be happening.

"Why, Chad?" Even as her mind refused to process what was happening, her body reacted in defense mode, conditioned by years of martial arts training. Automatically, she tensed and shifted to the balls of her feet. "I thought we had something special."

"I don't have any choice." The regret vanished . . . or maybe had never been there, just her wishful thinking. Instead, his steel-gray eyes hardened.

She judged the distance between them. A little closer would put her in striking range with her feet. "There's always a choice."

He shook his head. "Not this time. Put your gun on the ground. The one you carry at your back, as well."

"Is it money?" She had some savings. Maybe she could offer it to him.

"They're getting Noah for me."

Madison stared at him. Chad's ex taking his son away had sent him off the rails. "What Jeannie did to you was wrong, but—"

"You don't have a clue. You never had your son moved out of your life, two thousand miles away. Now do what I said, or I'll shoot you myself."

She knelt and placed her service gun on the concrete walkway, then removed the smaller semiautomatic from her back holster.

"This isn't the answer." When Madison stood, she inched closer to him, something he didn't seem to notice. "I know you,

Chad, and there's no way you can live with yourself if you kill me."

Her heart sank when his hard eyes didn't soften. "I'll manage. At least I'll have Noah."

"You won't get away with it."

"But I will. I have it all planned out. The plane is bringing Noah and then flying us to a little fishing village where we'll disappear."

A light bulb went off. Her informant was working with the cartel, feeding her just enough information to gain her trust. "There's no shipment coming in tonight. You wanted to get me out here."

Chad laughed. "Give the lady a gold star. They've moved on from here, anyway. It was getting too dangerous to use the airfield."

He planned to kill her, probably take her body with them and dump it over the ocean, and everyone would assume the traffickers had kidnapped and killed them both.

"But why kill me?"

"I know you. After I was presumed to be dead, you would've tried to track down my 'killer.' I couldn't take the risk that you might actually find me."

How had she let herself be duped by him? "How many times did you tip them off that it was safe to bring a load in?" Had to be a lot for this kind of payoff.

"Enough to get my son."

"Are you sure they'll come through with their end of the deal? You can't help them any longer if you're hidden away in some fishing village in Mexico."

"Shut up." For the first time, doubt crossed his face. When he shifted his eyes toward the airstrip, she used the distraction to move a little closer.

Chad checked his watch. Sweat beaded his face.

"They're late. Maybe they're not coming at all." Almost within range. Her standing flying kick wasn't as good as the running one she usually practiced, but she had to work with what she had.

Madison prepared herself mentally for the maneuver, but at the same time, she had to keep him off guard. Maybe if she pushed his buttons a little harder . . .

"And Noah . . . Have you thought about what this will do to him?"

"I said to shut up." The gun wavered in his hand. "He's four—he'll get over it."

Madison's heart lurched when she heard the faint drone of an airplane. Chad jerked his head toward the runway, and Madison pivoted, jumped up, and kicked both feet into his chest.

Time slowed. He turned toward her, his eyes wide, mouth open. As she knocked him off his feet, he brought the gun around and fired. The bullet went wide and came nowhere close to her. Madison landed on her feet and scooped up her gun.

Chad fired again. The bullet whizzed close enough to her head that she felt the heat. Madison returned fire, hitting him squarely in the chest. He dropped his Glock and crumpled to the ground. She kicked the pistol away and knelt beside him, pressing two fingers against his neck. His pulse was weak and thready. He'd be lucky to make it to the hospital. Her heart hurting, she turned her attention to the small corporate-type jet that had just circled the airstrip to land. She and Chad had been partially hidden by the hangar, and she was pretty sure the pilot hadn't seen what just went down.

It didn't matter if he had. If Noah was on that plane, she had to get him safely off. A plan came to her, but if she couldn't pull it off, they both might be killed. First she called the sheriff. "I need help." She quickly explained what happened as the plane came in for the landing.

"I have a unit five miles from you," the sheriff said.

"But I thought Chad called you."

"He did, but I'd already notified the FBI response team. When I called for them to abort the mission, they informed me Chad was under investigation. The team is on its way in a helicopter."

"No! You have to stop them. Chad's son is on the plane, and they might kill him if they hear a chopper." The plane taxied to a stop. She had to get out there before they took off again. "I gotta go!"

She hung up and quickly shed the holster at her side, breathing a thanks that there hadn't been time to dress in her NPS uniform when the informant called.

Madison slid her backup gun into the holster at her back and pulled her T-shirt over it. With more bravado than she felt, she sauntered past the concrete barriers on legs that felt like overcooked noodles and tried not to think what would happen if the pilot had a photo that identified her. With the safety of the barriers behind her, she forced her legs closer to the runway.

The door near the cockpit dropped down, with steps leading into the plane. A bearded man appeared with an AK-47 in his arms.

"Chad Turner sent me to pick up his son." She was surprised at how strong her voice sounded. "Did you bring him?"

At his side, a woman appeared with a sleeping boy in her arms. Madison recognized Noah's red curls. "Who are you and where is Turner?"

"He had car trouble and sent me. I'm his new wife."

"You're lying. Turner would have let us know if he had a wife." In a smooth motion, Bearded Man swung the AK-47 around and fired.

Madison dove for the ground and rolled, barely dodging the bullets that sprayed around her. She fired, and Bearded Man pitched forward on the tarmac just before the cabin door closed. Seconds later the engines screamed to life.

They still had Noah. She had to stop them. Madison rolled over on her belly and aimed her gun at the jet's tires. Two quick shots, and the plane settled on the tarmac.

They were going nowhere.

2

MARCH, FOUR YEARS LATER

Every mile south that Madison drove on the Natchez Trace brought more dogwoods in bloom due to the early spring. Even more than had been in Jackson, Mississippi, where she'd spent most of Tuesday with the Ridgeland district law enforcement ranger and Hugh Cortland, lead for the FBI team she would be working with on this new case. They'd all been so helpful, especially the analyst, Allyson Murphy. It was a bonus to be on good terms with someone who could get information quickly.

For the past four years she had buried herself in fraud and theft cases, sifting through hard drives and recovering deleted files—anything that wasn't a violent crime. Both Madison and the Investigative Services Branch had been surprised to discover she was even better at solving white-collar crimes than she had been the other.

Madison shuddered, remembering her last violent-crime case that ended with the FBI agent she'd partnered with dead. The same agent she'd fallen in love with. At least she'd saved his little boy.

She brushed the thoughts away and concentrated on driving the lonely road. Huge trees arched their limbs across the two lanes, creating a canopy that allowed little sunlight through. She could only imagine how spooky it would be at night. No way did she ever want to drive the Trace after dark.

In the distance, Madison noted a white SUV approaching from the south. It was the first vehicle she'd met in five miles. Once it passed, she dismissed it and shifted her thoughts to the case in Natchez. It was her first in this area, and she was anxious to dig into a possible theft and kickback scheme. Not to mention spending time with her grandfather.

A minute later, she glanced in her rearview mirror, and her heart seized. Blue-and-white lights flashed in the grill of a quickly approaching white SUV, probably the one she'd just met.

Immediately she let off on the gas pedal and glanced at her speedometer. *Oh rats.* She hated getting tickets, but sixty-five on the Natchez Trace was a no-no, or so someone had said yesterday.

Madison always kept her creds in the inside pocket of her uniform jacket and felt for them before remembering she wasn't wearing it. This was an undercover assignment, and she was dressed in business casual—black pants and a white blouse. She'd stashed her ID in her bag.

Why was the park ranger checking speed at eight o'clock in the morning, anyway? Didn't he have staff meetings or something? Grudgingly she flipped her right signal light and pulled the Chevy Impala rental to the shoulder of the road. Madison found her bag and took out her credentials along with her driver's license while the ranger walked toward her vehicle.

The scowl on his face raised her defenses. For miles and miles, the road had been perfectly empty until she met him. By the time she lowered the window, Madison was ready for him, but he didn't give her a chance.

"Ma'am, I clocked you at sixty-five miles an hour." He lifted an eyebrow. "Going to a fire?"

His sarcasm wasn't lost on her, but to refer to her as ma'am? She was only thirty-five and probably the same age as he was. She swallowed the retort on her tongue. Madison had learned a long time ago that a chip on her shoulder begged for someone to knock it off. She pasted a smile on her lips.

"I can explain." She held up the wallet with her ISB credentials.

"Is that supposed to mean something? Unless you're in hot pursuit . . ." He glanced up and down the road before returning his scowl back to her. "Since I don't see any vehicles for you to pursue, that badge doesn't excuse you from breaking the law. You of all people should know that."

Heat flushed her cheeks. He was right, but Madison didn't have time for this. She glanced at the name plate over his left pocket. Clayton Bradshaw. "Officer Bradshaw, I'm afraid I'm in a bit of a hurry," she said and glanced pointedly at her smart watch.

"Then I better get to writing your ticket," he replied. "License, please."

Madison handed over her driver's license and fumed while he painstakingly wrote out the ticket. Clayton Bradshaw. No . . . it couldn't be the same Clayton Bradshaw who hung out with her cousins when she came to visit her grandfather in the summers. The same one who'd bullied her along with her cousins every summer? Never would have figured him to become a cop. Madison eyed him again, noting his square jaw and fit body. He'd certainly grown into a fine specimen of a man.

The heat in her face intensified. Had she really thought that? But nothing else about him had changed—she imagined he took great delight in pulling people over and handing out tickets.

Evidently, he hadn't recognized her or her name, and she wasn't going to remind him. Why was the speed limit only fifty miles an hour anyway? She'd met so few cars they weren't worth counting. And now she was going to be late. Madison closed her ears to the little voice that reminded her she'd been breaking the law, something she wouldn't have been doing if she'd left Jackson a little earlier.

When he finished, he looked up with a smile that was even

more forced than hers. He handed her the license, along with the ticket. “What are you doing in Natchez?”

She stuffed her license and the ticket in her bag. Since it wasn’t known how far the possible corruption had spread, Madison and the two agents she had met with yesterday decided that only people with a need to know would be informed about her assignment. And Clayton Bradshaw wasn’t one of them. Madison went with her cover story. “Visiting my grandfather.”

“I hope you have a nice visit. Just keep your speed down.” He started to walk away, then turned back. “There’s a reason the speed limit is only fifty.”

“And I’m sure you’re going to tell me.”

The grim smile didn’t falter. “I am. The Trace is narrow and winding, and cyclists use it all the time, which you’ll discover in about two miles.”

“What do you mean?” A thought niggled in the back of her mind.

“There are ten bicycle riders up ahead and several curves. At your speed, you would have been on them before you realized it. Someone could have died.”

Blood drained from her face, leaving her lightheaded. Too late, she remembered that Hugh Cortland, the FBI agent she was meeting in Natchez, had warned her about the bicyclists if she drove the Trace.

He’d even advised her to take Highway 61, a route she’d had no intention of taking. The last time Madison had been on the River Road, it had been two lanes that went through the heart of every town between Memphis and Natchez. She ought to know—it’d been the route her type-A father had driven every summer when she was a kid for her yearly month-long visit with her grandfather. All the little towns must have driven Gregory Thorn crazy.

What if I’d killed one of the cyclists?

“I, ah . . .” She swallowed down the nausea coming up into her throat. “I’m sorry. It won’t happen again.”

"No problem." His face suddenly softened, and he tipped his flat hat. "I hope you make your meeting on time."

She sucked in a fortifying breath of air and managed a true smile this time. "Thank you. For everything."

"Yes, ma'am." He saluted her before he turned and walked to his SUV.

There was that *ma'am* again, but this time it didn't hold censure. After checking to make sure there were no approaching cars, Madison pulled out onto the Trace again and this time kept her speed at fifty. Sure enough, a few miles down the road, the cyclists Clayton had mentioned pedaled two-by-two in the southbound lane.

With a northbound car speeding toward them, Madison decelerated and then flashed her lights, hoping to slow the motorist down. The universal signal that a cop was in the area did the trick, and the motorist slowed. Once it passed, she pulled around the cyclists, feeling she'd done her good deed for the day. And tonight she would send Clayton a note of apology for her rudeness.

3

The rich smell of freshly ground coffee beans wrapped around Clayton as he pocketed his change from the barista. "Thanks, Chrissy," he said and accepted the cup of freshly brewed Kona she held out.

"Your croissant should be ready in five," she said. "And your table is available."

Ignoring her grin, he nodded and checked out the back wall. Yep, the table was empty, and he strode to it. All the employees knew about his habit of sitting where he could see who came into the café. Clayton set the cup on the table and flipped off the lid. He hated drinking coffee through a lid.

After settling in the chair, he sipped the hot liquid, glad he'd made the time for a stop off. Coffee and More made the best coffee in town—almost as good as the diner the coffee shop had replaced. Clayton still missed the home cooking that had been served up in the building.

True to her word, in five minutes, Chrissy brought his croissant. *Whoa.* He'd forgotten how big the breakfast croissant was—bacon, cheese, avocado, and eggs. But since it was already after ten, it should hold him over until tonight when he had dinner with his sister and six-year-old niece.

As the southern district supervisor on the Natchez Trace, he rarely worked patrol, but it'd been a productive morning, changing a flat tire for an older woman and giving two warning tickets—one for a driver doing sixty on the posted fifty-mile-an-hour Trace and Madison Thorn's. He cut the croissant in half, thinking of the pretty ISB special agent. At first he'd thought she was full of herself, but once she learned of the cyclists, her attitude completely changed. And that parting smile she'd given him. It was still wowing him, and since she was going to be in Natchez a while, maybe he'd see her again.

Clayton hadn't bought her reason for being in Natchez, so he called his district supervisor, but he was unavailable. Since ISB agents often worked with the FBI, he'd called his friend in the Jackson office. Hugh Cortland confirmed he and Madison were working a case for the National Park Service, but hadn't offered any details. It kind of stung that Clayton hadn't been informed. He handled everything from traffic violations to murder investigations.

He sipped his coffee. Why did Madison Thorn's name ring a bell? Clayton didn't recall ever meeting her, something he definitely would have remembered.

It wasn't like him to give someone driving sixty-five on the Trace a warning, and he hoped she was pleasantly surprised when she finally looked at the ticket. He took a bite of the croissant as the door opened and Judge William Anderson entered the coffee shop.

The judge scanned the room, briefly nodding when his gaze landed on Clayton, then he took a seat that was almost out of Clayton's line of sight. He checked his watch. Too early for a break in court; then he remembered court wasn't in session this week.

Growing up, Clayton had been friends with the judge's grandsons, who'd long since left the area. This was years before Anderson's judicial appointment. The image of a girl with blond pigtails a couple of years younger than the boys popped into his mind. The judge's granddaughter. Back then she'd visited every summer, but he couldn't recall her name. Spunky little thing. He did remember the grandsons picking on her until he'd made them stop, at least when Clayton was around. A memory tried to surface . . . something about the girl taking martial arts training.

Another customer entered the coffee shop, a woman probably in her fifties. Clayton had never seen her before and probably wouldn't have paid her any attention, except she held herself erect, like someone in the service. He judged her to be half a foot shorter than he was, so about five six. Then she purposefully strode to the judge's table and sat opposite him without waiting for an invitation. Even though dressed casually in jeans and a pullover, she was definitely military of some sort.

Clayton shifted his attention back to his food and took his time finishing breakfast. Jesse Ritter, his new field ranger, had a dental appointment but was now patrolling the Trace, and Clayton intended to take advantage of a chance to relax after spending a month of supervisory training the freshly minted ranger.

He placed his fork and knife on the now-empty plate and glanced once again at the judge's table, where the woman now leaned toward him, her palms open, like she was imploring the judge. Clayton could barely see the judge as he shook his head. The woman, who was young enough to be his daughter, sat back, her face almost stonelike. Suddenly, she stood and said something. The judge held out his hands in an it's-out-of-my-hands motion. The woman stared at him briefly, then said something else, loud enough for Clayton to hear this time. "You'll have to live with the decisions you've made."

As the woman marched to the door, Clayton felt like there was something familiar about her. Short-cropped brown hair, heart-shaped face. But no one in particular came to mind. He stood and put two dollars down for Chrissy before ambling over to Judge Anderson's table.

"Morning, sir," he said.

"Clayton." He acknowledged him with a nod and set his cup

down. Clayton had never noticed the judge was left-handed. "How are you?"

They exchanged pleasantries, then Clayton asked about his grandsons. "Do you hear much from Buddy and Joe?"

"Not often," the judge replied. "I think they're too busy for me."

"They don't know what they're missing." He wished his grandfather were still alive. Clayton felt a presence at his elbow and turned, recognizing the older woman who waited expectantly. "Sorry, Mrs. Winslow, I didn't mean to block your way."

Judith Winslow barely came to his chest. Her wispy hair forming a silver halo around her head was the only indication she was in her sixties.

The administrator of the local orphanage stared at him with a can't-quite-place-you look in her eyes.

"Clayton Bradshaw," he said, helping her out. "My mother volunteers at Bright Horizons."

Recognition lit Judith's eyes. "Ramona. She is such a blessing. How is that precious granddaughter of hers? Ava, I believe?"

"Ava's good. I'm having dinner with her and my sister tonight."

"Such a pity about the birthmark on her face."

"Yes, ma'am." Ava was a beautiful child, inside and out, and it broke his heart that the first thing anyone thought about was the port wine stain on her cheek.

"I'll tell your mother I saw you."

He grinned and turned to the judge. The look in his eyes as he stared at Judith stopped Clayton cold. He'd seen the same expression in one of the unbroken horses he'd worked with in his college days when they put a saddle on his back. Wariness. Just as suddenly as the look had been there, it disappeared, and the judge shifted his gaze to Clayton.

"Good to see you again, son."

"Same here."

Anderson extended his hand, and Clayton shook it, then walked away. At the door, he glanced back at the table. Judith was seated in the same chair as the judge's previous visitor, and the older man was emphatically shaking his head to something Judith had said. Clayton didn't know what was going on, but Judge William Anderson was not happy to see Judith Winslow.

William Anderson glanced away from Judith, his face schooled not to reveal the turmoil raging through him. He'd sown the wind and now the whirlwind had come to collect.

She stood. "I didn't put my order in. Be right back."

He started to tell her not to bother, that he didn't have time for her today, but for someone in her sixties, she moved very fast and was out of hearing range before he got the words out.

William stared at the chair she'd vacated. It'd been in this very room thirty-five years ago when he signed a pact with the devil . . .

"All right. You'll get the $50,000 at the exchange," he'd said to her. "And not a second before."

"Didn't expect anything else." Judith Winslow smoothed her skirt and leaned forward in the chair. "And you'll never hear from me again."

"I have your word on that?" Like her word was worth anything. When she nodded, he said, "All right. It's a deal."

"Good." Then without skipping a beat, she said, "Now for my brokerage fee. I believe $10,000 today will do it."

"Brokerage—" He snapped his jaw shut on the rest of his response and took a deep breath. "Taken out of the $50,000, I presume."

She shook her head. "The fifty grand is for the . . . package. The ten is my fee. For brokering the deal."

His fingers itched to slap the smile off her face. "What assurance do I have you'll give the fifty to—"

"You disappoint me if you think I would cheat someone out of what was rightfully theirs."

His stomach roiled as he took his checkbook from his coat. "Do you have a pen?" He wasn't about to use his favorite Montblanc. She handed him a cheap ballpoint, and he scribbled out the check. "Do me a favor and don't cash it here in Natchez."

"I'm not that stupid."

He wasn't too sure about that, but it was always better to let the adversary think they'd won.

While Judith Winslow had discovered his weakness and cashed in on it, she'd greatly underestimated how much he would've paid to save his daughter. He just hoped this did it.

"I never want to see you again." His parting words.

"Don't worry. Just make sure you sign both documents," she'd said, pocketing the check. Then she'd stood and walked out of the diner.

He should have worried—that one transaction had allowed Judith Winslow to get her hooks into him. Ever since that fateful day, he'd had to deal with her over and over. He just hadn't expected to have to deal with her today. Not with Madison coming to stay with him.

Judith sat opposite him and took a long sip of coffee. "What did my daughter want?" She'd dropped the soft tone she'd used when Clayton was at the table.

"You saw her?"

"What did she want?"

"She wanted me to introduce her to Madison."

"You told her no, of course."

He nodded curtly. "I did."

Even though his own daughter could no longer be hurt by what he'd done, like his daughter, Madison knew nothing about the details of her adoption. She was all he cared about now, and he did not want to see her life turned upside down.

"Good." She took a file from her oversized purse and opened it. After shuffling through the papers, she drew a sheet out. "I need a signature."

He took a deep breath. "No. I'm done."

She shook her head. "You're not done until *I* say you're done."

Judith laid the paper on the table and shoved it toward him as she stood. "Take it to your pal, Judge Billings. Let him know there'll be a sizable donation to his reelection campaign once he approves the adoption."

He pushed the paper back to her side of the table. "I can't do it any longer."

"How can you walk away? Think about all the good we've done. God gave us this opportunity to give children a better life."

The woman actually believed she was doing God's work. He shook his head.

"William, do you know how many children have had a decent chance at life because of what we've done?" she asked, passion cracking her voice. "If they'd been left in the squalid conditions they were born into, they would never have lived up to their potential."

"You don't—"

"Give me a break. Do you think Jonathan Rivers would be in London as a Rhodes scholar if I hadn't arranged for his adoption? A sixteen-year-old mother could not have given him the kind of life he's experiencing because of me."

"But—"

"Where would your own granddaughter be? Certainly not an elite law enforcement ranger."

"Don't you ever wonder—"

"No. God always showed me the special children, the ones who needed to be given to special parents."

Special children were those with birth mothers who could be guilted into giving up their babies to special parents who could afford to pay Judith's asking price. If she thought God approved her thievery . . . The coffee in his stomach soured.

The furrow between her brows deepened and her lips compressed in a tight circle. "Do you regret denying an appeal that kept a man in prison so he'd get 'rehabilitation'?"

A slow burn started through his chest. How dare she compare what he did to her thievery.

"Don't give me that sanctimonious, holier-than-thou stare. It all started with you."

Her words were like a knife slicing his heart. He'd been trying to save his daughter from spiraling into the depths of depression. And he had. For a while.

"I am sorry about Sharon . . . her suicide," Judith said, touching his arm.

Anderson flinched, barely able to stand the woman's fingers on his skin. By sheer willpower, he masked the anger that consumed him. A mother who cared nothing for her own granddaughter certainly had no feelings for his daughter.

"She did not commit suicide."

Judith frowned. "But the paper said—"

"I know what the paper said." Somehow a reporter in Natchez had gotten the autopsy results, and the newspaper had broken its usual code of silence regarding the cause of death. The judge had yet to accept it. For all he knew, the worthless womanizer Sharon had married could have killed her.

Gregory Thorn had certainly contributed to her death. Thank God the judge hadn't shown her the report from the private investigator he'd hired to follow Gregory. He probably shouldn't have threatened to expose his son-in-law to his company at the funeral, though. With their strict morals clause, Gregory would've been gone in an instant.

Revenge wasn't like him at all, but his daughter was dead, and he wanted someone to pay.

He raised his gaze and pointed to the paper she wanted him

to get his colleague to sign. "No more. Not today, not tomorrow, not ever again."

"Think about it. And think about what you have to lose if you don't." She stood and walked away.

When he was alone again, the judge slumped in his chair. Madison. Judith would use his granddaughter for leverage.

He had to tell Madison the truth, make her understand. He couldn't wait one more day. Something could happen to him, and the papers in his safe-deposit box would tell the harsh truth without him there to explain that he'd done it all to save his daughter.

Just thinking about what he had to confess made him sick.

5

At 10:05, Madison pulled into the parking lot at 314 State Street. Just before she reached Mount Locust on the Trace, she'd received a text from FBI agent Hugh Cortland that their meeting had been pushed back to ten. With an hour to kill, she'd stopped off at the historic site and lost track of time. Now she was once again late, but as she scanned the parking lot, she didn't see Hugh's car.

Madison stared at the old Victorian structure and then read the sign. Adams County Historic 1891 Jail. Below that was another sign. Adams County Administration and Board of Supervisors Building.

Good for you, Natchez. Instead of tearing down the historical building, they'd repurposed it. She'd seen more than one of these types of buildings destroyed in the name of progress.

Hugh had chosen the county supervisor's office to discuss the investigation because it was larger, and they would draw less attention than at the National Park Service maintenance building.

Madison looked around as another dark sedan pulled into the parking lot. Cortland. She climbed out, then reached for her bag, and the ticket the ranger had issued fell out. Tempted to let it lay on the floor, she almost shut the door, but the neat freak in her wouldn't allow it. With a sigh, she retrieved the ticket, glancing at it before stuffing it back in the bag. "Well, I'll be . . ."

She closed the car door and turned to Hugh. "Good morning," she said, envying the Styrofoam cup he grabbed after he stepped out of his car. Like her, he wore business casual—khaki pants and a blue shirt with no tie.

"Happy Hump Day," he said, handing her the coffee. Swallowing her surprise, she took it, and he reached back inside his car for another cup. "Thought you might need it after I heard you had a detainment on the Trace."

Heat infused her face as she imagined the laugh the agent and Clayton Bradshaw probably had at her expense, and almost handed the coffee back to him. Except she needed the caffeine desperately. "So the ranger called you and tattled?"

"Not exactly. He wanted to know what an ISB agent was doing in Natchez, and I told him we were working together on a case," Hugh said. "Don't get your hackles up about the ticket, although I think I did warn you about the Trace."

"You did, and I should have listened." She took a sip of the coffee and regrouped. "Truth be known, if he hadn't stopped me, I might've plowed right into a group of cyclists. I can't believe he only issued me a warning."

His eyes widened briefly before he nodded approval. "He's a good guy, and now you know if you drive the Trace, keep your speed limit to about fifty-five—rangers rarely bother anyone going five over. Any faster and I doubt he'd give you grace again."

"Believe me, it'll be right on the speed limit." She took another sip of the coffee. "Do you know this Paul Davidson? Or Deon Cox?"

"I know Paul, and he's a straight shooter."

Hugh's words confirmed what Madison had discovered in her research on the county supervisor. "How about Cox?"

"Never met Deon, but when I talked with Paul, he spoke highly of him."

Cox, who was the National Park Service maintenance supervisor for the southern district, had been the one who made the initial contact with the Ridgeland district supervisor for the Natchez Trace last Wednesday. Cox reported a theft ring that involved both the National Park Service and Adams County employees.

The maintenance division was based at Rocky Springs on the Natchez Trace, and normally the district ranger would handle the case, but because of Madison's expertise in white-collar crimes, Evan McCall had called the Investigative Services Branch and asked for her to be assigned to the case instead of Clayton Bradshaw.

She nodded toward the supervisor's office. "You ready to become an insurance salesman?"

That was their cover to anyone who was interested. When Hugh nodded, she turned and climbed the six steps to the gray-painted porch. Inside the building, a lemony scent mixed with the musty odor of an old building met her. It looked as though whoever renovated the old building used much of the original material and tried to keep the character of the Victorian building intact.

"I'd love to tour this place," she murmured.

"Maybe you can before the case is over," Hugh said. "The trapdoor where they hanged criminals is still in place."

Madison shuddered. That, she didn't want to see. When they entered the supervisor offices, a woman in her late thirties looked up from her computer, and the plastic smile forming on her lips froze.

"We're here to see Paul Davidson," Madison said when the secretary remained silent. She glanced at the name plate on the woman's desk. Vivian Hawkins, administrative assistant. Where had she heard that name?

"Is he in?" Hugh asked.

The assistant's perfectly shaped eyebrows lowered briefly, then she shook her head. Madison was beginning to wonder if the woman talked at all. "You're sure?" he asked.

Vivian Hawkins thinned her lips. "I'm very sure."

She *could* talk, but her tone made Madison want to hold her hands up and say *whoa*. Instead, she tried again. "It's just that we had an appointment with Mr. Davidson at ten to discuss insurance."

"You were supposed to be here at nine. He probably assumed you weren't coming."

Madison had no intention of explaining herself to the woman, but Hugh cleared his throat. "The meeting time was changed."

"Mr. Davidson didn't alert me to that fact."

Before either of them could ask when he would return, the door opened, and a lanky blond-haired man wrestled a rolling cart loaded with a carafe and mugs through the doorway. Madison recognized Davidson from a campaign photo she'd found on the internet.

"Sorry I wasn't here to meet you. Somehow I thought it'd be a simple matter to make a pot of coffee for our meeting." He towered over the cart as he straightened. "I never bargained on this cantankerous thing."

Vivian Hawkins sprang to her feet. "I could have done that . . . Let me help you."

Davidson waved his secretary off. "I have it."

Then he turned to the FBI agent and extended his hand. "Good to see you again, Hugh." After the two men shook hands, he turned Madison's way. "You must be Ms. Thorn."

"Yes, sir," she said, accepting the hand he held out. "Feel free to call me Madison."

"Will do. Come on into my office, and we'll get down to business." He turned to Ms. Hawkins and gave her a warm smile. "Hold my calls, Vivian, and thank you for offering to help."

"Anytime, Paul . . . I mean, Mr. Davidson," she said, her voice soft. Like flipping a switch, Vivian Hawkins's striking face had transformed from guard dog to Southern belle, a feat Madison had never managed. "Do you have everything you need for coffee?"

The woman practically purred. Madison kept a poker face as Davidson asked if either of them wanted cream and sugar. "Black," Madison said and Hugh echoed her choice.

"Then we're good." Davidson pushed the cart into his office.

She followed Hugh into the room. Once they were seated across from the Adams County supervisor, he poured coffee and handed each of them a mug. "Deon will be here shortly."

For a few minutes the supervisor and Hugh talked about March Madness and which team would win the college basketball championship. Then the FBI agent included Madison in the conversation. "Did you ever see Paul play pro football?"

"No, but I think I recall seeing him play for the University of Kentucky," she said. Madison had always preferred college games over pro.

"Those were fun times." Davidson stood when three raps sounded at the side door. "That should be Deon."

He opened the door, and a wiry man a couple of inches taller than Madison's five six entered the room. He quickly removed his green park service cap and ran his hand over his close-cropped hair. "Sorry I'm late, but we had trouble with one of the machines this morning."

After the introductions were made, the soft-spoken maintenance supervisor grabbed a cup of coffee and took a chair. "You always have good coffee," he said, turning to Paul. "Appreciate you letting us meet here. Wouldn't be any way to get you three into my office at maintenance headquarters without someone wanting to know why you were there."

Paul nodded. "Although I've found Vivian to be very close-mouthed, I still told her that Hugh and Madison are here to pitch a new county insurance proposal. Shall we get down to business?"

Hugh nodded for Madison to take lead, and she took out a notebook. Some agents used a tablet, but she liked being able to write all over the page. She turned to the park service worker first. "On the phone, you mentioned equipment was missing."

Deon nodded. "Just last month we lost three commercial string trimmers and three power saws. Two of the power saws had never been cranked."

She turned to Paul. "And you?"

"Basically the same thing, but we have different types of equipment missing, and we may be dealing with kickbacks."

"Kickbacks?" Hugh uncrossed his legs and leaned forward.

Paul nodded. "I campaigned on transparency, so no vendor has approached me directly. However, I happened to be at the yard when a vendor brought in a load of bridge lumber. The invoice didn't match the board footage on the load. When I figured it up, a quarter of the lumber was missing, but 100 percent had been billed for. I figure the vendor slipped someone part of that 25 percent in cash."

"Any idea who?"

The two supervisors exchanged glances. Deon spoke first. "That's just it. We haven't caught anyone actually stealing—the equipment just goes missing. I think the kickbacks involve someone higher up, but we both feel they are part of the theft ring."

"Our records show a purchase order, the company that ordered, and the amount delivered, whether it's equipment, lumber, or gravel," Paul said.

"Gravel?" Madison raised her eyebrows.

"That's the easiest item to steal," Deon said. "It's easy enough to short a load or put down two loads of rock or gravel when only one was delivered."

"And when I questioned the guy at the yard about the lumber discrepancy," Paul said, "he indicated he'd questioned a supervisor once and was told the question was above his pay grade."

Madison raised her eyebrows. "In other words, don't ask questions."

Both men bobbed their heads.

"Did he say who the supervisor was?"

Another nod. "The one I just replaced."

Paul Davidson had only recently won a special election after George Spencer, the supervisor from the fifth district, died in an automobile accident after his brakes failed.

"So far no one has proven George's brake line was loosened, but I'm being extra careful before I accuse someone of accepting kickbacks or stealing," Paul said somberly. "And you better do the same in your investigation."

Hugh carried the files out to Madison's Impala and stored them in her trunk. "Want to grab a bite to eat?"

"No, thanks. I want to unload my things at my grandfather's house and get started on these files."

"I understand. What do you think about the case?"

"I think it'll be easy enough to see if the requisitions and invoices match up. I assume you'll dig into who's stealing the equipment."

"Sounds good. I'll check in with you later today." Hugh climbed into his car.

Madison's cell phone rang just as he drove away. She didn't recognize the Texas number and almost let it go to voicemail. At the last second, she slid the button. "Madison Thorn."

"Madison. I'm glad you answered. I didn't want to leave a message."

The voice was familiar . . . and created dread in her stomach. She opened her car door and slid across the seat. "Who is this?"

"I'm sorry. Steven Turner."

Chad's brother. She gripped the phone tighter. No wonder he sounded familiar—his voice was very similar to Chad's. "How did you get my number?"

"It was in Chad's phone."

She should have changed her number after what happened in

Texas. Madison had only met the former Delta Force operator once—at the hospital the night Chad died. Why would he be calling her?

Almost like he read her mind, he said, "Please, don't hang up. I need to talk to you."

"About?" Like she had to ask. The only thing they had in common was his brother, who died from the bullet she'd fired.

"My dad has cancer, and he's asked me to talk to you."

She hadn't been expecting that. "I don't understand." His silence stretched from a few seconds to almost thirty. "Are you there?"

"Yeah . . . this is harder than I thought it'd be," he said, his voice tense.

"What do you mean?"

"My brother tried to kill you, and I'm not sure how to ask you to meet with me and listen to what I have to say."

Meet with him? Every nerve in her body screamed no. Yet, something held her back. "I haven't hung up yet." When he hesitated again, she added, "Maybe you could tell me over the phone."

"No, I need to talk to you face-to-face. Could you meet me for lunch? I'm here—in Natchez. I'd like to personally thank you for saving Noah, if you'll give me the chance."

He was in Natchez? And he wanted to thank her? That was the last thing she expected. "How did you know where I am?"

"Your location shows up on Chad's phone. It showed you were in Jackson yesterday and I booked a flight out of Dallas with the intention of calling once I got to Jackson to see if you'd go to dinner, but my flight was delayed, and it was after nine when I arrived. Have you had lunch yet?"

"No, I planned to grab a burger at one of the fast-food places."

"I understand the hamburgers at the Camp Restaurant are excellent."

Madison hadn't eaten at the restaurant located in the Natchez-

Under-the-Hill district, but several of the people she met yesterday recommended it. Steven had aroused her curiosity. She didn't believe for a minute he'd gone to all this trouble to track her down just to thank her for his dad, and the restaurant would be a very public place to meet with him. "All right. I'll meet you there. What time?"

"How about now?"

She might as well since she probably wouldn't get much work done until she satisfied her curiosity. When they finished, she could go to her grandfather's house and work. "See you in ten minutes."

Madison stuck her phone in the cupholder and drove the short distance to the restaurant and parked on the side of Silver Street. When she gave her name, the hostess took her upstairs to a table by the windows. Steven stood when she approached.

"Thanks for coming," he said and pulled out her chair.

From where she sat, Madison had a great view of the Mississippi River and the *American Queen* steamboat docked at the bottom of the hill.

"I thought about a place on the deck, but it might get a little chilly with the wind off the river."

"This is perfect." The room was over half full. Plenty of witnesses if he had something besides an apology in mind. She gave her drink order to the server, and when they were alone again, Madison took a breath and studied him. He looked a lot like Chad—same light brown hair, same gray eyes, same dimple in his right cheek when he talked. But there were some differences. Steven was heavier and more muscular. Judging by the size of his chest and arms, he worked out.

"You said your dad has cancer. How is he?" She'd met Robert Turner several times, and his gruff manner had always made her uneasy. And while she'd shot Chad in self-defense, Madison imagined it would be a hard thing for the man to get past.

"It's pancreatic cancer, and while they've made great strides in treating the disease when it's caught early, his was diagnosed at stage 4."

"I'm so sorry."

"Thanks."

They both fell silent as the server brought her tea and took their orders of hamburgers and fries.

When they were alone again, he tilted his head. "How are you?"

She lifted her shoulders in a noncommittal shrug. "Good." His arched eyebrow challenged her. "Really," she said, and his features softened.

"I'm glad. I worried when I learned you'd moved out of violent crimes since you were so good at it."

Madison traced a finger down the condensation on her glass. "How did you know I moved?"

"One of the FBI agents in Chad's office told me."

"I see. I suppose he was bragging about how they'd run me off."

"It wasn't like that. He thought it was a shame the way some of the men refused to work with you."

Any park ranger or ISB agent assigned to the vast Big Bend area of Texas needed the FBI's collaboration, and the men in Chad's office made it plain they wanted nothing to do with her. "I needed a change of scenery. And I like white-collar crimes. Most of the time no one dies."

"I'm sorry I brought it up. Could we start over?"

"I don't know." She cocked her head. "Why are you reaching out to me now?"

"Dad. He wanted to make sure you knew how much he appreciated you risking your life to save Noah."

"Really? I got the impression he never liked me."

"Unfortunately, that's my father. Until people get to know him, they perceive him as a little bit arrogant." He reached into his shirt pocket and pulled out photos and handed them to her. "But he sent you these."

Noah had lost his mom and dad within a day of each other. His mother when the men Chad hired to kidnap the boy killed her, and his dad to Madison's bullet. She flipped through photos of the boy riding a horse, swimming, playing with his friends, and saw no signs of trauma in the now eight-year-old boy's face or eyes.

"How much does he remember?"

"None of it, thank goodness—he's adjusted really well. My sister adopted him, and they live just outside of Dallas in a small house next door to Mom and Dad. Noah gets ongoing counseling, and so far, he seems okay."

"Good." There hadn't been many days that she hadn't thought about the boy she'd rescued, and she was relieved to know that he appeared to be whole. She slid the photos across the table to him. "Thank you for showing those to me."

He slid them back in front of her. "Dad thought you might like to have them."

"Thanks." She must have misjudged the elder Turner, and the gesture touched her. Madison tucked them into the side pocket of her bag. The waitress approached and set their burgers and fries in front of them. "This looks good."

He picked up one of the crispy fries and bit into it. "The fries at least are as good as they look."

She followed suit and agreed with him. Both fell silent as they sampled the food. The burgers were as tasty as the fries.

When Steven polished off the last of his burger, he sat back in his chair. "How long do you expect to be in Natchez?"

"However long it takes for the case I'm working on."

He laughed. "Spoken like a true agent, whether FBI or ISB."

She couldn't keep from smiling at his remark. "It won't be all business, and it'll be a chance to spend time with my grandfather since I'll be staying with him."

"Judge Anderson."

She tensed. How did he know who her grandfather was? Her

shoulders relaxed. Chad, probably. She'd talked about the judge to him. "And you? I don't expect you came all the way from Texas just to see me."

"I have friends in Natchez, so like you, I'll combine this with getting together with them. Terri, an old Delta Force buddy, is driving up from the coast and should arrive sometime this afternoon. We haven't seen each other in a long time. We're having breakfast tomorrow."

"You never hear much about women being in Delta Force."

"I know, even though they've been in since the nineties when they were recruited to engage the female population in Afghanistan. She's G squadron instead of a regular D operator, and we served on several missions together. I wish you two could meet."

"Who knows, maybe we will." The woman sounded interesting.

"Like me, she's retired," he said. "Lives near the Alabama line on the coast. I offered to drive down, but she had business in Natchez to see about." He picked up the dessert menu. "Want anything?"

Madison held up her hand. "I'm full. So what have you been doing since you left the army?"

"Right now I'm taking care of Dad. Trying to put things in order for him."

"And I'm one of those things."

His face turned somber. "Yes, you are."

Darkness was falling as soft murmurs of conversation filled the Mediterranean restaurant in downtown Natchez. Dani Parker set her fork down. A tingly sensation spread down the back of her neck. Nonchalantly, she blotted her lips with the linen napkin and lifted her gaze.

Across from her, the teenager with five stainless-steel studs in each ear and John 3:16 tattooed on her wrist laid her fork on the table as well. "You feel it too," the girl said, looking around.

Dani barely nodded. She'd purposely chosen a corner table at the Guest House Restaurant, a habit of hers so she could keep the entire room in view. It'd been especially important tonight since she was delivering Briana Reed, or Bri as she preferred to be called, to a safe house in Jackson.

"Do you see anyone you recognize?"

Bri scanned the room as though she were looking for the waitress, then shook her head before she picked up her fork again and dove into her dessert. "I doubt anyone I know would be having dinner at a place like this," she said between bites.

Dani continued to survey the room. Two men sat to her left, both watching a basketball game on the screen. Past them, a man she assumed to be a father focused on his daughter's animated dialogue while the mother picked up her purse and stood. Earlier,

Dani had looked his way and caught him staring at her, but not in a way that would give her this eerie feeling. Three tables over, a lone woman sat engrossed in a book. Evidently feeling Dani's gaze, she looked up and frowned.

Dani smiled and received a cold stare back. Dismissing the woman, she studied the other people sitting at tables in the restaurant. Another lone woman, older than the book reader, a family with two kids, two men engrossed in conversation . . . None of them seemed to be paying attention to her and Bri. Maybe she'd been wrong and it was simply her anxiety playing tricks on her. When Bri finished her last bite of chocolate pie, Dani attempted to get the waitress's eye. "Be right back," she said to the girl and caught the waitress before she left the room.

"Could we take care of my bill?" she asked, taking her credit card from her bag. "I need to get on the road."

"It's been taken care of," the waitress said with a smile.

"What do you mean?" Anxiety raced through her body.

"That gentleman just leaving—he said you'd understand."

She jerked her head toward the door as the girl and her mother walked out into the courtyard. The man made eye contact with Dani and winked before he turned and joined his family.

Dani had never seen the man before in her life. Could it have been meant for Briana . . . ? No, he'd winked at *her*, and told the waitress she'd understand. It was like he knew her, but she'd never been to Natchez before. Uneasiness slid down her spine.

Maybe it was simply a random act of kindness. She'd read about that lately, where someone pays for another person's meal. But that usually happened in a drive-thru. Perhaps she could catch them before they got out of sight. She stuffed her wallet in her bag and hurried back to the teenager. "Do you need to stop by the restroom before we leave?"

"I'm good," she replied. "But that was quick."

"Evidently the man with his wife and little girl paid for us."

"You're kidding." Bri gave her a sidelong glance. "People don't do that . . . unless they want something in return, and isn't he, like, married?"

It broke her heart that circumstances had made Bri so cynical. Dani buried her own suspicions. "Maybe it was the wife's idea. Besides, there are some good people in the world," she said softly and hoped this was one of those times.

By the time they reached the street, the family had disappeared into the March night. She pulled her jacket close against the cold west wind as they hurried to where she'd parked her Honda Civic. She wished she could have at least thanked them. Another instance of being too late.

Dani had been disappointed when she'd called the Natchez Trace district supervisor's office in Jackson earlier in the day and learned Madison Thorn had left Jackson. The person she talked to wouldn't give any details of where she'd gone. Maybe if she dropped by the district office in the morning and talked to the supervisor in person, he would help her connect with Madison.

Bri buckled her seat belt. "How long 'til we get to Jackson?"

"A couple of hours. Should be there by nine." She'd meant to make Jackson before dark, but it had taken longer to connect with the organization that rescued Briana than Dani counted on. Beside her, the teenager sighed.

"Nervous?" Dani asked. The girl answered with a shrug. Until now, Bri hadn't exhibited any sign of anxiety.

"A little. It's always hard going into a new situation."

"You'll do fine." Dani navigated the one-way streets out of downtown Natchez. She'd been pleased at how well the two of them had connected the last two hours of the three-hour drive from New Orleans. That first hour, it'd been like pulling teeth to get the girl to talk.

But once Bri realized Dani didn't look down on her for the life she'd been forced to live on the streets, the girl opened up. Dani learned that even though she looked much younger, Bri was twenty-one and a new Christian. Wings of Hope in Jackson would be the perfect place for her to grow in her walk. "If there's anything I've learned about you since we left New Orleans, it's that you're a survivor. You haven't let what you've been through destroy you."

Bri sat a little straighter. "Thanks. Sometimes I just want to crawl into a cave and stay there. But then I realize if I did, they'd win."

"Good for you." The social worker in New Orleans had told Dani that the organization was working on getting Bri's record for prostitution expunged since she'd been forced into it.

Dani ignored the GPS that directed her to Devereux Drive and instead took a right at Forks of the Road, weaving around to Liberty Road and the entrance to the Natchez Trace. She'd looked at the map, and it was a straighter shot to Jackson than Highway 61 or I-55 with a lot less traffic.

They hadn't traveled far on the Trace when Bri groaned.

"What's the matter?"

"All that tea I drank—I should've gone to the restroom like you said. Do you think there's someplace on this road we can stop?"

"I'm sure there is." Bri wasn't alone in her request. Dani had been so taken aback by the man paying their bill, she'd ignored her main rule for traveling—always visit the restroom before hitting the road. "Use my phone and see if you can find a map of the Natchez Trace."

A few minutes later, the teen sighed. "There's no service of any kind."

"Guess we'll have to keep driving. Keep checking to see if we get service."

She edged past the posted fifty-mile-an-hour speed limit until she noticed headlights in her rearview mirror and eased off the gas pedal in case the person behind them was a park ranger. No need to risk getting a ticket. Ten minutes later, they passed a sign announcing Mount Locust in one mile. "Maybe there's a restroom there."

At the historical site, Dani pulled off the road, but a gate blocked their way and she backed out.

"Wait!" Bri said. "I have a signal. Give me a second." Her fingers flew over the phone. "Oh, good. There appears to be something at Coles Creek. Looks like it's a couple of miles."

"Let's hope there's no gate there."

Just down the road, a sign indicated Coles Creek was a mile ahead on the left. A lone light shone outside the small brick building when they pulled into the parking lot.

The girl shivered. "Looks spooky."

Dani agreed with her. "We can keep driving—maybe find a town nearby."

Bri shrugged. "We're here. Might as well make the most of it."

Dani took the phone Bri handed her and dropped it in her purse, then she grabbed her keys and locked the car doors after they climbed out. Inside the bathroom, one of the two stalls had an out-of-order sign on it, but otherwise the facility was clean. There was a lock on the outside door, and for a second she was tempted to lock them in.

"You go first," Bri said.

A few minutes later, Dani exited the stall and washed her hands in cold water. "I'm going back to the car. I have sanitizer in the console."

It'd gotten colder since the sun went down, and she pulled her jacket closer. That's when she noticed a car had pulled into the parking lot behind them, but it was impossible to see if anyone was inside.

A tingling raced down her neck just like at the restaurant, only this time her sixth sense screamed to run. She turned and dashed toward the restroom. If she could get there, she could lock the door—

There was a loud pop, and her right shoulder stung. Another pop, and she stumbled as a second bullet knocked her forward.

The concrete walk came up to meet her head. Dani fought to stay conscious as footsteps approached. *Pretend you're dead.* That might not be hard to do . . .

8

Gunfire erupted just as Bri turned off the cold water. They'd found her.

Frantically, she looked for a place to hide. *Out of order.* It was her only hope. Not wasting a second, she slipped inside the stall with the sign on it and slid the lock in place before she hopped up on the rim of the toilet.

The outside door scraped open. Bri's heart beat so hard she was certain the person could hear it. She didn't dare breathe.

The door in the next stall slammed against the wall. She clamped her hand over her mouth to keep from crying out. The door to her stall shook. If the lock didn't hold, she had only one choice and prepared to tackle the assailant.

Instead, the outside door scraped open again. She waited, expecting the person to return. When a motor fired up and tires screeched away, she almost fainted with relief. Ignoring her trembling legs, Bri climbed off the toilet and rushed outside. Dani lay facedown in front of the building.

She sank beside her. Blood. So much blood. "Please don't be dead."

Tears streamed down Bri's face. She had to get help . . . her phone—she could use it to call 911. She slipped it out of her jeans pocket. Only one bar. What if the call didn't go through? With shaky fingers, she punched in 911.

"What is your emergency?"

The operator's voice sounded broken. "My friend. She's been shot. I . . . she might be dead!"

"What . . . location?"

Bri pressed her hand to her head. Where were they? "The Natchez Trace! Coles Creek. We stopped at the first restroom."

"—On the line . . . sending help—"

When the phone fell silent, Bri looked at the screen to see if the operator had disconnected. No. It looked like they were still connected. She sucked in a breath of air.

The phone came to life again. "Still there?"

"Yes!"

"Assistance is on the way, but I need you to check your friend for a pulse."

Suddenly the call was clear. "H-how do I do that?"

"Which is easier to access? Her neck or wrist?"

"She's facedown and blood is everywhere!" Bri's voice ended in a wail.

"Okay. I need you to stay calm. My name is Gloria. What's yours?"

How could she stay calm when Dani looked like she was dead? Bri shuddered a breath and told Gloria her first name.

"And your friend, what's her name?"

"D-Dani . . ." What did she say her last name was? Bri had only half listened when the counselor in New Orleans had introduced them.

"Okay, Bri, let's try her wrist," the operator said. "Can you place your index and middle finger on the inside just below her thumb?"

Bri scooted over to where she could cradle Dani's hand in her own. It was so still. Hesitantly, she placed the fingers Gloria instructed her to use against Dani's wrist. "Okay . . ."

"Can you feel a pulse?"

"No! All I can feel is a bone! She's dead!"

"You're too high. Move down an inch, maybe two."

She moved her fingers and caught her breath. "I feel something!"

"That should be her pulse. Can you count it?"

"It's too fast."

"She's probably in shock. Do . . . have blanket . . . something . . . her?"

The call was breaking up again, and Bri shook her head and then realized Gloria couldn't see her. "She had an overcoat. It's in the car." But where were the keys? *Think.* Dani had them when she got out of the car.

She scanned the area in the dim light from overhead. Something glinted by the trash can, and Bri scrambled to the other side of the sidewalk and grabbed the keys and ran to the car for the heavier coat. A faint wail reached her ears as she laid Dani's parka over her still body.

What if they think I shot her? Her hands curled. With her arrest record, that's exactly what the police would think. Bri would rather die than go back to jail.

The siren drew closer. Help wasn't far away . . . She stared at the keys in her hands and then at the Honda. Dani wouldn't need her car, not until she was better and could tell the police what happened and that Bri hadn't shot her. Thank goodness she hadn't given the 911 operator her full name.

9

Clayton's heart dipped as six-year-old Ava climbed out of her car seat and wrapped her arms around his neck.

"Fank you," she whispered in his ear.

"You're welcome." He tried to keep his thoughts away from the laser surgery she faced to remove the birthmark on her cheek. Not that it would be anytime soon since Jen's insurance had a ten thousand dollar deductible—if the procedure was even covered by her insurance. They would have to come up with the money first. Now that he had his gambling debts paid, he could start saving for her surgery.

"Yes, *thank* you," Jen echoed, narrowing her eyes at Clayton. Probably for not correcting Ava when she regressed to her four-year-old speech pattern.

He didn't care. The kid had enough going on with her father abandoning the family a year ago. It didn't help that Jen worked long hours just to keep the power turned on because the man she'd married took what little savings they had and blew it on drugs before he walked out of their lives. "Mind your mom, and we'll do this again soon."

"Pwomis?" When he raised his eyebrows she said, "Promise?"

"Yes."

Satisfied, Ava released him, and he set her on the drive. "Thanks for dinner," Jen said as she took her daughter's hand.

Clayton reached for the two hundred dollars he'd pocketed before he picked the two up and handed it to his sister.

Tears shone in her eyes. "Clayton, you don't—"

"Indulge me."

Her shoulders squared. "We'll pay you back every penny you've given us."

"Who's keeping count?" he asked with a smile. The smile faded as they walked to the small bungalow next door to his mother's craftsman house. He wished he could do more for Jen, but what she needed wasn't so much money as answers, like why her husband skipped out without even a goodbye.

Once they were safely inside, he walked back to his truck and turned his phone on as he pulled away from the drive. It had been a good outing, made even better after he'd picked up the tab for Madison Thorn.

Clayton's phone buzzed, breaking into his thoughts. "Bradshaw."

"Oh, good. I've been trying to raise you on the radio, and you're not answering your phone."

He immediately recognized field ranger Brooke Danvers's voice. Had to be something bad for her to call on his night off. "Sorry, I'm in my pickup. I took Jen and Ava out to eat and just now turned on my phone. What's going on?"

"Dispatch notified me that we have a shooting at the Coles Creek rest area. I'm still about five minutes out and right behind the ambulance."

Clayton groaned. Something like this happened every time he took a few hours off. "I'm on my way. Did you call Ritter?" Jesse Ritter was Clayton's other field ranger.

"He's up near Jackson, so it'll be a while before he can get here."

Brooke could handle this—she was a seasoned ranger and was always on top of everything. Her dad, Big John Danvers, had been one of the best district law enforcement rangers around and had trained Clayton. He was now trying to fill the legendary ranger's shoes.

"I'll be there ASAP." Clayton pulled a portable emergency light from his console and popped it on his dash before he executed a U-turn and sped toward the Natchez Trace with the blue light flashing. Brooke was married to Luke Fereday, a ranger with the Investigative Services Branch, and it might not be a bad idea to pull him into the investigation. Except, he remembered Brooke saying Luke was in Washington for a conference.

Twenty minutes later, he pulled into the parking area at Coles Creek as paramedics hurried a gurney toward the ambulance. Brooke met him at his truck. "How bad?" he asked.

"Paramedics say it'll be touch and go. Loss of blood, erratic pulse . . . She was shot in the back and shoulder area."

"Has she said anything?"

"A couple of times she asked about somebody named Bri."

He nodded and moved closer to the ambulance where he could see the victim's face. For a second, he didn't breathe. ISB special agent Madison Thorn? He'd paid for her dinner not an hour ago.

Could he be wrong? He stared at her. She wasn't dressed the same as this morning, but it was the same blond hair and the same heart-shaped face with a slight cleft in her chin that he'd noticed at the restaurant.

Her eyes fluttered open, and she locked gazes with Clayton. Same blue eyes.

"Agent Thorn, did this Bri person shoot you?" Clayton asked.

She frowned. "Bri . . . you . . . find her."

Her eyes closed, and for a second, she struggled to open them again.

"We're ready to load," the medic said, and Clayton stepped away from the gurney.

They slammed the doors to the ambulance shut. "Are you taking her to Merit?"

"Yeah. It's the closest hospital. They'll probably airlift her to Jackson if they get her stabilized."

From his expression, the paramedic didn't think she'd make it, and Clayton lifted a quick prayer heavenward before he turned to Brooke. From the look on her face, she'd done the same thing. He scanned the parking lot for the light-blue Chevy Impala he'd pulled over this morning. "Where's her car and the girl?"

"What girl?" Brooke frowned. "And there was no car here when I arrived. Haven't found a purse or a cell, either."

"I saw the victim at the restaurant in the Guest House B&B around 6:45 with a female who looked like she might be in her late teens or early twenties." He kicked himself for not going over and talking to her and finding out who the teenager was. But he had no way of knowing she would get shot.

Brooke tapped her iPad. "A female who gave her name as Bri called the shooting in to 911 at 7:30."

"That's the name the victim spoke." Clayton rubbed his jaw as he did the math. Forty-five minutes. "Allowing fifteen minutes to get out of Natchez and on the Trace, and then the time to get here—they must have left soon after I did and didn't make any stops."

Brooke tilted her head toward him. "You know the victim?"

"I issued her a warning ticket for speeding, but there was no teenager with her," he said. "She must've picked the girl up sometime between eight this morning and when I was with Jen and Ava at the restaurant."

"So you have her tag number?" Brooke asked as the ambulance pulled out onto the Trace with red-and-white lights flashing.

"Yeah." He started toward his pickup and turned back with a grimace. Since he only gave her a warning, he hadn't entered it into his iPad. "The information is in the ticket book in my SUV."

Clayton quickly called Sheriff Nate Rawlings to issue a BOLO for a late-model blue Chevy Impala with a rental license plate and a young adult female driving it.

"I'll pass this along to the police chief and get him to issue a BOLO as well," Rawlings said. "And I'll send my chief deputy to help with the investigation."

"Good. Once I reach my SUV and get a plate number, I'll call you back." After he disconnected, Clayton dialed Hugh Cortland's number. When he'd talked to him earlier in the day, Cortland had indicated he was working with the ISB special agent. Maybe Cortland had her plate number. When the FBI agent answered, Clayton explained the situation.

"That's impossible. Last time I talked to her, she planned to meet someone for lunch and then go to her grandfather's house in Natchez and work. She was spending the night with him and she shouldn't have even been on the Trace. Are you certain it's Madison Thorn?"

"The victim's car is missing with her personal effects, but I'm pretty sure it's her. A woman who looks like Ms. Thorn leaves an impression."

He pictured the woman at the restaurant with her blue eyes and blond hair in a ponytail. She'd been dressed in jeans and a pullover instead of the white blouse and slacks from earlier in the day. Could he be wrong? The image of the woman he'd given the ticket to had popped up in his mind all day, and he believed it was the woman who just left in an ambulance.

"I have her cell number—let me call her," Hugh said. "If she doesn't answer, I'll make some calls and get the license plate number." There was hesitation on the other end of the line. "You know if it is Madison, I'll want the investigation," Hugh said. "The FBI has more resources."

Clayton straightened his shoulders. He was the law enforcement officer for the Natchez Trace, but the FBI had jurisdiction over criminal activity in a national park and they held a higher rank than he did. That meant if Cortland wanted it, he could take the lead since the Trace was a part of the National Park Service. "Yeah, I know, but we've always worked well together on cases in the past." Clayton saw no reason they couldn't in this matter.

"Absolutely."

"I'll be here at Coles Creek looking for spent slugs until my other field ranger or Rawlings's chief deputy shows up," he said. "Once you have that plate number, call it in to the sheriff."

Clayton pocketed his phone and looked for Brooke. She had her high-beam flashlight out, sweeping it over the parking lot. "Find anything?" he asked when he reached her.

"No. Been thinking. Why would this girl call 911 if she intended to rob the victim and steal her car?"

"Good question." An SUV with the Adams County Sheriff's Department logo on the side pulled into the parking area. "I'm going to the hospital to see if I can get some answers."

10

The clock on Judge William Anderson's wall inched toward 8:15. He'd been sitting in his office almost three hours. His gaze was drawn to the headline again.

"Local Natchez Man Killed at Parchman." William laid the paper on his desk and leaned back in his leather chair. He'd read and reread the article detailing how Blake Corbett had been found in his cell at Parchman Penitentiary, dead from a knife wound to the chest.

No one could find the prisoner's brother, and the US Marshals office had already called to let him know the marshal assigned to him was outside his door and would escort him to his car and follow him home tonight.

The judge leaned forward, pressing his fingertips to his temples. He was getting too old for this job. So many times he had no choice in the sentences he imposed. The Corbett case had been one of them.

Corbett's brother would take his death hard. Anderson had felt for the man during the trial. He'd totally believed in his brother's innocence—so much so that he'd come unhinged when the jury returned their verdict, and had to be restrained. That potential existed again.

His cell phone chimed.

Where are you?

Madison. He'd completely forgotten she was at the house. He texted back.

On my way.

He stood and texted the marshal that he was leaving. The judge shoved his chair in place, and a thought rooted him to the floor. Could Corbett's brother go after Madison for retribution?

11

Madison folded her cloth napkin and placed it beside her plate. "Thank you, Grandfather. That was very good," she said.

It wasn't really an untruth, but nine o'clock was way past when she normally ate a heavy meal like steak and potatoes. Usually if she ate this late, it was cottage cheese or something else light. She scooted her chair back to stand, wishing she could excuse herself and get ready for bed but knowing it wouldn't be possible. Besides, her grandfather had been acting strangely ever since he arrived home, and she wanted to know why.

Her grandfather stood as well. "Nadine made her New Orleans bread pudding especially for you. I'll have her bring it to the study." He used his bench voice that brooked no argument.

She moaned. No matter what time it was or how full she was, Madison could never turn down Nadine's bread pudding. The recipe had been handed down from her grandmother back in Jefferson Parish, Louisiana, and it was to die for. Besides, turning down her grandfather's invitation to join him in his study would be tantamount to refusing an invitation from the king.

"While we eat, you can tell me what brought you to Natchez, and then, uh . . . I have a matter I want to discuss with you."

Again the feeling that all was not well with him. She turned her phone from off to vibrate as she followed him out of the dining room. Taking a call during dinner was definitely a no-no here, but now that they were finished, she didn't think Grandfather would mind if her phone buzzed.

"I apologize again for not being here when you arrived," he said once they were seated in front of the fire. Ever so briefly, worry crossed his usually impassive face. "Something came up at the last minute."

"It wasn't a problem." As a law enforcement officer, she knew how that went, and she'd used the time to study the invoices. More than once her thoughts had returned to her lunch meeting with Steven Turner. She'd enjoyed talking to him and was glad to see Noah was doing well, but there was something off about it.

Her grandfather sighed, and she turned to him. Something was bothering him, and she couldn't help wondering if it was what had held him so late. Her grandfather, the Honorable William Anderson, rarely allowed a court session to go beyond five, and if court wasn't in session, he was home early. Not only that, he'd been jumpy ever since he'd walked through the door. "Are you all right?"

"I'm fine." He ran his left hand through his thick white hair. "Did Nadine get you settled in the guest room?"

"She did." It was the same room she'd stayed in when she and her mother visited in the summers.

After a light knock at the door, the housekeeper entered with a tray that she set on a table. The strong aroma of chicory filled the small room.

"The bread pudding is a little dried out," Nadine said, self-reproach in her voice.

She had been with the family for as long as Madison could remember, living in a small apartment beside the garage. Though small in stature and just past her eightieth birthday, Nadine Broussard ran the judge's house like a precision watch. She was probably the only person in the world who could boss her grandfather around.

"I apologize again for being late, but I'm sure it will be fine. And don't hang around waiting for us to finish. I'll bring the dishes to the kitchen," her grandfather said and helped himself to a cup of coffee and a serving of dessert. "Coffee, Madison?"

"Not if I want to sleep tonight." It wasn't the chicory in Nadine's coffee that would keep her awake, it was the naturally caffeine-rich Kenyan beans she used. Besides, Madison had tried chicory once and hadn't liked the bitter taste.

Once Nadine left them, he stirred cream into his coffee. "So, when are you going to get married and give me great-grandchildren?"

She stared at him. That was the last thing she'd expected him to say. "What?"

"You heard me. All you ever do is work. I think it's high time you got interested in someone and settled down, preferably here in Natchez."

"Unfortunately, I haven't found anyone as interesting as my job." The one time she had, it'd turned into a disaster. Been there, done that, she wasn't trying it again.

"Just consider it." Her grandfather took a bite of the pudding. "Nadine was wrong," he said. "This is not dry."

Neither of them spoke as they enjoyed the sweet treat, then her grandfather set his half-eaten dessert on the table. "Speaking of your job, what brings you to Natchez?"

"A case involving theft and kickbacks." She was glad to be off the subject of her matrimonial prospects, or rather her lack thereof. Not that she would be sharing any details of the case. "How about you? What happened today that made you late?" She took another bite of the bread pudding.

He studied her a minute. "You're getting good at evading questions."

"Comes with the territory." She waited expectantly.

He picked up his coffee and sipped it before answering. "A man I sentenced to Parchman was killed there yesterday. Blake

Corbett," he said softly. "Always claimed he was innocent, even took a chance on a longer prison sentence rather than plead guilty."

"I'm sorry."

He continued like she hadn't spoken. "The US Marshals notified me that he'd recently made more threats against me. His brother has, as well. I was late because I went over the transcript of his trial to make sure I'd made no errors."

Madison could never be a judge, often deciding a person's innocence or guilt and then their fate. "What was your conclusion?"

"The jury believed the prosecution's case was stronger than the defense lawyer's and found him guilty. With mandatory sentencing for his crime, I had no choice. According to the US Marshals, his brother, Aaron, doesn't see it that way. I, as well as the members of the jury, have been notified of his death and advised to take precautions. A US Marshal followed me home and will arrive early tomorrow morning to accompany me to court."

Madison frowned. "Shouldn't there be someone here tonight?"

He shook his head. "This place is like a fortress, and I have my .38. I'll be fine."

He was right about the house. Steel burglar bars adorned each downstairs window, and he had a state-of-the-art security system. The cup and saucer rattled as he set it down. He wasn't as calm as he'd like her to think.

"Do you get these often? Death threats?"

"Often enough," he said. "Let's talk about you. How long will this case keep you here?"

"I'm not sure."

"You'll stay here, of course."

"That's my plan. Tomorrow I'll pick up additional records and bring them back here to work on."

"You indicated you were working with the FBI on this. Did you say which agent?"

She'd forgotten she'd mentioned that during dinner. "I don't think I did. I'll be working with Hugh Cortland."

"Good man." He rubbed his chin. "I saw someone today you probably knew as a little girl—friend of your cousins. Clayton Bradshaw."

Strange coincidence. "I remember him all right. He was Buddy and Joe's friend and always hanging around when I came to visit in the summers." She turned to him with a smile that was more like a grimace. "He gave me a warning ticket for speeding on the Trace."

"Were you?"

Her shoulders dropped. "I'm afraid so."

"Then count yourself blessed that he only issued you a warning. So, you recognized him?"

"No. His name was on his shirt. And before you ask, he didn't recognize me, either."

Her grandfather fell quiet, and she tried to think of something to fill the void. But she didn't get the chance.

"How have you been dealing with"—his jaw tightened, and sadness settled in his face—"your mother's unfortunate . . ."

Madison understood that he couldn't bring himself to say the word *overdose*. She had trouble with it herself. "I'm coping."

He closed his eyes briefly. "In spite of all her problems, I'm having trouble believing she deliberately ended her life."

12

Grandfather, the blood tests don't lie." How Madison wished they did. It pained her to know her mother was so unhappy she saw no way out other than death. If only Madison had paid closer attention, she could have prevented the overdose from happening.

But what haunted her the most was she hadn't been enough for her mother to want to live. Just like she hadn't been enough for her birth mother to keep her.

She pulled herself away from the dark thoughts and turned to her grandfather, immediately catching her breath. He'd picked up the porcelain cup again and gripped it so tightly in his left hand, his fingers had turned white. "Grandfather, if you don't let go of that cup, you're going to shatter it."

He stared down at the cup.

"Are you all right?"

"If she killed herself, Gregory drove her to it," he said. "Or he could have put something in her wine. She'd lost her sense of taste and wouldn't have noticed it."

His eyes . . . the look on his face . . . Her stomach squeezed in a knot. "Surely you don't mean that. Dad was taking her on a cruise."

For five long seconds, he said nothing, then shook his head

as though coming out of a trance. "He'd never taken off work before." He held her gaze. "Why then?" Then he laughed, but there was nothing happy about it. "But he ended up not having to take off, didn't he?"

She didn't have an answer for him. Her father was a type-A workaholic. He'd never had time for vacations before, other than driving Madison and her mother to Natchez every summer. He always returned to Memphis the next day, not coming back until the end of their month stay to take them home.

Until she turned twelve. That's when her father had bought the horse, and she started riding lessons and competitions that were mostly in the summer. Looking back, it was easy to see it'd been so he could keep her away from her grandfather. It hadn't worked quite the way he'd planned, though.

She'd been surprised about the upcoming cruise that had brought her mother out of her depression, and Madison never questioned him about it. They'd both seemed excited. It was one reason the overdose had shocked her like it had.

He raised his eyebrows. "If there really was a cruise, why weren't you going? Were you even invited?"

"I was, but I had to work." She stared at the last bite of bread pudding in her bowl. Their conversation had taken her appetite, but Nadine would be disappointed if any was left. Madison managed to get it down and set the bowl on the tray before she turned to her grandfather.

Weariness etched the lines of his face. He took a breath and released it slowly. "You've been mostly happy, haven't you? I mean, with your parents, growing up in Memphis . . ."

This was the strangest conversation she'd ever had with her grandfather. "You mean about being adopted?"

Her parents had told her even before she was old enough to understand that she was adopted—chosen, they said.

He frowned. "Not exactly. Are you happy in general?"

Was she? Growing up with a bipolar mother and a workaholic

father who barely gave her the time of day had been difficult. But, like someone once said, what doesn't break you makes you stronger. After she was grown, Madison realized her childhood had taught her critical-thinking skills and probably led to her career in law enforcement. But was she happy?

"In general, yes." Where was he going with this? "Why do you ask?"

Her phone vibrated in her pocket, and she pulled it out. Hugh Cortland? And he'd called several times before this call. "I'm sorry," she said. "I need to take this."

She didn't miss the look of relief on her grandfather's face. Madison stood and strode out of the room. "What's up?"

"I've been trying to reach you for the past two hours."

"I had my phone turned off."

"Where are you?"

"I'm at my grandfather's, like I told you I would be. What's going on?"

"Clayton Bradshaw has a gunshot victim he swears is you."

"I don't think so."

"Since you answered, I agree, but she must be a dead ringer for you. The woman was shot at Coles Creek on the Trace, which is National Park Service property—you'll probably be called in to work it."

"I doubt it. FBI gets first dibs, and if you don't want it, Clayton Bradshaw and Evan McCall are next in line to investigate—not me. Besides, the Investigative Services Branch doesn't come in and work on a case unless we're asked, and I don't think either of those two have asked."

"Clayton thinks you've been shot. He only called me because I told him we were working together on a case this morning. I guarantee you'll be getting a request from Evan, asking you to look into it."

Hugh and Evan both knew she didn't work violent crimes, not after what happened in Texas.

"You know you want to check out this woman who looks like you. She's at Merit not ten minutes from you."

The local hospital. Madison's heart beat a little faster. She did not want to get caught up in an attempted murder case. "You say Bradshaw mistook the victim for me?"

"Yes. I'll text you his number."

"Okay, only to prove this woman doesn't look that much like me." It looked like whatever was going on with her grandfather would have to wait. She hung up and slid her phone into her pocket before she stepped back inside the study. "Hugh Cortland wants me to check out a shooting victim."

"You have your key in case I've gone to bed when you return? And you remember the security code?"

"I do. It's my birthday. Are you going to set the alarm when I leave?"

He nodded.

"I don't think I'll be gone long, but if you've gone to bed, I'll see you in the morning at breakfast."

"Be careful."

"Always."

With her grandfather's concern about Aaron Corbett fresh in her mind, Madison scanned the grounds for anything suspicious as she pulled out of the drive. Anyone could lurk among the ancient oaks in the front yard and she wouldn't be able to see them.

And neither would his neighbors since his house sat in the middle of five acres on the edge of Natchez. It would be hard for neighbors on either side to know if a break-in happened. She shook her head, dismissing her fears. He had a security system, and he was armed.

She wasn't that familiar with Natchez but did know where the hospital was and quickly drove the short distance across town. Madison found a parking space under an overhead light and climbed out of the Impala. Even with the light, it was dark in the parking lot, and she looked up. Either clouds were obscuring the moon or there wasn't much of one. She called the number Hugh had texted her as she hurried to the hospital entrance.

"Bradshaw."

"This is ISB Special Agent Madison Thorn—"

"You can't be Thorn. I'm standing at the foot of her bed right now."

"And that's impossible. What's the room number?"

"Room 224 in ICU on the second floor. I'll meet you in the waiting room."

"I'll be right there."

13

William Anderson poured himself another drink from the almost-empty bottle on his desk and checked his watch. No word from Madison, and she'd been gone almost two hours. He leaned back in his chair, a headache starting in his temples. Maybe it was better that circumstances interrupted his time with her.

She has a right to know.

And he would tell her. He was just relieved he didn't have to tell her tonight. It wasn't like he hadn't wanted to in the past, but because of his daughter, he hadn't felt the freedom to share Madison's beginnings with her. Now, with Sharon gone, he had no excuse to wait.

Sharon. With her it was too little, too late. If he'd shown her the report from the private investigator, would his daughter still be alive? Or would it have pushed her over the edge? Now he had to decide what to do with the evidence of infidelity the PI had brought him.

His lips curled in a tight smile at Gregory's reaction when he'd confronted him. After Gregory's initial bluster, he'd owned up to his infidelity, his tone practically groveling.

Had Gregory killed Sharon after that? Thinking she might divorce him if she found out? Gregory would get a lot more from

Sharon's estate than he would have from a divorce settlement. But of course, there'd been no divorce.

And then there was the problem of *what* to tell Madison. Anderson stood and poured himself another glass of bourbon. Corbett hadn't been the only reason he'd been late to dinner. He'd been looking over copies of her adoption papers, papers he'd wanted to discuss with her tonight.

Even though there was nothing illegal in the papers, he'd never told his daughter the details of the adoption. Not just how he'd arranged it, but what it had cost. And that had allowed Judith Winslow to get her hooks into him. He quickly downed the drink and poured the last of the whiskey. Madison being called away had only prolonged the inevitable. This morning's meetings had made that plain.

He drained the glass and set it down. The alcohol had done nothing to blunt the dread in his stomach.

The floor outside his study creaked. "Nadine?"

No answer.

With a start, he realized he'd forgotten to reset the alarm after Madison left and opened the desk drawer on his left, where he kept a Smith & Wesson .38 Special.

Clayton disconnected from the call from the woman claiming to be Madison Thorn and stepped outside the ICU room as the deputy assigned to guard the victim's room returned from the cafeteria.

"I was about to call you," Clayton said. "I'll be right back."

And he would be, as soon as he dispatched the imposter claiming to be Madison Thorn. She had to be playing some kind of sick joke because the person Clayton had given a warning ticket to this morning was the same person he'd been holding a vigil over for the last half hour.

Clayton stepped through the double steel doors as the woman entered the waiting room. He blinked and then stared with his mouth gaped.

The woman strode across the room while he gathered his thoughts. How was this possible? He examined the credentials she held out, the same ones that had identified her as Madison Thorn this morning. "You didn't tell me you had a twin sister," he blurted.

She frowned. "That's because I don't."

"Really? Follow me." He turned and walked back inside the unit.

"Wait."

He turned around, and her blue eyes held him.

"Exactly what am I walking into?"

They had stopped near the nurses' station. He probably needed to prepare her. "I'm not sure. I have a gunshot victim with no identification but who looks just like you."

"You say there's no ID?"

"None. Did you eat at the Guest House tonight?"

Madison shot him a confused look before she shook her head. "I met someone for lunch then went straight to my grandfather's house. Judge William Anderson. I never left until now."

Surprise made him take a step back. This was the judge's granddaughter? He stared at her, trying to see a resemblance to the girl with pigtails. He should have recognized those blazing blue eyes and the stubborn tilt of her chin this morning when he pulled her over.

To her credit, Madison had not tried to use the toughest and most well-respected judge in Adams County to get out of her ticket.

"So," she said, "you finally recognize me."

Heat flashed in his face. "You knew who I was when I pulled you over?"

"Not then, but when I saw your name tag, I figured there weren't too many Clayton Bradshaws in Natchez."

He thought back to his first summer in Natchez. "I was only ten and you were, what? Six?"

"Seven."

"I must have made quite an impression on you."

"You did. How could I forget how you and my cousins bullied me every summer?"

"Whoa!" He raised his hands. "I never bullied you—"

"But—"

"No buts. Think back. The first time I met you, they were teasing you, calling you names, and I made them stop. Later I told them I'd give them a knuckle sandwich if I caught them doing it again."

She frowned and folded her arms across her chest. "That's not how I remember it."

"If you don't believe me, ask your cousins." Warmth spread through Clayton's chest as he remembered Madison standing up to the boys. "You were a plucky little thing."

It'd been hard to take a stand against them. He'd just moved to Natchez from Jackson after his dad died, and they were the only boys his age he knew. Funny thing was, they'd respected him for it. "They were jealous, you know."

"You're kidding."

A memory of her throwing one of the boys over her shoulder flashed in his mind. "Wait—you put one of your cousins in his place. Buddy, wasn't it?"

She pressed her lips together, but not before a tiny grin tugged at them. "They wouldn't let me in your stupid club because I was a girl and I wasn't 'real' family—but they let *you* in. Said I had to whip one of them. Like that was going to happen—they were older and bigger.

"So I did what all little girls do—I tattled to Grandfather, and he paid for me to take martial arts training. I'd been practicing that move all winter."

"You did good. I'll never forget the look on Buddy's face when he hit the ground."

Her face softened. "I can't believe he went on to become a preacher."

"You stay in touch with them?"

She nodded. "Mostly through Facebook. Except for my dad and grandfather, they're the only family I have."

She might be wrong about that, but he wasn't sure how to broach the subject. Instead, he asked if she still practiced judo.

"Not judo so much, but I reached a level three in tai chi before life got busy. I still practice, though."

"That's . . . ?"

"It's for self-defense and keeping me in shape." She grinned. "I'm really good at flying kicks."

"Remind me not to make you mad."

Madison stared into space for a minute, then tilted her head. "I still don't understand why you thought it was me at Coles Creek."

"You'll understand when you see the victim—who's now a Jane Doe. I really thought it was you at the restaurant tonight. The woman I mistook you for was with a girl who could've been in her late teens or early twenties. I'm sure she wondered why I bought their dinner."

"You bought someone's dinner thinking it was me?" Madison propped her hands on her hips and held his gaze. "Why?"

His heart stuttered. Did she not feel the chemistry between them? For him it was like electricity. He hadn't been able to get her off his mind all day, even though he fought it—acting on those feelings was the old Clayton. He stood straighter. "I was a little rude to you this morning. It was my way of apologizing."

Her blue eyes softened, and for the first time, he noticed her cheeks were flushed and they hadn't been when she first came into the waiting room. Maybe the feeling *was* mutual.

"Well, thank you. I'd like to see this person now, if you don't mind," she said and waited expectantly.

15

Madison followed Clayton down the lighted hallway, past rooms with critically ill patients in them, but her thoughts were everywhere except where they should be and surprisingly mostly on him. What was up with that?

She didn't do relationships. She didn't have time for one even if she did, not even with someone as appealing as the ranger. How had her memory of him been so wrong? Or had he made up his defense of her?

No, he wasn't faking the hurt her accusation caused. Or the fervor in his voice when he denied bullying her. She searched memories of her summers in Natchez, trying to remember a specific time he'd been part of her cousins' bullying. It surprised her that nothing surfaced. There were plenty of times when it was just her and the cousins, though. She owed him an apology. Again.

She shifted her focus back to the reason she was here. Was it possible? No, there was no way this woman could resemble Madison enough to be mistaken for her. It just didn't happen in real life . . . did it?

Except . . . all her life, she'd felt something was missing. In spite of her parents always telling her she'd been "chosen," she never quite felt accepted. Madison brushed the thoughts aside. She'd come to terms with being adopted years ago. But what if that family she always wondered about included a sister? The thought almost stopped her in midstride.

Clayton rounded a corner and spoke to a nurse stationed outside a room before turning to Madison. "She's on a vent and hasn't regained consciousness from surgery."

"Surgery?"

"She was shot twice in the back. One was a through-and-through in the shoulder, and the other lodged near a rib, but it missed vital organs. The surgeon gave me this when he finished." He pulled a small plastic bag from his pocket. "My guess is it's a 9mm, and I believe it's in good enough shape to determine the gun it came from. I thought you might get Hugh to run the ballistics report."

Madison examined the mushroomed projectile. She agreed with him that it probably came from a 9mm gun, maybe a conceal-and-carry type. "You want me to ask the FBI to run the ballistics?"

"The sheriff offered, but Jackson is backlogged. I figure it'd be quicker if the FBI ran it, and I also figure Hugh will do it if you ask."

He was probably right, and if the gun used in this shooting had been involved in another case, the ballistics team would find it.

"Gotcha. Hugh said he'd be down tomorrow." She handed the bag back to him.

Madison entered the softly lit room. It was hard to tell much about the victim's size. Not that she noticed other than having a bare impression. Everything in the room faded except the face on the bed. She found it impossible to look away. The face was identical to hers.

"I-I don't understand." She released the breath trapped in her chest. The room tilted, and she swayed.

Clayton steadied her. "I did warn you she could pass for your twin."

It still hadn't prepared her for seeing an exact replica of herself down to the hint of a cleft in her chin.

"You weren't aware you might have a twin?"

Madison licked her dry lips. "No. There has to be an explanation."

"There's always an explanation," Clayton said. "Even though you might not be prepared for it."

She studied the woman again, her gaze stopping at the bandage that covered her shoulder. "How bad are her injuries?"

Clayton motioned for her to step out of the room, and she followed him. Once they were in the hallway, he turned to the deputy standing guard. "I'll be in the cafeteria if you need me." Then he turned to Madison. "That's if you'll join me for a cup of coffee."

All she could manage was a nod. Madison needed the caffeine. It'd been a long day and it might be a long night.

In the cafeteria there were plenty of tables to choose from, and Clayton pointed toward a corner. "How about that one? You look kind of done in, so why don't I grab the coffee?"

She must look bad for an almost total stranger to notice. "Thanks."

"Creamer, sugar?"

"Black."

A few minutes later, he brought two steaming Styrofoam cups to the table. "They made a fresh pot." He handed her one.

Madison wrapped her hands around the cup and took a sip, pleasantly surprised that the coffee tasted pretty good.

"You okay?"

"I'm getting better, but it was quite a shock." She took another sip of the hot liquid. "It must be pretty bad if you didn't want to discuss the patient's condition in the room."

"It's not good, for sure, and while I don't think she can hear us, you never know. I talked with the surgeon . . . she lost a lot of blood and her blood pressure is extremely low. He indicated there could be organ failure if it doesn't come up." He took off his jacket and laid it on the back of a chair.

"Optimistic sort, huh?"

"I know." Clayton stared into his coffee, then looked up. "He did say she seemed to be a fighter. Personally, I think if she makes it through the night and an infection doesn't set in, she'll recover."

"Have you spoken to her?"

"Briefly. She came to when they were loading her in the ambulance. I asked if she knew who shot her, but she asked about someone named Bri—probably the girl I saw her with."

"Do you think this Bri person shot her?"

"I don't know. Our Jane Doe's car is missing along with her ID, and I don't know if Bri shot her and took the car and ran, or if someone else shot her and stole her car. Even if she improves overnight and regains consciousness by morning, I doubt we'll get much information from her until sometime tomorrow afternoon."

Suddenly his eyes widened. He snapped his fingers and took out his phone. "I need to cancel the BOLO or an Adams County Deputy will be pulling you over."

"What do you mean?" she asked.

"When I thought the victim was you, I gave the sheriff your license plate number."

"From this morning."

"Yep. Once I got it from my SUV." He walked to the coffee machine to make his call, and Madison took a notebook from her bag, her thoughts returning to the patient in room 224. Was it possible she had a twin sister? She knew absolutely nothing about her biological family, not that she hadn't tried after she went away to college. The DNA kits had just become available, and she ordered one and sent it off. She'd even marked that she wanted to participate in the DNA Relatives feature, but nothing ever came of it.

Clayton returned to their table with more coffee.

"Get it taken care of?" she asked.

"Yes. And I talked to Hugh and let him know we were working on finding out who the victim is."

Madison should have called him already, and she would on her way back to her grandfather's. "Fill me in on the details."

He hesitated. "Are you taking over the case?"

Was Clayton asking because he didn't want the Investigative Services Branch horning in? He was a district ranger in a supervisory position, which meant he had many years of experience. She didn't know what his problem was. Unless he expected her to come in and throw her weight around. Madison studied him, looking for the signs. Instead, she found herself admiring his broad shoulders, shoulders that might be good to lean on.

From what he said earlier, Clayton was older than she was by three years. His high cheekbones and straight black hair made her wonder if he was of Native American descent. As a kid she'd never really known him or his family.

He waved his hand in front of her face. "Clayton to Madison . . ."

Heat flashed up her neck and into her cheeks. "Sorry. Fell down a rabbit hole there for a second." What were they talking about? Oh yeah. "Would you have a problem with it if I did take over the case?"

Clayton stared at her a moment, then he visibly relaxed. "I'm hoping we can work together on it—we're both National Park Service officers, even though you're in the *elite* group." He made air quotes around *elite*.

"Me too." She tilted her head to the side. From his relaxed posture, it was evident Clayton was comfortable with who he was. "I want to know who this woman is," she said. "And I believe we can work together. Now fill me in on the details . . ."

She made notes as he took her from seeing the victim at the restaurant to when he arrived at Coles Creek. When he finished, she reviewed what he'd told her. "Evidently the two had a destination—Jackson, probably. It's too early to be looking for a missing persons alert, but I'll check with Allyson Murphy, the FBI analyst I met yesterday in Jackson."

"That sounds good." Clayton glanced at his watch. "We've been gone almost an hour. If you're ready, I'd like to see her one last time and call it a night."

Madison was ready to do the same thing. They returned to the ICU wing, and while he spoke with the deputy on guard, she slipped back into the room. Now that she was alone, Madison took more time to study their Jane Doe. *Their* Jane Doe? She'd warmed pretty quickly to working with Clayton.

She tried to estimate how tall the unconscious woman would be if she were standing. About Madison's height . . . and weight. She peered a little closer at the roots of the ash-blond hair fanned out on the pillow. It was either recently colored or, like Madison, she'd never colored her hair. Either way, the blond shade was the same, and it appeared to be shoulder length, like her own. "Do you wear your hair in a ponytail?" she asked softly. It was Madison's go-to style.

How surreal, looking at a mirror image of herself. Even the woman's fingers were like Madison's. Piano fingers, her mother called them.

"Who are you?" She cradled the right hand that didn't have an IV. The patient's fingers curled around hers, sending a shock wave through Madison.

"Is there any chance she could be your twin sister?" Clayton asked as he joined her side.

She hadn't heard him enter the room, and her heart skipped a beat, then took off like a dog after a rabbit. *Stop it!* Madison pulled her attention back to their Jane Doe and released her hand before turning to him. "I'm adopted, so I suppose it's possible."

"Is there any way you can find out?"

"DNA swab?"

"You can't ask your dad?"

"No. Dad, he—" Madison stared at her clenched hand. "He's never been the easiest person to talk to."

"Did you ever discuss your birth parents with your adoptive parents?"

She shook her head. The only time she'd broached the subject, her mother had gone to pieces, and her father insisted that she never bring the subject up again. Not that he was ever around for her to ask again.

"*You've been mostly happy, haven't you? I mean, with your parents, growing up in Memphis . . .*" Her grandfather's question from earlier popped into her head. "I can ask my grandfather," she said just as her phone vibrated in her pocket. She fished it out and frowned. Nadine's name was on the ID. The housekeeper never called her. "I need to take this."

She stepped out of the room again and punched the answer button. "What's wrong, Nadine?"

For a few seconds, there was no answer. Was Nadine crying? Madison's heart thumped wildly in her chest.

"It's . . . the judge. You must come, chère. He's . . . he's . . . the paramedics are here!" The housekeeper's voice rose to a wail.

"He's what?" Blood drained from Madison's face and she leaned against the wall to keep from falling. "Nadine! What's going on?"

"I hear a gun shoot. I come into the back door and go to the study, and I find your grandfather slumped over the desk. You must come now!"

"Is he . . . ?" She couldn't say the word.

"I don't know! You come now!"

He couldn't be dead. She clung to the thought. "What hospital are they taking him to?"

"I don't know if they will, chère . . . I fear he is gone . . . and they didn't think I heard them, but one said something about him taking his own life."

16

When Madison didn't return to Jane Doe's room, Clayton stepped outside, searching for her. Where had she gone? He turned to the deputy. "Have you seen the woman I was with?"

"Last I saw, she was running toward the elevators."

"Do you know why?"

The deputy shrugged. Madison would not have left unless it was an emergency. Clayton dashed down the hall. When he rounded the corner, the elevator area was deserted, and he jogged to the exit. Hoping to catch her before she reached her car, he bounded down the stairs two at a time. At the hospital doors, he spied her hurrying under the covered pull-thru at the entrance.

"Madison!" She kept running as though she hadn't heard him. Clayton dodged a car and ran toward her as she approached the Impala. "Madison!" he called louder.

This time she stopped and turned around, her face the color of chalk. He quickly closed the gap between them. "Hey," he said softly. "What's going on?"

Tears glistened in her eyes. "My grandfather . . ." She sniffed. "He's . . . been shot, possibly dead . . ."

Judge Anderson, shot? That didn't seem possible. "I'm sorry . . . what happened?"

She shook her head. "I don't know. I'm on my way now to

find out. His housekeeper, Nadine, called a few minutes ago. She heard a gunshot and went to investigate." Madison bit her bottom lip. "She overheard the paramedics say he may have tried to kill himself."

"No way." The man Clayton knew from the bench would never try to kill himself.

"My feelings exactly. He was upset at dinner but not depressed. He'd gotten news that a man he'd sentenced to prison had died, but nothing about my grandfather tonight pointed to . . ." Shuddering, she closed her eyes, then seemed to catch herself. "I have to go."

"Look, you're in no shape to drive. Let me take you."

"Then I would be stranded." Madison opened her car door and hesitated. "But you can follow me, if you'd like."

He'd take that. "Give me a second while I get my SUV."

Clayton knew where the judge lived, but he followed behind Madison. They met an ambulance with red-and-white lights flashing just minutes away from the judge's two-story antebellum house. Madison braked as though she might turn around and follow them, then continued on to the circle drive, where Police Chief Nelson's SUV idled empty beside a slew of other Natchez police cars. At least the white Adams County Coroner van was absent.

Clayton frowned as he parked on the street. Two attacks in one night were not the norm for Natchez. Then he corrected his thinking. The judge's shooting could be an attempted suicide, but he found that hard to swallow. Anderson had been fine when he saw him at the coffee shop earlier today.

Or had he? The meetings he had with the two women hadn't appeared to be happy meetings—the first woman left with what looked like an unresolved issue, and the judge had seemed wary with Judith.

He climbed out of his SUV and met Madison in front of the house. Before he could bring up seeing her grandfather at the coffee shop, she said, "Maybe I should follow the ambulance back to the hospital."

"You wouldn't be able to see him—if there's a bullet wound, he'll go straight into surgery," Clayton said. "Why not find out what happened and then go?"

"Good idea. I should have thought of that." Still she hesitated.

"Would you like me to come in with you? You look like you could use a friend." What was he thinking? He didn't need to get involved in Madison's problems. He had enough of his own. Evidently from the way she pressed her lips into a thin line, she felt the same way. So, what was he doing invading her space and patting her arm?

Her eyes searched his face, looking for . . . he didn't know. Maybe that friend?

"I know we only met today, and I gave you a warning ticket for speeding, but . . ." He gentled his voice. "I hope you'll let me be the person who stands in the gap for you like when we were kids."

Her shoulders relaxed, and she gave him a wan smile. "I suppose I've had worse friends. But thanks, and you're welcome to come with me."

It was a starting point. To what? Clayton didn't know, but he felt inexplicably better than he had a few minutes ago.

He followed her up the steps to the house and waited while she explained to the officer standing guard that she was the judge's granddaughter. Clayton recognized the older man—Jim Burney, who'd been a patrol officer when Clayton was a teenager. When he shook his head, Madison showed her ISB credentials.

"Little lady, I don't care who you are. Chief Nelson said no one was to get past me, and until he says otherwise, you're not getting in."

Clayton winced when the officer called Madison "little lady." He figured that was like baiting a mama bear. She pulled herself up to her full height, which couldn't be more than five six.

"I'm an ISB special agent with the National Park Service, and I don't need your permission to enter a crime scene. I only asked out of professional courtesy," she said through gritted teeth. "Get Chief Nelson out here now, or I'm walking through that door."

The older man tried staring her down.

"You have one minute."

Reluctantly, he pulled out his phone and called the chief.

"I have a lady who wants in. Says she's some sort of special agent with the National Park Service." He listened for a minute before he hung up. "Chief Nelson will be right out."

The look he gave them said it wouldn't do her any good. In less than a minute, Chief Pete Nelson came through the door, and they followed him to the other side of the wraparound porch. As always, the chief's white shirt and khaki pants looked as though they'd just been pressed. Clayton didn't know how he did it.

He looked from Madison to Clayton. "What's going on?" the chief asked, addressing Clayton.

"This is Special Agent Madison Thorn with the NPS, and she's Judge Anderson's granddaughter." Clayton had known Pete ever since high school when he was a quarterback for the Natchez Bulldogs, and he was a fair man. "She wants to know what happened to her grandfather."

Pete Nelson rubbed his shaved head. "Agent Thorn—"

"Call me Madison."

He nodded. "I'm sorry for the confusion. When Officer Burney called, he didn't say you were Judge Anderson's granddaughter."

Seconds ticked off as she seemed to process his apology before she gave him a curt nod. "What was his condition when he left here?"

"Critical. Gunshot wound to the chest. Apparently, he shot himself."

She jutted her jaw out. "There's no way my grandfather shot himself. He simply would not do that. Where did it happen?"

"In his study."

"Can I see the crime scene?"

"I'm sorry, but the park service has no jurisdiction here."

"I understand that, Chief Nelson, but I'm an ISB ranger with more than enough experience in investigating crimes." Her voice was soft but firm. "I'm in Natchez working a joint investigation with FBI agent Hugh Cortland, and I may be able to help you—no one else here knows that room the way I do."

The chief studied her for a minute and nodded. He turned to Clayton. "What's your interest?"

"Just moral support for a friend."

Nelson continued to study them both. "Very well. Follow me."

Clayton's shoes echoed on the polished wood floor as he followed Madison and Nelson into a huge entry hall. "Have you called the marshal assigned to Judge Anderson?"

The chief paused at the hall doorway and turned to face them. "Just before you arrived, I called both the marshal and Hugh Cortland. I informed them it appeared to be a self-inflicted wound, but I'm sure they'll conduct their own investigation if it proves otherwise. At this point, they're deferring the case to me."

"What makes you think he shot himself?" Madison asked.

"The position of the gun. It looks as though after he fired the gun, it fell to the floor less than two feet from his chair. And there's a note."

She froze as the chief handed her a plastic bag with a paper in it. "We found it in his printer."

Madison. I'm so sorry to do this, but with Sharon dead, I can't go on. Please accept this decision. Love, Granddad

She stared at the note. "My grandfather did not write this. I would bet my life on it." She raised her head. "If he had intended to take his life, he would have written a personal note, not typed it on a computer."

"I know this is difficult—"

Madison crossed her arms. "I never, ever called him Granddad. And when he wakes up, he'll tell you who shot him." She looked toward the kitchen. "Where's Nadine? She'll tell you the same thing."

"In the kitchen. One of my officers is trying to get her complete statement, but so far all she's managed is that you had dinner with him. By the way, I'll need your statement as well before you leave." He took out a notepad. "Can you tell me what his emotional state was when you left him?"

"He seemed fine, although he was upset that a man he'd sentenced to Parchman had been murdered yesterday. And he mentioned something about the man's brother making threats against him."

Pete winced. "Blake Corbett and his brother, Aaron." The chief rubbed the back of his neck. "Did he think Aaron might show up here?"

"He wasn't too worried about it—said this place was like a fortress, and he had his .38." She furrowed her brow. "Thinking back to dinner, Grandfather was a little unsettled, but nothing that indicated he might take his life. I can't believe he shot himself. I want to see the room."

Without waiting for an okay, Madison brushed past Nelson and hurried down the hall to a room at the end. At the threshold, she hesitated.

"Wait, Madison." Clayton hurried to catch up. After what she'd already been through tonight—coming face-to-face with a Jane Doe who could be her twin—he didn't want her walking into the room without someone by her side. She turned, and the dark circles under her eyes and the paleness of her face underscored her vulnerability.

"What?" The question came out more a whisper.

"You don't have to do this. Chief Nelson is very competent. I promise, he won't miss anything, and I'm sure Hugh will be here tomorrow with a crime response team."

"No, he won't, not if the chief rules it attempted suicide." Madison wavered, then squared her shoulders. "I have to do this. No one knows his study the way I do except Nadine, and it sounds like Nadine isn't able to help. If anything's out of place, I'll know it."

Weight pressed on Madison's shoulders. Clayton seemed to sense the sudden dread that filled her. Did he think she couldn't handle it?

Could she? This was the only grandfather she'd ever known. Her heart faltered. It'd be so easy to let Nelson take care of it. No one would blame her. Except . . . because of the note, the chief believed her grandfather had shot himself. If a piece of evidence contradicted what he believed, he might dismiss it, not on purpose but because it didn't fit his preconceived idea.

"I have to see the crime scene for myself," she said, standing taller. Somehow she had to find something that countered the note because someone had killed her grandfather and made it look like suicide. She turned to the chief, who had joined them. "No offense, Chief, but there may be something you're missing."

"No offense taken, but this is family," Chief Nelson said gently. "Can you treat this like you would any other investigation? Otherwise, I can't risk you destroying evidence. Only way I'm letting you inside that room is if you can detach yourself and not think of the victim as your grandfather."

"I can do that." She had to.

He nodded. "Just remember you're doing this as an officer of the law."

She inhaled slowly, hesitating. Now that Madison had the

go-ahead, doubt crept in. It'd been four years since she'd investigated a violent crime—instead, she dealt with numbers, embezzlement, and kickbacks, not death. Could she go through that door and look at the room where her grandfather was shot without falling apart? The room that had been her special place in his house?

Even though she'd only seen him in the summers and occasionally at Christmas, William Anderson had been a big part of her life. The time he'd spent writing short notes and calling her at least once a week was more time than she got from her dad.

Like a photo album, memories flipped through her mind. The summer he'd taught her to swim . . . and to fish . . . reading in this very room . . . the martial arts training he'd encouraged and paid for . . . the times he'd driven to Memphis just to see her. And then after she quit coming to Natchez, he'd driven to Memphis or wherever she was showing her horse to cheer her on.

A tight band pressed her chest until she almost couldn't breathe. There was no way her grandfather tried to kill himself. He wouldn't do that to her.

She could do this. If he didn't make it—and Madison didn't think she could bear that, but if he didn't—it might be the last thing she did for him. She would make sure nothing was overlooked. With another deep breath, Madison straightened her shoulders. "Do I need some type of booties for my feet?"

"Hold on." A black case sat outside the door, and the chief pulled out three pairs of disposable foot covers. "My crime scene investigators were vacuuming when I left to talk to you. I don't hear them, so they must be finished, but it's still a good idea to wear these." He replaced the ones he'd worn to the porch with a new pair as they donned theirs.

Madison's shaky legs appreciated Clayton's steadying hand under her arm as she walked inside her grandfather's study. The crime scene tech dusting for fingerprints on the bookcase looked around and nodded.

Her gaze immediately went to the desk where she'd seen her grandfather sit so many times. A pool of blood circled the floor under his chair, and to her left as she viewed the scene lay a revolver. The room swam, and her knees threatened to buckle.

"I'm here." Clayton's arm steadied her again.

She had to get a grip. *Look at it like any other crime scene.* Except now her crime scenes were records instead of actual places where someone had been shot. Madison flexed her calf muscles to get blood to her legs and forced her gaze away from the desk and around the room. She ticked off every piece of furniture, every painting, even the articles on his desk, settling last of all on the table where their bowls and his coffee cup had not been moved.

"When I left him, he was sitting here." She touched the leather chair that was to the right of the table. Something wasn't right, but she couldn't put her finger on it. "He had coffee, and we both ate some of Nadine's bread pudding."

Chief Nelson leaned forward. "And then . . . ?"

"I received a call from Clayton about my doppelgänger and went to the hospital to see for myself," she said, turning to the chief.

"Excuse me?"

"There was a shooting at Coles Creek around seven thirty," Clayton said. "When I arrived, I identified the victim as Agent Thorn. But as you can see, I was wrong. They could be twins, though."

Pete Nelson snapped his fingers. "The BOLO." He turned to Madison, frowning. "You're involved in two different crimes tonight? That's a mighty big coincidence."

She didn't believe in coincidences, but neither did she think the two separate incidents were connected.

"Have you identified the victim?"

Clayton shook his head. "And as far as I know, the girl traveling with her hasn't been found, either. If the victim doesn't regain consciousness by morning, I'll get her prints and see if she's in AFIS."

"You think she might have a criminal record?" Madison asked. The Automated Fingerprint Identification System would give them her name—if she was in the system.

"It's possible. I'll also shoot them to Hugh. If she's ever had a background check, then the FBI should have her prints stored."

"I could—"

"Let me take care of that for you," Clayton said.

After a hesitation, she nodded. "I believe we've gotten sidetracked."

"I believe we have too," Pete Nelson said. "You left him sitting in the chair . . . at some point, he walked to his desk, took out his .38, and pulled the trigger."

"No! That did not happen." Madison turned and stared at the empty chair beside the table with a coffee cup and their bowls.

With her jaw clamped tight, she allowed her gaze to follow the path he would have taken if the scenario was as the chief said. Something nagged at her . . . What was it? "Have you moved anything?"

"No," Nelson replied. "Is something missing?"

"I don't think so. It's just that . . ." She turned back to the small table, replaying their actions. She caught her breath and held it. That was it.

"What?" the chief asked.

Madison held up her finger and walked to the desk. "You're sure nothing has been moved?"

"I'm sure."

"Then my grandfather didn't shoot himself."

18

Bri pulled the Civic into the hospital parking lot. When she googled hospitals, Merit Hospital in Natchez had been the closest, and she figured the paramedics had brought the lady who picked her up in New Orleans to this hospital. She stared at the building. She hoped and prayed that Dani hadn't died. Bri had only known her a few hours, but they'd, like, connected.

Why did someone shoot her . . . and leave me alive?

The thought had chased itself around in her head for the last four hours. She wished she'd stayed and waited for the police. But she'd been afraid they would arrest her, and she was *never* going back to jail.

If Dani died, no one would ever believe Bri hadn't shot her. If only she'd seen the shooter. As it was, she couldn't even give the police a description.

Her heart pounded. When Bri didn't show up at the rehab center, they would call the police and report her missing. But they didn't know what kind of car she was in. And no one knew she had a different cell phone. Bri had trashed her Tracfone because she was afraid that after using it to call 911, the police could track her with it. She'd picked up a burner at a Love's Travel Stop with some of the cash she'd borrowed from Dani's purse. Money Bri would pay back once she had a job.

She needed to hit the road . . . but where to? And what would she use for money? Bri didn't want to use any more of Dani's money. She stared at the iPhone and purse. At one time in her life, she wouldn't have thought twice about taking what money was in the purse or selling the phone.

Trust God from the bottom of your heart . . . don't try to figure out things for yourself. That's what one of the other girls who'd been captured said when she told Bri about Jesus.

Her name was Julie, and by the time she finished, Bri had been blubbering like a baby, but she'd asked Jesus into her heart. The peace that flooded her after that—she'd never felt anything like it before. Like everything would be okay. And it had been. Right after that, they'd been rescued from the men who held them prisoner.

Then the judge had released her to Wings of Hope, and now, eight months later, she'd been looking at a fresh start. *Why did this have to happen?*

Someone had told her that no matter what happened, God would make something good from it, but she didn't see how even God could make anything good out of this.

A twinge stung her heart again, and she glanced at the hospital building. If Dani were unconscious, no one in the hospital would even know who she was. Maybe Bri could call and say . . . what? *That woman who was shot . . . her name is Dani Parker.* That's what was on her driver's license.

Didn't hospitals have information desks when you walked in? She could take Dani's purse and leave it. Her driver's license had her photo on it. Bri's heart sank. No one would be there at 11:00 p.m. unless it was security guards. And if they saw her with a purse like Dani's . . . with Bri's body art and five earrings in each ear, they would automatically think she stole it. They would arrest her for sure.

A yawn stole up on her. She hadn't slept much last night thinking about moving to Jackson, and she was so tired. Maybe she could move the car to the edge of the parking lot and take a nap. It'd be easier to think after she got some sleep.

Bri eased the car through the lot and found a space away from the overhead lights and reached into the back seat for the coat Wings of Hope in New Orleans had given her. Just a short nap. That's all she needed.

19

Madison turned to Pete Nelson and Clayton. "When I saw the gun on the floor, it bothered me, but until now, I didn't know why."

Both men waited expectantly.

"My grandfather is left-handed. He wouldn't have used his right hand to shoot himself."

"Are you sure?" the chief asked as Clayton walked to the desk.

"Yes."

Clayton snapped his fingers. "He was using his left hand to drink coffee when I saw him at the coffee shop this morning."

Madison turned to him. "You saw him where?"

"He was at Coffee and More not long after we met on the Trace. Besides me, two other people stopped and talked to him. Judith Winslow and a woman I didn't recognize." Clayton walked to the desk. "His pens are all arranged on the left side." He opened a drawer. "And his notepads are in this left drawer."

"He kept his revolver in that drawer as well, so he could easily access it with his left hand. That's proof he didn't kill himself." Weight lifted from Madison's shoulders. "Ask Nadine—she'll back me up."

Pete turned to his crime scene investigator. "Check with Miss Nadine," he said as his phone rang. He answered, and after a brief conversation, he disconnected. "That was one of the paramedics who transported the judge."

Madison's heart banged against her ribs. "Is he . . ."

"He's in surgery now. The paramedic gave the OR nurse my number—she's supposed to call with an update as soon as the surgery ends."

He was still alive. She closed her eyes briefly. His life was in the surgeon's hands . . . and God's. Madison looked up when the officer returned.

"Miss Nadine confirmed he was left-handed," he said.

"The killer must have put the gun in his hand and fired it again so he would have gunpowder residue on his skin." Clayton glanced toward the ceiling. "Have your techs found a second bullet?"

"We weren't looking for one," Nelson said. "Hugh Cortland will be taking over the case. He'll bring in his own team, and they'll comb every inch of the room to find it." He instructed the crime scene tech to seal the room. "I don't want *anyone* in here."

After they stepped into the hall, the chief turned to Madison. "Did you see anything unusual when you left the house?"

"No, and I checked the grounds because of Grandfather's concerns about the prisoner who was murdered." Of course, she'd had her mind on other things. Like why Clayton had thought she'd been shot. "Have you issued a BOLO on Corbett's brother?"

"I've sent a detective to his home to interview him."

If only she hadn't left. Madison shook her head. She couldn't think that way—she hadn't known something like this would happen. "What's next?"

"Right now, I'm going to see what Miss Nadine can tell me."

"I'll go with you." Knowing the housekeeper, she would have a pot of coffee going, and Madison needed more caffeine.

"Mind if I tag along?" Clayton asked as they left the study. "I've known her most of my life—we attend the same church. Good Shepherd."

Madison glanced sharply at the ranger. "She didn't go to St. Matthews with my grandfather?"

He shook his head. "She's a charter member of Good Shepherd."

More surprises.

When they entered the kitchen, Nadine sat primly at the table. She nodded at each of them, then took a sip from the cup she held.

"That'll keep you up tonight." Then Madison cringed. Her grandfather had just been shot. Why had she said something so inane?

The older woman squeezed her hand. "It won't be coffee that keeps me awake. I will never believe the judge did such a thing."

Madison exchanged a glance with Clayton and gave him the barest nod. He sat across from Nadine and took her hand. "We don't think he shot himself. We believe that someone else did, and now we need your help in catching this person."

Nadine gasped. "I knew it!"

"They made it look like he tried to take his life, but whoever shot him put the gun in the wrong hand," Clayton said.

"Yes!" She clasped her hands together and pressed them against her lips. "That's what it was! My mind, it kept telling me something was wrong, but I did not understand until now." The older woman lifted her gray head heavenward. "Thank you," she murmured. Then she turned a troubled gaze to Madison. "But why? And how did they get in? Didn't you lock the door when you left?"

"No. That door locks automatically when you close it. I didn't think I needed to."

"Something was wrong with the lock, and the judge kept saying he would get it fixed, but now you must use the key to lock it. Didn't he tell you?"

"No, he only reminded me to set the alarm when I came in." If he'd told her to use her key, she didn't remember. Nadine's voice held no criticism. It didn't have to—Madison's conscience made up for it.

"Miss Nadine," Clayton said, "can you describe what happened?"

"Again?"

Chief Nelson nodded. "It's very important."

"Starting . . . ?"

The chief took out a pad and pen. "With when you last saw Judge Anderson."

"Then I need to fortify myself with more coffee." She rose and walked to the coffeepot. "Anyone else want a cup?"

"None for me," the chief said.

"I'll take one, without chicory if possible," Madison said.

"Me too," Clayton added.

Nadine gave them both disapproving looks, then shook her head. "Black for you, Clayton, if I remember correctly from Sunday," the housekeeper said and turned to Madison. "And for you as well."

Clayton looked surprised that Nadine would remember that, but from Madison's experience, an elephant's memory had nothing on the housekeeper's.

Once Nadine was seated at the table again, she said, "I last saw the judge when I took the bread pudding and coffee to his study. You were with him, chère. He told me not to wait for you to finish, so I went to my apartment and prepared for bed before I watched the ten-o'clock news on TV."

"What happened next?" Madison asked.

"I had just settled in and was almost asleep when I heard gunfire."

"Could you tell where the sound came from?" Clayton asked.

"It wasn't loud, and I knew the judge had a gun in his desk drawer . . . I assumed it came from the house."

"How many gunshots did you hear?"

Nadine stared into her cup, then looked up. "One, I know.

Then I heard something else, but I can't say for sure it was gunfire."

"How far apart was the noise?" Madison asked.

The tiny woman pinched the bridge of her nose. "The time it took me to get out of bed, get my slippers and robe on."

Madison calculated how long it would take to put the revolver in her grandfather's hand and fire the gun a second time. "Would you say the sounds were two minutes apart?"

"Probably." Nadine tilted her head. "Have you called your daddy?"

"Not yet." Madison glanced at her watch. Half past eleven. A couple of days ago, she'd called his office and his secretary told her he was away on a business trip and hadn't known exactly when he would return. It had frosted Madison that she had to learn he was out of town from his secretary. But what else was new?

Madison hoped he was already home and took out her phone. When she dialed his cell number, it went straight to voicemail. Evidently, he'd turned off his phone. She left a message, asking him to call her, and then turned to face the others. "I'll try again in the morning if he doesn't return my call."

Even though there was no love lost between the two men, there would be the devil to pay if her father first heard about her grandfather's shooting on the news. *The press.* She turned to Chief Nelson. "Can you keep this out of the news until I can get in touch with my dad?"

"Should be able to. Our radio system is fully encrypted, so only our scanners pick up the transmissions, and I'll tell everyone involved to keep it quiet. But you know as well as I do, this isn't something you can keep quiet for long."

"I know, but thanks." She shifted her gaze to Clayton. "And thank you for helping tonight."

"No problem. Have you talked to Hugh?"

Hugh! Her face flushed—she'd meant to call him after seeing the Jane Doe, but then Nadine had called . . . and while Clayton and the chief had called Hugh, he would expect a call from her as well.

It was late, but she didn't want to wait until morning. Madison fished her phone from her back pocket, but before she could make the call, the chief stood. "I'll notify the US Marshals as well as the FBI in Jackson that this is a criminal investigation."

"I'm calling Hugh now," she said.

"Tell him I've sealed the room until morning—I know him, and he has his own way of doing things."

She nodded. The FBI and US Marshals would work together on the case, with the FBI taking lead because that's what the FBI did—investigate. Both offices would work with Chief Nelson and his team, but after tonight, she'd be out of the loop.

Madison walked across the room for privacy as she dialed Hugh Cortland's number. He answered on the first ring. "I'm sorry about Judge Anderson."

"Thanks." Madison hated the way her voice hitched.

"I know how close you are to him." He was quiet for a second. "What's his condition?"

"Critical. He's in surgery now to remove the bullet."

"Chief Nelson indicated it was self-inflicted, so he'll—"

"The chief was wrong. Whoever tried to make it look like suicide put the gun in the wrong hand."

She filled him in on the details.

"That makes quite a difference. How about the marshals? Have they been called in?"

"Chief Nelson is notifying them now, and he's sealed the house and is shutting down the investigation for tonight."

A tapping sound came through the phone. Hugh was already typing out a memo. "It'll take a couple of hours in the morning to put together an evidence response team and get down there," he said. "I'll let Nelson know we should be there by noon. In the meantime, is there anything I can do?"

The shock was beginning to wear off, and his offer brought a response she didn't expect. Tears. Blinking them back, she swallowed down the lump in her throat. "Thank you, but I'm fine."

"I doubt that," he said. "Madison . . . it's okay to not be fine."

No, it wasn't. Gregory Thorn's daughter had to suck it up and not show emotion—that had been ingrained in her every time she didn't finish in first place, whether it was a riding competition or martial arts.

When Madison didn't say anything, Hugh blew out a breath. "I'll see you by noon. You're not staying at the house, are you?"

"No. When I leave here, I'm going to the hospital."

"Good. And we'll reschedule our next meeting with Paul and Deon. You do plan to take off the next few days, don't you?"

Madison hadn't thought that far ahead. "No. If I just sit around, I'll go crazy. I received a text from Paul earlier that they had the rest of the financial records ready for me to pick up at Paul's office. I'll do that in the morning and get started on reviewing them."

When they finished, she disconnected and returned to the others, where she passed on the information from Hugh. Then she turned and gave Nadine a gentle smile. "You look tired. Come on, and I'll walk you to your apartment before I go to the hospital."

"Thank you, chére. Will you call when you find out how your grandfather is?"

"Yes, and I'll probably stay with you tomorrow night, if you don't mind."

"Of course not. Having you here will be a comfort, but do you mean tonight?"

Madison glanced at the kitchen clock. Past midnight. It was Thursday already. "Yes. I'll grab my clothes from my room after I get you settled."

Nadine squeezed Madison's hand as they walked out the back door. "Your grandfather is very proud of you."

"What if he dies?" She hadn't meant to just blurt that out.

"Then it is God's will, but . . ." The older woman held up her finger. "Don't get ahead of him."

Madison didn't think she could bear that. Grandfather had been her rock. He'd told her often how much he loved her. Tears burned her eyes, and she swiped her face with the back of her hand.

It was only a few feet to the apartment, and when they reached Nadine's door, Madison flushed under the older woman's steady gaze.

"Who is this woman who looks like you?"

"You heard?"

"My eyes may not see twenty-twenty, but I can still hear a pin drop," the housekeeper said gently.

"But we were in the study, and you were in the kitchen."

Nadine dropped her eyes. "I may have come to the study door to see if any of you wanted coffee, but when I got there, I couldn't go into that room again. You didn't answer. Who is she?"

"I don't know." But she was going to find out . . . and if there was any connection between the woman and her grandfather's shooting, Madison was going to find that out as well.

20

Madison walked ahead of him as Clayton rolled her suitcase to her car instead of Nadine's small apartment behind the big house. She wanted her clothes with her in case she stayed at the hospital for more than what was left of the night. He wasn't sure what to think of the ISB agent. After she got over the shock, Madison had shifted into cool, calm, and collected—almost like she had ice water in her veins.

She stopped at the car and moved the garment bag to her left hand. "You didn't have to stay and bring my suitcase, but thank you."

"No problem."

She tilted her head. "You say that a lot."

"What?"

"No problem. You said it just a little earlier, and I believe this morning as well."

"I guess I do." She remembered what he'd said this morning? Something he didn't even remember? His heart warmed when Madison's mouth quirked upward for what could pass as a tiny smile before she hung her clothes in the car. Her hand brushed against his as she reached for the suitcase, sending a rush through him. "I'll put it in the trunk for you."

Even after he closed the trunk lid, the electricity that her touch ignited stayed with him. Had Madison felt it? Probably not with everything she had going on. He tried to ignore it and turned to her. "I'm really sorry about your grandfather. He's one of the good guys."

"He's going to be all right."

Even though her voice was firm, her eyes turned even bluer as tears formed in them. Clayton ducked his head. He hadn't meant to make her cry.

"Are you coming to the hospital later this morning?"

He looked up. Clayton didn't know how she got herself under control so fast. "My first stop. Maybe your lookalike will be awake by then and can answer questions."

"I'll be at the hospital. I'll try to catch you there."

He studied her. Most people would take a few days off in a situation like this.

She held up her hand. "I know what you're thinking, but I can't sit and do nothing."

"Do you ever stop? You know, turn the job off?"

"And do what? Being an ISB agent is my life."

"No close friends?" *Or boyfriends?*

"I have lots of friends, but none particularly close since I move around a lot."

She wasn't going to volunteer whether she had a boyfriend, so it was time to quit fishing. "No one special in your life?"

"I haven't found anyone who'll put up with my crazy schedule. Right now I'm based at the Hot Springs National Park, but I travel all over the US. I never know how long I'll be in one place."

Madison was holding back something, but he wasn't sure what. "When do you expect your dad?"

She suddenly looked very tired. "Not today, I'm sure. My call to his cell phone earlier went straight to voicemail, and I left him a message but he hasn't called back. I don't know where he is or if he'll even come. He and Grandfather didn't have the best relationship."

"Where do you think he might be?"

"He could be anywhere. His law firm represents clients all over the States."

"But his office will know . . . right?"

She blew out a hard breath and nodded. "I doubt they'll tell me. They'll figure if he doesn't answer my calls, he doesn't want to talk to me. Maybe they'll at least get in touch with him for me."

He frowned. "They won't tell you where he is?"

"Nope. He's always kept business and family separate. I'm not sure Mom always knew where he went on his business trips." She turned to open her car door. "Well, again, thank you."

"Wait," Clayton said. "You have my cell number, but I don't have yours."

"It should be on your cell phone from when I called you earlier."

"Give it to me again." He added the number she rattled off to his contacts. "I'll call you in the morning . . . I mean this morning when I get to the hospital and let you know if our victim is awake."

"Thanks."

Clayton waited until Madison pulled out of the drive before he turned and walked to his SUV. Not many people he knew could've handled the problems she'd had thrown at her tonight. But then, something told him Madison Thorn wasn't like any person he'd ever met.

Clayton rolled his shoulders to stretch out the kinks before getting behind the wheel. He was wound tighter than a steel drum. After he pulled away from Judge Anderson's house, Clayton thought about the two cases. Both involved Madison, but were they connected?

A few minutes later, he glanced up and with a start realized he'd driven almost straight to the casino. In the past, blackjack was how he'd unwind from a hard day. His heart raced as he stared at the dark street up ahead that led down the hill to the gambling boat.

All he had to do was take a right, park his SUV, and amble inside. The day's worries would be lost in a haze of smoke and the excitement of waiting for the next card to turn or the next roll of the dice. Clayton gripped the steering wheel, his hands sweaty.

He was a new creation. Gambling was the old thing. He shook himself, and when the light changed to green, he pressed his foot to the gas pedal, his tires squealing.

The strong lure of the game had slammed Clayton from out of nowhere. While it was a war he waged every day, he hadn't had such a strong pull to the casino in a while. Now wasn't the time to let his guard down.

When he pulled into his drive, he went inside and quickly changed into running clothes and shoes. A few minutes later the rhythmic slap of his feet as they hit the pavement freed his mind. Usually after a mile he slipped into the "zone" as he ran the two-mile circuitous route he'd mapped out in his neighborhood. But not tonight. He couldn't shake how he'd felt when he saw that he was about to turn into the casino.

Clayton hadn't been back to the casino since the night he encountered Luke Fereday there two years ago. The Investigative Services Branch ranger hadn't come out and accused Clayton of having a gambling problem, but there'd been a question in Luke's eyes.

That week Clayton faced facts for the first time—he'd maxed out his credit card to the tune of ten thousand dollars, all in gambling debts, and he'd turned to alcohol to lessen the pain.

Clayton hadn't always lost money, and it wasn't like he'd blown the money he'd won. He'd taken the money and applied it to his mom's loan on her house. Therein lay the problem after the cards turned against him—until that night with Luke Fereday, he'd thought if he kept playing, the cards would eventually fall in his favor.

He'd quit gambling and drinking cold turkey and paid off the debts. And he'd found a therapist who specialized in addictions.

She'd been the one who explained that he needed a substitute for his gambling habit. That he couldn't just quit a bad habit without something to take its place. Running had been that replacement.

Clayton thought about calling his sponsor. No, it was much too late to bother him, and he decided to wait until their regular meeting later in the week. Besides, he was okay now. Instead, he focused on clearing his head with running.

Most nights he ran the route once. Tonight, it took two rounds to calm his nerves. His chest heaving, he shed his clothes as he walked inside his house and then hopped in the shower.

It had been a long day and sleep came quickly, but if it hadn't, he was prepared to recite Scripture verses until it did.

When Clayton's alarm went off at six thirty, he crawled out of bed and grabbed his Bible and a cup of coffee. Last night he'd been blindsided when he realized he'd driven straight to the casino, and he needed reinforcements. He camped out in the first few verses of Isaiah 26. Twenty minutes later, he closed his Bible and breathed a heartfelt prayer for help.

At eight o'clock, his phone rang, and he checked the caller ID. Hugh Cortland. When he answered, the FBI agent got straight to the point.

"How did Madison Thorn handle the two shootings last night?"

"Fine, as far as I could tell, but why are you asking?"

Hugh hesitated. "Since Evan McCall has requested that she work the Coles Creek shooting with you, I need to fill you in on her past so you won't be caught off guard if it comes up."

Clayton listened as Hugh related the details of the shooting in Texas four years ago. "Even though she killed Chad Turner in self-defense, Madison hasn't worked a violent crime since, even though she received the Medal of Valor for saving Chad's son and shutting down the human trafficking ring."

"I totally get it that she wouldn't want to work violent crimes, but from what I observed last night, she won't let her past get in the way of doing a good job with this case," Clayton said. "I don't see a problem working with her on it."

"Good, because there were problems in Texas after the shooting. Some of Turner's buddies thought what happened at the airstrip could have been handled differently, that she didn't have to kill him."

"You're kidding." From what he'd seen in Madison, he was pretty sure she would've done everything in her power to keep from having to shoot a fellow officer of the law. "I appreciate you telling me, but like I said, I don't have any reservations working with Madison."

"I thought you'd feel that way."

Another call beeped in on Clayton's phone. Merit Hospital. He'd asked to be notified of any change in Jane Doe's condition and had left his number with the nursing staff in the unit. "I have another call I need to take. I'll see you later today." He quickly switched to the second call. "Bradshaw."

"Good morning, Clayton," the caller said. "This is Rebecca Temple in Surgical ICU at Merit. I thought you'd like to know our Jane Doe patient is waking up."

Good. "Thanks. Is she still on the vent?"

"We're weaning her off." Rebecca chuckled. "This lady is a fighter. According to her chart, she's had a remarkable turnaround, but she's still very weak."

"Has she remembered what happened? Or if there's any family we can notify?"

"Come on, Clayton," she said. "You know as well as I do our communication is mostly limited to yes and no answers until the vent is removed. But the best I can tell, the patient has no memory of being shot. When I put a pad and pencil in her hand, she was able to write 'What happened?' I imagine she's very confused."

"Will I be able to talk to her?"

"That's what I was hoping for. It'd be good if you could tell her what you know."

"I'll be there in fifteen."

Clayton quickly ran his electric razor over his face and then dressed in the park service gray-and-green uniform and strapped on his service pistol. On the way out the door, he grabbed a protein bar and ate it on the drive.

Five minutes later, he pulled into a parking space at the hospital and jogged to the front door. Rather than wait for the elevator, Clayton took the stairs two steps at a time to the waiting room.

21

Madison groaned as she returned the recliner she'd slept in to an upright position. By the time she'd gotten to the ICU waiting area, all the sofas were taken by the family members of other critical patients. She'd been lucky to find the recliner.

She stretched and then smoothed yesterday's clothes that she'd slept in.

"Coffee's over in the corner."

She turned and nodded to the older woman who'd spoken. "Thanks."

"You're new," she said. "I'm Caroline. My son's been here a week today."

"I'm so sorry." Madison followed her to the refreshment center.

"Me too. He was riding a motorcycle, and a car turned right in front of him. They say if he lives, he'll never walk again, but I don't care about that, just that he makes it through this." She poured a cup of coffee and handed it to Madison. "Who are you here for?"

"My grandfather." She wasn't ready to share that he'd been shot.

Caroline nodded. "Oh, by the way, there's a shower in the bathroom around the corner—just knock before you open the door."

It would feel good to get out of the day-old clothes. "Thanks."

A man came out of the bathroom with water dripping from his hair. "Better grab it while everyone is in the back visiting," Caroline said.

"You go ahead."

"I'm going to take a walk while my husband's here. Fresh towels and washcloths are on a shelf just inside the door."

"Okay . . . thanks." Madison rolled her suitcase to the bathroom. Twenty minutes later she walked out, amazed at the difference a shower and clean clothes made. Another cup of coffee would only make it better. Then she'd check and see where Clayton was.

After pouring her coffee, she turned and almost dropped it. "Steven?"

He and a woman stood not twenty feet from her, scanning the room. Surprise flashed in his face when he saw her. "Madison?"

"What are you doing here?"

They'd spoken in unison and Steven said, "You go first."

"My grandfather is here. What's your reason?"

"I think I told you yesterday I have friends here. Terri and I were just finishing up breakfast . . . I told you about her too." He nodded to the woman standing next to him. "Anyway, I got a call that one of my friends had been brought to the hospital. The person who called told me he was in ICU and some of the family should be in the waiting room, but I don't see anyone I know. Except you."

Terri nodded toward the desk. "Why don't you ask the receptionist?"

"Good idea. Be right back."

A wave of exhaustion swept through Madison, but she managed a smile at Terri. There was something very familiar about Steven's friend. "Do you mind if we sit?"

Silence fell between them after she settled in one of the chairs and Terri on the opposite sofa. "Is the person in the hospital your friend as well?"

Terri shook her head. "I wouldn't have come with him, but he practically insisted, saying he needed the moral support. I'm sorry about your grandfather."

"Thank you."

Terri glanced at the cup Madison held. "I didn't get to finish my coffee at the restaurant. Think I'll grab a cup."

"The machine is in the corner."

"Can I bring you another one?"

"I'm good." Madison took a sip and made a face. The coffee was cold. "On second thought, please."

The way Terri stood and strode toward the coffee machine reminded Madison that she was a Delta Force G squadron operator. When she returned with the coffee, Madison said, "Your first time in Natchez?"

"No." She didn't offer any other information, instead sipped her coffee. "We were going to drive out to Rodney and see the ghost town before it gets too hot."

Madison had never been to the town that had almost become Mississippi's first capital only to die when the Mississippi River changed course, taking away the profitable port at Rodney. "If you're into that sort of thing, be sure to go by the Old Jail here in Natchez."

"A jail? I don't think I want to visit that one," Terri said as Steven rejoined them. "Did you find him?"

"The receptionist said there was no record of him being here. I called the guy who said he was. Turns out he was taken to Jackson." Steven scowled. "How much trouble would it have been for him to call and let me know?"

"I'm sorry," Madison said.

"It's not all bad," Steven said. "At least I ran into you. How is your grandfather? Was it a heart attack?"

For a brief few minutes, Madison had put aside why she was

sitting in the ICU waiting room. She didn't want to go into the details, though. "Not a heart attack, but he is critical. I haven't been back to see him yet."

She looked up as the doors to the waiting room opened, and Clayton strode in. He stopped and scanned the room. "Over here," she called, raising her hand.

He approached, giving Steven a once-over before shifting his gaze to Terri, and a light frown creased his brow. Madison introduced them, apologizing when she didn't remember Terri's last name.

"It's Davis," she said. "Terri Davis."

"We were in Delta Force together," Steven said, shaking the hand Clayton extended.

Clayton turned to Terri. "Did I see you at Coffee and More yesterday?"

"It's possible—they have great coffee."

"So, how did you two know where to find Madison?"

Why was Clayton giving them the third degree? "Steven was mistakenly told a friend had been brought here. How's our patient?"

"Waking up. I thought I'd see if she could answer a few questions."

"And I think that's our cue to leave," Steven said. "You have my number on your cell—call me if you need anything. I'm staying at the Grand, so I can quickly be here."

"Thanks."

"Are you staying at the Grand as well?" Clayton asked.

Terri hesitated. "No, I'm at the Hampton by the Mississippi bridge." She turned to Madison. "It was good to meet you. I hope we run into each other again, under better circumstances, of course."

"Me too." Madison meant it. Terri was the kind of person she enjoyed being around.

After they left, she turned to him. "What was with the third degree?"

Clayton shrugged. "Just curious. This Steven Turner . . . any relation to Chad Turner?"

Her breath caught in her chest. "How do you know about Chad?"

22

Clayton cringed. He'd planned to wait and let her bring up what happened in Texas and fished around for words to tell Madison he'd been discussing her past with Hugh.

She folded her arms across her chest. "You haven't said how you know about Chad."

"Hugh told me."

"I see."

"Madison, you had to do what you had to do."

"Thank you." She took a deep breath. "Okay. I'm glad it's out in the open, then."

"Good, but I still want to know why Chad's brother is here." Clayton turned and stared out the door the two had exited. His suspicion radar pinged off the charts.

"I told you about his friend."

And that smelled like two-day-old fish. Clayton was certain Terri was the same woman who'd had a serious discussion with Judge Anderson at Coffee and More. The woman's military background matched his impressions of the judge's visitor, but he hadn't wanted to question her about it with Madison present.

"How well do you know Steven?" He'd seemed pleasant enough . . . except Clayton didn't like the underlying tension he got from the man. Of course, since Steven was a former Delta

Force operator, that could be normal. But he didn't get the same tension from the woman, and she was former Delta Force too.

"Until yesterday, I hadn't said ten words to him." Frown lines appeared on her forehead. "I thought he held me responsible for killing his brother."

"Since he's here, I assume he doesn't, but if you haven't had communication with him until yesterday, what happened to change that?"

"He called me, said he was in Natchez and needed to talk to me."

"How'd he know you were in Natchez? Or get your number?"

"Chad's phone on both accounts. I'd forgotten he had an app that kept up with my location. I was curious about what Steven wanted and agreed to meet him for lunch at the Camp Restaurant. I'm glad I did. Finding out the boy I saved that horrible day is doing well was worth any reservations I had in meeting Steven."

Learning Turner's reason for coming eased his suspicions somewhat.

The doors to the ICU opened, drawing their attention to a man in a lab coat scanning the room.

"It's Grandfather's doctor. I asked him for an update," Madison said, raising her hand.

The doctor started toward them, and Clayton felt she needed privacy. "I'll be in our Jane Doe's room if you want to talk once you finish with the doctor."

He squeezed her hand and quickly walked through the same ICU doors the doctor had exited. Clayton was much later than he'd told Rebecca he would be and hoped she was still around. He relaxed when she was at the desk and looked up as he approached.

"Good. You're here," Rebecca said.

"Took a few minutes longer than I thought it would, and then I stopped by the waiting room to speak with Judge Anderson's granddaughter."

The nurse nodded her understanding. "If you spoke to Madison, I'm sure you know it's still touch and go with him. As for your Jane Doe, she's very weak and slipping in and out of consciousness."

Clayton followed Rebecca into the room where the patient lay with her eyes closed. In his mind, he'd taken to calling her Jane.

"Good morning again," the nurse said softly.

Jane turned her head toward them and blinked her eyes open. They were as blue as Madison's, and after spending several hours with the ISB agent last night and just leaving her now, it was surreal to see another person with the same features.

While the charge nurse checked Jane Doe's IVs, the patient moved restlessly in the bed. It was evident she was struggling to stay awake, but after a few seconds, she closed her eyes and slipped back into sleep. He studied her face, looking for a difference in features, and even with the vent tube pulling on her mouth, the resemblance to Madison was strong. It would help if she were here for him to compare the two.

Almost as if he'd conjured her up, there was a knock at the door and Madison walked in. Rebecca hurried to her and whispered something, and the two walked out into the hallway. Clayton followed them.

"Since you weren't aware of this person's existence, I'm not sure our Jane Doe is aware of you, either. It might be quite a shock for her to see you," Rebecca said. "I'd like to prepare her first."

"I totally understand," Madison replied. "Can she talk at all?"

"No, but like I told Clayton, we're weaning her off the vent. If all goes well, she should be able to speak later today. In the meantime, she has a pad and pen and can write and does seem to comprehend what I say to her."

Another nurse approached them and requested Rebecca's help. "Be right back," she said and walked away.

"How's your grandfather?" he asked.

"He's extremely critical. He's around the corner in room 211." Madison's phone buzzed. "It's Hugh."

Clayton nodded and returned to the room to give her privacy. He looked for a chair to move closer to the bed so that if Jane Doe roused, he wouldn't be standing over her. He winced when he bumped the bed with the chair.

She turned her head toward him and opened her eyes again. They were much clearer this time. She lifted a notepad that was on the bed, scribbled on it, and pushed it toward him. "*Who are you?*"

"Clayton Bradshaw," he replied. "I'm a law enforcement ranger on the Natchez Trace. That's where you were found. What's your name?"

Her brows lowered, and she hesitated. Clayton thought she was drifting off to sleep again, but then she scratched out letters on the notepad. When she finished, the pen relaxed in her hand. Clayton waited a second before he tore the sheet from the notepad.

Lindsey Tremont. She roused again, and he smiled. "It's good to have a name—I've been calling you Jane Doe."

A frown shadowed her face, and she wrote, "*Why? Purse. ID.*"

"Unfortunately, both are missing, as well as your car and the young woman you were with."

She groaned and shook her head.

He patted her arm. "Don't try to talk, it'll only frustrate you."

The frown deepened as she tried to open her eyes, but sleep won out, and her face relaxed again into a deep sleep. At least he had a name now. Lindsey Tremont. Clayton stood and strode to the door. A background check should give him answers. And a certain ISB agent could probably get a more thorough report than he could. And quicker.

23

Madison gripped her phone. The call from Hugh quickly became a conference call with the FBI agent and Evan McCall, the district law enforcement ranger at Ridgeland, and David Sowell, her ISB superintendent in Hot Springs. Their suggestion that she take the next few days off hadn't been one she wanted to hear.

"I need to be busy," she said. "Sitting at the hospital all day won't help my grandfather. Besides, the US Marshal posted outside his door promised if there's any change, he'll call immediately."

"Okay," McCall said. "Since you want to be busy, I'd like for you to assist Clayton in the shooting at Coles Creek."

"What?" Surely she'd misunderstood him. He knew she didn't do violent crimes. "Clayton can handle the investigation by himself."

"I know that, but you're there, and two well-qualified officers are better than one," McCall said.

She swallowed hard. The last time she'd worked a violent crime had been a disaster, both personally and professionally, and if something went bad with this case, Madison didn't know if she could take that again. "What about the kickback case with the supervisors?"

"Just do what you can on that," Sowell said. "I understand

Davidson pulled the necessary records for you to go over. You can do that in your sleep."

She directed a question to Hugh. "What time will you arrive in Natchez?"

"Around noon," he said. "Have you spoken to the Coles Creek victim?"

"No, she's still on a vent."

"Does she really look like you?" Hugh asked.

"She could be my twin," she said. "Evan, are you sure you want me to take lead?" Seconds ticked off as she waited for him to answer. Surely, he was reconsidering this assignment.

Her ISB supervisor answered instead of Evan. "It's not a matter of who takes lead. Just work with Clayton Bradshaw on this, Agent Thorn."

Sowell wasn't changing his mind, and by using her formal title, he was reminding her what she signed up for when she joined the Investigative Services Branch.

"You have what it takes to investigate this crime." Sowell's voice was soft but firm.

She appreciated his confidence. Madison stood taller and squared her shoulders. She would not blow this investigation and end her ISB career. "Okay. I'll check back with you later."

She glanced at her phone after the two supervisors had disconnected. "You still on the call, Hugh?"

"Yeah. I just wanted to pass along that Clayton's a good investigator and you can trust him to have your back."

She already knew that about him, especially with the way he reacted to learning what happened in Texas.

"Just be wary of his charm," Hugh added.

That she didn't get at all. "What do you mean?"

There was a brief pause. "He has quite the reputation with the ladies."

On that note, Hugh ended the call, promising to keep her in the loop about the investigation into her grandfather's shooting.

Madison pocketed her phone. Clayton was a ladies' man? She hadn't seen that side of him, but she probably wasn't his type.

"Bad news?"

She turned. Clayton was leaning against the wall, apparently waiting for her to finish. Thank goodness the call hadn't been on speaker. "Depends on how you look at it," she said. "Looks like we'll be working together—Evan McCall just assigned me to work with you."

"I can use all the help I can get. Do you have any pull with the FBI analyst in Jackson? We need a background check."

"On . . . ?"

"Our patient. Says her name is Lindsey Tremont," he said. "And she was concerned that the girl and her purse and car were missing."

"I'll call and see. When I met with Hugh at his office in Jackson on Tuesday, he introduced me to the rest of his team, and they all said they'd help in any way they could. The analyst was really nice, and while this has nothing to do with the investigation Hugh and I are working, maybe she can check Lindsey Tremont out. If she can, we should get a preliminary report back by this afternoon."

"Sounds good. Did you get an update on your grandfather's case?"

"Only that the crime scene response team will be here by noon. Right now I have to drive across town and pick up some files from the county supervisor's office. Then I thought I might drive to Coles Creek." If she had to investigate the crime, she needed a feel for what had happened, and the only place she could get that was at the crime scene.

"Are you sure you want to leave the hospital?"

"I can't accomplish anything by staying here other than worrying. The doctor said Grandfather would probably be out of it all day." She hesitated. "Want to ride to Coles Creek with me?"

"Sounds good," he said. "But let's take my SUV."

"Why?" What was it with men wanting to be in control?

He raised an eyebrow. "Just thought it'd be easier since I'm familiar with Natchez and you're—"

"I have GPS," she said.

"But it doesn't always work on the Trace." He tilted his head, studying her. "Just like a cell phone doesn't. It'd be easier for my people to get hold of me on my radio in the SUV."

She didn't know what was wrong with her. First, she'd accused him of bullying her when she was a kid, and now she'd taken offense at his suggestion that they use his vehicle, which was perfectly logical since he knew the area.

It had to be Hugh's remark about his charms—that he hadn't used on her. Her face flushed. Had she really just thought that? Madison immediately erased it. "Sorry. It's just . . ."

He lifted an eyebrow. "You're not one of those people who *have* to be in the driver's seat, are you?"

She gave him a wry smile. "Your SUV is fine."

"Good," he said, grinning. "Let me find Rebecca and ask her to call if there's any change in our patient."

While Clayton went to find the nurse, Madison dialed the Jackson FBI office and asked for Allyson.

"Need something already, Madison?"

Apparently Allyson didn't waste words. "Yes, but it doesn't pertain to the case I'm working on with Hugh. Can you still help me?"

"Whatcha need?"

"A background check on a Lindsey Tremont."

"I can do that. Do you have an address? Or date of birth?"

"No address. Ms. Tremont had no ID on her." For DOB Madison hesitated, then impulsively gave her birth date. She'd read somewhere that twins happened in 3 percent of all births. And Lindsey Tremont appeared to be about Madison's age, so it wasn't out of the realm of possibility that she and Lindsey were at least related and possibly twins. They certainly looked enough alike for it to be true. "But get information on anyone within five years either way."

"I'll get right on this," Allyson said. "If she's in the system, I should have something by this afternoon."

"Thanks."

"You're welcome . . . and Hugh told us about your grandfather. I'm really sorry."

The sincerity in Allyson's voice brought tears to Madison's eyes. It was the unexpected kindnesses that undid her. "Thanks," she choked out. "But he's going to make it." After she disconnected, Madison fished a tissue from her bag and blotted her eyes.

"You okay?" Clayton asked.

She whirled around. "I didn't hear you come up."

"I'm like Sylvester the cat."

Madison blinked. "You watched Tweety Bird cartoons?"

He laughed. "Guilty as charged, and I still do—I have a six-year-old niece, and she loves Tweety Bird."

"So do I." She grinned, then asked, "Did you find the nurse?"

"I did. You want to leave your car here? Or would you rather drop it off at your grandfather's house?"

"The hospital parking area is fine." She would be coming back to the hospital anyway.

Madison grabbed her briefcase from the Impala and climbed into Clayton's Ford Interceptor. While she fastened her seat belt, he phoned his field ranger to meet them at Coles Creek in an hour.

Neither of them spoke on the short drive downtown. When he pulled in front of the Old Jail that housed the supervisors' offices, she climbed out. "Be right back."

The administration office was quiet when she opened the door. "Anyone here?"

"Be right there." The muffled voice came from behind a closed side door. An old closet, maybe?

The door opened, and Vivian Hawkins hurried into the room,

her arms loaded with files. She took one look at Madison and caught her breath. "What are you doing here?"

She would not let this woman get under her skin. "I believe you have some files for us."

Vivian set the files she carried on her desk and uncapped a bottle of Perrier. She took a long sip and then turned to Madison. "I thought the other person with you yesterday was picking them up."

"No, you got me." Madison noticed a box sitting on the same rolling cart Paul Davidson had used the day before. "Are these the files?"

"I suppose. Paul left the box out here this morning and said someone would be picking it up—I assumed it'd be your partner."

"Why?"

She shrugged her shoulders. "You'll have to sign a form that you're taking the box. It's on the top."

"Yes, ma'am. And I'll get the records back to you as soon as I can." She would be up late tonight comparing the invoices with the actual deliveries, but at least it would give her something to think about other than her grandfather's injuries. The secretary drummed her fingers on the desk as Madison signed the paper and handed it over. She turned to pick up the box and tried to figure out what she'd done to the secretary to produce such an intense dislike on her part.

Vivian cleared her throat. "If the FBI is trying to pin something illegal on Paul Davidson, it's a complete waste of time and taxpayer dollars."

Madison's hands stilled on the box. The supervisor had said he wasn't telling anyone he'd called them in, so how did the secretary know one of them was FBI? On the other hand, if Vivian thought the FBI was investigating the boss she seemed infatuated with, it would certainly explain her animosity. Madison turned to face the woman. "I'm not with the FBI. What made you think I was?"

Vivian's nostrils flared. She dropped her gaze to the desk and focused on paper-clipping several sheets of paper together. Madison waited.

She raised her head and held Madison's gaze. "I recognized your partner. He spoke at a Rotary Club meeting last year about the FBI, and if he is an FBI agent, I figured you were too."

"I see," Madison said. "I'm afraid I don't know anything about any Rotary Club meeting because until Tuesday, I was at a ranger station in Hot Springs, Arkansas. But I dare say your boss would appreciate it if you didn't broadcast that an investigation is going on."

"I still think it's a waste of money to investigate Paul."

Paul Davidson would have to be the one to inform his secretary that no one was investigating him . . . but if Vivian did spread the news that the FBI had been called in, it would suit their purposes better if she thought the investigation was directed toward Davidson rather than the stolen machinery and kickbacks. "We'll see."

The secretary's eyes narrowed. "You really like digging up dirt on people, don't you?"

"If someone breaks the law, they need to be held accountable." Madison kept her voice even.

"Do you ever consider the people you hurt when you throw baseless accusations around?"

"I don't throw accusations around—I go by what the numbers tell me, and numbers don't lie—they speak for themselves. Now, if you'll excuse me, I have work to do."

"I bet you do."

Madison bit back the retort on her tongue and walked out the door. Some people had to have the last say, and she wasn't getting into a spitting match with Vivian Hawkins.

24

Clayton checked his watch. Madison had indicated that grabbing a few files wouldn't take a minute. A news alert on his phone dinged, and he quickly scanned the messages, his heart turning sick.

Another mass shooting, this one in St. Louis. He flinched when the cargo lid to his SUV opened. He hadn't even seen Madison come out of the building.

Once she stowed the box, she climbed into the Interceptor and took one look at him. "What's wrong?"

"Somebody went crazy at a mall in St. Louis. Killed eight people."

She took her phone from her bag and typed something in a search engine. A minute later she leaned back against the seat. "Oh no. Certainly makes my problems seem insignificant."

He glanced at her. Madison's cheeks were red, and the lines around her mouth were tight. As bad as the shooting was, he didn't think it was the reason for her reaction. "Didn't go so well in the office?"

She shrugged.

Clayton waited. Madison Thorn played her cards close to her chest and would tell him what was going on in her own good time. It quickly became evident by her silence now wasn't that time. "Fasten your seat belt, and we'll be on our way."

She quickly complied, and he pulled away from the curb.

Thoughts of the shooting lay heavy on Clayton's heart. If he were truthful, he felt some relief that it hadn't happened in his territory where he would be sure to know some of the victims. God help those who were touched by this tragedy. Prayers were the only course of action he had.

Madison had fallen silent, probably thinking the same thoughts he was, if she had a relationship with God.

"Why do people do this? Shoot people randomly?"

He wished he had an answer other than "I don't know." And telling Madison they lived in a dark world was no better.

When he didn't answer, Madison continued, "It just seems so senseless. Why doesn't God keep things like this from happening?"

Clayton stopped for a red light and glanced at her, his heart cracking at the pain in her face. She didn't have to tell him she was referring to her grandfather's shooting.

"I wish I knew." Why did God stop some evil and not others? He hesitated. "It's taken me a while to understand, but there are some questions we won't get answers to this side of heaven."

She slumped in the seat. "I know. But that doesn't help right now."

He understood that. The light changed to green, and he gunned the Interceptor through the intersection. Neither of them spoke until they were almost to the Trace. "What did you think of the Old Jail?" he asked.

Her dark expression lifted. "I'm glad they repurposed it. I'd love to tour it."

"Maybe I can make that happen."

"Really?"

He grinned. "You actually don't need my help. I think the mayor's office can set you up with a tour." He turned onto the Natchez Trace. "You know there's a ghost associated with the building?"

"You're kidding."

"Nope. It's even been featured in one of those ghostbuster shows."

"You don't believe in ghosts, do you?"

He took a second to glance her way and almost laughed at her wide-eyed expression. "Of course not. I figure all the noises come from rodents and maybe bats."

"The chief bat would be Vivian Hawkins," Madison muttered.

"What happened back there?"

"She hates me, and I don't have a clue why."

"You want to talk it through?"

"Not really." She tapped her fingers on the armrest. "Okay, I've been told I can be a pain sometimes, but she bristled as soon as she saw me."

"Did she give you a reason?"

"She thinks we're investigating her boss, Paul Davidson."

He nodded toward boxes in the back. "Are you?"

She hesitated. Madison knew Clayton well enough now to clue him in on why she was in Natchez. "Not Davidson. He's the one who called us about a theft ring and kickback scheme, but he wants to keep that on the Q.T. We portrayed ourselves as insurance agents. Unfortunately, she'd seen Hugh in his official capacity—"

"And that made you look like liars."

"Yeah. But why would that ruffle Vivian's feathers?"

"I've met a few personal assistants who were bulldogs when it came to their bosses, and she's evidently very protective of Davidson."

"Well, I hope I don't have to deal with her much longer."

Clayton had been to the supervisor's office, and he brought up a mental image of Vivian Hawkins. What he remembered was a pleasant woman with dark hair and large eyes. His experiences with her had not been bad at all, but it seemed there was something else he should remember . . . "I think her bark is worse than her bite."

"No, it isn't." She sighed. "You would've had to have been there."

"Does this happen with you often?"

"No," she said a little too quickly. "At least not until someone gets to know me better."

He laughed. "You must be one of those hard-nosed special agents who always follows the rules."

Red crept into her face. He'd hit a nerve.

"Nothing wrong with rules," she said. "How far to Coles Creek?"

"Seventeen and a half miles, which will take about twenty minutes."

Evidently, Madison didn't wish to discuss Vivian Hawkins any further. A few miles on the narrow two-lane road lined with budding dogwoods. Then it came to him what he'd wanted to remember about the personal assistant. "Vivian Hawkins really isn't a bad person. She even coaches the county's 4-H shooting team."

"What?"

He repeated what he'd said. "I worked with her a couple of years ago. She came home to Natchez after a terrible tragedy—something about the man she was going to marry. I'd have to ask my mom for the details."

"That still doesn't explain why she doesn't like me."

"Maybe she's just having a bad week, and don't forget, she thinks you're investigating her boss."

"I guess." She glanced out the window and sighed. "This truly is a beautiful drive. I was too worried about being late yesterday to appreciate it."

"Yeah. I like driving the Trace any time of the year, but it's especially pretty in the spring." *Like you.*

The thought came out of nowhere, and with the road straight and not a car in sight, Clayton cut his eyes at Madison. Their gazes met, and her blue eyes softened, hitching his heart. The moment vanished as she looked away and clasped her hands in her lap.

What just happened? He didn't know, but he was pretty sure Madison had felt whatever *it* was, as well. In the past, that one shared look would have been enough for him to take it a step further and ask the woman out on a date, which always ended with a kiss . . . sometimes more.

It was tempting to take that step—Madison was a beautiful woman, and even more, she was strong and comfortable in her own skin. They even shared a passion for justice. But he'd vowed before God—no more casual relationships.

Was it time to think about a long-term commitment? Had God brought Madison in his life for that purpose? The thought scared him. More than likely it was a test to see if he'd really meant his vow.

Silence filled the SUV, but not the comfortable silence of before. He fished for something to break the tenseness, but his mind refused to cooperate.

"What made you become a ranger?" she asked.

And just like that, the tension in the SUV evaporated. Or maybe it'd been in his imagination. He glanced at her again. She'd turned slightly toward him. At least she wasn't trying to put distance between them.

"The usual reasons," he said. "I like being outside with nature, and I like being in law enforcement. Being a ranger combined the two."

"Did you know from early on that's what you wanted to do?"

His chest tightened. He didn't like to think about his childhood. "I joined the Youth Conservation Corp when I was fifteen and worked most summers at St. Catherine Creek until I turned eighteen . . . although I did work one summer at a riding barn during college."

"Is that what you studied when you went to college? Wildlife management?"

He laughed, and the tightness eased. "Nope. Much to the chagrin of my family, I got a criminal justice degree."

"They didn't want you in law enforcement?"

"My mom had a hissy fit. My dad died when I was ten, but before that he made it plain he wanted me to do something in the higher-pay-scale range."

She frowned. "That was a lot of pressure on you so early."

"Yeah, and Mom picked up his mantle. Even now, my job isn't something we discuss around the dinner table at holidays."

"But you persevered."

"I did."

"What did your parents want you to do?"

"From my earliest years in school, I was good in math, so Dad wanted me to be a CPA. He thought they made a lot of money, and maybe they do, but I never saw myself sitting in an office all day."

"Interesting." She leaned toward him slightly. "Why did he want you to earn a lot of money?"

"He used to say he grew up so poor he couldn't pay attention. He didn't get to go to college." Because Clayton had come along and ruined that dream. "He wanted more for me than the low-paying jobs he had to take."

They passed the marker for Loess Bluff. Before she could ask him another question, he said, "And you—were your parents happy about your career choice?"

"Probably about as happy as yours." Her foot tapped against the floorboard.

They had that in common too.

"My dad wanted me to become a lawyer like him."

"Why did you go against his wishes?"

Madison shrugged. "I joined mostly to prove to myself I was good enough to get in."

He could understand that. "I didn't know the Investigative Services Branch even had a special agent who focused on white-collar crimes until I met you."

Her foot stilled. "I've heard that before." After a significant pause, she said, "How much farther to Coles Creek?"

"About five miles." Clayton didn't understand why she was working white-collar crime after getting the Medal of Valor. Did she have some sort of PTSD from the shooting in Texas? "Do you like it? Working white-collar crime?"

"I'm good at it. I seem to have a talent for spotting bookkeeping irregularities."

"That didn't answer my question."

"I like it fine," she said matter-of-factly.

He glanced her way, and she was staring out the side window again. He counted two mile markers in the growing silence until she sighed.

"Just another couple of miles," he said as the turnoff for Mount Locust came in sight.

"Any word on the person who was with Lindsey Tremont?"

"Afraid not."

"Maybe Lindsey will be alert enough to tell us where to look for the girl when we return to the hospital."

"Here's hoping." He turned off the Trace into the Coles Creek rest area and drove past his field ranger's Interceptor that partially blocked the drive.

Clayton parked on the other side of the vehicle, and they climbed out of the SUV. He waved to Brooke, who was sweeping a metal detector back and forth over the parking area.

"Lindsey was shot near the restroom," he said as they walked toward his field ranger.

The only response he received was a curt nod. Madison was already scanning the area, her whole demeanor tense. She reminded him of a bloodhound on the scent. He sensed she had the natural instincts to investigate a crime like this, so why had she stopped?

The lady had a story, and he wanted to hear it.

25

Even though Clayton knew what had happened in Texas, Madison did not want to discuss why she'd joined the white-collar crime division. It was hard enough being drawn into this case without reliving an old one.

Instead, she focused on the introduction he was making and smiled and nodded to the field ranger. "I look forward to working with you," Madison said.

"Same here. You'll be the first ISB ranger I've worked with other than my husband," Brooke said, her smile genuine.

Madison had almost forgotten that Brooke was married to Luke Fereday, since Brooke had kept her maiden name professionally.

"What can you tell me about last night?" Madison asked as Clayton walked away from them. Brooke took out her iPad and read the report she'd written.

"Thanks. Can you send that to me?"

"Sure, but take my tablet for now so you can refer back to my notes."

Madison nodded. "Let me have a few minutes to process everything." Once Brooke joined Clayton, who was in the shade of the brick building, Madison scanned the area. In her mind's eye, she could see Lindsey Tremont pulling off the Trace and parking.

Madison walked inside the building. One working stall, one with an out-of-order sign. Since the girl had called 911, she was with her and may have offered for Lindsey to go first. Going on that assumption, Madison retraced the victim's steps, exiting the restroom.

From Brooke's notes, it appeared Lindsey was facing the door, probably trying to return to the building when she was shot. Madison stilled herself and focused on how the crime may have gone down. What she could "see" was Lindsey exiting the building, maybe realizing something was wrong, and running back to the restroom when someone shot her in the back.

She glanced around and tried to recall if there'd been a moon visible last night. No. Madison distinctly remembered looking for one when she arrived at the hospital. She approached the two rangers.

"Was this light working last night?" Madison thumbed toward the light on a wooden post in front of the restroom.

"Yes," Brooke said. "But it's the only one here. Anyone could have hidden in the shadows beyond the light's reach, and the victim wouldn't have seen them when she came out of the restroom. I figure she came out alone to wait for Bri—that's the name the girl gave the 911 operator."

"What's your take on her? Do you think she shot our victim and stole her car?"

"I don't think so. The 911 operator indicated she was scared and tried to help."

They had so little to go on. Was she a relative? Or someone Lindsey had picked up, maybe doing a good deed? Madison glanced at her phone, willing the FBI analyst to call with information on this Lindsey Tremont. Only one bar? "Is there no phone service here?"

"Very little," Clayton said. "You might get a text through. Or I can contact dispatch on the radio to make a call for you."

"I'll wait." Even if she had Allyson's report, there was nothing she could do with it out here. She searched Brooke's notes to see if there was anything about how far away the assailant had been and didn't find anything. "Any guesstimate on the distance between the victim and shooter?"

"It was really overcast last night so it was very dark. I'm thinking ten, twenty feet at most." Brooke turned to her boss. "What do you think?"

Clayton nodded. "I agree."

A gun that used 9mm ammo was accurate to thirty yards, but that was with daylight conditions. Madison was inclined to agree with Brooke as well. "Did you find any casings?"

"Nothing last night. I had just started sweeping the area again when you arrived." She pointed to the metal detector leaning against the brick building.

Madison waved her away. "By all means, go back to it, and let me know if you find anything."

"Are you ready to leave?" Clayton asked.

"As soon as I take some photos." Madison took out her phone and quickly snapped shots of the area. Having a visual would help when she wrote her report.

Once they were in Clayton's SUV and headed south again, she leaned back against the seat.

"I don't imagine you got much sleep last night, so take a nap if you want to."

"I wish. I can't turn off my brain. Why did they stop *here*? Where's the girl? Where were they going? Why would someone shoot her?" She turned to him. "You ever have that problem?"

"All the time."

Her phone dinged with a message. "We must be back in cell phone range." She checked her phone. Not a message but a voicemail from Allyson. Madison punched the playback button and put it on speaker.

"Call me when you get this. Interesting information on your Lindsey Tremont."

"Maybe we're finally getting somewhere," Clayton said.

"I hope so. How long will we have reception?"

"Mount Locust is just ahead. There's good reception at the maintenance building. I'll pull in there."

A few minutes later, Clayton pulled off the Trace and drove around to a low white building and parked. Madison hit redial and put the call on speaker. "What do you have?" she asked when the analyst answered.

"I emailed you the report. Didn't you get it?"

"I'm on the road." She didn't want to try to read it on her phone. "What's in it?"

"Lindsey Tremont grew up in Mobile, Alabama. Mother died from cancer, but the father is still living. And her DOB is the date you gave me."

Madison's heart almost stopped. That couldn't be a coincidence. It was impossible to comprehend all that meant, and she pushed the information to the back of her mind. "Anything else?"

"I'm getting there, just setting the backdrop. Lindsey Tremont was a social worker until four years ago, when she died—killed in a car crash."

"What?" Madison glanced at Clayton. He looked as puzzled as she felt. "Do you have a photo of her?" She wanted to make sure they were talking about the same person.

"It's in the report."

"Allyson, I don't have the report." She tried not to sound impatient. "Can you text it to me?"

"Give me a second. One thing you should know—about a month before she died, Tremont was the key player in bringing down a big human trafficking ring in the panhandle of Florida, and there was a contract on her life."

Another piece to the puzzle. Within seconds her phone dinged, and she hit the home button and clicked on the photo in the analyst's text. It was their patient, all right.

"I didn't know you had a twin," Allyson said.

"Neither did I," she replied dryly and showed Clayton the photo. Anyone who knew Madison would assume it was her—like he had. "And Lindsey Tremont isn't dead, at least she wasn't a couple of hours ago."

"So, what's the story?"

"I'm not sure. When I am, I'll fill you in." Madison ended the call and slumped against the seat again. "Why can't anything be simple?"

"You don't really expect that, do you?" Clayton asked.

She liked the undercurrent of amusement in his voice. In fact, Madison could like everything about him. *Get your mind back in the game.* She straightened up. "No."

"This is one of two things—either our Lindsey Tremont is in the WITSEC program and someone found her, or—"

"She was transporting a victim and she had a new bull's-eye on her back." Was Bri a victim of human trafficking? And did the person who shot Lindsey have Bri now?

Madison massaged her temples. It was easy to believe Lindsey was in the witness security program if she helped to shut down a human trafficking ring. She could see her changing her name, but why not change her looks as well? And why get involved in helping victims of human trafficking again?

Clayton pulled back onto the Trace. "Hopefully she'll be up to telling us what's going on when we get to the hospital."

26

After they had exhausted the subject of Lindsey, Madison took Clayton up on the chance to snooze on the way to the hospital . . . or at least make him think that's what she was doing. Her whole life had been upended with this Lindsey Tremont and then her grandfather's shooting.

She needed time to process the fact that she might have a twin sister. The thought boggled her mind. Why hadn't it shown up on the DNA test she'd done? Maybe because Lindsey hadn't taken the DNA test until recently? But then again, when was the last time she'd opened an email from the testing site?

Madison had called the hospital before they left Mount Locust and checked on her grandfather and Lindsey. He was critical and still unconscious. However, her possible twin was off the vent, and while mostly sleeping, she was alert when awake. Maybe Madison could get some answers . . . but then again, Lindsey might be clueless as well about their connection. She wouldn't be clueless about her identity, though, and they could discover why she was listed as dead.

At the hospital, Clayton parked near the entrance, and they hurried inside and opted for the stairs instead of the elevator. When they reached the ICU doors, Clayton stopped her. "Let's find out if Lindsey has been told about you before we descend on her—we don't want to get kicked out of the hospital."

As much as Madison wanted to barge right in and question Lindsey, Clayton was right. If she didn't know she had a twin, seeing Madison for the first time might be a shock. "You check with your friend while I check on my grandfather."

He gave her a thumbs-up, and she walked to her grandfather's room. A different US Marshal sat outside the door. She showed her ID. "Do you know how he is?"

"Nurse says he's about the same."

"Still unconscious?"

"Yes."

"I'm going to step inside just a minute." Even though she'd spent the night at the hospital to be close to her grandfather, she hadn't actually seen him. Since her mother's death, Madison wasn't good with visiting sick people, much less critically ill family members she loved.

She slipped into the room and stopped at the sight of her grandfather hooked up to more tubes and wires than she'd ever seen. Madison squeezed her eyes shut. Her mother hadn't lived to get to the hospital, and she hadn't seen her this way.

She couldn't do this.

Her grandfather had always been so strong. Her champion. Madison did not want this picture imprinted in her mind.

He's always been there for you. Now it's your turn. She wanted to put her hands over her ears, but the voice had come from inside her head.

Take a deep breath. Hold it. Blow it out. She repeated the process until she could approach the bed.

The whoosh-whoosh-click of the ventilator broke the quiet of the room. She avoided her grandfather's face and instead slipped her hand in his and looked up at the monitor someone must have silenced. Heart rate was one hundred. Madison supposed that wasn't bad. Blood pressure—not too bad either for his condition.

A slight pressure on her fingers surprised her. "Grandfather? I'm here."

More pressure, and she finally lifted her gaze to his face. It was the color of the sheet, but his eyes flickered like he was trying to open them. Madison moistened her dry lips and bent closer. "I'm here, Grandfather."

A groan came from his throat.

"Don't try to talk. Just rest and get better."

There was no response.

The door flew open and a nurse rushed in as code blue sounded from the overhead system. "Clear the room!"

"Why—" Her heart hammered in her chest. Madison dropped his hand and backed away from the bed.

"Go!" The nurse swung the glass wall open, and someone with a crash cart barreled in.

The US Marshal led her from the room into the hall. "He's coded. Let's get out of their way."

This couldn't be happening.

A nurse closed the door and pulled the curtain so Madison couldn't see what was going on. She strained to hear what they were saying, but words and sounds came at her too fast.

Madison felt someone by her side and looked up into Clayton's blue eyes, concern etched on his face.

"What happened? I heard a code blue and came to check on you."

"I think his heart stopped," she whispered.

He wrapped his arms around her, and she leaned into him, resting her head on his chest, feeling the steady beat of his heart.

"I'm so sorry. You want to sit in the waiting room?"

"I'm not leaving."

A nurse came out of the room, and Madison stepped out of his arms and faced her. "How is he?"

"We're stabilizing him."

"H-he's going to be all right?"

"At least for now." The nurse squeezed her arm. "And you

might as well return to the waiting room or even go home and rest—it'll be a while before you can see him again."

"Thank you." Madison took a cleansing breath and turned to Clayton. "How is Lindsey Tremont?"

"It's complicated."

"What do you mean?"

"I tracked down Rebecca, and there are some developments."

"What did she say?"

"One, that she's quite a fighter. And if she knows about you, she's not talking. When Rebecca asked about family, she clammed up. But the kicker is, she emphatically claims her name isn't Lindsey Tremont."

"I can see that if she's in the witness security program. She might deny that's who she is, but why tell you her name in the first place?"

"The anesthesia, maybe."

That made sense. "Did she give another name?"

"Dani Parker."

Madison's head ached, and she massaged the back of her neck. This case kept getting stranger and stranger. "I want to go in to see her, but first I'd like to get Allyson to do a background check on Dani Parker."

"I saw a coffeepot around the corner. You want a cup?"

Madison would about kill for one right now and nodded as she took out her phone and dialed Allyson and explained what she wanted.

"It won't be a full report, but if you'll stay on the line, I'll run the name," the analyst replied.

"I'll hold." A smile came to her lips when Clayton returned with a Styrofoam cup.

"You there?" Allyson said.

"Yep."

"It's weird. There's a file on a Dani Parker, but it's password protected. However, we received a missing person alert for someone by that name just last night. She was supposed to arrive at Wings of Hope here in Jackson around nine with a young woman by the name of Briana Reed, but they never showed."

"What's Wings of Hope?"

"It's an organization that rescues victims of human trafficking."

"Thanks. Can you check around and see if either Lindsey Tremont or Dani Parker is in WITSEC?"

"I'll try my connection at the US Marshals office."

"Thanks, Allyson. I owe you one." Madison was so thankful for the connections she'd made. "We have movement on the case," she said, turning to Clayton. He handed her the cup of coffee, and she took a sip before she relayed what she'd learned.

Clayton took notes, and when she finished, he said, "I don't understand why she got involved in an organization that's working to stop human trafficking after what happened before. And I certainly don't see the US Marshals going along with it."

"I hope she's up to telling us."

"Are *you* up to hearing it?"

"Absolutely." Madison found the US Marshal standing guard at her grandfather's room and asked him to notify her if there was any change, then she followed Clayton to the nurses' station, where he asked Rebecca if they could go into her room.

The charge nurse put down her pen. "She indicated if Clayton returned, she'd like to speak to him."

"How about me?" Madison asked.

"Maybe I better go in with him, and the two of us can lay the groundwork for you to talk to her."

Madison agreed. As much as she wanted to question Lindsey/Dani or whatever her name was, she didn't want her to be so shocked that she had a heart attack.

27

Clayton followed Rebecca into the ICU room. Lindsey, or Dani, whichever her name was, lay in the bed with her eyes closed.

"Hello, sweetie," Rebecca said. "You want me to raise the head of your bed?"

"Please," she whispered. As Rebecca elevated her head, Madison's lookalike opened her eyes and turned toward him, frowning when their gazes locked.

"You were here earlier," she said.

He had to step closer to hear her. "Yes. You told me your name was Lindsey Tremont."

"So that's where . . ." She coughed, and then sucked air from the cannula. "Mistake . . . shouldn't have said that."

"May I move a chair closer to your bed so we can talk without stressing you?"

"Sure."

She searched his face as if trying to place him, then her eyes widened. "You bought our dinner. Thank you."

"Glad to do it." He didn't tell her he'd thought she was Madison. Clayton slid a white plastic chair beside her bed. "Lindsey Tremont . . . that *is* your name?"

"Lindsey Tremont died."

He scooted closer to avoid missing her breathy words. "And Dani Parker was born?"

She nodded and closed her eyes. He wasn't certain she'd fallen asleep until her breathing became even. Clayton let her sleep.

Now that the vent was out, he could see that the resemblance to Madison was even stronger.

Rebecca's rubber-soled shoes squeaked as she came to stand by him. "She may sleep a while," she said softly. "Would you like me to let you know when she's alert again?"

Before he could respond, Lindsey said, "Not asleep . . . just resting my eyes. Bri . . . she okay?"

"I don't know. We haven't found her. Was she the person who shot you?"

"No. She wouldn't do that."

"Did you see your assailant?"

"Afraid not." She fell silent again.

He didn't want to exhaust her, so he stood up to go. "Tell her I'll be back."

"Wait . . ." Her voice was stronger. "There's . . . a National Park Service agent . . . Madison . . ."

Clayton froze where he stood. "You want to see Madison Thorn?"

"You know her?"

He sat back down. "Yes. Is she your sister?"

"Pretty sure."

"She's here, at the hospital. Would you like to—"

"Yes."

"I'll be right back." He stopped at the door. "Which name would you like for me to use?"

Uncertainty clouded her eyes, and then she seemed to come to a decision. "We better stick with Dani."

28

Madison checked her watch. Clayton had been gone ten minutes. What was taking him so long? She found the refreshment station, and her hand shook as she poured another cup of coffee. Maybe Lindsey/Dani didn't want to meet her.

After all, her birth mother hadn't wanted her . . . Another thought struck her. Had Lindsey/Dani—she groaned. Madison couldn't keep calling her by two names. Dani. She settled on that. If Dani was her sister, had their mother given Dani up as well? Maybe Madison had been a cranky baby, too much trouble. Like the dog her parents had adopted and then returned.

And what about their birth dad . . . Was he in the picture at all? A sigh escaped her. All her life she'd wondered about her birth family. If she had brothers and sisters—

"There you are."

She jumped, then swung around. "How is she?"

"She's weak, but she wants to see you."

Tension released in her shoulders even as the back of her throat tightened. She swallowed past the lump. "Really?"

"Yes. Evidently she's aware of who you are because she asked for you by name."

"You're kidding."

He took her by the hand. "Let's find out what's going on."

She didn't move. It was like her feet had rooted to the floor as suspicion found purchase in her mind. Why was Clayton so interested in this case?

Almost as though he knew what she was thinking, he said, "The sooner we can learn more about Dani Parker, and she does want to be called Dani, the sooner we can find out who her assailant is."

What was her problem that she questioned Clayton's motives? Chad Turner was her problem. Ever since he'd betrayed her, she'd had trouble trusting men.

"Coming?"

She shook off the doubt. "I'm right behind you."

The door opened, and Rebecca stepped out of the room, closing it behind her. "She's weak, so don't stay too long."

"We won't." He indicated Madison should go in first, and she shook her head. She'd thought her grandfather's shooting had upended her life, but if it turned out Dani was her sister, possibly her twin sister, her life would be changed forever. A real family. Blood kin that would love her without reservation.

Not that Mom and Dad hadn't loved her, but as a kid, Madison had never been able to shake the feeling that if she didn't perform well, if she wasn't perfect, they would send her back. Like the puppy.

"Ready?"

With a deep breath, Madison straightened her shoulders and stepped inside the room behind Clayton. Her gaze went immediately to the person in the bed who lay sleeping.

Having the same birthday had left no doubt in Madison's mind that they were twins, but that didn't prepare her for the reality. Why hadn't she sensed that she had a twin? Her breath caught in her chest. Could that be the feeling she got sometimes that something was missing?

Dani slowly opened her eyes. "Madison . . ."

She could barely hear Dani say her name, so she approached the bed.

"I didn't mean for us to meet this way," Dani said.

"I'm going to grab another chair," Clayton said, "and I forgot to tell you—sometimes she even sounds like you."

Since Madison didn't have a clue how her voice sounded, she'd have to take his word for it. "I . . . am afraid you have me at a disadvantage. How do you know more about me than I do you? I'm not even sure who you are."

"Dani Parker . . . now." She breathed in deeply through the cannula and released it. "And according to Ancestry.com . . . your identical twin sister."

Twin sister. So it's true. Madison's knees turned to Jell-O, and she grabbed the chair beside the bed and plopped into it. It didn't matter how many times the thought that they *might* be sisters had crossed her mind, the reality was still hard to take in.

Madison found her voice. "Ancestry. That's the same DNA test I took, but it didn't tell me anything about you. But that's been years ago. Maybe you weren't in the system yet." She stopped her rattling when a tiny smile quirked the corners of Dani's mouth. "I'm talking too much and too fast. Always do when I'm nervous."

"Me too. And I only took the test recently," Dani whispered, and then a coughing fit shook her body.

Madison shot a frantic look around for Clayton, but he hadn't returned yet. She didn't want to wear Dani out, but neither did she want to leave yet.

"Give me a minute," Dani said. "Maybe a sip of water?"

Madison grabbed a cup and filled it. "Straw?"

"No. Let me sip it." When she finished, she lay back on her pillow, her face white against the sheet. "Thanks."

As much as Madison wanted to know more about their relationship, her primary concern needed to be solving the case of who shot her sister. *My sister.* The thought filled her with a desire to protect this fragile woman in the bed.

Madison leaned forward. "You're getting tired, and I'm sure

it's showing up on your monitor. Before they run me out, could we talk about the shooting?"

"You don't want to know—"

"Of course I do, but whoever did this to you might try again." She took out her notebook and pen. "We can talk family after you're safe . . . and stronger, okay?"

"I'd rather talk . . . about us now . . . but, I guess you do need to know what happened last night." Amusement twinkled in her blue eyes. "Just a thought—looks like you're the practical one."

"I've been called worse." Madison's mind jumped all over the place. Where was Clayton? She needed him here when she asked the questions.

Just then, he opened the door and brought in a chair. "Sorry it took so long, but I had to 'borrow' one from another room." He scooted it next to Madison's.

"We're discussing the shooting," she said, imploring him with her eyes to take over.

Clayton dipped his head, then shifted his gaze to Dani. "What do you remember?" he asked.

She stilled in the bed and closed her eyes again. No one said anything as the seconds ticked off, then she stirred. "I picked Bri up in New Orleans . . . we left around three."

Her voice was low, and Madison strained to hear it. "Who exactly is Bri, and why were you picking her up?"

"Briana Reed. I was taking her to the Jackson campus of Wings of Hope Wednesday . . . Was that yesterday?" Dani coughed. "More water . . ."

Madison jumped up and held the cup to her lips. "Yes—this is Thursday."

"Good stuff . . . where was I?"

"Briana Reed and Wings of Hope," Clayton said. Madison picked up her pen again.

"We stopped in Natchez to eat. Since it was getting late, I

notified the rehab we'd be late. Didn't make a pit stop at the restaurant . . . that's—"

"Why you were at Coles Creek," he said.

She nodded. "That's all I remember."

"You're certain this girl wouldn't hurt you?" Clayton asked.

"She wouldn't. If I had my phone . . . it has her number in it . . ."

"Where's your phone?" Madison asked.

"My purse. Bri used it to find a restroom on the Trace, and when she finished, that's where I put it."

"And your purse is in your car." Madison rubbed the back of her neck. "Do you think she would answer it?"

Dani's eyes lit up. "She might. Let's try."

She rattled off her number, but before Madison dialed it, Clayton stopped her. "Don't! If it rings, she may not answer and might even get rid of it. Call that analyst—she can pinpoint the location."

"You're right." Madison should have thought of that. She redialed Allyson's number and had her on the line in less than a minute and gave her the phone number.

Quicker than Madison expected, Allyson came back on the line. "You're not going to believe this."

"What?"

"It shows the phone is where you are—Merit Hospital in Natchez."

They both stood and turned to Dani.

"What make and model car do you drive?" Clayton asked.

"What does she look like?" Madison asked at the same time.

Dani shrank back, probably because of their strident tones.

"I'm sorry." Clayton gentled his voice. "Let's try this again. Your car—"

"Beige Honda Civic. It's a 2015 model."

"And how will we recognize Bri?" Madison asked.

"Just look for someone five sixish, lots of earrings, dressed in black . . . spiked hair, also black, and a few tattoos. But . . ." She tried to raise up and fell back on the bed.

Madison hovered over her. "Are you all right?"

"Yes. Bri is very fragile, especially when it comes to men." Dani took a breath. "Madison . . . maybe you could approach her."

"I don't have a problem with that. You?" She exchanged glances with Clayton.

"It's a good idea." He tilted his head toward Dani. "Do you keep a weapon in the car?"

"Yes . . . but it's locked up. I have a permit." Dani gripped Madison's arm with her free hand. "Please. Don't let Bri get hurt."

She hesitated, hating to promise something she might not be able to do. "Could she have gained access to the gun?"

"No. Combination safe." Dani's voice became weaker with each word.

Madison squeezed her hand. "If we find your car, I'll make sure she's not hurt."

She barely heard the thank-you as she hurried after Clayton. Neither spoke until they stepped through the front entrance. "She'll probably be parked in a far corner," she said.

"Why don't we take my SUV?"

She eyed him with a raised brow. "And advertise who we are? How about my Impala?"

"Good idea."

A few minutes later they cruised around the parking lot, looking for a beige Honda Civic. "Is that it?" Madison pointed to a tan car parked under a huge oak with thin tendrils of Spanish moss hanging from it.

"Could be. Park right there." He pointed to an empty space behind a tall van. "Do you see anyone in the car?"

Madison shook her head. "I'll approach and knock on the window. If she's inside, I'll ask if she can help me—I'll tell her I locked my keys inside my car."

"And I'll get out now and wait behind the van. If she pulls the gun—"

"I know what to do." Why had she promised Dani no harm would come to Bri? She climbed out of her car and cautiously approached the Civic. Front seat was empty. Just as she peered into the back window, a shout came from across the parking lot.

"What are you doing? Get away from my car!"

Madison whirled around. A thin girl with spiked hair the color of a raven rushed toward her, murder on her face.

"Whoa!" Madison palmed her hands up while at the same time checking for a gun. Nothing obvious, but the baggy black pants Bri wore could hide several guns.

Suddenly the girl stopped. Her eyes widened and her mouth formed a big *O*. "Dani! You're not . . ." Bri clamped her hand over her mouth, then she raised her eyes toward the sky. "Thank you, Jesus!"

Why hadn't it occurred to her that the girl would think she was Dani? Was she slipping? Then again, she wasn't used to being a twin. She should tell her she wasn't Dani, but first Madison wanted answers to a few questions. Out of the corner of her eye, Clayton edged around the van, and she waved him back.

Suddenly, Bri threw her arms around Madison, sobbing. The poor thing needed comforting, yet Madison hesitated. Should she hug her or just pat her on the back?

It's going to be all right. The words her mom said when she held and rocked Madison after she skinned her knee. The memory was embedded in her mind because comfort from her mother so seldom happened. And never from her father. Madison did the only thing she knew to do.

"It's going to be all right," she murmured and rubbed Bri's back. The girl was so thin, it was like rubbing a washboard. Dani was right—Bri wasn't her assailant. "Dani will be—"

She realized her mistake when Bri stiffened.

The girl jerked out of her embrace and stared at her. "Wait a minute . . . you're not—" She pivoted and took off running.

"Wait!" Madison sprinted after her. If only Bri had run in Clayton's direction.

Bri was fast. Impossible to catch her. Had to find another option. "Dani wants to see you!"

She wasn't sure the girl heard her until she slowed to a stop and turned around. "You're not lying to me, are you?"

"No." Madison braced her hands on her knees and breathed deeply. She'd used her last breath to yell at the teenager, and the girl wasn't even winded.

"Who are you? Her sister or something?"

"Or something." Madison straightened up. She took a step toward the teenager and held out her credentials. "I'm a law officer—I won't let anyone hurt you." When she didn't respond, Madison said, "Do you want to see Dani?"

"She's really okay?" Bri wiped her forehead with the back of her arm.

"Yes. Why don't we go see her."

Bri shifted her gaze to her hand and shook her head.

This wasn't working. "Why did you run?"

Bri gave her a "you've got to be kidding me" look. "I'm sure everyone thinks I shot her."

"Did you?"

"No!" She glowered at Madison. "Dani was nice to me. Said what happened to me wasn't my fault."

"She was right." Madison palmed her hands. "I don't think you shot her."

Bri looked past Madison, and her eyes widened like a rabbit caught in a trap.

Madison turned to follow her gaze. Clayton. And he was fast approaching them. She wished he'd waited a few minutes. Of course, with him fearing Bri might have Dani's gun, it was understandable that he didn't.

"I've got this," Madison called to him, then turned back to Bri. "It's okay. The guy that's about to join us—he's a National Park Service ranger like me, and he won't hurt you."

The wariness remained. Bri shifted her feet away from Madison. She was getting ready to run again.

"Dani trusts him, I promise."

"Men only hurt you."

What terrible things must have happened to this young woman for her to feel that way.

29

In a van across from the hospital, the sniper pulled the backpack from the floorboard into the passenger seat and unzipped the gray bag. With precision that comes only from practice, the sniper had the Sig crossover together in less than a minute.

Then the sniper lifted a pair of binoculars and scanned the hospital entrance a quarter of a mile away. Movement came from near the street where a tan Civic was parked. The driver's side door opened, and a thin girl emerged.

"Where did you come from?" The question broke the silence in the van. The rumpled black T-shirt, the bedhead, and eyes that looked as though she'd just woken answered the question. It was apparent she'd been sleeping in the car.

The girl finger-combed her short black hair. Probably dyed since it contrasted sharply to her pale skin. The girl scanned the parking area, then turned and stared toward the van, almost like she sensed being watched.

The sniper shrank back, feeling foolish—no way the girl could see through the tinted windows. The girl turned and walked toward a gas station. *If* she had slept in the car, she was probably going for something to eat.

Fifteen minutes passed. Then, Madison Thorn and the ranger exited the hospital and walked to a late-model Impala. Excitement coursed through the sniper's veins as the Impala backed out of a parking slot and circled the parking areas, first the employee, then the visitor, slowing when it reached the tan Honda. Seconds later, the Impala pulled into a parking spot near where the girl's car was parked, and Madison and the ranger exited the vehicle.

A quick glance showed no one was around, and the sniper lowered the van window and settled the rifle on the window frame just as the girl returned.

Impossible to get a clear shot. Nothing to do but wait. After a few minutes, the three walked toward the hospital entrance. The sniper's finger itched to pull the trigger but couldn't get the right shot. Then the trio disappeared behind a short strip of hedge.

A minute turned into ten.

Then the girl reappeared, followed by Madison Thorn with the ranger bringing up the rear.

It'd be like picking off blackbirds perched on a power line.

"Vengeance is mine, not God's . . ."

30

One of Clayton's jobs when he worked his way through college had been at a horse barn where there'd been a few high-strung horses, and he'd learned to come at them gentle-like. Same thing applied here with the antsy teenager. He kept his posture relaxed and smiled at the girl. "Hey, Bri," he said, his voice calm. "Looks like you've had a rough time."

Much like the horses had, she watched him warily.

"All we want to do is find out who shot Dani," Madison said.

Bri looked from Clayton to Madison. "She never said she had a twin sister."

"Could be because we hadn't met."

She shifted her feet toward the street again.

"Dani wants to see you." Clayton held out his hand. He would rather she came voluntarily, but either way, she was coming with them.

"You'll take me to see her?"

"Yes," Madison said.

Bri hesitated, then took his hand. Clayton released the breath he was holding in and smiled at her. "Let's go see Dani."

Madison visibly relaxed.

"It's not too far. Mind walking?" Clayton asked. When both agreed, he nodded toward the Impala. "We can pick up your car when we leave."

“Works for me,” Madison said. ”Let me grab Dani’s purse.”

He had questions he wanted to ask before they got to Dani’s room. When they passed a wooden picnic table with seats, it looked like a good place to talk. He turned to Bri. “We need to know what happened last night. Why don’t we sit here a minute where we have privacy?”

“I figured this was coming,” Bri replied. She stared down at the asphalt a minute and then nodded.

He sat on the outside of the bench next to Madison, and Bri sat opposite them. “What were you two doing in Natchez?”

She clasped her fingers in front of her on the table. “Dani picked me up at Wings of Hope in New Orleans. She was taking me to their Jackson campus.”

Wings of Hope. The place that reported Dani and Bri missing. She was so young, his heart broke for her. “How old are you, Bri?”

She dropped her head. “Twenty-one,” she whispered.

He would have guessed younger. Madison reached across the table and squeezed her hand. “It’s going to get better.”

“I know.” She raised her head. “The good thing is, I found Jesus while our pimps had me. It was the only thing that kept me going sometimes.”

“What do you mean?” Clayton had never thought of anything positive with human trafficking.

“One of the girls—she was a Christian, and she was different. Julie had a peace that I wanted.” A small laugh escaped her lips. “And she was the reason we were rescued. Her parents hired a private investigator who found her . . . and the rest of us.”

Bri shook her head as if throwing off a blanket. “Anyway, we stopped in Natchez to eat and . . .” Suddenly she stared at Clayton. “Wait a minute—you’re the guy who paid for our supper! Why’d you do that?”

“Ah . . . I . . .” Heat crept into his face. “I thought Dani was”—he glanced at Madison—“someone else.”

“But you were with your wife and little girl.”

"Wife?" Madison gave him a sharp look.

He held his finger up. "My sister and niece." They all laughed, breaking the tension. "What happened after you left?"

Bri bit her bottom lip. "We stopped at this place to go to the restroom. One of the stalls was out of order, and I told Dani to go first. I thought I heard a car pull in, but nobody came into the restroom. When Dani finished, she said she was going to the car.

"When I was washing my hands, that's when I heard two gunshots. Someone came into the restroom, but I'd locked myself in the stall that was out of order." She wrapped her thin arms around her body and laid her head on her knees. "They found me. I'm the reason Dani was shot."

"No, you're not," Madison said. "Evil people do evil things."

"But if she hadn't been taking me—"

"No." This time Madison took both of the girl's hands in hers. "Do not blame yourself for this. We have no idea who shot Dani or why. Besides, even though I haven't known her but a few hours, I know she wouldn't want you to feel that way. She's very worried about you."

The sense of being watched raised goose bumps on the back of Clayton's neck, and he glanced around. Nothing looked out of the ordinary. He turned back to the women. They'd gotten about all the information Bri had. "Why don't we get you up to see her?"

"Good!" The girl jumped up.

They stood as well and once more started toward the hospital entrance. "Did you see anything that would identify the shooter?" Clayton asked.

"No, I—"

The air buzzed between Clayton and Madison a millisecond before wood splintered from the picnic table.

"Get down!" Clayton pulled his gun and hovered over Madison and Bri and at the same time scanned the parking lot. Another buzz, and a bullet kicked up concrete three feet from them. He listened for the rifle crack that never came. The shooter must be using a suppressor, and he was probably a good distance away. "Are you hit?"

"No, but we're sitting ducks." Madison nodded toward a nearby tree. "Run for the oak!"

She ran for the live oak tree in a median strip while Clayton covered her and searched for the shooter. Everything looked normal. No one screeching off. No one running. Except him when he made a dash for the tree. He flattened his back against the trunk and dialed 911.

"We have an active shooter in the parking area at Merit Health," he said when the operator answered, then quickly identified himself. Once he hung up, he asked, "Where's Bri?"

"She took off toward the entrance." Madison eased around the tree. "I think he's gone."

"He? Did you see the shooter?"

"No, but a shot like that—had to be a rifle."

"Cavalry is here," he said as sirens came at them from all directions. Clayton holstered his gun and Madison did the same. It wasn't long before the parking lot was filled with flashing blue lights led by the chief himself.

Once they were satisfied the gunman was gone, Madison left to track down Bri, and Clayton laid out what happened to the chief.

"Any idea why someone would shoot at you?"

"Not a clue." Clayton helped search for spent bullets while Nelson's men triangulated the spot the shots came from.

Madison approached them, and he looked past her for Bri. "Couldn't you find her?" he asked as Chief Nelson joined them.

"I found her, all right—in Dani's room—but she wouldn't come with me. She believes the shooter was after her and still is. I left her my card with Grandfather's address on the back and told her she was welcome to stay there."

Her cell phone rang, and Madison looked at the caller ID. "I have to take this."

When Madison stepped away, Chief Nelson turned to Clayton. "Who's the girl?"

"Briana Reed. Dani Parker, the shooting victim on the Trace, had picked her up in New Orleans yesterday morning." He gave Nelson the background on the case.

"So it's possible the shooter was after the girl and tried again today?"

"Anything's possible. Think your officers will be able to get a trajectory on the bullet that plowed into the picnic table?"

"They're working on it."

Clayton turned as Madison pocketed her phone and hurried toward them. "I have to go to my grandfather's house. Something about the investigation."

31

Madison started for her car. Nothing Hugh had said made sense.

"Wait up," Clayton called to her, and she stopped until he caught up. "What's going on?"

"Hugh's team just finished processing the crime scene, and there's no trace of a second bullet or even a fragment."

"That means—"

"Nothing." She hadn't meant to snap at Clayton. "I'm sorry. It's just, I know he didn't shoot himself. Hugh's team missed the spent bullet. It's the only answer."

She wouldn't let herself think any differently, not until she could talk face-to-face with the FBI agent, and she tried not to think of how she would view this new evidence if the victim hadn't been her grandfather.

Clayton bit his lip, then took her hand. "Once your grandfather regains consciousness, he can tell you what happened."

She latched on to that thought. *But what if he doesn't wake up?* No. She would not even consider that possibility.

"Want me to go with you?"

Madison shook her head. Clayton couldn't quite hide the doubt that surfaced in his face, and doubt was the last thing she needed right now. "I'd rather you check and make sure Bri is okay. She was a basket case when I left Dani's room."

He hesitated.

"Please," she said. "You can be more effective interviewing the two of them. We still have to find Dani's shooter. And whoever just took shots at us."

Reluctantly he nodded. "Call me when you know something."

After promising she would, Madison hurried to her Impala. By the time she arrived at her grandfather's house, her jaw ached from clenching it. Hugh met her at the front door. Before he could present his case, she said, "My grandfather did not shoot himself."

The look on his face said it all. "I'm sorry, Madison." He held her gaze. "I know you don't want to believe that, but there's no other explanation. Come inside and look at the evidence."

She followed him to the study. "Have you checked out the brother of the man killed at Parchman?"

Hugh nodded. "He has a solid alibi—he was at a bar burying his sorrow. The bartender and at least two customers saw him there."

Drinking buddies might lie for a friend; the bartender not so much, unless he was a friend as well.

Hugh stepped inside the room and palmed his hands. "We've looked everywhere for a second bullet—the floor, the walls, the ceiling. Nada."

"Maybe whoever shot him took it with them."

He raised an eyebrow. "The shooter would have had to dig it out." Hugh swept his hand around the room. "And there are no holes anywhere."

"Maybe they came prepared—brought a block of wood and carried it off with them." Even to her ears it sounded like she was grabbing at the wind.

"Think about it," Hugh said. "The gun used was his own, and it contained one empty round and four .38 caliber bullets, all identical *and* a match to the other fifteen bullets in the box we found in his desk."

No law said the killer hadn't replaced the casing with a cartridge from the desk, but if she said that to Hugh, he would tell her she was reaching. And maybe she was. "Did you check the box for fingerprints?"

"Of course."

"And?"

"Found a few smudges." His voice sounded a little defensive. "But that's not uncommon. It was practically a new box."

"How about the bullets in the gun?"

He shook his head.

"Sounds like someone wore gloves when they loaded the gun."

He sighed. "Madison, you know how seldom fingerprints are found on cartridges. The only prints we found anywhere were yours, Ms. Nadine's, and your grandfather's. His were the only ones found on his gun."

Madison clenched her teeth again, and pain shot from her jaw down her neck. She forced the muscles in the side of her face to relax. Somehow, she had to make Hugh see that he was wrong. "How do you explain the gun falling on his right side? He was left-handed."

"Madison . . ." Hugh huffed a sigh. "Maybe after he fired the gun, he fumbled it and grabbed it with his right hand, then lost consciousness."

He couldn't just abandon this case. "I don't understand why you keep insisting he shot himself."

"The evidence . . . or lack thereof," he replied. "There was no sign of forced entry, the neighbors have been questioned and you are the only person seen coming or going last night, and a few of the neighbors have indicated he was very depressed about his daughter dying. Even Chief Nelson confirmed he was despondent over her death. And you're forgetting about the suicide note."

"I keep telling you he didn't write that note, and once he wakes up, he'll tell you himself."

Hugh shifted his gaze away from her. “We’ll see,” he said just as her phone rang.

Madison glanced at the caller ID. Merit Medical. Her mouth dried. There was only one reason Merit would call her—there’d been a change in her grandfather’s condition. Her heart pounding, she punched the answer button. “Madison Thorn.”

32

After Madison drove away, Clayton tracked down Chief Nelson at the parking lot a good thousand feet away from the picnic table. One of his officers held a black screen about the height of a pickup or van, and in the center of the screen was a laser beam.

"You think this is where the shooter was?" he asked.

"Yes. We inserted a rod where the bullet hit the picnic table and eyeballed where it might have originated. Then we inserted a laser in the rod, and it confirmed our estimate." Pete removed his hat and wiped his shaved head with a handkerchief. "Have you talked to Hugh?"

"No, but from what Madison said, he thinks Judge Anderson shot himself."

"That's what I got from him too." Pete cocked his head. "What's your take on it?"

"I just don't see Judge Anderson doing something like that."

Pete blew out a hard breath. "He's been pretty depressed about his daughter lately."

Clayton didn't know what to say. "I knew she died recently."

"Four months ago. Overdosed, and while the Memphis medical examiner ruled it accidental, I don't think it was."

"What do you mean?"

"It would have been hard to accidentally get the amount

of Oxycontin found in her system." Resignation settled in the chief's face as he adjusted the gun on his belt. "Judge Anderson is a good man—mentored a good many boys down at the Boys and Girls Clubs, including me. If it hadn't been for the judge's letters of recommendation, I probably wouldn't have gotten a scholarship to Southern Miss."

The judge had helped Clayton get into the same university.

"He was so proud when I became police chief . . . our relationship changed from mentor-mentee to friends. We met for coffee at least once a month."

Clayton and the judge hadn't stayed close, not like Pete had. Yesterday at the coffee shop had been the first time he'd seen the judge in a couple of months. "He talked to you about his daughter's death?"

Pete nodded. "I thought he was coming out of his depression. He was so excited about Madison's visit. I never saw suicide coming."

"We don't know that for sure, yet. The judge made a few enemies over the years." And from the looks on the faces of the two visitors Clayton saw him with yesterday, there were at least two women who didn't particularly care for him.

Clayton checked his watch. He should be hearing something from Madison soon, and she would want to know how Dani and Bri were. "If you hear anything, let me know."

He jogged across to the hospital entrance and climbed the stairs to the second floor. After being buzzed in, he checked on Judge Anderson first, and his nurse indicated there'd been no change. That was a good sign . . . wasn't it?

When he reached Dani's room, he knocked softly and was bid to come in. "Where's Bri?" he asked when he noticed that only Dani occupied the room.

She sighed. "I'm afraid after my heart rate spiked, they asked her to leave. She said she'd be in the waiting room. Wasn't she there?"

He hadn't seen her there and tried to remember if he'd seen Dani's car when he jogged across the parking lot. "Did she still have your keys?"

"Yes." Her eyes widened. "Oh no. She's taken off again. It's all my fault."

"No, I should've taken the keys." He turned to leave.

"She thinks she led them to me, that my shooting is her fault, and they'll come back."

"Running away won't help. I need to talk to her and find out just who she thinks is looking for her."

"Her pimp."

"If she'd stuck around, we could have at least gotten a drawing of him."

A code blue sounded through the unit, seizing Clayton's heart. Outside the room, footsteps pounded down the hall. What if it was Judge Anderson? "I need to check and see what's going on."

When he reached the hallway, the doors to the judge's room had been thrown open and a crash cart rolled beside the bed. He inched closer. The monitor had flatlined, and a nurse pumped his chest. Clayton balled his hands as he prayed for the line to jump back to life.

Rebecca grabbed his arm. "You shouldn't be here."

He jutted his jaw. "Not leaving."

She left him alone, but seconds later someone closed the door and curtain to the judge's room. He stood sentinel until a doctor arrived, and seconds later the nurse he'd seen giving CPR stumbled from the room, tears in her eyes. She stopped short when she saw him.

"He didn't make it," Clayton said.

She shook her head and hurried down the hall.

He squeezed his eyes closed. Madison would take this hard. He had to get to her, be there when she got the word. Or tell her himself.

Clayton found Rebecca at the nurses' station. "Can you hold

off on notifying Madison about her grandfather until I can reach her?"

Tears glistened in the nurse's eyes. "It's . . ." She bit her lip and then wiped her eyes. "It's not up to me. Once my boss tells me to make the call, I'll have to do it."

Then he had no choice but to try to reach Madison first. "Give me a little time, if you can." He spun on his heel and rushed out of the unit.

33

Madison . . ."

Immediately she recognized the charge nurse's voice, and when Rebecca's voice cracked, Madison steeled herself.

"Are you still there?"

"Yes."

"I'm afraid Judge Anderson had a massive heart attack . . . we weren't able to revive him."

Madison stumbled to a chair and collapsed in it. "I thought his condition was improving. . . ." The scene from when he crashed earlier was embedded in her memory.

"He was, but his heart slipped into an abnormal rhythm, and the stress was too much. I'm sorry."

"Thank you for notifying me. I'll be right there." She stood and turned to Hugh. "I have to go to the hospital."

"What's wrong?"

Ignoring the buzzing on her phone, she slipped it in her pocket. The room turned into a blur. "Grandfather just died."

"I'm sorry, Madison."

Numbly she nodded. "Thank you."

"If there's anything—"

She held up her hand, cutting him off. "Someone shot my grandfather and if you won't find them, I will—if it's the last thing I ever do."

"Madison—"

"I mean it, Hugh."

"You have bereavement time with the park service. Take it. We'll sit down later and go over this," he said. "Right now, you have things to take care of. Is there anyone who can help you arrange the funeral?"

Funeral. She'd have to contact her cousins, but she doubted Buddy and Joe would be much help, living so far away. She didn't remember the last time they came to visit Grandfather.

The room closed in on her. She had to get out of here. Madison nodded to whatever he'd said after "funeral" and rushed from the room and down the hallway. When she flung the front door open, Clayton stood there.

Without thinking, she threw herself into his arms and burst into tears.

"I'm so sorry," he murmured against her hair. He repeated the words as he slowly patted her back.

When her tears were spent, she looked up. "I have to go to the hospital, but afterward could we go somewhere? Somewhere quiet and peaceful?"

He took her hand. "I'll take you to the hospital, and then I know just the place."

Madison allowed him to take her arm and guide her to his SUV and help her in. Once he pulled out of the drive, she held herself erect—it was the only way to keep her emotions together. Too soon they were pulling into Merit.

For the next hour, Madison operated on automatic pilot, sitting at a desk across from Rebecca, answering the charge nurse's questions. When Rebecca asked which funeral home should be called, Madison stared blankly at her. Grandfather had never talked to her about his funeral, and she doubted he'd talked to her cousins either. Maybe she should call them. She scrolled through her phone, the names and numbers a blur.

Clayton had accompanied her inside the small room and spoke up. "Would Nadine know?"

Nadine. Of course. She would know everything. Madison should've already called her. No . . . "She's eighty years old. I-I can't spring something like this on her over the phone."

He turned to Rebecca. "Can we call you with that information as soon as we get it?"

"Absolutely." She patted Madison's hand. "Again, I'm so sorry."

Barely acknowledging her sympathy, Madison stood and took Clayton's hand again as they walked out of the office. "Do you mind taking me back to Grandfather's?"

"Of course not."

Within fifteen minutes, they were breaking the news to Nadine in her apartment.

"God rest his soul," the older woman murmured, gripping the arm of the chair she sat in. Then Nadine sat straighter. "I heard you and your boss talking earlier. He's wrong. William Anderson never would have taken his own life."

Teary-eyed, Madison leaned over and hugged her. "I know. And it looks like I'll have to prove it. But first I need to know what funeral home to call."

"Peebles. That's who handled the arrangements for getting your mama down here. Your grandfather left a letter for you."

Madison raised a troubled gaze to Nadine's. "It's only been four months. How could I have forgotten Peebles handled my mom's funeral?"

"Don't be so hard on yourself," Clayton said. "A lot has happened since then."

"Yes, chère," Nadine said. "I doubt your father was much help in settling your mama's estate."

Madison's heart warmed. Nadine had always been her champion, just like she'd been her mother's. "Wait. Did you say Grandfather left me a letter?"

"Yes. Let me get it." A few minutes later, the spry octogenarian handed her a large envelope.

"Do you know what's in it?"

"Not from reading it, but your grandfather and I discussed what he would write. I'm sure he mentioned Peebles in it."

Madison stared at the envelope. She'd thought it would be years before she had to deal with her grandfather's funeral. When she didn't reach for the letter, Nadine pressed it into her hands. If paper could burn, her hands would be on fire. She placed the envelope on the table near the door. "I'll read it later. Right now, all I have to know is the name of the funeral home."

Clayton took out his phone. "I can call Rebecca for you."

"Would you?" One less thing for her to do. She still had Buddy and Joe and her father to notify.

Clayton glanced at Madison then Nadine. "Why don't we step outside on the patio?"

Nadine seemed to have shrunk since they delivered the news. She probably needed time to herself. "I'll check on you later," Madison said and hugged the older woman again.

"My prayers go with you, chère."

The patio was pleasantly warm when she sank into a black wrought-iron chair. While Clayton walked toward the house to call the hospital, Madison tried her father's cell phone one more time before she resorted to calling the office. He answered just as she was about to hang up.

"I'm in a meeting. What is it?"

Usually it didn't bother her that he never sounded like he wanted to hear from her, but today it did. "Call me back when you have time to talk."

"Madison, why did you call me?"

The muscle in her jaw throbbed. "Grandfather is dead."

Absolute silence met her announcement. "You're kidding."

"No, I'm not." Like she'd kid about something like that.

"I'm sorry. You . . . just caught me at a bad time. And I'm sorry about your grandfather. I know you cared for him."

And you didn't. But she bit back the words on the tip of her tongue. "I wanted to let you know before it hit the news."

"Thank you," he said. "I assume you'll be going to Natchez tonight?"

"I'm in Natchez." She gripped the phone. "Why didn't you call me back? I left a message when Grandfather was shot."

"What are you talking about? I never got a message from you."

"But I called."

"Well, I didn't get it." His voice was sharp—typical. "Where will you be staying?"

Madison had told Nadine she'd stay with her, but the house had been cleared. She could stay in her old bedroom, but she wasn't sure she could do that. "Probably with Nadine."

"I'll be there by seven tonight to help any way I can."

So much for staying with Nadine.

"I'll be fine. No need for you to make the five-hour drive."

"It's only two. I'm in Jackson, have been for a couple of days," he said. "I'll see you tonight. Love you, pumpkin."

Madison was left holding a dead call, her heart tugging at his pet name for her. It'd been years since he'd called her that.

Clayton joined her back at the patio. "You okay?"

She gave him a shrug. "My dad will be here tonight."

"That's good." He frowned. "Right?"

"I suppose. Our relationship is . . . complicated."

"Aren't most?"

"I don't think he wanted to adopt me."

34

What makes you say that?" Clayton asked. From his own experience, kids knew when they weren't wanted. It was one reason he watched over Ava the way he did after her dad skipped out.

"A lot of little things, but one in particular." Madison stood and walked to the edge of the patio. She turned and rubbed her bare arms. "We'd gotten a puppy that was too much trouble—according to my dad. I don't remember everything that was said . . . but one word led to another, and pretty soon my parents were screaming at each other. It ended when he yelled, 'Getting this kid was supposed to fix your problem!'"

Madison stared down at her hands. "We took the dog back to the pet store the same day."

He wasn't sure what to say. While his dad had been difficult, Clayton never felt he didn't love him. Just wanted to control him. "You thought they would give you back if you caused trouble."

"H-how did you know?"

"It's what I would have thought. Do you have any happy memories with him?"

She seemed to consider his question and gave him a wistful smile. "Precious few. He was this important businessman, and Mom always told me not to bother him. When he was home it was like tiptoeing on eggshells, but at least he wasn't home much."

Clayton had thought his childhood was bad, but hers topped it. "That had to have been painful."

"Staying with Grandfather in Natchez every summer was the best part of the year."

He tilted his head. "I don't remember you being here as a teenager."

"I quit coming when I was twelve."

"Why?"

"I didn't have time after my dad bought me a horse. He thought I should take dressage lessons, and of course I loved that horse, loved riding. I think he only bought him so I wouldn't want to spend summers in Natchez with Grandfather. But the shows were always on weekends, and Grandfather always showed up to watch me."

"Sounds like there was a lot of competition in your family."

"You could say that."

They both turned when Nadine's back door opened and she stepped out onto the patio with her phone in her hand. "That was your grandfather's pastor. Some of the ladies of the church will be by with food for tonight."

Clayton's stomach growled, reminding him he hadn't eaten lunch. He doubted Madison had either. He turned to Nadine. "Is there something in the kitchen to make a sandwich?"

"Lunch meat is in the refrigerator and bread is on the counter."

He grabbed Madison's hand. "Come on. We're going to have a picnic."

"What?"

"I promised earlier to take you somewhere peaceful. You need a break, and I know the perfect place for it."

Half an hour later, Clayton parked on Broadway in front of a grassy area near the river trail.

"We're going to eat here?" Madison said.

"Yep. And watch the sun set over the Mississippi." He hopped out and came around to her side of the SUV, not believing she'd actually waited for him to open her door. He offered his hand, and she took it. Already the worry lines around her eyes had faded.

"Thanks," she said.

He grabbed the small picnic hamper that Nadine had filled after she shooed him out of her kitchen. He couldn't wait to see what she'd put in it. He grinned at the plaid throw the housekeeper had included when she handed him the basket.

They walked across the grass to the bluff's edge. "You want to sit on a bench or spread out the throw?"

She looked at the ground, then the bench, and then at the river. "The bench. That way we can watch the boats on the Mississippi."

He set the basket between them and opened it, taking out a sandwich. "Looks like pimento cheese." He reached in again. "And she put in chips and drinks."

Madison took the sandwich and drink. "Nadine makes the best pimento cheese."

They ate and watched the sun drop behind a bank of clouds, brilliant beams of light fanning upward.

"That's so beautiful," Madison said softly. "Grandfather always brought me to the river bluff when I came to visit in the summers. I remember looking at the Mississippi and thinking about where the water had been and where it was going." She smiled. "It was too much for my young brain."

He understood what she meant. "There's something about the Mississippi River that gets to you. Have you ever seen it at flood stage?"

She shook her head.

"I have, and it reminds me that there are some things I can't control."

She was quiet a minute. "Like my grandfather's death."

"Yeah. And the port wine stain on my niece's face."

"Your niece has a birthmark on her face?"

He nodded.

"Can't they remove it?"

"Maybe. But my sister has a ten thousand dollar deductible on her insurance, and it's doubtful the company would even approve it. I hate it that when people think of Ava, the birthmark is all they see."

"I'd like to meet her sometime."

"She'd love to meet you too." They'd finished their sandwiches, and he looked through the basket again. Clayton was sure that Nadine put some kind of dessert in the basket. Maybe in the little tin box he found. Sure enough, the tin box held four cookies—two were chocolate chip and two were oatmeal raisin.

He offered Madison first choice, and she took an oatmeal raisin and bit into it. "Mmm. That's so good."

"I like the chocolate chip." He glanced toward the river. "Oh, look . . ."

The sun had escaped from the clouds and hovered like a giant red ball over the horizon. Beside him, Madison sucked in a breath.

"Oh wow," she murmured.

Neither of them said anything until the fiery ball sank out of sight, leaving a red glow in the sky. She turned to him, her eyes soft. "Thank you for this."

He grinned. "I don't think I can take credit for the sunset."

The cookie had left crumbs near the corner of her mouth, and he gently brushed them away, the touch like an electric current to his fingers. She leaned into his touch, and his gaze fell to her lips. He brushed them with his thumb. At that moment, all he could think of was how much he wanted to feel his lips on hers.

A car backfired, and Clayton jerked his hand away. What was he thinking? "We need to go." He threw their trash in the basket and pulled Madison to her feet.

"What happened?"

"We're out in the open, exposed. Whoever fired at us this afternoon could have easily followed us."

She quickly scanned the area. "You're right."

He hurried her to the SUV. This was why he didn't need to think about a relationship, especially one with the person he was working a case with. His carelessness could get them both killed.

35

Thank you." Madison smiled and accepted the caramel cake from a silver-haired member of her grandfather's church and handed it off to Nadine. It seemed like most of the food that had been dropped off in the last two hours came from the older ladies at St. Matthews. "I don't think I caught your name."

"Judith Winslow," she said. "Your grandfather and I go way back."

"Good evening, Judith," Clayton said as he appeared by Madison's side.

"Clayton. I'm surprised to see you here. I didn't realize you and the judge's granddaughter were that close." Then she looked from Clayton to Madison and tapped her head. "Of course—I hardly noticed you're both wearing park ranger uniforms. Are you working together?"

"Sort of." He turned to Madison. "Judith runs Bright Horizons, a pregnancy center. My mom is a volunteer there. If y'all will excuse me," he said, taking the cake from Nadine, "I'll take this to the dining room."

"Wait." Madison held up her hand. "Set it on the island. I'd like a slice before I go to bed." Just then the doorbell rang. "That's the front door—would you see who it is?"

"Sure."

After Clayton left, Madison studied the thin woman dressed

in business attire. Was it possible Judith's pregnancy center could've had something to do with Madison's adoption? "How long has Bright Horizons been in operation?"

"Later this year will be thirty-four years."

Then she couldn't have had anything to do with Madison's adoption. Disappointment hit her harder than she expected. "Well, thank you for the cake."

"I'll keep you in my thoughts," Judith said. "The next few days will be difficult. Let me know if there's anything I can do to help—if you handle his estate, you may come across my name quite often in his files."

Madison frowned, trying to make the connection, and it must have shown on her face.

"Your grandfather helped me get started with Bright Horizons and signed off on a lot of my adoptions when he was a chancery judge."

"Thanks for the information. If I run across anything I need clarification on, I'll give you a call."

"Madison," Clayton said, coming in from the hall. "Your friends from this morning are here."

Who was he talking about? Frowning, she turned toward him, and her eyes widened. "Steven?" she said as he stepped inside the kitchen. Terri hovered behind him. "What are you doing here?"

"We heard about your grandfather and wanted to see if there's anything we could help you with."

They were the last two people she expected to see. "Thank you for coming, but there's nothing anyone can do."

She paused as Terri stared across the room. Madison followed her gaze to Judith Winslow, who'd lost all color to her face. "Do you know Judith?" she asked Terri.

The air in the room seemed to crackle with tension as Steven's friend slowly brought her gaze back to Madison. "We've met," she said.

Just then the back doorbell rang, and Judith smiled apologetically. "I have a million things to do, and that's my cue to leave. Good meeting you all," she said and hurried out the door.

"Be right back." Madison needed time to regroup after Steven and Terri showed up, and she walked to the back door with Judith. She'd been almost as shocked to see them as the older woman appeared to be. "Are you okay? You seem . . . a little flustered."

"I'm fine. Terri reminded me of someone I knew a long time ago."

"Thank you again for the cake." Madison waited while Judith chatted briefly on the back porch with an older lady who held what looked like a casserole in her hands. A few minutes later, Madison returned to the kitchen with the casserole. Nadine and Clayton were talking to the new guests as they surveyed the kitchen counter that held barbecue, casseroles, and an array of vegetables.

"Have you ever seen so much food?" Madison turned to Steven and Terri. "Have you two eaten?"

"Yes." They both spoke at the same time.

Madison shifted her gaze to Nadine. "What will we do with all this food? Can't you put the word out that we don't need anything?"

"I can try, chère, but a lot of people loved your grandfather, and bringing food is their way of expressing their love." Nadine glanced at the counter. "When your dear mama passed away, we gave most of what people brought to the mission. I'll call and see if they need food tonight."

Madison did not remember that about her mother's funeral, but then she'd been barely aware of anything. She squeezed Nadine's gnarled hands. "Thank you."

After Nadine left, Madison turned to Steven. "Did you ever find your friend?"

"He was in Jackson. He thought he was having a heart attack, but it turned out to be anxiety, and they didn't keep him."

"I'm glad it wasn't serious." Madison was on autopilot, somehow her brain was coming up with the right words. "I appreciate you coming."

Terri smiled softly. "I wish there was something I—I mean we—could do to help, but I see you have a lot to do." She exchanged glances with Steven. "We need to be going."

Again, kindness almost undid Madison. "Thanks," she choked out.

They started to leave, and Terri turned back. "Could I give you a hug?"

When Madison nodded, the woman wrapped her arms around her. "It's going to be all right, and in time, it will get better."

"Thanks."

Steven squeezed her hand. "If there's anything we can do . . ."

While Clayton showed them out the front door, Madison sat at the breakfast table and rested her head in her hands. Her brain was numb except for occasional bursts of sadness. Somehow her grandfather's death was worse than her mother's. Not worse, really, just that it had been only four months since she lost her mother, and now this.

"You okay?" Clayton asked softly when he returned.

"I don't know," she said truthfully. "I was surprised to see Steven and Terri."

"I wondered if you knew they were coming by."

"No. I should have asked how they found out."

"It was on the evening news," Nadine said as she stepped inside the kitchen. "And the pastor at the mission said he would take some of the food. He'll be here shortly."

"Good. I hate to see it all go to waste."

Clayton sat across from her while Nadine boxed up food. "You look beat. Why don't you get some rest?"

She shook her head and glanced at her watch. "I'll have to wait on my father. And now the pastor."

"Did your dad say when he would arrive?" Clayton asked.

"Absolutely not."

A grin spread across his face. "That's mighty definite."

"*I think it's high time you got interested in someone and settled down.*" Her grandfather's words the last time she saw him stabbed her heart.

Heat flooded her face. What was she doing laughing and flirting with Clayton like nothing was wrong?

36

The front doorbell rang, and her heart sank. If it was her father, he was early. It was probably another dish. Neither of which she wanted to deal with right now.

"You want me to get it?"

Most of the church members bearing dishes had come to the back door. "No. It's probably my dad, and if it is, he would be insulted if I didn't meet him at the door." At least he wouldn't expect her to have her arms wide open.

"Would you rather I leave?" Clayton nodded toward the back door. "I can go out that way."

Madison was not ready to be alone with her father. "Please, stay. I'll be right back."

The doorbell pealed once more before she got the door opened. "You made it. Come on in."

A briefcase in one hand, her dad pulled luggage with the other as he brushed past her. "Where were you?"

Same old Dad. She caught a scent she didn't associate with him—it was more floral. "In the kitchen waiting for the mission pastor to pick up some of the food that's been dropped off."

"Of course. The Methodist ladies." Then he stood his luggage up and squeezed her hand. "I am sorry about William. I know he meant a lot to you."

She blinked back a rush of tears. "Thanks. Have you eaten? There's plenty."

"I grabbed something at the hotel before I left. I'll take a cup of coffee, though."

"Sure." She eyed him. Something was different. His hair? Maybe a little longer on top . . . but more than that. Then it hit her—he looked younger. The gray was gone except for a tiny bit at his temples.

He cleared his throat, and she swallowed her surprise. He must have said something. "I didn't catch that."

"Maybe because you weren't listening? I asked which room."

"The one you and Mom always used—I put clean sheets on the bed. While you're stowing your things, I'll put on a pot of coffee."

"No chicory," he said over his shoulder.

"Right." They did have that in common.

Clayton looked past her when she entered the kitchen. "He's putting his things away and will be here in a minute. Thanks for hanging around."

"No problem."

"I'm making coffee. Would you like some? And maybe a piece of that caramel cake I've seen you ogling?"

"I thought you'd never ask. How'd it go?"

"As usual." Actually, better than she expected. Madison poured water into the grind-and-brew coffeemaker, then scooped in beans and turned it on. The tantalizing aroma of freshly ground coffee perked her up. She should have made coffee an hour ago.

"I didn't know you had company."

Madison flinched. She hadn't heard her father come into the kitchen. "Sorry, I forgot to mention Clayton was here. Clayton Bradshaw, my father, Gregory Thorn."

Clayton extended his hand. "Pleased to meet you, sir."

She almost laughed at the way the two men sized each other up as they shook hands. Her dad had left his jacket in the bedroom, and the slim-fit dress shirt hugged a trim body. Evidently, he'd lost weight and had been working out.

Clayton was no slouch in the looks department, either. Even

in his uniform, it was easy to tell he was fit. He had a rugged appeal with a strong, clearly defined jaw. She'd noticed more than one woman turn and take a second look at him. Maybe in part because Clayton's face held kindness. Where her father's face usually held a stony wariness.

"So, you're a park ranger?" her father asked, glancing at the gun on Clayton's belt then hers.

"Yes, sir. Supervisor for the southern district on the Natchez Trace."

"Do all the rangers around here wear a gun?"

"Only the law enforcement ones."

"Even when they're off duty?"

Madison rested her hand on her pistol. "I hadn't thought about it, but if it bothers you, I'll take it off."

"I can as well," Clayton said.

Her dad pinched the bridge of his nose. "No, I shouldn't have said anything. How do you know each other?"

"We're working a case together," Madison said.

"Oh, good. For a minute there I thought . . ."

Madison hadn't thought about it, but her dad would hate it if she married another ranger.

"I don't think Madison has told me what you do . . . sir."

Hiding a smile, she turned to get cups for them. Clayton could hold his own with her father.

"I'm a corporate lawyer, and right now I'm representing a textile manufacturer who is thinking of opening a plant in Jackson."

"That sounds good. We need the jobs in Mississippi," Clayton said. He tapped the counter next to the caramel cake. "You did say we could cut this?"

"Yes." She handed him three plates.

The pastor arrived not long after to pick up the food. Later the tension eased as her father warmed up to Clayton and his stories of speeders on the Trace, including hers. All too soon, Clayton rose to leave.

"Would you like for me to go with you to the funeral home in the morning?" he asked. "Unless Buddy or Joe is coming to help you."

"I talked to my cousins earlier and they're happy to let me handle everything." For a blessed few minutes, she'd put all thoughts of the funeral from her mind. As well as the letter from her grandfather that she needed to read before she talked with Peebles. Madison had no idea whether she could even hold it together to make the arrangements, and she certainly didn't want Clayton to see her come unglued again. "I'd rather go by myself."

"I'll accompany her."

Her father's words were like an iron fist clamping her lungs. "Why would you do that? You couldn't stand Grandfather." The thoughts in her head blurted from her mouth. She really needed to get a filter when it came to her father.

He had the decency to blush. "To make sure old man Peebles doesn't take advantage of the situation like he did when your mother died." He shook his head. "He way overcharged for his services."

Her mother's funeral had been a reflection of her personality. Quiet, beautiful, and tasteful. How would he even know what the service cost? She'd seen her grandfather write the check to Peebles without a complaint.

The thought of her father haggling over prices with Mr. Peebles . . . Madison scratched a small welt on her arm. "I do not need or desire anyone's help. It's the last thing I'll ever do for Grandfather." She lifted her chin to look her father in the eye. "And I want to do it by myself."

"I was only trying to help."

"I know, but I'm a big girl now." She shifted her gaze to Clayton, encouraged by the admiration in his eyes. "I appreciate both of your offers, but I can handle this."

Clayton stopped at the door. "Call me if you need me."

"Thanks. I'll be busy the next few days, but keep me in the loop about Dani."

"No problem."

His favorite words. When the door closed behind him, the kitchen seemed empty, and she quickly cleared the bar of the plates and cups just to hear the noise. Which was ridiculous.

"If you don't need anything else," she said to her father, "I think I'll go to bed."

"Can we talk a minute before you do?"

"Can it wait? It's been a very tiring day."

"No, it can't. Do you mind sitting back down?"

"Let me do something with these dishes first." Madison used the time putting the stoneware in the dishwasher to calm her nerves. In the past, whenever her father wanted to "talk," it never ended well.

With her face as blank as she could make it, she sat on a barstool across from him and waited.

He loosened his tie, then caught her gaze and held it. "I'm getting married next month."

37

Clayton had met men like Gregory Thorn. Controlling. Narcissistic even came to mind. Madison hadn't seemed comfortable with him. Maybe he should've stayed longer.

No. She probably had things to discuss with her father. He checked his watch. A little after eight. ICU had an 8:00 visitation. He would check on Dani and see if she'd heard from Bri.

It was the last visiting time until morning, and the ICU waiting room was empty when Clayton walked through the opened doors and around to Dani's room, shifting his gaze away from the room where the judge had been.

"How is she?" he asked the nurse outside her room.

She looked up from her computer. "I believe she's sitting in the chair. Why don't you ask her?"

Nice way of getting around HIPAA rules, and he grinned. "I believe I will."

Clayton tapped on the door.

"Come in." Dani's voice was still low, but she sounded much stronger.

"Look at you," he said when he stepped inside the room. "You look great."

"I think you need glasses." Then she sobered. "I overheard two nurses discussing Judge Anderson's death—they thought I was asleep. How's Madison?"

"So-so. She was close to her grandfather." He sat on the side of the bed.

"I thought she might've been."

Neither of them mentioned *adoptive*, but the word hung in the room. "How did you discover you had a twin sister?" he asked.

"One of the ancestry DNA sites."

Dani wasn't going to volunteer more than she was asked. She shifted in the chair and winced. Clayton stood. "Would you like me to help you get back in your bed?"

"Oh, that would be great. I started to ask the nurse just before you arrived, but she's so busy with a new patient, I hated to bother her."

He held out his hand, and when he pulled her up, Dani groaned and pressed her hand against the bandage on her chest.

He froze. "Did I hurt you?"

"No. There's pain any time I move. Thank you for helping me." Once on her feet, she took a minute to straighten her back before she sat on the side of the bed. Another groan came when she lay back against the pillow. "The doctor said the pain would get better, but I don't know."

"I'm sure it will."

"Have you ever been shot?"

"No, but I broke my arm once."

"I believe they call that apples and oranges. And would you please sit down? You're making me nervous, hovering over me."

He laughed and took out a pad and pen as he sat in the chair beside the bed. Dani and Madison shared more than physical traits—they both had a good sense of humor.

Clayton jotted a few questions to ask and looked up. "Were you adopted as well?"

Her blue eyes darkened briefly. "Yes."

"It wasn't a happy situation?"

"I didn't say that."

"You didn't have to." Was the two women's tendency to clam up hereditary? "You're a lot like Madison, you know."

She raised the head of the bed. "What do you mean?"

"Neither of you show your cards."

Her eyes twinkled. "And you know a lot about card playing?"

Clayton hadn't meant to go there. "Unfortunately, I once did."

"But no longer."

"That's right. You are evading my questions, Ms. Parker. May I ask why?" Seconds ticked by, and he tried to think of a way to reframe the question.

"Habit."

He lifted an eyebrow. "Habit?"

She sighed. "Yes. Partly because of what happened when I had to change my identity, and partly because I'm a social worker and accustomed to respecting my clients' right to privacy."

"I can understand that, but I wasn't asking out of curiosity. I have a shooter to catch—your shooter—and any information you can give me will help."

"You think someone might not have wanted Madison and me to connect?"

"It's occurred to me."

Her expression was thoughtful. "I'd hoped to explain all of this to Madison first, but you're right. It may be days before she and I can talk. I need to be helpful, although I don't believe the fact that Madison and I are twins has any bearing on my shooting."

"Why don't you let me be the judge of that." He flipped the page on his notepad. "How long have you known about Madison?"

"Let's see . . . this is, March, right?" When he nodded, she said, "Four months. Right before Christmas."

"Why didn't you contact her then? Give her a call?"

"It wasn't something I wanted to do over the phone." Dani bit her bottom lip. "I didn't know enough about her—not everyone wants relatives coming out of the woodwork. I didn't know if she was aware she'd been adopted. I couldn't barge into her life and say, 'You have a twin sister.'"

"I suppose not."

"It was only recently that I was comfortable with getting in contact with Madison and had planned to connect with her once I dropped Bri off." She grabbed the cup of water and took a sip.

"Have you heard from Bri?"

Dani shook her head. "The girl is scared to death. I can't imagine where she's hiding out. I called Wings of Hope to let them know why we never made it to Jackson. As soon as I know where she is, I'll call, and they'll send someone to get her."

Clayton nodded. "I snapped a photo of your car tag, and I'll have Chief Nelson issue a BOLO for her. When she was here, did you discuss where she might find a safe place to stay?"

"No, but Madison gave her a card with her grandfather's address on it. Bri was freaked out about the shooting, and then she freaked out about a marshal being here. I told her it was for Madison's grandfather, that he was a judge, and the police thought someone might have shot him. That's when I went into A-fib, and they asked her to leave."

He leaned forward. "I hope this isn't stressing you."

"It's not. Putting everything in order is actually helping me clear my mind." She frowned. "But I'm not sure where I left off."

"You planned to contact Madison once you dropped Bri off . . ."

"Oh yeah . . . Bri and I had only gotten to Natchez when you saw us at the restaurant. By then I had decided to try and see Madison on my way back to Mobile."

"Is that where WITSEC set you up to live?"

"No. WITSEC was very much against me moving back to Mobile, so I'm not in the program any longer. They also didn't want me to continue my work with human trafficking victims, and I wasn't about to give that up. Like Bri told me yesterday, that would've let the bad guys win." She grinned. "So far just changing my location and name has worked."

"I'm not locked into human traffickers being your shooter. They would have known Bri was with you and taken her."

"Good point, but who else could it have been?"

"We're working on it."

"Is Madison still working the case?"

"Not officially. Pretty sure her supervisor will take her off if he hasn't already, since it's been determined you two are family. She'll be tied up with the judge's funeral and settling his estate for the near future." He scanned his notes. "Have you found any other family members?"

When she didn't answer, he looked up. Tears streamed down her face.

"I'm sorry! I didn't mean to make you cry." He grabbed the tissue box on the tray table and handed it to her.

"It's . . ." She stuttered a breath. "Not you."

Dani pulled tissues from the box and dabbed her eyes. He waited until she regained control.

"I'm sorry."

He patted her arm. "Nothing to be sorry for."

Dani gave him a weak smile. "To answer your question. I've found our mother on the DNA site, but her information is private. I sent an email to the address on the company site, but I haven't gotten a reply."

"So you have no information on her?"

"All I know is that her Tree gave Ocean Springs as her location, but no address, and I'm not sure if that's even valid. And if it is, I wonder if we've met. Ocean Springs is only about an hour from Mobile." She stared down at the sheet. "I wonder if Madison can pull in some of her resources and find her?"

Madison had seemed reluctant to talk about her birth mother. "You could ask her. Was there any other information on the site that might help you find her?"

"No. I can send you the report when I get to my computer."

"I would appreciate it."

She was quiet a minute. "I do know she was fifteen when she had us. That was one of the few things my parents told me when I questioned them about my birth mother." Dani gave a wry grin. "Can you imagine having twins at fifteen? We were split up and adopted out to different families."

It seemed to Clayton some effort should have gone into keeping the girls together. He noticed that the dark circles under Dani's eyes had deepened. She needed rest, and besides, the bell notifying visitors it was time to leave had sounded a good ten minutes ago. He was surprised the nurse hadn't run him off. He stood. "Time I was going."

"Can you stay a little longer?"

Was that fear in her eyes? Or just exhaustion? "You'll be safe here in the unit, and I'll be back in the morning."

"I'm not afraid. Well, maybe a little, but the nurses have assured me no one will get in this room that they don't know. Bri couldn't even get in here until the nurse confirmed I wanted to see her."

"Do you know when they'll move you out of ICU?"

"The doctor talked like it would be tomorrow or the next day."

He wished she could stay in the unit. The police chief had pulled the security detail off Dani since this part of the hospital was secure. The floor wouldn't afford the same safety measures. Clayton planned to ask if the detail could be returned, but he doubted Nelson had the resources to assign her an officer.

"Give me your number, and I'll call to see where you are before I come. You did keep your phone?"

She nodded and pulled it out from under her pillow. "A nurse loaned me her charger."

"I'll pick one up for you tomorrow." Clayton punched in the number she rattled off, and her phone rang. "Now you have mine."

"Thanks. I'll put it in my contacts,"

He did the same. "Call me anytime, day or night, if you need me."

"I will, and if I hear from Bri, I'll let you know."

Clayton stopped outside the room and gave his phone number to Dani's nurse and asked her to contact him if there was a problem. A minute later he jogged to his SUV to chase the chill off the cool night air.

When he pulled to the edge of the hospital parking lot, he hesitated. Hampton Inn wasn't far, and now might be a good time to interview Terri Davis. Clayton turned toward the bridge and drove to the hotel.

The front desk clerk wouldn't give him Terri's room number, but he did call her room. Terri agreed to see him, and he quickly walked up the stairs. "I hope it's not too late," he said when she opened her door and invited him in.

"No. I've been expecting you."

He sat in the club chair she gestured toward. "So, you admit to being at Coffee and More yesterday?"

She sat on the edge of her bed. "I never said I wasn't."

"You kind of danced around it."

She lifted a shoulder in a slight shrug. "I didn't think it was any of your business."

"Maybe not, but evading the question makes you a good suspect in the judge's shooting."

"I did not shoot the judge. I was with Steven most of the evening."

"Until what time?"

She thought a minute. "Maybe nine-ish. What time was he shot?"

"Around ten."

"I was here, alone. Pretty sure the security cameras will show what time I came to my room and that I didn't leave."

He nodded. "What did you see Judge Anderson about at the coffee shop?"

She fingered the cross around her neck. "It was a private matter."

Clayton crossed his arms. "We can do this here or downtown at the jail with Chief Nelson present."

Terri tried to stare him down, but she was the first to look away. "Oh, all right. I've only recently learned his daughter had passed away, and I wanted to give my condolences."

"How did you know the judge's daughter?" Terri was too young for them to have been friends growing up.

"Before she married and left Natchez, Miss Anderson was my fifth-grade teacher." She slid the cross back and forth on its chain. "I came from a single-parent home where I went to bed hungry a lot of times. I had three outfits for school, and kids made fun of me, but Miss Anderson changed all that. She made me her helper, made me feel important, and I'm pretty sure she's the one who left a mysterious package right before Christmas break that year. It had two new outfits in it."

She closed her eyes, and a tiny smile played around her lips. "There was no name on the package—if there had been, my mother would have made me return it." Terri opened her eyes. "And that's why I wanted to express my condolences to the judge."

Clayton studied her for a minute. He believed her . . . partly, but he sensed there was more to the meeting than she was telling.

38

Clayton left Terri Davis with the certainty she hadn't shot the judge, but he wasn't quite so sure she and the judge only talked about his daughter. He was climbing in his SUV when his cell phone rang. Jen.

"Nothing's wrong, is it?" he asked.

"I'm checking on you since you haven't made your nightly call," his sister replied.

Clayton scraped his hand over his jaw, the stubble prickling his fingers. He couldn't believe he'd forgotten to call. Yes, he could. It'd been a crazy day. "Working a case. How's Ava?"

"She's fine. Missing you."

"I'm sorry. Mind if I stop by a minute?"

She hesitated. "I'd rather you didn't."

Something in her voice bothered him. "Why not?"

"I don't want you to wake her up."

"I won't. I just want to see her." When Jen reluctantly agreed, he pointed his SUV toward his sister's house. She let him in with a finger to her lips and then glanced over her shoulder.

"Keep your voice down," Jen said, her voice not much more than a shaky whisper.

A tense undercurrent filled the room. "You okay?"

"Why wouldn't I be?"

"I don't know. You tell me. Do you need money?"

She shook her head and shooed him down the hall. "And remember—don't wake her up," she mouthed.

"Yes, ma'am." Now she had him whispering. Clayton tiptoed to his niece's bedroom. She'd kicked her blanket off and lay curled in a ball. It was all he could do to keep from stroking her hair as he tucked the blanket around her.

His gaze traveled to the red birthmark on her cheek. The pediatrician had said it would fade before she started school, but it hadn't. Clayton had researched and discovered some never faded. If Jen's worthless husband hadn't quit his job, it could've been fixed a year ago, before she started school. Jake's insurance company had been one of the few that didn't consider a port wine stain on the face cosmetic surgery, especially in a child.

He bent over and lightly kissed her head, then eased out of the bedroom. Jen sat on the sofa, her hands working furiously with her knitting needles. She looked up when he returned to the great room, and for a second, she seemed to hold her breath.

"How are you fixed for money?"

"I've already told you that we're fine." She glanced toward the hallway again, then finished the row and laid her work aside. "Thanks for coming by."

"Why are you in such a hurry to get rid of me?"

She shifted her gaze to the floor. "Clayton, I'm beat. It's been a long day, and every other customer I checked out found something to complain about. Either the price of lettuce was too high or the meat had too much fat . . . like I could do something about it."

Jen was downright jittery. Something wasn't right. He scanned the room, and his shoulders tightened. Someone had draped a black leather jacket over the back of a kitchen chair. Not just someone. "Where's Jake?" he asked through clenched teeth.

Silence filled the room until a man stepped from the kitchen.

Jake Prescott. Pressure started in Clayton's chest and shot to his head. "What are you doing here?"

Jake glanced at Jen. "I told you I shouldn't hide." He planted his feet squarely on the floor and took a deep breath. "This is my family. I have a right to be here."

"You have no rights." Clayton glared at him. "You gave them up when you walked away from your family."

Jake's face flushed. "I know that, but I wouldn't have done it if it hadn't been for the drugs. I'm clean now."

Clayton ignored the pleading in his former brother-in-law's eyes and turned to Jen. "Tell your ex he's not wanted here."

"He's not my ex. We're still married."

Clayton stared at his sister, not comprehending her words. He had been there when she went to court. "What do you mean, you're still married?"

Jen crossed her arms. "I . . . withdrew the papers before they were final."

Her words hit him harder than any fist could have. He stepped back. "That doesn't mean you have to let him back in your life."

"He's changed. Give him a chance."

Clayton balled his hand. "When pigs fly."

Jake stepped forward. "I have changed, and if you'll let me, I'll prove it to you."

He took out his wallet and pulled out a wad of cash. "Here's a down payment on the money you've given Jen and Ava."

"I don't want your money." Clayton knocked Jake's hand away, scattering the money over the floor.

"Uncle Clayton?"

Ava. He jerked his head toward the hallway as his niece ran toward him and grabbed Clayton's hand that was still balled in a fist.

For a second, no one said a word, then Ava ran to her father, dragging her blanket behind her. Jake bent down and lifted his daughter into his arms as Jen joined them.

So that's how it's going to be. "Call me when you come to your senses." Clayton turned and marched out the door to his SUV.

He fastened his seat belt and pushed the ignition, but before he could back out, Jen rapped on his window. Clayton punched the down button. "I don't want to talk about Jake."

She stared at him, tears falling down her cheeks. "He really has changed. He's a Christian now."

Clayton would believe that when he saw it. He gripped the steering wheel until his knuckles turned white. "Why are you giving him a chance to leave you again?"

"I'm telling you, he's changed. He said—"

"Words are cheap, Jen."

She jutted her chin. "The old Jake would have torn into you with his fists, and that's not all. With the money Jake's been sending since he got out of rehab, I don't need you to pay my bills any longer."

"I see. How about Ava's operation. Can he pay for that?"

Jen ducked her head. "Not yet, but when he gets insurance—"

"Unless he's working for the same company as before, it might not cover the operation she needs."

"His old company took him back."

There was no use talking to his sister, and he shook his head. "I can't believe you'd put Ava through this. Do you know what it'll do to her when he starts using again and leaves you high and dry?"

"Jake loves us, and he won't go back to using."

How could his sister be so blind?

Jen backed away from the SUV. "If you can't accept Jake, then just stay away from us."

"You don't mean that."

"I do."

Clayton threw the SUV into reverse and floored the gas pedal. He couldn't feel any worse if she'd cut his heart out with a knife.

39

Her father was remarrying? The words bounced around Madison's head like a pinball.

"Did you hear me?"

She mentally shook her head to clear it. "I heard you all right, just not sure why you felt the need to tell me this tonight."

"I don't like having secrets between us."

As usual it was all about him. "That's one secret I would have preferred you kept until a later time." She stared at her father. "Did you even love my mother?"

"Of course I did."

His answer came a little too fast and way too loud. "Isn't this a little sudden? How long have you known this woman?"

"That's hard to answer."

Ever the lawyer. "I don't see why. Days, months, years? That doesn't seem so difficult."

"She works for the company but . . ."

The picture was becoming clearer. "Were you having an affair before Mom died?"

"No!" Then he repeated the word a little softer. "No. I loved your mother, but our marriage wasn't the easiest—you should remember that. We fought all the time."

How well she did remember. Weariness pressed her shoulders down. She rubbed her eyes. "I'm too tired to deal with this tonight. Can we discuss it in the morning?"

He patted her arm. "Sorry to drop it on you like this, but—"

She pulled away. He wasn't sorry, and Madison didn't want to hear him justify his actions. "I'm going to bed."

He took a step back and stared at Madison like he'd never seen her before. And maybe he hadn't.

"I hope you sleep well," he murmured.

"You too." Without another word, she strode out of the kitchen. Once in her bedroom, Madison collapsed on the bed. *He's getting married?*

Something poked her in the back, and she pulled it out. The letter from her grandfather. Nadine must have put it there. Another thing she couldn't deal with tonight or at least until she had a shower.

Half an hour later, Madison laid the unopened envelope on her dresser and crawled into bed. *Tomorrow . . .*

A creak outside her bedroom popped her eyes open. Had she even been asleep? The lighted clock on her dresser showed 1:00 a.m., so she'd slept a little.

She cocked her ear toward the door. There were three or four boards on the stairs that made a noise if someone stepped on them. She listened for more creaks. Hearing nothing, she climbed out of bed and grabbed her gun.

The hallway was empty, as was the stairs. Her imagination? Probably. Just as she turned to go back to bed, a light bumping sound from downstairs arrested Madison. She held her breath, waiting, and another bump rewarded her—like the sound a file cabinet made when it was off track.

She thought about calling for her dad and dismissed it. If he was the one prowling around, she wanted to know why. Madison eased down the stairs, avoiding the creaky boards, and tiptoed to the entrance hall. A faint glow came from the end of the hall . . . the kitchen or the study? Maybe her dad had gotten hungry. She peeked around the corner.

The light plainly came from the study and was probably only

her dad. If not, she had the element of surprise on her side. Madison crept down the hallway, sidestepping other boards that she remembered creaking.

From the doorway she had a plain view of her grandfather's file cabinet and her father rifling through it. The sight rooted her to the floor. Part of her wanted to burst into the room and demand to know what he was doing, but the investigator in her overruled the impulse. She silently retreated to her bedroom.

Madison returned her gun to its holster, then slipped into a terrycloth robe and opened and closed her bedroom door loud enough to be heard. This time when she reached the entry hall, the light came from the kitchen.

She mentally smoothed the frown from her face and walked into the room. "Couldn't sleep, either?"

Her father looked around from where he sat at the bar, a piece of the caramel cake in front of him. If nothing else, he thought on his feet.

"No. I, ah . . ." He pushed the cake away. "It bothered me that I dropped my wedding plans on you at a time like this."

As well it should have, if she could believe it. She held his gaze as he studied her face.

"What's your problem?"

"I fell awake. Came to get a glass of water."

Confusion crossed his face. "You what?"

She shrugged. "If you can fall asleep, why can't you fall awake?"

"I don't believe I've ever heard that expression before, but it's logical."

"I think so." She wanted to ask what he was looking for in her grandfather's files. What was he hiding from her? Madison filled a water glass and sipped it. "Shall we try this again?"

He stiffened. "What do you mean?"

She wanted to laugh. He was wondering if she'd seen him in the office, but he couldn't ask. What a strange dance they were doing. "Sleep. What did you think I meant?"

"That. You just sounded funny."

That's what a guilty conscience did for you. "See you in the morning."

"I was serious when I offered to go with you to the funeral home."

"And I was serious when I said I could do it alone."

He cocked his head. "You've changed since your mother died."

"Maybe I've just grown up." If she hadn't at thirty-five, when would she? "Good night, again."

Back in her room, Madison picked up the letter from her grandfather. As much as she didn't want to read it, it was time. She was too wired to sleep, anyway.

She noticed for the first time that the back had an unbroken wax seal across the flap, and this made her smile. Even though her grandfather was a busy man, he always made time for her. One summer they'd spent several days researching and making wax seals. She slid her fingernail under the seal, broke it, and opened the envelope. Slowly she withdrew the papers inside. Two pages in his handwriting.

Another smile. She recognized the fine lines from his favorite Montblanc fountain pen.

Dear Madison,

If you are reading this, then we never had the opportunity to speak of what you should do when I pass. But first I want you to know how much I cherished and loved your mother, then you.

She quickly skimmed the missive as he detailed the funeral service, agreeing with his choice of music. The last paragraph dealt with the settling of his estate, and the attorney she should contact.

I'm depending on you to take care of these matters.

The second page was written with a different pen, and she frowned as she read it.

Madison, I want you to go through my files and find one labeled James M. Hargrove. If it's not there, then forget I mentioned it. But if you find it, please take the entire file to James. He'll know what to do with it.

No matter what happens, always remember that I loved you and wanted the best for you.

Grandfather

She blew out a long breath. The details about the funeral service helped immensely, but Madison wasn't sure what to do about the second letter. Was that the file her father had been looking for?

Madison leaned against the headboard. She wanted to know who Hargrove was. She picked up her phone and typed the name James M. Hargrove into a Google search. Several hits popped up, but one in particular caught her eye.

James M. Hargrove, Private Investigator, Natchez, Mississippi.

40

When Madison read the last page of her grandfather's letter, her first impulse had been to go to the study and comb through the files. Instead, she waited until she no longer heard her father moving around in his bedroom.

She did not want him to catch her going through the files, in case she found Hargrove's folder, and let another hour pass before she slipped into her robe. Madison eased out of her room and down the hall, once again avoiding the boards that creaked. Instead of her gun, Madison held her phone, using it as a flashlight.

Inside the study, she went straight to the four-drawer file cabinet and shined her light on it. The drawers were labeled on the outside—top one was labeled Miscellaneous, second was Clients, third was a nonprofit he was involved in, and the fourth was labeled Projects.

Which of the drawers would Grandfather have picked to store the Hargrove file? She eased the bottom drawer open. There weren't many files in his Projects, and it didn't take long to search through them. No Hargrove. She skipped the nonprofit drawer and skimmed through the files in the client drawer. Again, only a few files and Hargrove wasn't in there, either.

She eased the first drawer open, grimacing when it hung up with a resounding bump. Then just like she did in her Hot Springs office, she gently lifted the drawer over whatever blocked it and stared at the magnitude of files.

There was no way to get one more file in this drawer. She flipped through them as quickly and quietly as she could and found nothing. That meant the file—if Grandfather hadn't already destroyed it—should be in the one she skipped. Madison should have known that the very last drawer she chose was where it would be.

Fearing something might block the drawer, she gently pulled on it, happy when it slid quietly open. Not quite as many files as the first drawer, but again nothing.

In her memory, she scanned the room, wishing she could turn the light on. But her dad might see it and come investigate. Madison rolled her shoulders. Might as well go back to bed.

Or check the top drawer again. What better place to hide a file than among hundreds of files? She eased the drawer open again and this time slowly went through each file.

By the time she got to the *P*s, she was ready to give it up. *Wait*. Was that a file that had slipped down? Or had it been purposefully hidden? Madison tugged the accordion folder sandwiched between two other fat files so she could read the label. "Hargrove, J" was written in her grandfather's neat lettering. Of course—*P* for private investigator.

She slipped the file out of the cabinet and eased the drawer shut. As tempting as it was to stand there and scan the contents, she didn't want to risk her father coming downstairs and finding her. Madison tucked the file under her robe and secured it closer to her body with the terrycloth belt.

A minute later she climbed into bed with the file, eager to read it. What if the file contained information on his killer? Madison pulled out the contents, and photos slipped from her fingers and fell onto the bed. She picked up one and dropped it like it was a hot coal. Her stomach churned, and she ran for the commode, heaving what little food she had in her stomach.

Madison wet a cloth and pressed it to her mouth, wishing she'd never looked in the folder. While the photos didn't show an adulterous relationship, it did show two people who were obviously in love with each other. Two people who weren't her mother and father but her father and another woman.

When were the photos taken? Before her mother died. Madison was certain of that—Grandfather would not have concerned himself with her dad's affairs unless Mom had still been living. She steeled herself and examined the pictures. Her father and the woman were in a restaurant setting . . . and evidently were having a private moment. While not conclusive proof of an adulterous affair, the pictures showed the intent was there.

Another thought roiled her stomach. The file was what her father had been looking for earlier. She'd have to give him points for not wanting her to discover the photos. An invisible band squeezed her lungs.

What if . . . no.

Her dad had not killed her grandfather for the file.

Would she be so quick to dismiss him as a suspect if he wasn't her father? "*If she killed herself, Gregory drove her to it. Or he could have put something in her wine. She'd lost her sense of taste and wouldn't have noticed it.*" Her grandfather's words roared back into her mind. What if her dad had killed her mother and then discovered Grandfather had this report? And then killed him to get the report. He'd certainly been searching for something in the file cabinet earlier tonight.

No. She refused to believe her father had killed her mother or grandfather. Madison's fingers shook as she scooped up the offending photos and deposited them back in the accordion folder.

That left the typewritten report to deal with.

Not tonight.

Madison jerked it up and stuffed it in the folder as well. She was too close to this, but she couldn't show the file to anyone else. Sleep. And time. That's what she needed.

She also needed to get through the next few days, starting with the funeral arrangements and then Grandfather's burial. People would be there to pay their respects and she had to represent him well.

In the letter, he'd told her he was depending on her to work with his lawyer to settle his estate, and to do that, she'd have to go through the contents in the filing cabinet.

What other secrets did it hold?

41

Clayton worked his shoulders. If he didn't, his neck would be so stiff he wouldn't be able to turn it by morning. He looked at the clock. Two a.m. It was already Friday morning. Unable to even think about sleeping, he'd been hunched over the laptop since he arrived home. He'd found articles on Aaron Corbett, the man whose brother had died at Parchman, and all kinds of articles on adoption.

Turned out Corbett was a sniper in Afghanistan back in 2008, and since returning home, he'd had several run-ins with the law for domestic violence and fighting at a local bar. Clayton found a Facebook page that was mostly rants against the government and the judicial system, Judge Anderson in particular. But the chance he was the sniper yesterday was remote. Why would he shoot at Madison? Would he even know who she was? He'd check with Hugh and see what he'd come up with on Corbett.

Until he had Dani's DNA file, he couldn't take that search any further. Clayton sat behind the computer again and once more googled finding birth parents. There was a plethora of sites that could help with that, and he clicked on links he'd skipped earlier. Nothing. Exhaustion weighed on him. Perhaps their mother would respond to Dani's email.

Clayton believed their birth mother had put her DNA out there for them to find. Could be she was a very private person and wanted to meet them on her own terms.

Own terms. Made him think of Jen. He blew out a long breath. At some point, Clayton had to call her and talk sense into her. He couldn't believe she'd trusted Jake again.

"Why not? I trusted you."

The voice wasn't audible but was loud and clear in his head. He wanted to plug his ears, like it would do any good. "Men like Jake don't change," he muttered to the empty kitchen.

"You did."

Had he? When he left Jen's house, he'd driven straight to the casino to lick his wounds. In time Jake would do the same thing—revert back to his comfort zone.

"You didn't go in."

No, but he'd wrestled with himself for a good thirty minutes before he called his sponsor in spite of the time. At least this time he'd been able to drive away, but the bomb was always there, ticking.

"Maybe Jake needs a friend who understands what it's like to have an addiction . . . like you."

No way. Clayton banged the glass on the countertop. *Focus on Dani's case.* She would be leaving the safety of the ICU soon and needed to be his first priority. The police chief had already turned down his request to put an officer outside her door due to lack of manpower.

All the more reason to get this case solved. There was an option he hadn't played yet, and he took out his phone and scrolled to the Fs. Silas Fletcher. Clayton hit dial.

"Don't you ever sleep, man?" From Fletcher's croaky voice, Clayton could tell he had woken him up. "What do you need?"

"Need you to check the dark web to see if anyone's put out a contract on a couple of people. Briana Reed and Dani Parker, who sometimes goes by Lindsey Tremont."

"Care to give me a clue where to look?"

"Both would be of interest to human traffickers."

"Got it. I'll contact you as soon as I know something."

"I owe you one."

"You owe me more than one," Fletcher growled. "Now let me get back to sleep."

Clayton ended the call and stared at his phone. Fletcher would find out if there was a contract on Dani. And if there wasn't, he needed to look in a different direction in the case.

Maybe he needed to anyway. Dani hadn't been the target at the hospital. That left either Bri or Madison. The teenage girl's background with human trafficking could easily have made her the target—if her pimp had tracked her down. But why shoot Dani and leave Bri at the rest area? If the pimp had followed them from New Orleans, he would have known the girl was with Dani . . .

He shifted to Madison. If she was the target, could someone have mistaken Dani for her? But why would Madison be anyone's target? That's the question he needed to ask her later today before she left to make funeral arrangements.

Clayton would definitely miss working with Madison on the case. He thought about the two women, so much alike yet different. It seemed odd how he was drawn to Dani as a sister. Definitely not the way he felt about Madison. Which was strange, given their features and many of their personality traits were identical.

Clayton blew out a breath. Women had been almost as addictive to him as gambling. It was different with Madison, though. But was it genuine attraction or the same-old-same-old? How would he ever be sure? The argument raged within him. He shook it off. *Focus.*

Maybe Clayton could get Judith Winslow to help him find Madison's and Dani's birth records. Was it possible she'd even handled the adoption? He googled both Bright Horizons and Judith Winslow. While there were plenty of hits that connected her to Bright Horizons, there was only a small amount of personal information on her.

He logged back into the Mississippi Secretary of State website and looked up Bright Horizons. Judith had started the pregnancy center thirty-four years ago as a 501(c)(3) nonprofit. That would have been a year after the twins were born. He clicked the link to more information. While the site didn't give her salary, it listed almost as much in administration expenses as in receipts and income. Over $400,000. Since the center operated mostly with volunteers, if he were still a betting man, he'd bet she had a hefty salary.

He leaned back in his chair, not sure exactly how what he'd learned fit together. How did Judith Winslow's meeting with the judge Wednesday fit with his information? At the time, Clayton had assumed it had something to do with a legal matter, like an adoption, but thinking back he wasn't so sure. In the first place, Anderson no longer handled adoptions. That ended when he went from being a chancery judge to a judge on the state supreme court, and five years later he was nominated by the president to become a district federal judge.

What had Winslow wanted from the judge? When Clayton had been at the door and looked back, Anderson was adamantly opposed to something she was saying.

He wondered if Madison's grandfather was on Winslow's board of directors. Probably not if the judge had signed off on any of Bright Horizon's adoptions, but he checked anyway. His assumption was correct—Anderson's name wasn't on the list of board members.

Clayton closed his computer and rolled his shoulders. He'd like to know more about Judith Winslow before he asked for her help, but who to ask? His mother. She should be able to help him.

Did his mother know about Jake? His stomach tightened. Of course she did—Jen lived next door to her. Why hadn't she told him? Because she knew how he'd react. His gut tightened.

Was he going to let Jake ruin his relationship with his family? He replayed the scene from earlier. "*If you can't accept Jake, then just stay away from us.*"

Clayton couldn't lose his family . . . especially Ava. His shoulders slumped. Could he accept Jake Prescott? With that question weighing on his heart, he headed to bed.

Sunlight woke him instead of his clock, and Clayton groaned. He hadn't set his alarm. It had to be almost eight. He checked his watch. No, just 7:30, but too late to grab his Bible for his usual study. He'd have to settle for a verse or two, and as long as he didn't make a habit of it, it would be better than nothing.

While he waited for his coffee to brew, he thumbed through his email for one of the devotions that dropped into his inbox every day and clicked on the first one he came to.

The way things were going with him, it'd probably be about forgiveness. He breathed a sigh when he saw it was from the third chapter of John. "For God so loved—"

His phone buzzed with a call. Madison. "Hello?"

She didn't answer right away.

"Are you okay?"

"Sorry. I thought I heard my dad come downstairs."

"What's going on?"

"Can we meet? I need advice, and I need it yesterday."

He ran his hand over the stubble on his chin. "I haven't eaten. Want to meet me at the Guest House for breakfast? It's near both of us and quiet."

"I'm not familiar with it, but it sounds perfect."

He gave her directions. "It's also where I first saw Dani."

"Okay. See you in about ten minutes," Madison said and disconnected.

Clayton took his coffee to his bedroom and gulped it in between showering and dressing in his park service uniform. Seven minutes later, his hair was still damp as he strapped on his P229 and walked out the door. When he arrived at the restaurant, he saw that Madison's Impala was parked on the street, and he pulled in behind it. A chill hung in the air, and he was glad he'd worn his park service jacket. Madison sat at a table in the outer courtyard in a lightweight down jacket zipped to her chin.

He took a chair across from her. "Are you sure you won't be too cold out here?"

"It'll be more private," she said. "I've already ordered a pot of coffee."

"Good." That first cup hadn't given him nearly enough caffeine. "You must have been ready to walk out the door when you called."

"I was."

He leaned back as a waitress approached with a carafe of coffee and two cups. "Are you ready to order or would you prefer the buffet?"

"Could you bring me a yogurt?" Madison asked.

Clayton needed something more substantial. "I'll take the full breakfast with scrambled eggs and ham." He eyed Madison. "You sure you don't want something heartier?"

"I'll do good to get the yogurt down." When he raised his eyebrows, she sighed. "Okay. How about an order of oatmeal?"

After the waitress left, he picked up his cup. "This is the best coffee in town."

"As long as it has caffeine and it's hot, tasting good is a bonus."

Neither of them spoke for a minute. He looked up and caught Madison studying him. "Sorry—I didn't have time to shave."

The corners of her mouth quirked up in the hint of a grin. "You do the day-old beard well."

Madison didn't miss the way Nadine's lips pressed together. "He said seven, but knowing him, he'll work until at least five, which should put him in Natchez between seven thirty and eight."

"That soon?" Nadine murmured. "I'll be in my apartment if you need me. Are you still staying with me?"

Madison checked her watch. How did it get to be seven? "No, but thank you." She did not want to leave her father alone to prowl around her grandfather's house.

She hugged Nadine. "I don't know what I'd do without you."

"You'd do just fine, chère," she said, returning her hug.

Once they were alone, Clayton said, "You want me to stay until your dad gets here?"

"I'm sure you have a life." It surprised her she didn't want him to leave.

"Not so much. Ava and my sister are busy tonight, and other than getting in a run, I'm free."

"No hot date?" Madison clamped her lips together. What was she thinking? But unless she was mistaken, Clayton had been about to kiss her when the car backfired at the park. She couldn't deny the way her heart raced now as she waited to know whether he was dating anyone.

He was staring at his hands folded on the table. "I don't date. I made a commitment a while back not to trifle with a woman's affections." He raised his head, and their gazes collided. "At least, I try not to."

Her heart thudded in her chest. Had he been trifling with her affections this afternoon? Then a thought made her smile. "Have you been reading Regency romances?"

He burst out laughing. "No. I'm just not quite sure how to put something like that into words. I thought it sounded pretty good myself."

"You're not ever getting married?"

"Didn't say that, just not playing the field like I used to. How about you? Are you dating anyone?"

42

Sorry. That's off topic." Why did Madison even notice Clayton's day-old beard? She needed to keep her focus on her mission. "And I'm sorry to drag you out so early, but I need your help."

"No problem."

That made her smile. "Nothing is a problem for you."

Madison pulled a copy of the Hargrove file from her bag and laid it on the table. She'd taken a chance and copied it this morning before she heard her dad stirring.

"What's up?" He eyed the folder.

"The letter Nadine gave me yesterday mentioned a file I'm supposed to deliver . . ."

"Is that it?"

"A copy." She bit her bottom lip. "I'm pretty sure Grandfather didn't want me to read it, but—"

"You did."

She nodded and pushed the file toward him. "It's about my father."

Clayton opened the folder, and his eyes widened. "This is—"

"I know. The photos predate my mother's death so it's evidence of my father cheating on her."

"Does he know this file exists?"

"I'm sure he does." She explained seeing him rifle through her grandfather's file cabinet. "I quietly returned to my room and pretended to come out again, slamming the door. When I got downstairs, he was in the kitchen."

"But he hasn't seen this?" He tapped the file.

She shook her head. "If he had, he would've taken it so I couldn't find it. He's probably looking through Grandfather's files again as we speak."

Clayton flipped through the pages of the report. "Do you know the woman involved?"

She clenched her jaw so hard, pain shot through it. "Not by name, but it's probably the woman he told me about last night. He's getting married again."

He looked up from the file. "Didn't your mom just die?"

"Four months ago." She looked toward the street to check her emotions, then turned back to Clayton. "My grandfather had something he wanted to discuss with me Wednesday night. Before he could, Hugh called about Dani, and I had to leave. I wonder if it was this?"

"Do you think your mother knew about the affair?"

"I don't know. She had issues, and they didn't have the best of relationships. She never mentioned it to me, but she wouldn't have."

Clayton refilled his cup and nodded at her empty cup. "More?"

"Please." She waited until he set the carafe back on the table to ask the question that was uppermost on her mind. Madison hated that she even let the thought take root. "What if he killed Grandfather to get this?" Last night she'd been certain he was innocent, but this morning doubts had crept in. "He was less than two hours away. And he would have known where Grandfather kept his revolver."

Clayton thought a minute before he responded. "Is your dad proficient in firearms?"

She blinked. "I-I don't know. I've never seen him with one."

"He never fired one of yours?"

"Good grief, no. He made it plain that I was wasting my talent with the National Park Service. He would've viewed shooting my gun as tacit approval."

"Does he carry one when he travels?"

"I'm sure he doesn't unless he packs it in his checked bag, and even that would be a hassle. You don't think he shot him?"

Before Clayton could respond, the door to the restaurant opened and the waitress brought out their food.

She set Madison's yogurt and oatmeal in front of her, then Clayton's full plate. "Aren't you two chilly?"

"We're fine." Madison inhaled the hearty aroma of the biscuits and country ham on his plate. She hadn't known it came with that kind of ham or biscuits.

"Want me to share?" he asked with a twinkle in his eye.

"No," she said too quickly and glanced down at her food. "Maybe just a tiny corner of that ham . . . and half a biscuit."

He laughed out loud and cut the slice of ham in half. "Here you go," he said, forking it to her plate. Then he added a biscuit. "I have plenty."

Both were every bit as good as she thought they would be and much more satisfying than what she'd ordered. "Thank you." She wiped her fingers with her napkin. They had let the subject of her father drop, and now it was time to return to it. "You don't think my dad could've shot my grandfather?"

"I've been thinking it over while we ate, and while it's not impossible, I don't think so. He seemed very uncomfortable that we wore guns last night."

"True," she said. Madison was relieved, but eliminating her dad put her back at square one. "Once I have the funeral arrangements finalized, I plan to stop by James Hargrove's office. Any chance you could meet me there?"

He nodded. "Unless an emergency comes up. Just give me a call."

"Shooting for eleven-ish."

He gave her a thumbs-up as his cell phone rang. "I need to take this."

"Why don't I run to the restroom while you talk."

"Thanks."

Clayton was answering as she strode to the entrance. While she was inside, Madison took care of the check and answered a call from her grandfather's attorney. The judge had made her executor of his will, and the attorney wanted to meet with her Monday at nine to go over the details. She was not looking forward to that.

When she returned and reclaimed her chair, he'd finished his call and the server had cleared their table. "I guess I better not keep you any longer," Madison said.

He leaned forward and put his elbows on the table. "I want to run something by you."

She tilted her head and waited.

"What if someone mistook Dani for you here in Natchez like I did, right here in this restaurant? And they followed her to Coles Creek and shot her, thinking it was you."

The sensation of falling made Madison grip the table even though she was sitting. Once she was steady, she let Clayton's words roll around in her brain. Thoughts that had been hovering in the back of her mind crystalized. Thoughts she'd kept at bay until now. But first she wanted to know why he brought it up. "Why do you say that?"

"Couple of reasons. First, I believe you were the target at the hospital. If it was Bri, the shooter could have taken her out earlier, when she left Dani's car to get something to eat."

Madison stared down at her hands and let his words sink in.

"Another thing," Clayton said. "I had a confidential informant check the dark web for a contract on Bri or Dani. There wasn't one under her current name or the Lindsey Tremont identity, and there's no chatter about either of them. That leaves you. My next question is, who in your past would want you dead?"

Madison raised her head and found strength in his blue eyes. The thoughts she'd kept silent about spilled out. "Maybe someone wants both of us dead."

He leaned back. "I haven't considered that possibility. Any thoughts who might want you both out of the way?"

"Hardly. I'm still dealing with the knowledge that I have a twin sister."

"Well, now that you've put it out there, we need to explore the possibility and the threat you might pose to someone."

Any number of reasons came to her mind. "Maybe someone stands to lose a great deal if we connected with our birth parents."

He chewed his bottom lip. "Or if your birth parents kept your birth a secret all these years, there could be all sorts of reasons they might not want you to find them."

She palmed her hands up. "Neither of them has anything to worry about from me—I have no desire to meet the people who never wanted me."

43

Clayton rubbed his jaw with his thumb. He was tempted to tell Madison what Dani had found out about their mother—that she'd taken the DNA test and how young she'd been when they were born. It might help Madison understand why she'd given the twins up. But he hesitated. Even though Dani hadn't sworn him to secrecy, he didn't feel comfortable sharing the information.

"There's another possibility," he said. "What if there's another sibling who stands to inherit a great deal of money and doesn't want to share it?"

"Has Dani indicated we have more brothers and sisters?"

"No," he said truthfully. "But I think it's time you two sat down and discussed what she's learned."

"I agree . . . it's just that the timing is all wrong." Her gaze dropped to the table, and when she lifted her head, her eyes were wet. "I have so many things to do, I don't even know where to begin."

"You know how to eat the hippopotamus, right?"

"Hippopotamus?" She burst out laughing. "Don't you mean elephant?"

"Same difference." He grinned. "Anyway, it's one bite at a time. Or as I say, 'Do the next thing.' So what's the next thing?"

"The funeral home."

"There you have it. Are you certain you don't want me to go with you?"

"Don't you have work to do?"

"I want to take time to go with you."

Madison's eyes teared up again, and she waved her hand in front of her face. "Thanks." She sniffed. "Sometimes it's hard to accept kindness."

He smiled. "I'd already committed to going to the private investigator's office with you, and then I thought we might stop by and talk to Dani again. See if she's remembered anything and let her know she's not on any hit list. Are you ready?"

When she nodded, he stood. "No need to take two vehicles—you want to ride with me? We can drop your car at the judge's house."

She frowned, and it was easy to see the wheels turning in her mind. "Don't forget," he said, "if you need your car, we're only ten minutes from anywhere in Natchez."

Madison gave him a wry grin. "I'd forgotten."

"I don't want to overlook any possibilities," Clayton said as they walked to their cars. "Be thinking about any past cases you've investigated where someone might hold a grudge."

"I will, but I'll need to go through my files to refresh my memory."

"Do any cases jump out at you?"

She shook her head. "No, but anytime you arrest someone, there's a possibility they'll seek revenge."

"True." He opened her car door and ignored the pointed look she gave him. "Are you wearing a protective vest?"

Her eyes widened. "No. I was in such a hurry to get away from the house, I totally forgot."

"Then you can run in and put one on when we drop your car off," he said. "What rating is your vest?"

"IIIA."

"Not enough." He frowned. "You don't have one with a higher rating?"

"Yes, but I don't want to wear it all day."

He held up his hand. "You have to wear one with a higher rating."

Madison pressed her lips together. "How about a compromise? If we're out in the open, like yesterday, I'll wear an outer vest, otherwise it'll just be the one under my shirt." When he agreed, she tilted her head. "How about you?" she asked.

"I'm wearing one now under my uniform."

"What rating is it?"

She knew as well as he did that any body armor that could be worn under clothes wouldn't provide protection against a sniper. "IIIA, same as yours. But no one is shooting at me."

"You don't know that. Why couldn't you have been the target yesterday?"

"I suppose I could've been. But ISB special agents investigate ten serious crimes to my one. Although I did give a certain ISB ranger a warning ticket for speeding."

He got a grin with that. "All right. I'll give you that," she said grudgingly and started her car.

Clayton followed her to the judge's house and waited in his SUV while she changed. Then they drove to the funeral home, where Madison finished making final arrangements for the judge's funeral while Clayton waited in the lobby. When she came out, she informed him it would be held at two o'clock Monday afternoon at the Methodist church where her grandfather was a lifelong member.

"He would've liked having it at St. Matthews," she said as they drove away. "And I need to call Buddy to let him know the funeral arrangements. I talked to him last night, and Joe is in Nicaragua so he definitely won't be coming."

Clayton had wondered why the cousins weren't here to help her with the funeral, but they'd never been as close to their grandfather as Madison. He wished she could fast-forward through the next few days. Madison had reverted to the shell-shocked expression she'd worn right after learning the judge had died. "Do you still want to stop by Hargrove's office?"

"Yes," she said. "He's expecting us." He shot her a questioning look, and she added, "I called while I was at the funeral home."

At the private investigator's, they were quickly ushered into his office. Both the waiting area and his office advertised his success. Leather chairs—not the thin stuff like Clayton's recliner at home, but real leather. And the mahogany desk probably cost at least five grand. He knew because he'd been looking for one and had quickly changed his mind.

After Madison introduced herself and Clayton, James Hargrove leaned back in his chair and templed his fingers. "I'm truly sorry about Judge Anderson."

She nodded. "Thank you."

"I understand there's a question about how he died."

Madison crossed her arms. "He did not kill himself."

"I agree, and if there's any way I can help, let me know . . . or is that why you came today?"

"Not exactly." Madison handed him the file folder. "I believe you did the work on this case."

He scanned through the documents. "I did. Your grandfather wanted proof of what he'd suspected for a long time and hired me to find it."

"Do you know how long the affair had been going on?"

"My guess is two years at least. That's how long the rental agreement for the apartment where she lives has been in effect."

"Is it in her name or his?" Madison picked at her cuticle.

"His."

"You're telling me this affair went on for twenty months before my mother died?"

Hargrove nodded somberly.

"How long did you observe him?" Clayton asked. Even without

explicit photos, the fact that he'd been paying her rent for two years spoke for itself.

"Every day for six weeks."

That should be long enough to know the man. He glanced at Madison to see if she wanted to ask the question they'd discussed earlier, and she gave a slight nod. Clayton leaned forward. "Do you think he's capable of murder?"

The question didn't seem to surprise the investigator. "Are you asking if I think he murdered his wife or Judge Anderson?"

"Both," Madison said.

Hargrove tapped his fingers together. "I found no proof that your father killed your mother with an overdose—it appears she accidentally ingested too many Oxycontins. In his report, the medical examiner indicated he'd found an empty bottle of the prescribed medication on her bedside table. The prescription was for twenty and had been filled only the day before for a tooth extraction. I believe his ruling of an accidental overdose is correct and that she lost track of how many she'd taken."

Madison chewed her bottom lip. Unfortunately, her mother's mindset had often been if one pill was good, two were better.

"As for your father shooting the judge, Gregory Thorn didn't strike me as the type to get his hands dirty."

Madison didn't know whether to be relieved or not. But the thought that kept running through her mind was that her father had out-and-out lied to her when she'd asked if he had an affair before her mother died. And he'd done it so easily. If he lied about that, what else had he lied about?

"Do you know if he owns any guns?" Clayton asked.

"I'm sure he doesn't. Judge Anderson had already told me he hated guns. Now the woman he was seeing . . . she was a different matter."

Madison leaned forward. "What do you mean?"

"Once the judge knew he was seeing someone, he wanted

more information on her, and I did a background check, interviewed former friends and the like. She is very skilled with both rifles and pistols—it's a hobby with her."

He sorted through the papers and frowned. "There should be a file on her included in this one." He picked up his phone. "Maxine, could you bring me all the files for Judge William Anderson?"

A few minutes later, Hargrove's personal assistant scurried in with an armful of files and placed them on his desk. He thanked her, then sorted through them. "The judge hired me to investigate several things for him. Here we go." He pulled a thin folder from the stack and opened it. "Margo Ellington. Works for the same law firm as your dad as a paralegal. Age forty-two."

Madison gasped. The woman was only seven years older than her. Surely this wasn't the woman her father intended to marry. Why hadn't she asked her name? Did she really need to? Her dad said he'd met her at the firm—that she worked there.

Madison's stomach churned. She stood. "Your restroom? Could I—"

"Of course." He stood and opened the side door that led into a hall. "Third room on the left."

In the bathroom, she wet paper towels with cold water and pressed them to her face, managing to keep her breakfast down. This was like a nightmare she couldn't wake up from. Her legs shook, and she dropped onto a stool beside the sink. As soon as she felt her legs would hold her up, Madison stood and dried her face. Then she returned to Hargrove's office.

"I think I've heard enough for today," she said. "Could we come back another time?"

"Anytime. I made a copy of Ms. Ellington's file and gave it to Clayton."

"Thank you."

"When is Judge Anderson's funeral?" Hargrove asked.

"Monday at two." She barely choked out the time.

Clayton filled him in on the funeral details, and then he

slipped his arm in hers as they walked out of the building into the sunshine.

"I don't know what's wrong with me," she said.

He squeezed her arm. "Madison, your world's been rocked with one shock after another since Wednesday night. You're not a robot without feelings."

At least he hadn't said that she was a woman and entitled to have an emotional breakdown. But normally she was neither emotional nor a crier. She had to get ahold of herself—she'd been on the verge of tears for the past two days.

When they reached his SUV, she grabbed the door handle and opened it before Clayton could. *Time to buck up. Thorns don't cry in public.* How many times had she heard that as a kid whenever she hurt herself? As she thought about it, she realized her dad had raised her like a boy—telling her that crying was for sissies, telling her to be tough, to not let anyone know when they hurt her, to always win . . . Suddenly it all made sense—it was obvious her dad had wanted to adopt a boy. Why hadn't she seen it before?

Madison tried to wrap her mind around this revelation as she fastened her seat belt. Seconds later Clayton opened the driver's side door and slid across the seat.

"Let's grab a bite, and then if you're up to it, we'll go see Dani."

"Let's skip the food for right now." She'd like to skip going to the hospital too. "And let's keep our conversation with Dani strictly on the shooting. I don't think I can take any more personal revelations."

"We can do that if you'll promise to eat once we leave the hospital—your body needs fuel to run on."

"I'll try."

"I do want to say that if I'd been through what you have, I don't know that I could handle it as well."

He was only trying to make her feel better, and nothing but time would accomplish that. If only her mind would stop spinning. One more piece of information in her head, and it would explode.

The drive from the PI's office to the hospital was short. Clayton stopped under the covered entrance. "So you won't have to put on the heavier vest."

"Thanks." She drew a shaky breath and turned to him, drawing strength once more from his kindness. "I'm not usually this fragile."

"I know that. You don't rescue a small boy and get a Medal of Valor for doing nothing."

Madison didn't know how to respond to his statement, so she nodded and quickly climbed out of the vehicle. Saving Noah had been the only good thing to come out of that day four years ago. After Chad's death, it was like she became a pariah—no one would work with her in the Texas office, not even on white-collar crimes. Their attitude had been the driving force for her relocation to the Hot Springs, Arkansas, office for her investigations. Dani's was the first violent crime she'd investigated in four years.

Once inside, she adjusted the vest under her shirt, her mind still on the Texas debacle. Chad hadn't worn a vest that day, and she'd often wondered why. If he had, he'd still be alive, albeit serving prison time. Maybe that was why.

She focused on Clayton as he jogged toward the building. He seemed different from other men she'd dated, not that there'd been that many or that she'd even dated him. But she wanted to. The thought took her breath. *Don't go there. He'll only let you down.* That had been her experience with men, starting with her dad.

But could Clayton be different?

"Men only use you. They play all nice until they get you hooked, and then they walk all over you." Her mother's words when she was in one of her depressive states had haunted the few relationships Madison had. And they had always proven to be true.

Clayton strode through the entrance. "You okay? You look like you're a million miles away, and not in a good place."

Madison relaxed her tight jaw and forced a smile. "Thinking about something my mom once told me."

"Must not have been good."

"It wasn't important." She tilted her head. "Stairs or elevator?"

"Stairs—I didn't get a run in this morning."

She followed him through the door to the stairs. "So, you're a health nut?" she asked, her voice echoing in the stairwell.

"Me? I'm not the one who ordered yogurt and oatmeal for breakfast."

Her heart warmed at the way he made her laugh. "Does Dani know we're coming?"

"I called her after I parked, so yes. She's been moved out of ICU."

After they located the room, they paused outside the door, and Clayton turned to her. "I'm going down to the cafeteria for a cup of coffee." When she started to protest, he said, "I think it's important for you to have time alone with Dani. It'll be fine."

Madison wasn't so sure. She was already shaky after talking with Hargrove.

"Trust me on this." He gave her a hug.

After he left, Madison took a second before she pushed the door open, knocking as she entered. "It's just me. Madison."

Dani sat in a recliner by the window and returned the chair to an upright position before she turned toward Madison with a smile. Madison's heart stuttered. For the first time since she'd learned of Dani's existence, it hit her that this was real—she actually had a sister. A knot formed in her throat, and she took a deep breath to relax it.

"I saw Clayton jogging across the parking lot," Dani said. "I'm assuming he let you out at the door?"

"Ah . . . yeah," she said, finding her voice. "After the shooting here yesterday, we decided that was the best tactic." When Dani's gaze went to the door, Madison added, "He went downstairs for coffee . . . to give us a little time to ourselves."

"He's a good guy."

Madison sat in the chair opposite the recliner so Dani didn't have to keep looking up.

"How long have you known him?"

"Two days?" It seemed much longer to Madison. "Oh, wait, a hundred years ago, he was friends with my cousins, and I would see him when I came to visit Grandfather in the summers. I was probably about eight the first time, and until recently I thought he was a bully."

Dani gave her a puzzled look.

"My cousins liked to pick on me. I sort of lumped him in with them until he made me remember that they didn't do that when he was around—he'd threatened to pummel them if they did."

"Hasn't changed much, has he? Still the knight in shining armor." Dani sobered. "I haven't had the chance yet to tell you how sorry I am about your grandfather's death."

"Thank you."

They both fell silent.

"You're a park ranger," Dani said.

"You look much better today," Madison said at the same time, unable to stand the silence. It looked as though they were alike in temperament as well. "Do you do that too? Rush to fill a void?"

Dani nodded with a sigh. "Especially when I'm nervous. What did you say?"

She was nervous too? Hard to tell from her calm demeanor. Madison repeated what she'd said.

"Oh dear." Dani felt her cheek. "I've looked in the mirror. I must have looked awful yesterday, and I'm sure it can't be blamed entirely on this lovely hospital gown."

"I'm not going to lie," Madison teased. She couldn't get used to looking at someone who had her same features. Same hair, same blue eyes, same dimple in her chin. "How tall are you?"

"I'm assuming you're always that direct, like me?" Dani said. "But to answer your question—five six."

"Same here," she said with wonder in her voice. "How long have you known about me?"

"A little over four months."

"Why did you wait so long to contact me?"

"When I googled your name, one of the hits was your mom's obituary." She shrugged. "I just didn't feel it was the right time . . . and I was still getting used to the fact that I had a twin sister. Don't get me wrong. While it was awesome knowing I had a sister, I'd always known I was adopted. What if you'd never been told?"

"I'd just been through a traumatic loss," Madison said softly. "And you didn't want to add more pressure. That was kind of you, since I'm pretty sure you were anxious to make contact."

"Oh, I was."

"I've always known I was adopted. Have you found . . ." Madison stared at her hands gripping the plastic arms of the chair, not sure if she was ready to know the answer to the question on her mind. But wondering was just as bad. "I mean, who else have you found?"

"No more siblings, at least none that have run their DNA."

Madison raised her gaze. There was a "but" in Dani's voice. "Have you found our parents?"

"Only our birth mother."

"The woman who gave us away," she said bitterly.

"She may not have had any choice."

"People always have a choice."

"I don't mean to cause you more distress," Dani said. "But she was only fifteen when she had us."

"Fifteen? That's just a child." Madison's grip loosened as she tried to wrap her mind around a fifteen-year-old giving birth. She'd never considered her birth mother may not have had a say-so about what happened. "Have you contacted her?"

"She only recently showed up on Ancestry. I emailed her about a month ago, but I haven't heard anything." Dani rested her head on the recliner. "I assume since she did the DNA test that she wants to connect with us, but it's always slow getting information."

That made sense. Madison noticed how weak Dani looked. Something she should have noticed earlier. "You're tired. Let me help you back into bed."

"I don't like being an invalid, but if you would, I'd appreciate it," she said. "By the way, I've put you on my HIPAA form so the doctors and nurses can discuss my case with you."

"Good." Madison helped her stand, then rolled the IV pole as she offered her arm to Dani. "Any idea when they'll release you? Or where you'll go?"

Her shoulders slumped. "No to both questions."

"I think I can solve the last one. You'll come to my grandfather's house and stay with me."

Dani faltered. "Are you sure?"

"Yes." Madison helped her into bed and elevated the head.

"Thank you." Dani lay back against the pillow. "Do you think you could use your connections to find our birth mother?"

"Without a name, I don't see how I can." Did she even want to dig into the past right now with everything else happening in her life? She glanced at Dani, who waited expectantly. Yes, she did.

"Send me your file from the DNA company. Maybe my friend at the FBI office in Jackson can help."

46

Clayton hesitated outside Dani's door. He'd given them a good thirty minutes to break the ice with each other. He rapped softly, and when someone said come in, he pushed the door open, looking to see how Madison was. He wasn't sure how she'd react if Dani brought up what she'd learned about their birth mother.

Madison's body language told him nothing except she was tense. "So . . . everything good?"

She tilted her head. "Did Dani tell you she had a lead on our birth mother?"

"She did."

"And you didn't tell me."

"It wasn't my place. Did you tell her the good news?"

A frown creased Madison's forehead, and she gave a small gasp. "I cannot believe I forgot."

"What good news?" Dani asked.

"There's no contract on the dark web for you."

Her eyes widened. "You checked? How?"

He grinned. "I know people who know people. Nothing about Bri, either."

Relief swept across her face, instantly replaced with fear. "But that means . . ." She looked from Clayton to Madison. Her hand went to her mouth. "If no one is after me, the shooter at Coles Creek thought they were shooting you."

Madison nodded slowly. "And the sniper here at the hospital yesterday was probably shooting at me."

"Do you have any idea who it could be?" Dani asked.

"With my line of work, it could be any number of people."

"But which of them would have known you were in Natchez?"

"The bad guys can usually find you. Or it could be someone already here in Natchez. How did you discover I was here?"

"After I learned who you were, I googled you, and your name came up in a news report in Texas about the FBI agent who tried to kill you."

That story would follow Madison for the rest of her life, and Clayton hated that for her.

"The article said you were an ISB agent with the National Park Service and linked to another article that listed you as now working at the national park in Hot Springs. I called there to see if I could get an appointment with you, and the volunteer who answered told me that you were either in Jackson or Natchez."

That volunteer should have checked with Madison first before giving out that sort of information. What if she'd told the wrong person and that person was here in Natchez? "You need to access your files as soon as possible," Clayton said. "How long will it take to get them?"

"I'll request them as soon as I get back to my computer."

"Then, it's time for you to leave," Dani said.

Madison stood and hesitated, then squeezed her twin's hand. "I'll try to get back later this afternoon."

"Just figure out who's trying to kill her," Dani whispered as Clayton bent over to pat her hand.

"We will," he promised, wishing he felt as confident as he sounded.

Clayton had just picked Madison up at the entrance when his

cell phone rang. He glanced at the ID. "It's Hugh Cortland," he said and quickly answered. "What's going on?"

"I've been trying to call Madison. Is she with you, by any chance?"

"Right here." He handed her the phone and pulled the SUV into a parking slot. "He's been trying to reach you."

"What do you need?" she asked, taking her phone from her pocket and grimacing. "Sorry. My phone's on silent."

She listened, then said, "Hold on a minute. Can I put this on speaker so Clayton can hear this? I'll tell him what you say, anyway." Madison pressed the speaker button. "Go ahead."

"Like I said, I owe you an apology, and I'm reopening your grandfather's case."

"Why?"

"The medical examiner called and gave me a preliminary report. He's ruled it a homicide."

"What?" She glanced at Clayton, her eyes wide and an I-knew-it expression on her face. "Based on . . . ?"

"The angle of the bullet, for one thing, and the absence of tattooing at the wound site."

Clayton nodded. It meant the gun had been at least three feet from the judge when it was fired.

"Direct muzzle contact leaves a speckled pattern around the entry wound from the soot and unburned powder," the FBI agent continued. "There was no tattoo, meaning the muzzle of the gun wasn't resting against his chest like you'd have in a suicide."

"I see." Madison pressed her lips together.

Hugh cleared his throat. "There was one other thing . . . the suicide note wasn't printed from the judge's printer."

"I knew he didn't write that note, but how do you know it didn't come from his printer?"

"Manufacturers put identifying marks on all color laser printers like the one the judge owns. These marks identify a specific printer model and unit, and the note didn't have any marks.

Which means it was either printed on a monochrome printer or one made before the 1990s."

"If the person who wrote the note knows this information," Clayton said, "they could have turned the color off, whether on their own printer or the judge's."

"That's a possibility, but the judge's printer is set to 'use the last settings' and that was color," Hugh said. "Besides, I don't think the shooter took the time to write and print out the note the night of the shooting."

Clayton didn't either.

"What's the next step?" Madison asked.

"I have a search warrant, and my team will be there in the next couple of hours to go through the judge's home files as well as his office files. Will someone be at the house?"

"I'll be there," Madison said. "But you didn't need a search warrant."

Clayton wasn't surprised at the warrant. It made the court case so much cleaner once they caught the culprit. Once the call ended, she handed the phone back to him, and neither spoke while he drove to the judge's house.

A text on Madison's phone broke the silence as they pulled into the drive. "It's from Deon Cox. He has more invoices he wants me to pick up at the supervisor's office." She blew out a breath. "Do you ever feel like you don't know where to start?"

"Sometimes." He pulled into the empty drive and parked. Evidently her father had left. "You want to talk about it?"

She nodded. "Before we go in, though. I don't want to take a chance of my dad coming back and overhearing us." Madison pressed her fingers to her eyes. "I just don't know which case to start with."

"I could pick up Cox's files, saving you a trip."

"That would be great, thank you. That way the files would be here, and I could work on the case after the funeral or when I need something to do."

"I know you want to investigate your grandfather's murder, but you know Hugh's not going to let you get involved in it." He turned to her. "If you're asking my advice, I'd say we work on finding Dani's shooter as well as investigate who might be out to get you—I have a feeling they're one and the same."

"You're right, but it'll take forever to go through my files." She unfastened her seat belt.

"Maybe I can help you."

Now that there was proof the judge's death hadn't been a suicide, Clayton needed to tell Hugh about seeing Judith Winslow at the coffee shop with the judge on Wednesday. Maybe he shouldn't have held back, but he'd had no proof the meeting was anything out of the ordinary. He hadn't wanted to send Hugh down a rabbit hole, especially since he could have imagined the judge's irritation—appearances weren't always what they seemed.

Clayton had to admit he hadn't wanted to point a finger at the pregnancy center's founder—she did a lot of good work in Natchez, and one word of scandal could do irreparable damage. He really couldn't see Judith being the one who shot the judge.

Combing Madison's files for evidence of who might be out to get her seemed the more urgent thing to do.

Madison and Clayton entered the house from the back door. "Wait here, and I'll grab my computer from my bedroom," she said, her stomach growling.

"We never ate. Do you mind if I warm up something from your fridge?"

"Sounds good."

She hurried to her bedroom and paused. Madison didn't remember leaving the door open. Not with her father here. She quietly pulled her gun and eased into the room. Empty. She holstered her Sig. Maybe she'd left the door open—she had been in a hurry to meet with Clayton.

Madison grabbed her computer and glanced at the box of files she'd picked up at the supervisor's office Thursday. Had it only been a day? Seemed like a month. The files in the box were neatly stacked, and she started out the door and stopped. Wait. She hadn't left a tan folder on top.

While she'd waited for her dad to go to sleep last night, she'd rifled through the box, trying to get a feel for the task she had to complete, and the last file she looked at was one from Deon Cox and it had been blue.

Her father! He must have come into her bedroom looking for the file she took to Hargrove. Fuming, she hurried downstairs.

Clayton took one look at her and asked, "What's wrong?"

"My dad—he went through the papers we picked up yesterday. Probably looking for the Hargrove file. I'll bet he searched through Grandfather's files again too." She turned and headed toward the judge's study. At least the door was still closed—she'd shut it behind her this morning after making a copy of the file.

Madison opened the door and gasped. The room was trashed with papers scattered everywhere. "No!"

Clayton pushed past her and stopped. "Your dad wouldn't have done this."

She started inside the room again, and he grabbed her arm. "You need to let Hugh take care of this." He took out his phone. "I'm calling him."

While he talked to the FBI agent, Madison surveyed the room from the doorway. Clayton was right. Her father would not have left such a mess. Who did this? And where was Nadine when it happened. "Nadine!"

Madison whirled around and rushed out the back to the housekeeper's apartment with Clayton on her heels. She banged on her door. "Nadine!"

Loud thumping came from inside the apartment. Madison tried the knob, and it turned. With her heart knocking against her ribs, she pushed the door open. "Nadine?"

More noise came from the closet that had a chair propped under the doorknob. Madison knocked the chair out of the way and jerked open the door. The eighty-year-old housekeeper was on the floor, bound with a hood over her head. Clayton pulled the hood off and scooped Nadine up in his arms and settled her on the sofa.

Madison knelt beside her and took off the restraints. "Are you all right?"

"Yes, chère." While Nadine's voice was calm, her normally hazel eyes had darkened to almost black.

"What happened?" Clayton wrapped an afghan around her shoulders.

She gripped Madison's hands. "After your father left, I tidied up the kitchen, and I came out the back door. I turned around to make sure it locked, and someone put that awful hood over my head and bound my hands before she made me walk to my apartment. Then she made me sit in the closet."

"It was a woman?" Madison asked. "Did she hurt you?"

"Yes, it was a woman, and no, she didn't hurt me. She kept saying how sorry she was. That someone would come along and let me out."

Clayton's phone rang. "It's Hugh." He listened a minute, then said, "Yes, she's all right. We found her bound in her apartment closet."

He listened again. "Will do." And disconnected. "He said not to touch anything in the office." Then he knelt beside Nadine. "Can I get you coffee? A glass of water?"

"Coffee would be good." She threw off the afghan. "But I will make it. I've had your coffee before, Mr. Weak-as-Water Coffee Man."

He laughed. "Then if you don't need me, I'll take photos of the judge's study from the doorway."

Madison gave him a thumbs-up and helped Nadine off the sofa, holding her arm until they were in her tiny kitchen.

"Stop hovering!" Nadine chided her as she plugged in her electric kettle. "I was not hurt and not even inconvenienced. I spent the time praying. Mostly for the woman," she said softly.

"Can you describe her at all?" Madison asked.

"She was taller than I am."

That would be about anyone in Natchez. "Was she skinny? Overweight? Average size?"

The aroma of chicory filled the kitchen as Nadine paused putting coffee in her French press. "Now how would I be knowing that with a hood over my head, missy?"

"Did she say what she wanted?"

Steam came out of the spout, and Nadine focused on pouring

water in the French press to let it steep. "Maybe she was looking for the same thing Gregory was looking for?"

Madison had known her father would search for the file she'd taken as soon as she left. "Do you know if he found anything?"

A smile tugged at the older woman's lips. "From how angry he was when he left, I'd say not." She tapped her forehead. "I almost forgot. He said he would not be back tonight. Maybe tomorrow. I suppose he's staying with his girlfriend."

"You know about that?"

She gave a curt nod. "Remember, my daughter, Nanette, is the head of housekeeping at the Westin in Jackson, and she saw them there the day after your mama was buried. Nanette was so angry—she and Sharon were practically inseparable growing up."

She remembered her mom telling her Nanette was maid of honor when she got married. Anger bubbled up from Madison's stomach. He'd stayed with that woman so soon after her mother died? "Did he see your daughter?"

"No, but I doubt Gregory would have remembered her, anyway—he made sure they didn't see each other after he took your mother off to Memphis. They only connected with each other in the summers when you came down."

And then her father had put a stop to that as well. "The person who attacked you—could it have been the woman he's marrying?" Maybe her father returned to do more searching and brought her to take care of Nadine.

"No." She pressed the plunger down and then poured the rich liquid into a cup. "You sure you don't want any?"

"No, thank you. How can you be sure it wasn't that woman? Do you know her name?" Madison couldn't keep calling her "that woman," and she couldn't be sure it was the same woman in the photos.

"Margo Ellington, and I can be sure because Nanette said the woman was very harsh when Gregory wasn't around and had a grating voice. Ordering her to bring towels and coffee . . ."

Madison barely heard anything past Nadine calling her Margo. Her father was marrying the woman he had the affair with. The woman who was only seven years older than Madison. She shook the thoughts off and tuned back into what Nadine was saying.

"The woman today was soft-spoken, and she was looking for something specific."

Madison studied the housekeeper she'd known since she was a child. She'd just realized Nadine had avoided answering her question earlier. "Do you know what she was looking for?"

"No, but . . ." Nadine averted her eyes, staring down into the dark liquid in her cup. "William Anderson had a good heart. He helped many babies find good homes and signed many adoption papers."

Madison heard a "but" in Nadine's voice. "What are you not telling me?"

"I don't think all the mamas wanted to give their babies away. Maybe this woman was one of them and maybe she thought she'd find something in his office that would tell where her baby was."

48

"Come in," Dani said to a soft knock at her door, and the nursing assistant who had been assigned her end of the floor came in to pick up her lunch tray.

"You didn't eat much," the twentysomething girl said.

Dani laughed. "You wouldn't either if they brought you a piece of chicken you could use for a hockey puck."

"I'm sorry . . . our main chef has been out with an emergency appendectomy. Can I get you something else? Maybe a cup of ice cream?"

"When you get time, Cathy. No hurry." She liked the young CNA. The girl had just gotten her certification for a level 2 nursing assistant and planned to go on to nursing school.

Cathy took the tray and disappeared out the door. Dani lowered the head of the bed. Maybe she could take a nap, but her thoughts drifted to Madison. Her heart warmed at her sister's offer for Dani to stay with her when she got out of the hospital.

She'd felt an instant connection to Madison but sensed reluctance on her part. Madison was probably protecting herself. She understood that—it was how she usually operated. But it'd been different from the first moments with her sister.

Sister. She loved the way the word wrapped around her heart. It sounded as though neither of their lives had been rosy, but perhaps this could be a new start for both of them.

Now if she would just hear from Bri again. She'd called early this morning, and Dani had tried to talk her into contacting Madison. But the girl was so afraid, and other than Dani, she didn't trust anyone. She'd have to turn her over to God. Briefly, she wondered where Madison stood with him . . .

Her eyes grew heavy and she let herself drift off to sleep. Dani didn't know what woke her unless it was the nurse who was checking her IV. "What are you giving me now?" she asked, her mind groggy.

The nurse mumbled something unintelligible.

The skin on the back of Dani's neck prickled, and she twisted so she could see what the nurse was doing. The person wore a white lab coat but their back was to Dani. She couldn't tell if it was a man or woman, but whoever it was stuck a needle into the port on the IV bag.

"What are you doing?" she demanded just as the nurse pushed the plunger on the needle.

"Flushing the port." The voice was low, rough, like a man's . . . or a woman trying to sound like a man.

Wait. Needles weren't used to flush a port . . . and Dani knew enough from her months caring for her adoptive mother before she died of cancer that continuously flowing IVs didn't need flushing. And that wasn't where you flushed a port, anyway.

The door opened, and Cathy bopped in. "I brought your ice cream."

The nurse quickly withdrew the needle, capped it, pocketed it, and with a ducked head, hurried out of the room. Cathy shot the departing nurse a quizzical glance and set the small cup on the table.

"Do you know that nurse?" Dani asked.

"No, but I haven't been here long, and we get new hires all the time. Do you know what the nurse did?"

"Flushed the port, but it looked more like the person was injecting medicine. Would you please check to see if the doctor ordered a new medication?"

As Cathy bolted from the room, Dani stared at the solution dripping from the bag into her IV line. Without flinching, she pulled the catheter from her hand and used a tissue to press against the vein. Better to have the catheter put in again than to risk dying if the nurse wasn't who they were supposed to be.

The door to the room flew open, and the RN who'd given her meds earlier rushed into the room followed by the gangly CNA whose eyes were as big as saucers.

"Oh, good. You pulled the catheter out," the RN said. "Whoever that nurse was, no one has charted that your IV was flushed, and from the description Cathy gave, that person doesn't belong on this floor. I've called security, and because of the shooting yesterday, they called the chief of police. Can you describe the nurse? Or did you notice a name badge?"

"No. The person kept their back to me, and I couldn't tell if it was a man or woman." She glanced at the RN's name badge dangling from a clip on her pants pocket with her photo and name clearly visible. "I didn't see a badge, either."

"Me either," Cathy said. "But the nurse had dark hair—that blue-black color—and was shorter than me and heavier."

The RN wound the tubing up and removed the IV bag. "You have antibiotics scheduled soon, and we need to get a new IV line in. I'll be right back."

She started to trash the bag, and Dani said, "No! Save that for the police."

"Of course. Don't know what I was thinking." The RN dropped it into a clear plastic bag.

Dani found her cell phone and texted Madison and Clayton about the nurse. Her phone immediately rang.

"What's going on?" Madison's voice was tight.

"I think someone just tried to kill me."

A gasp came over the phone. "What?"

"Yeah." Dani explained what happened. "The police are on

the way. Not sure how long it'll take to test for what the person injected in my IV bag, but I have a bad feeling about it."

"We'll be right there. Some interesting things have happened around here too. We'll be there in the next hour."

Ten minutes later someone rapped on her door, and she said, "Come in."

A muscular man stepped inside the room, his bald head shiny. "Ms. Parker? Police Chief Pete Nelson." He showed his ID as he approached the hospital bed.

She compared the photo on the ID to the man, and satisfied, she shook the hand he extended. "I wasn't expecting you this soon, but thank you for coming."

"I was already here, visiting a friend." His reassuring smile disappeared as he shook his head. "I wish I could've put a man on your door, like Clayton Bradshaw suggested. But with budget cuts, I just don't have the manpower. Rest assured, though, there will be someone out there now—the sheriff is loaning me a couple of his deputies."

That made Dani feel somewhat better. "I doubt an officer at the door would have stopped the person. Whoever it was dressed like a nurse." If only she'd gotten a look at the person. As it was, she couldn't swear whether it was a man or woman.

"I just now discussed your case with Clayton, and we're making a plan on how best to protect you while you're here in the hospital. He brought me up to speed on your case. I understand until this happened, he assumed your shooter mistook you for Madison Thorn."

"Yes." That assumption was definitely wrong. Why was someone targeting her?

49

Clayton disconnected from Chief Nelson's call and sighed. The case just reset to zero. Was Dani the target after all? Or were they both targets? He pocketed his phone and surveyed the disorder in Judge Anderson's study one last time. Were the shootings tied to what was going on here?

Clayton hated to leave before Hugh arrived, but he needed to find out what happened at the hospital. Good thing he'd already taken photos with his phone and transferred them to Madison's—once Hugh arrived, they wouldn't have access to the room.

"It's a mess, isn't it," Madison said, coming up behind him. She'd just come from the housekeeper's apartment.

"Yeah. How's Nadine?"

"Nadine is amazing. She's not going to let a little thing like being locked in a closet stop her—her words, by the way."

That sounded like the Nadine he went to church with. "You got the photos, right?"

She nodded. "I'll look at them later. Are you ready to go to the hospital?"

"I am. Did Nadine have any idea what the intruder was looking for?"

"Adoption papers."

He turned to her. “Why does she think that? Did the intruder mention adoption papers specifically?”

“Yes.” Madison took a deep breath. “Nadine seems to think some of the mothers who signed away their rights didn’t want to give up their babies.”

“I can’t believe your grandfather would have anything to do with something like that.”

“Me either, but something lay heavy on his mind that he said he wanted to discuss Wednesday night. I keep remembering how relieved he was when I left to meet you at the hospital.” She turned and walked toward the kitchen. “I’m going to let Nadine know we’re leaving and that an FBI team will be here soon.”

“I’ll be in my SUV.”

A few minutes later, Madison climbed into the passenger side and fastened her seat belt. When he queried her with his eyebrows, she laughed. “She’s fine.”

Clayton backed out of the drive. “I keep thinking about the sniper yesterday at the hospital and wonder if Hugh has totally ruled out Aaron Corbett.”

“The man whose brother died at Parchman?”

He nodded. “I’m not sure why Hugh ruled him out so quickly.”

“Hugh said he had an alibi, but maybe now he’ll look into it a little deeper.”

“Could he have been the nurse at the hospital today?” Clayton said.

“Anything is possible, but why? If he killed my grandfather, his vendetta would be over. Even if he thought Dani was me, he has no motive to kill me.”

“Unless he’s a sociopath, or his time in the war made him unbalanced. It happens.”

She took out her phone. “I’ll check and see if he’s posted anything lately.”

They were almost to the hospital when she whistled. “Wow! He’s posted a newspaper article about my grandfather’s death, and he's not broken up about it at all." She kept scrolling and caught her breath. "Here's one where he says Judge Anderson's family should experience what it's like to lose someone they love."

With both of the judge's children deceased and his two grandsons living thousands of miles away, that could be nothing but a veiled threat against Madison. But how would he know she was his granddaughter? "Do you know Aaron Corbett?"

She shook her head. "I was only in Natchez during the summer. Other than you and Nadine's family, I don't know anyone."

"Are there any photos of you and your grandfather on the web?"

She stilled. "He came to DC when I received the Medal of Valor. He could have been in the clips that were shown on the news outlets." Madison rubbed the back of her neck. "And there were the photos Mom took of us together and put on her Facebook page. Knowing her, she would have tagged us in the post."

"So maybe those photos would pop up for anyone searching Facebook for the judge's name."

A low groan escaped her lips. "Could Corbett have been at the Guest House that night you saw Dani and Bri?"

"I don't know." He hadn't paid that much attention to the people other than Dani.

"How about your sister? Would she remember the people there?"

He clenched his jaw, feeling the muscle jump. Jen was a people watcher. If he had a photo of Corbett, she might remember him. Except they weren't exactly talking to each other. This was something he needed to do in person, anyway. "I'll print out a photo of him and show it to her."

Clayton pulled under the pull-thru at the hospital, and Madison unbuckled her seat belt. "See you in a minute."

When they got to Dani's room, a deputy sat outside. They showed their ID and were allowed inside. Madison went straight to the bed that Dani had raised to a sitting position. "Are you sure you're all right?"

She nodded. "Chief Nelson took the IV bag to get the contents tested, but I'm not sure how long that will take."

"Did you recognize the nurse?"

"No. The person woke me up and their back was to me."

"Did anything stand out?" Clayton asked.

"I've been lying here going over what happened, but all I keep seeing is that needle going into the IV bag." She frowned, concentrating. "I have an impression the person was overweight, but the hands holding the syringe were thin. Cathy, the CNA, thought the person had blue-black hair."

"Maybe he or she was wearing padding, and the blue-black hair sounds like the kind of wig I bought to wear to a costume party." Madison turned to Clayton. "What do you think?"

Clayton shot an amused glance at Madison. "I haven't gotten past that you went to a costume party."

Her cheeks turned crimson. "I don't normally, but it was for a friend's thirty-fifth birthday. I do have fun sometimes—when people aren't trying to kill me." She glanced at Dani, who was laughing. "Or my newfound sister."

Clayton smiled. "I wasn't making fun of you, just glad that sometimes you relax."

"You two kill me," Dani said. "I can't believe you've only known each other less than a week."

Warmth filled his chest. She was right. It did seem as though he'd known Madison much longer. It hit him that he *wanted* to know her more, but it wasn't at all like the way he'd felt about someone he was attracted to in the past. Then his goal hadn't been about getting to know the woman. It'd been more about the thrill of the chase, and once that was gone, he'd move on to someone else.

Lately Clayton had been asking God for someone to share his life with . . . Could it be Madison? His heart thudded against his ribs as it hit him that he wanted the house with the white picket fence and the kids. And he wanted it with Madison. But did she want that? She hadn't given him any indication she did.

He looked up, and their gazes collided. Clayton could drown in her sea-blue eyes. Could Madison be the woman God had picked for him?

50

The hospital room faded as Clayton's gaze held her prisoner. The last man who'd made her feel even remotely the way Clayton did had tried to kill her. She stepped back, breaking the connection. "Where were we before we got sidetracked?"

Clayton was slow to answer, as though he had to remember what they'd been talking about.

"He could've been wearing a wig," Dani said.

"How about camera footage? Did the chief mention getting that?"

Dani shook her head. "He didn't say, but one of the nurses told me the hospital is in the middle of changing companies, and the cameras haven't been installed yet."

The door opened and Chief Nelson entered the room carrying a small bag. "I got a local lab to run a sample from the bag before I sent it on to Jackson. It contained potassium chloride, a drug that shouldn't have been there since none has been ordered for you."

Dani sank against the bed, her face the color of the white sheet. Madison was certain she didn't look any better—Nelson's words had hit her like a gut punch. "How much was in it?"

He pressed his lips together. "I'm sorry to say, but it would have been enough to kill her."

"Did any of the nurses recognize the person?" Clayton asked.

"No. No one other than the CNA got a glimpse. Whoever it was could have easily ducked into one of the restrooms and changed out of the disguise." Nelson's face hardened. "As long as you're in the hospital, there'll be a guard outside your door."

What if the person came back? A guard wouldn't be able to tell the difference between a real nurse and a fake one. "I think you need to be out of here and somewhere safe, like my grandfather's house. I can hire security to guard you there."

"The doctor won't discharge me—I've already asked. He said I needed at least three more days of IV antibiotics and maybe even a procedure."

"Home health can give you the antibiotics. I'm going to check with the nurse about getting you discharged—if you want to leave."

"I don't want to put you in danger."

"I'm already in danger. Someone wants to get rid of both of us, and maybe together we can stop him."

"Or get killed together," Dani pointed out dryly.

"Then, it's settled." She started for the door. "I'll go get the ball rolling."

"Wait." The chief set the bag he'd been carrying on the over-bed table. "I have your grandfather's personal effects from when he was taken to the ER. I just need you to sign off on them."

Her stomach clenched as the chief took the articles from the bag. Madison hadn't even thought about what her grandfather might've had with him when he went to the hospital. His wallet. Keys. The bone-handle pocketknife made her tear up. She remembered him peeling apples for her with this very knife when she was a child.

Nelson held out the paper for her to check off the items and sign. She barely glanced at the wallet or keys as she stuffed them in her bag, but the knife she held tightly in her hand briefly before slipping it in her pants pocket. "Be right back," she choked out.

Madison drummed her fingers against her leg while the charge nurse contacted Dani's doctor. The nurse turned to her and relayed the doctor's answer as to whether Dani could leave the hospital. "Absolutely not. She's only just had the drain tube in her chest removed, due to her collapsed lung."

Madison had forgotten about the lung issues. "Can I speak to him?"

"Are you on her HIPAA form?"

"Yes." If she'd looked at the chart, the nurse would have seen it. She took the phone and identified herself to the doctor. "Can you tell me how soon she can leave?" Madison asked. "I'm worried whoever attempted to kill her will try again."

"What are you talking about?"

After she explained what had happened, he said, "I'm sorry about that, but healthwise it would be even more dangerous for her if she were to leave the hospital. Her latest chest CT scan indicates she needs a procedure on her lung. Ms. Parker and I have discussed the possibility that she might need it, and I'm scheduling it for first thing in the morning. If it goes well, I'll consider allowing her to leave late Sunday."

A doctor who did surgery on Saturdays. She'd have to remember him. After answering a few more questions, the doctor ended the call, and Madison returned the nurse's phone.

She nodded to the guard on duty, then pushed the door open. Dani took one look at her face and said, "I figured he'd say no."

"Yeah. He's doing a procedure on your lung tomorrow." Madison looked around. "Where's Clayton? And the chief?"

"They went down to the cafeteria to discuss the sniper from yesterday, and someone named Corbett."

Clayton would fill her in on what information the chief had. "Have you heard any more from Bri?"

"I talked to her this morning and encouraged her to call you. I was hoping she had."

"She didn't call me," Madison said. "Have you talked to the people in Jackson? Wings of Hope?"

"I have and they'll call me if she shows up. But I don't expect her to go there." Dani dropped her gaze to the sheet she smoothed with her free hand. "I've released her to God," she said softly and looked up. "How about you? Where do you stand with him?"

Where did she stand with God? Church had been one of the few things her mother had been adamant about attending, taking Madison when she was a child, then dragging her when she entered her teen years. Somewhere along the way, it'd stuck, and when she first went to Texas, she'd found a church and attended regularly. Her faith was what got her through what happened with Chad, but lately she'd drifted away. "That's a good question."

"You want to talk about it?"

Madison stood and paced the room. Did she? A square envelope on the floor beside the IV pole caught her eye, and she stooped to pick it up. When she turned it over, her name was handprinted on the front. She showed it to Dani. "Is this yours?"

Her eyes widened. "I've never seen it before."

Madison winced. Picking it up had been a dumb move, but she'd thought it was trash. She dropped the envelope on the table and grabbed a pair of gloves from the box on the wall and pulled them on.

The ivory-colored envelope was good quality. She turned it over. The flap was barely stuck at the tip. *Possible DNA site?* Her fingers shook as she carefully tugged where it was sealed. Inside was a single sheet, the same quality as the envelope, and she slipped it out. More hand lettering.

Now you know how it feels to have people you love taken from you.

Revenge is mine, not the Lord's.

Sound faded as blood drained from her face, taking with it her peripheral vision. Her legs buckled and she stumbled to the chair and fell into it, barely hanging on to consciousness.

When she came to herself, Dani was on her phone, telling Clayton to come quick. Madison sucked in air, trying to regain her equilibrium.

She hadn't had a panic attack in three and a half years.

51

With the police chief on his heels, Clayton burst through the door to Dani's room. It'd taken him less than three minutes to dash up the stairs from the cafeteria, but it'd seemed like an hour. Especially since all he could get from Dani was that Madison needed him.

One of the RNs he'd seen earlier was taking Madison's blood pressure, and another had a wet washcloth to her forehead. He looked from Madison to Dani. "What happened?"

"She found that card on the floor and almost fainted when she opened it."

"This one?" Chief Nelson asked as he pointed to an ivory envelope and a folded sheet of paper on the rolling over-the-bed table.

"Yes."

He looked over the chief's shoulder as Pete used his pen to flip the paper open and slide the card out. Clayton's hands curled into fists as he read the handwritten words.

The nurse removed the blood pressure cuff. "It's better," she said. "Just sit there a minute."

Clayton knelt beside the chair. "Are you okay?"

Madison removed the wet cloth. "Physically—yeah. Did you see the note?"

"I did."

"Whoever did it thought Dani would be dead when I read it. Who would do such a thing? And why?"

He squeezed her hand. "I don't know, but it's their first mistake."

She stared at him, then comprehension lit her eyes. "We have a motive," Madison whispered.

"Yes. It's more important than ever for you to go through your files. See who might blame you for a loved one's death . . . or even incarceration."

Clayton stood as Pete Nelson slid the envelope into a plastic bag. "Do either of you recognize the handwriting?" the chief asked.

Both shook their heads. Madison pressed her lips together. "Someone wants to make me suffer. Is it possible the person who wrote this killed my grandfather? Because if it is, they've certainly made me suffer."

One killer instead of two? Clayton wasn't ready to combine the two cases. A glance at Nelson indicated he wasn't either. The police chief rested his hand on his gun. "I have an appointment, but I'll be in touch."

"You'll have an officer at the door?" Madison's voice held a touch of panic in it.

"Definitely. I wish I had the manpower to put someone inside the room too, but . . ." With a nod, he walked out, closing the door behind him.

Clayton searched his memory for someone they could hire. Hargrove. He turned to Madison. "Why don't you give James Hargrove a call—he probably has someone he can send or knows of someone."

Relief flooded her face. "Yes."

"I'll pay for it," Dani said.

Madison took out her phone and scrolled through the contacts. "We'll figure that out later."

Half an hour later, a plan was in place, and the first of James

Hargrove's female operatives walked through the door. They'd gotten lucky that he'd had a client postpone a trip, freeing up several of his bodyguards.

"Jane Blackwell," the woman said, introducing herself first to Dani then to Madison and Clayton. "I've been doing this for ten years, and I'll take good care of her."

Clayton had no trouble believing the warrior-like agent. She carried herself with the confidence that came from years of experience in protecting people. His phone dinged, and he glanced at it. "Hugh is arriving at the judge's house in fifteen minutes," he said. "We need to fill him in about this."

"Before you go, I want to show you photos of the team." Jane handed Dani her phone. "This is especially important for you—if someone shows up and says they're here to guard you, make sure it's one of these women. I'll AirDrop the photos to your phone in a minute so you can memorize their faces."

"Can you send them to us too?" Clayton asked.

"Planned to as well as exchanging phone numbers. Give me yours, and I'll call you, then you'll have mine."

Once she AirDropped the photos, Clayton scrutinized the women's faces. All, like Jane Blackwell, looked extremely capable. He waited while Madison hugged Dani and murmured something to her.

A few minutes later he picked Madison up at the hospital entrance. "Do we have time to run by the Old Jail?" she asked. "I'd like to pick up the files Deon Cox left. He indicated these should be the last ones, and I can get them sorted over the weekend."

He'd meant to pick the files up for her, but there'd been no chance. "Don't you want to take some downtime? You've had a bad week."

"If I do nothing, I'll start brooding about everything. Besides, my answer to a bad week has always been to stay busy."

That didn't surprise him. "Have you called to see if anyone is at the office? It's almost five."

"I'll do that now." She made the call. "Paul's there. He'll bring them out."

Ten minutes later, Clayton idled at the curb and Madison texted Paul that they were there. While they waited for the supervisor, he scanned the area and didn't see anything that raised his suspicion. When the supervisor approached the SUV with a box in his arms, Clayton hopped out and opened the back hatch.

"Thanks."

Once the files were secure, Paul tapped on Madison's window, and she lowered it.

"I'm sorry about your grandfather," he said. "Vivian would be here to express her sympathy, but she's been out sick since lunch yesterday. She's taken the judge's death pretty hard—they attended the same church."

"Tell her thank you."

As they drove away from the Old Jail, her phone chimed with a text, and she glanced down. "No."

"What's wrong?"

Madison had unfastened her seat belt when they stopped, and now she muttered as she clicked the metal in place. It almost sounded like she was counting to ten. "It's my father. He's bringing *that* woman to Grandfather's house tonight."

"Tell him you don't have time. That the FBI is there." He turned right at the next street and pointed the SUV toward the judge's house.

"Good thought." She quickly texted a message and groaned when there was a return text. "Now he's suggesting we eat at Monmouth's Restaurant 1818, and I didn't bring dressy clothes. And he wants to know why the FBI is there."

She typed out another text. "How does this sound? 'Too much to text and the nicest outfit I have is my uniform. Let's make this another time.'"

"Sounds fine, but why don't you just tell him no?"

The text made a swooshing sound as she sent it. "I've never

been able to do that, mainly because he simply doesn't accept it." Another text dinged. "See," she said. "He wants me to pick a place."

"Just tell him no and don't answer any more texts."

"You don't understand. Then he'd bring her to the house for sure. My father is used to getting his way—business, personal, whatever."

Her cell phone rang and she rubbed her temples. "It's him."

"You don't have to answer."

"You don't know him. I don't have the energy today to handle the fallout, and there would be fallout." She slid the button and put the call on speaker. "Hello."

"What is the FBI doing at the judge's house?"

"The medical examiner in Jackson has ruled his death a homicide."

"Why?"

She questioned Clayton with her eyes, and he shook his head. If Gregory Thorn wanted to know, he could call the ME's office himself.

"I don't have all the details," she said. "Only that the FBI will be investigating along with the US Marshals."

There was a brief silence on Gregory's end, then a sigh. "That means they'll go through his files."

The man must be worried the FBI would find Hargrove's report and photos.

"Yes," Madison said. "Someone trashed his study earlier today and locked Nadine in her closet, so it's a crime scene."

"You're kidding. Could she identify the person?"

Clayton frowned. Most people's first concern would have been if the older woman had been injured.

"She couldn't," Madison said.

Another brief pause. "Where would you like to eat tonight? I'd like for you to meet Margo."

Several cars lined the judge's drive and Clayton parked on the grass. The man thought of no one but himself. Maybe if Clayton told him—he caught himself before he said anything. Madison would not appreciate it if he fought her battle for her. She must have feared he'd say something and put a finger to her lips.

"I didn't bring anything nice enough for Monmouth. How about King's Tavern? We can get a flatbread. And I may bring a friend." She eyed Clayton as she spoke.

Her father hesitated. "All right. Seven?"

"Make it eight," she said. "I have several things I need to do between now and then."

Once Madison hung up, she blew out a hard breath before she turned to him. "Do you mind being the friend I'm bringing along?"

52

Madison held her breath, waiting for Clayton's answer.

"Sure, if you want me to."

She'd hoped he would say that. "Thanks—and since we're going to King's Tavern, we don't have to change out of our uniforms." They needed to get out of the SUV and go inside, except something about the conversation with her father bugged her. But what was it? "Did anything he said sound off to you?"

"Other than he showed no concern for Nadine?" Clayton's brows lowered as he considered her question. "His voice was tense when he asked if Nadine could identify the person who locked her in the closet."

That was it. "Nadine indicated Dad had searched the office before he left, and she didn't think he'd found what he was looking for. Do you think he came back and brought this Margo with him to neutralize Nadine?"

"He could've been afraid she might pop in and catch him."

"Maybe I should tell him he can quit looking—that I've already found the file he wants." She gave a short, mirthless laugh. "And I might just do that tonight."

Except . . . why was she so ready to believe the worst about him? He hadn't been a horrible father in the sense that he'd beaten her or worse. And while he was a master at put-downs, it wasn't like he singled her out—he talked down to everyone. Because it made him feel superior. And in charge. Didn't he realize that he made her feel like she didn't belong? And if she didn't belong at home, where did she belong?

Clayton unbuckled his seat belt. "Ready to go in and talk to Hugh?"

Madison pushed the thoughts away. "I want to check on Nadine first."

She climbed out of the SUV and grabbed the box of papers.

"Let me have those," Clayton said and took them from her.

When the housekeeper didn't answer the knock at her door, Madison tried the doorknob. Locked.

"She's probably in your grandfather's kitchen."

That was exactly where she found Nadine—making coffee and using a pie server to cut one of the pies church members had brought. "You shouldn't be working."

"Pssht," Nadine said, brushing her off. "I am fine. Would you like coffee and chocolate pie?"

Madison's stomach growled, a reminder that she hadn't eaten since breakfast and that was a long time ago.

"I think I want a sandwich first." She turned to Clayton. "Would you like a snack to hold you over until we meet my father?"

"Let me go check with Hugh first." He motioned to the box. "Where do you want me to put this?"

"In my bedroom." She told him where her bedroom was located.

Clayton gave her a thumbs-up and disappeared down the hall to the stairs.

Nadine laid the pie server down with a clatter. "You are meeting your father?"

"Yes. He wants me to meet Margo."

"Does he not know you have enough on you right now?" She waved her hands. "Oh, but we are dealing with Mr. Gregory, aren't we."

Madison bit back a smile. Nadine had never liked her father, and she was sure the feeling was mutual.

"You haven't told me about this woman who looks like you," Nadine said. "Is she your blood sister?"

She gulped, not sure she wanted to share Dani with anyone other than Clayton just yet. But this was Nadine . . . "Actually, my identical twin sister."

Nadine stood very still. "She looks just like you, then?"

"Very much." Madison eyed the older woman. She knew more than she was telling. Why had she never asked Nadine about her adoption? Probably because Madison didn't think she would tell her anything. The housekeeper believed in minding her own business. That's why she and her grandfather got along so well. But Grandfather was gone.

"What do you know about my birth mother? Do you know why she gave me, us now, up for adoption?"

Nadine took both of Madison's hands. "I know nothing for a fact, only that your grandfather was instrumental in the adoption. Anything else I might tell you would be the ravings of an old woman."

"Did you know I had a twin sister?"

"No, chère. Your adoption was a subject your grandfather and I did not discuss."

"How about my adoption papers? Do you know where they might be?"

"Let me think about it."

The papers weren't at the house in Memphis. Her father had delegated Madison to clean out her mother's bedroom and office, and there was nothing in either related to the adoption. She needed to ask Dani what she knew about her adoption.

She hugged Nadine. "My sister's name is Dani, and I'm bringing her here when she gets out of the hospital. We can get to know her together."

Madison turned toward the door as footsteps sounded in the

hallway and Hugh and Clayton entered the kitchen. "That coffee smells wonderful," Hugh said. "Pie looks pretty good too."

"Help yourself," she said as Nadine took out sandwich meat. "I can make you a sandwich, if you'd like. Any answers to what happened here earlier today?"

He waved off the sandwich. "Plenty of prints, but so far only those that should be there—yours, Clayton's, Nadine's, your dad's. Whoever trashed the room and put Nadine in the closet wore gloves."

Madison tilted her head at the housekeeper. "Do you think you would recognize the woman's voice if you heard it again?"

"Yes. After you left, I thought about it, and there was something familiar about the voice . . . like I've heard it before."

That eliminated only about half of Natchez.

After she'd eaten, Madison looked for something to do. She couldn't help Hugh, so she went to her room to sort through the papers Deon Cox had sent her. She paired the purchase orders with the receipt of goods that employees had signed off on.

A pattern emerged. One particular employee regularly signed off on the receipt of goods that did not match the purchase order. However, the final cost never changed from the original order. Did the man think they were stupid? That no one would notice? But there was no telling how long he'd been getting away with it.

She raised her head at a soft knock. "Come in."

Clayton stuck his head in the door. "It's 6:30, and since Hugh said he'd be here another hour, I thought I'd run home and shave and change."

That meant she'd have to change as well. Her gaze went to his now almost two-day beard. She could get used to the sexy look. Heat flushed her face. Where had that thought come from? "Uh, sure," she mumbled.

"Okay . . . see you around 7:45," he said, winking at her.

Her face grew even hotter. What if he'd noticed? He might

think she viewed tonight as an actual date. She barely managed to give him a thumbs-up and tell him she'd be ready.

After Clayton left, Madison searched through her closet for something to wear, discarding first one outfit, then another. Not that she had that many to choose from. Maybe she should've picked up something at one of the boutiques downtown. Like she'd had time. She finally settled on cropped jeans and a casual linen shirt.

Why was she dithering? Then it hit her. Because down deep, she had begun to think of tonight as a real date.

53

Clayton couldn't deny he was looking forward to spending time with Madison away from their problems. Well, his problems, anyway. Her problems with her father still existed, and he'd only been invited to be a buffer between Madison and her father . . . and the woman he was bringing.

Still, Clayton was glad she wanted even that. He got the impression Madison didn't trust many men. And after meeting her father, he could understand why. And then there was the FBI agent who tried to kill her. Rather than ask her about it, Clayton had looked it up on the internet. One article had talked about them being romantically involved. If it was true, it was no wonder she didn't trust men.

After he showered and shaved, he pulled on a pair of dark jeans and a red checkered shirt and rolled the sleeves to just below his elbow. Only 7:20. Still twenty minutes before time to pick Madison up. He drummed his fingers against his leg, not believing how nervous he was.

Do something to kill the time . . . His gaze settled on a photo of him kneeling beside Ava. *Call your sister.*

His stomach clenched. He hadn't gotten around to stopping by. Would she even answer, and if she did, what would he say? He did have an excuse to call her and ask if she remembered seeing Aaron Corbett at the Guest House Wednesday night. Not just an excuse, but a responsibility.

He took out his phone and opened the favorites menu and tapped Jen's number. After the fourth ring, he decided she wasn't going to answer and started to press the end button.

"What do you want?"

"I, ah . . ." *Apologize.* "How are you?"

"I've been better."

"Look, I know you don't want to talk to me, but I need to ask you something."

After a brief silence, she said, "What?"

"It's about a case. Do you remember any of the people who were at the Guest House the night we ate there?"

"No. Is that what you want?" Disappointment laced her voice.

"You didn't know any of the guests there? It's important."

Silence answered him, then Jen drew in a deep breath. "I remember seeing Mrs. . . . I can't remember her name. Mom volunteers at her place."

"Mrs. Winslow?"

"Yes. Her."

"How about any of the men that were there?"

"No. Why is it important?"

He pinched the bridge of his nose. "The woman I bought dinner for was shot and critically wounded right after she left the Guest House, and I believe it could have been someone at the restaurant."

Jen gasped. "That's terrible. Is she all right now?"

"She's improving." If someone didn't get to her and finish the job.

"I tell you what. I'll think about it and sketch the people I remember. Will that help?"

"Yes! That would be great." Jen had been sketching and painting since she was a kid, and she was very good at it. "And I'll text you a photo of a man I think may have been there. See if you remember seeing him."

"Okay."

"Thank you. And Jen, I'm really sorry about last night. I . . ." He took a deep breath. "I shouldn't have said some of the things I did."

"Thank you. And I promise, Jake has changed. You'd know it if you talked to him."

Talk was cheap, but he managed to bite back the words. "I hope you're right."

Jen promised to get the sketches to him by Sunday, and he breathed a sigh after they hung up. He truly did hope Jake had changed. He didn't know why she loved the sorry excuse for a man, but she did.

The same reason I love you. She sees potential in him.

Clayton winced as God laid the impression on him. He had the potential to be an addict just as much as Jake. Not "potential to be"—he was an addict, and he better not let himself forget that. Clayton had seen the destruction caused by gambling in the meetings he attended, and it was every bit as real as a drug addiction. That it hadn't destroyed his life was only grace.

Reach out to Jake. He needs a friend.

Clayton resisted the impression on his heart, but it persisted.

Okay. First chance he got, he'd talk to Jake.

He checked his watch. Time to pick up Madison. A few minutes later, he rang the front doorbell. When she opened the door, he almost lost his breath. "You look . . ."

"Mah-velous, darling?" she supplied in a Billy Crystal voice.

He laughed. "You're good with that accent. And yes, you look marvelous."

And she did with her blond hair framing her face. The blue shirt matched her eyes perfectly. And she wore a smidgeon of makeup. For him?

He'd like to think that, but it was probably to impress her dad, not that she would admit it. People did it all the time—tried to impress the difficult people in their lives.

"You do have body armor on?"

"Of course. And you?"

"Same." He held out his arm. "Your carriage awaits."

He opened the door and breathed in a light, clean fragrance as she climbed into the SUV.

"I miss your five-o'clock shadow."

Clayton ran his hand over his clean-shaven face. "I'll keep that in mind. Shaving every day gets to be a hassle."

An easy silence fell between them as they drove the short distance to King's Tavern. A car pulled out from in front of the restaurant just in time for him to grab its parking spot. "Wait until I—"

"Come around," she finished for him. "Yes, sir."

He checked out the surrounding buildings. There were several groups of people walking in the deepening darkness. They should have made the dinner for an earlier time. He hurried her inside the building, and immediately the aroma coming from the wood-fired oven caught his attention. King's Tavern had the best flatbread and pizzas around. Clayton scanned the room. Not too busy for a Friday night.

Beside him, Madison tensed, and he followed her gaze to where her father sat at one of the wooden picnic tables. The woman beside him was the same woman in the photos. While Hargrove's file said she was forty-two, she looked older . . . maybe it was the too-blond hair that aged her and gave her a hard look. Gregory surprised him by standing when they approached.

"Glad you could make it." He offered Clayton his hand. Then it looked as though he was going to hug Madison, but before he could, she sat on the bench that served as a chair and slid over to give Clayton room.

"Margo Ellington, my daughter, Madison, and her friend Clayton Bradshaw."

"Nice to meet you." Madison nodded, her lips tight with a plastic smile.

This was not going to go well. Clayton felt it in his bones.

54

I've been so looking forward to this," Margo gushed. "Your dad brags on you all the time."

"Really?" Madison clamped her jaw tight to keep it from dropping to the floor, then realized Margo had probably made the remark to break the ice. She couldn't help asking, "What does he say?"

"Oh, how proud he is of you. How successful you are, and that you're so busy you never have time to come and visit, that sort of thing."

Madison could believe her father's compliment since it explained why she never came home. She studied the slim woman. She had pale skin that her platinum hair washed out even more. Either she didn't listen to her hairdresser—because no stylist would willingly dye their customer's hair the color Margo's was—or she colored it herself. Madison opted for the former because the simple, just-below-the-chin hairstyle was salon perfect, and while the color didn't suit her face, the style did.

Margo was nothing like Madison's dark-haired and olive-skinned mother. "Do you plan to drive back to Jackson tonight?"

Margo's smile faltered slightly, and she shifted her gaze to Madison's father.

"No," her dad said. "Margo wanted to stay at one of the antebellum bed-and-breakfasts, and we chose the Burn."

An awkward silence fell on the table, until Clayton cleared his throat. "The Burn is my favorite," he said. "Be sure to pick up the book one of the original owners wrote. It's a fascinating read."

The Burn was only a mile or so from her grandfather's house. They could've walked there. Madison turned to Margo. "So, when did you get into Natchez?"

"This afternoon."

If that could be believed. Maybe Clayton knew the owners well enough to ask when they arrived. She still wasn't convinced her dad hadn't trashed the judge's study looking for Hargrove's file on him. And maybe Margo was the woman who locked Nadine in the closet. "Have you had a chance to tour Melrose?"

"We'll probably do that tomorrow. We took this afternoon to settle in and explore the bed-and-breakfast and a little of the downtown area."

Just then, the waitress appeared with a tray loaded with food. Her father cleared his throat. "I went ahead and ordered an assortment of flatbreads while we were waiting for you and unsweetened tea for both of you."

"Sounds good—it's what we planned to order, anyway," Clayton said.

"We got here early," Margo said quickly, her voice conciliatory.

Madison knew her father felt like she'd kept them waiting even though his words didn't actually say it. Nothing more was said while they sampled the food. The girlfriend's personality was not at all what Madison expected. Could she have been the woman who kept apologizing to Nadine for putting her in a closet, maybe so her dad could search the house for Hargrove's file? They certainly had opportunity.

Margo wasn't quite the shrew Nadine had painted her to be. Or was the platinum blond on her best behavior tonight to impress Madison . . . or her dad? She tilted her head toward the other woman. "How long have you two known each other?"

"Years," Margo answered for both of them. "When I was a paralegal, my office was just down the hall from his, so ever since I've been with the company."

Madison sipped her tea. "You're no longer a paralegal?"

A broad grin spread across the other woman's face. "I just passed the bar and will start work as a lawyer the first of the month. This trip is sort of a celebration, but of course, I never expect to be in the same league as your father—I'll continue my work in real estate."

Her dad leaned toward Margo. "You'll be very good at it too."

Color flushed her face and she beamed. "Thank you."

Madison had to get as much information from her as she could. "So, what do you do when you're not working?"

"Oh, a little of this and that."

"Nothing you're passionate about?"

Margo shifted her gaze briefly to Madison's father. "Your father hates it, but I dabble in skeet shooting, and I'm on a rifle team. We compete all over the state."

Clayton snapped his fingers. "I've been trying to remember where I've seen you and that's it. We've competed against each other."

"Clayton Bradshaw." Margo said the name slowly. "Yes, I do believe I remember you."

"You're an excellent shot," Clayton said. "And don't you compete in the bull's-eye category at some of the meets?"

"You have a good memory," her dad said.

"I just remember the people who beat me," he said with a smile.

Margo Ellington was a crack shot, but was she in Natchez the night her grandfather and Dani were shot? Or at the hospital the next day? Could she probe a little without making them suspicious? "Is this your first time to Natchez, Margo?"

Margo shifted her attention from Clayton to Madison and shook her head. "I've been here a few times. How about you? How long will you be in Natchez?"

"Good question. I'll have Grandfather's estate to settle, and there's still the case that brought me here."

Conversation shifted to her father's next trip to the West Coast. Exhaustion washed over Madison as she tried to pay attention. Putting up a false front was wearing on a day that had already been grueling. She placed her napkin on her plate and flashed them both a smile that she was sure didn't reach her eyes.

"This has been nice." She glanced at Clayton, and he nodded. "But I have a full day tomorrow, so if you'll excuse us, we'll be going."

"So soon?" her dad asked, his voice polite but not warm. "Maybe we can do this again sometime."

Not in this lifetime. "Perhaps."

She stood and Clayton followed, extending his hand to her dad. "Thank you for dinner."

"My pleasure," her dad murmured. "I think we'll stay and have dessert."

At the door, Madison glanced back at the couple. Her father was more relaxed than she'd ever seen him. Had he ever looked at her mother the way he was looking at Margo? Not that Madison remembered. But then, with her mental and emotional problems, her mother wasn't the easiest person to get along with.

That still didn't excuse him from having an affair.

"That wasn't so bad," Clayton said as they walked out of the restaurant.

"If you say so." The night air was comfortable and warmer than it'd been for the last few days . . . probably a storm brewing.

He opened her door and she slid across the seat, then he walked around to his side and climbed in. "Want to take a ride? Or go to your grandfather's?"

"I should go home and see if I have access to my cases . . ."

"But . . . ?"

Madison sighed. "I don't know if I can focus. Tonight . . . this was hard. I actually might have liked Margo in different circumstances, and that makes me feel guilty since she was having an affair with my dad before my mother died."

"Let's take a drive," he said and pulled away from the curb. "I know a spot where you can relax. It's a place I found after I stopped gambling, and it's not far—about ten miles up the Trace."

"Sounds perfect."

Once they were on the Trace, Clayton asked, "Your parents' marriage. What was it like?"

Madison leaned her head against the seat with her eyes closed and let the memories wash over her. "Like all marriages, there were highs and lows. They yelled a lot . . . no, that's not true. Mom yelled a lot when she was in her manic phase. Then there was Dad—he was like this immoveable rock, especially as her bipolar disorder progressed."

"Your mom was bipolar?"

"Yes. I thought you knew." She'd blocked so much of her childhood memories. "I never had many friends because I was afraid they'd want to have a sleepover at my house, and I never knew which mom would meet me at the door when I got home from school. The one full of energy and laughing . . . until something happened to make her angry. Or the one who cried all the time."

"I'm sorry. Sounds like you had a rough go as a kid."

"I survived." Madison didn't know why she was telling Clayton all of this, except he was easy to talk to. Somehow, he made her feel safe. "Grandfather was my rock. He called and checked on me a couple of times a week. Wrote me notes. Came to my martial arts competitions and my horse shows, something my dad rarely ever did even though he'd bought me the horse."

He turned off the Trace onto a narrow road, and then in a couple of miles he turned into a lighted parking area. The headlights flashed on a sign. "Emerald Mound?" she said.

"Yes. Ever been here?"

"No. What is it?"

Clayton killed the motor. "Emerald is the second largest ceremonial Indian mound in the States. It was built between 1300 and 1600 AD. Want to walk to the top?"

She glanced around. "Do you think it's safe?"

"I checked—we weren't followed from Natchez, and no one could know we were coming here. The moon should be rising soon, and you can see it much better from the top of the mound."

Madison unbuckled her seat belt. "Let's do it."

By the time Clayton came to her side of the SUV, she was already climbing out. The air was still, and somewhere to her left an owl's lonely hoot was answered by another owl. "This way." He clasped her hand in his.

His touch sent a delicious shiver through her, but as they climbed the mound, she realized it hadn't been a romantic move—it was to steady her for the ascent. He shined a light on the path, and Madison was puffing a little by the time they made it to the top.

Clayton flicked the flashlight off, and darkness surrounded them. "Close your eyes."

She did as he said and felt his hands on her shoulders as he turned her.

"Now open them and look up."

When she did, it took her breath. As far as she could see, an immense span of blackness provided a velvety backdrop for the stars that were like a million fireflies floating in the air.

When I consider your heavens, the work of your fingers, the moon and the stars which you have set in place . . . The verse from Psalms filled her heart. Madison leaned into Clayton, and he put his arm around her waist, pulling her closer.

"It's beautiful, isn't it?" he said softly.

How did he know this was exactly what she needed? "Look!"

A streak of light raced across the sky—a shooting star, the first she'd seen since she was a kid.

"Did you make a wish?"

"I always do." It was always the same wish—to belong. But tonight she added another wish—some way to keep the sense of peace she felt. Suddenly a tiny thread of fear encroached on that peace. Somehow Clayton had found a crack in the wall she'd built around her heart. She should step away, tell him to take her home, but the night sky held her captive.

He bent his lips closer to her head. "Now look this way."

She turned, and the full moon, the color of a pale pumpkin, filled the eastern sky. "It's huge."

"A super moon."

The magical night wrapped around them as they watched the huge orb rise. She'd never seen anything so beautiful. Or maybe it was who she was with. Madison turned and faced him, placing her hands on his chest. He was solid. Strong. Caring. "Thank you."

Clayton slipped his other arm around her waist. Madison breathed deeply, drinking in the strength she found in his presence. But something else too. He was going to kiss her. The realization created a stirring in her heart she'd never felt before.

Her lips parted slightly, and she slid her hands behind his neck as he gently pulled her closer. She melted against him as his lips claimed hers.

55

Clayton had kissed many women but had never tasted a kiss so sweet. His heart swelled at the desire consuming him to protect Madison. He broke away and traced his fingers along her jaw.

"You're beautiful," he said softly. He hadn't come to Emerald Mound with the intention of kissing Madison, but he couldn't stop himself.

She closed her eyes, and a small moan escaped her lips when he kissed them, then he lifted her chin, seeking her lips again. She responded, melting into his arms.

"Where did you learn to kiss like that?" Madison asked breathlessly when they pulled apart.

Her words were like ice water, and he stepped back, the vow he'd made two years ago haunting him.

"What's wrong?"

The trust in her eyes seared his heart. "You're vulnerable right now . . . I shouldn't have taken advantage of you."

"I see." She stepped back.

Madison had taken his words as rejection. Clayton could see it in her face and the way she hugged her arms to her waist.

"Can you take me home?" Without waiting for an answer, she turned and marched down the mound.

Regret burned hotter than a coal in his chest as he followed her. Anything he said would make it worse, so Clayton said nothing. But once they were on the Trace again, the thought of driving back to Natchez in icy silence made him try. "I didn't mean to hurt you. It's just—"

"I don't want to hear it. It's evident we made a mistake, and since we have to work together, we'll simply pretend tonight never happened."

He took a breath to refute her words.

She held up her hand. "Please. Don't try to explain."

Clayton clamped his mouth shut. Maybe she would be willing to listen to him by the time they reached Natchez. When they reached the judge's house, he pulled around to the back door. "I'd like to explain."

"There's nothing to say. You kissed me and regretted it. Plain and simple."

"That's not true."

She turned and looked at him. "You're saying you don't regret kissing me?"

"Not the way you mean it." He couldn't just say he'd taken a vow not to kiss a woman and leave it at that—he would need to explain why. She probably wouldn't believe him anyway.

Madison shook her head and opened her door. "I'm too tired to decipher your meaning tonight."

"It isn't you, Madison." He couldn't let her leave thinking she was lacking in anything.

She rolled her eyes. "Not the old 'it's not you, it's me' routine?"

"This time it's true. You don't know this about me, but at one time I wouldn't have cared that I took advantage of you. That all changed when I quit gambling and drinking. Do you remember me telling you I'd made a commitment that I wouldn't trifle with a woman's affections?"

"And I accused you of reading Regency romances. I thought you were joking."

"I wasn't, and it was a little more than a commitment—I took a vow before God, that unless I was ready to propose to a woman, I wouldn't touch her. That meant no kissing."

She gave him a sarcastic glare. "And you want me to believe that I made you break your vow? I had no idea I had that much power."

He knew he would make it worse. "That's not what I meant."

She rubbed her forehead. "Look, let's end this while we're still speaking to each other."

"Please, just—"

"No. I'm done tonight, and I still have to comb through my files." She climbed out of the SUV and slammed the door.

Clayton unlocked the gun safe in his Interceptor and grabbed his Sig. "Wait." He reached the back door before she got it unlocked. "I want to clear the house."

Madison stilled, and a protest formed on her lips.

"You're not even armed," he said.

She held up her hands in surrender and allowed him to go in first. He cleared the downstairs, then, with Madison following, cleared the upstairs. By the time they returned downstairs, she didn't seem quite so angry.

"Thank you," she said grudgingly.

"No problem."

That brought a tiny smile to her lips. Madison tried to smother a yawn, and rolled her shoulders.

"You're exhausted. I've been thinking about all the cases you need to go through . . . What would you say to letting someone else read through them and cull all but the obvious ones?"

Hope lit her eyes. "That would be great. Do you have anyone in mind?"

"Brooke Danvers."

"She won't mind?"

"No, I'm sure she won't, and I'm sure Evan McCall will approve it. We'll get it set up tomorrow, so go to bed and don't worry about going through the files."

"Thanks, Clayton."

Madison might not be as angry, but the sad aura that he was responsible for remained. He opened his mouth to tell her that he was sorry for jumping the gun at Emerald Mound, but he left the words unsaid. He was only trying to relieve his conscience. Maybe in time she would understand that he had taken their relationship too fast.

What relationship? And therein lay the problem. They didn't really have one.

"I'll touch base with you in the morning." He walked to the back door, and she followed him, this time not even trying to smother a yawn. "And be sure to set the alarm."

After Clayton pulled out of the judge's drive, he turned his SUV toward his sister's house. He couldn't do anything about the mess he'd made of tonight, but he could try to fix the problem with his sister.

He parked in her drive and sat there. What if she didn't let him in the house? What if he and Jake got into another shouting match and scared Ava? What if . . .

He could "what if" all night. He was reaching for the car door when his cell phone rang. Jen.

"Why are you sitting in front of my house?"

He sighed. "Getting the courage to call and ask if I can come in."

"Oh, Clayton, of course you can come in."

"Is Jake there? I'd like to apologize to him."

She didn't answer right away. "He went to an NA meeting, and he and his sponsor were going for coffee afterward."

Relief that he didn't have to face his brother-in-law poured through him. "Is Ava still up?"

"No, but you could tiptoe in and take a peek at her. She asked about you earlier tonight."

"I'll be right in."

Jen met him at the front door and let him in. "She's kind of restless. If she wakes up, just talk to her a minute, and she should go right back to sleep."

He walked quietly down the hall to Ava's room. She'd kicked off her blanket, and he spread it over her again. Ava's eyes blinked open.

"Uncle Clay. Will you tell me a story?"

"You know I will." He sat on the edge of her bed and smoothed her hair back. "What story do you want to hear?"

"Tell me about the princess."

Clayton knew the story she wanted and began the story of the princess and the pea. "Once upon a time . . ."

It wasn't long before Ava was asleep again and he eased out of her room and returned to the living area. "Did you remember who was at the restaurant Wednesday night?" he asked his sister.

Jen reached for a sketch pad on the table and handed it to him. "I know there were more people at the restaurant than these six, but they're the faces I remember. And the photo of the man you sent me? I don't remember him being there at all."

That meant Corbett probably hadn't been there. Clayton scanned the paper Jen handed him. She'd sketched Dani and Bri, two men sitting at the bar, and two women, one at least twenty years older than the other, sitting at separate tables. He recognized Judith Winslow, and the other woman looked familiar, but he couldn't come up with a name. And as for the men watching TV, they didn't ring a bell at all. "Thanks."

Jen tapped the sketch of the older woman. "That's Judith Winslow."

"I recognized her. Do you know who the other woman is?"

"No, and I'll keep thinking about the people who were there—sometimes faces will come to me when I'm washing dishes."

Gravel crunched in the drive. "Jake?" When she nodded, his stomach took a dive. He turned to face his brother-in-law as he came in the door.

"Clayton," Jake said, nodding. "I saw your SUV."

"Yeah. I stopped by to talk to Jen . . . and to apologize to you if you were here. I'm glad you got home before I left."

Jake stared at him warily.

"Jen says you went to an NA meeting?"

"Yeah. At church. Then my sponsor took me to the Waffle House for coffee. He's been a lot of help."

Clayton didn't know the church was sponsoring the meetings. "How's it going?"

Jake gave a slight shrug. "Pretty good."

"Who's your sponsor?"

"Tim Markowitz."

"He's a good guy."

"How do you know him?"

"He comes to my Gamblers Anonymous meetings. A lot of people have cross addictions."

Jake stared at him, then shook his head. "You have a problem with . . ."

"Gambling," Clayton said. "It's why I got so angry with Jen for letting you come back—while I don't know how hard it is to quit drugs, I do know what an addiction is like. It won't be easy."

"I know, but I swear to you, I'll never hurt Jen and Ava again."

"Don't say that—it's just tempting the devil. And you can't do it for them—you have to do it for yourself." Clayton sighed. "I know we don't trust each other yet, but if you ever need help and Tim isn't available, give me a call."

"Are you serious?"

"I am. With the help of some good people, and a lot of prayers, I got my act together again. It wasn't easy then and it isn't easy now. I fight temptation every day."

"Yeah, I know what you mean." He dropped his gaze to the floor where Ava's teddy bear had fallen and stooped to pick it up. "Does it ever go away?"

"Nope, but if you stick to the program and give control of your struggle to God, it gets better."

"That's what they tell me in the meetings, but I'm not sure what that means."

Clayton searched for the right words. "For me, it's admitting I don't have the power within me to stop gambling, but that God does."

56

Saturday morning Madison woke to sunlight streaming into the bedroom. The early morning sun had been one of her favorite things about her room when she was a kid. Her grandfather had always teased her about not wanting to waste her daylight hours. She glanced at the clock. Had she really slept until eight?

She curled up under the Dutch girl quilt that was as old as she was. Nadine had made it for her, and Madison savored the love that had gone into every stitch. Until her grandfather died, this house only held fond memories for her.

She would miss him. He'd been the only constant in her life. The only man Madison had totally trusted. The only man who hadn't rejected her.

Until now she'd held last night's memory of Emerald Mound and Clayton at bay. It'd been such a magical time with the night sky and then the full moon. She hadn't expected him to kiss her, but when he did, it'd been like fireworks exploding inside her.

Why had she thought Clayton might be different? She must have "stupid" stamped in giant letters on her forehead. Did he really expect her to believe he'd taken some vow not to kiss a woman? Men didn't do those kinds of things. At least none of the ones she'd ever known.

Except . . . he'd looked so guilty and sad. Almost as sad as she'd felt.

No! The truth was he'd lied to her like every other man in her life. Except her grandfather. Now she and Clayton had to work together to find out who was trying to kill Dani.

Workplace romances rarely worked out anyway, not that she was looking for romance. Her face grew hot remembering the way she'd returned that first kiss and then wanted more. She'd known better than to get involved with Clayton. Once they wrapped up Dani's case and she finished the original case that brought her to Natchez, she'd be leaving.

But until then, they would be spending a fair amount of time together. Maybe she should google how to maintain a business relationship after a kiss. Groaning, she threw back the quilt and climbed out of bed. Staying there only brought more thoughts that she didn't need.

Madison called Dani to check on her, and the call went to voicemail. Alarmed, Madison quickly dialed the room phone and the bodyguard answered. "Is Dani okay?"

"She is. The doctor came by and canceled whatever he was going to do this morning and said she could take a shower. An aide brought a shower chair, and that's where they are."

If the procedure had been canceled and she'd been cleared to shower, she would probably be discharged in a day or two. Madison asked the bodyguard to relay a message that she would be by to see Dani by noon—at the rate Madison was moving, it would probably be that long before she could get out the door. But first, coffee and breakfast.

She slipped into a robe, and the wonderful aroma of coffee met her as she padded downstairs. Nadine must be in the kitchen. She was, but she wasn't alone. Bri sat at the island, her hair a tangled mess, and looking as though she could use a shower.

"Good morning," Madison said.

Nadine handed her a cup of black coffee. "This young lady was asleep in a small car in the drive. Says her name is Bri. Not sure what kind of name that is, though."

"It's short for Briana," the younger woman said. "My mom thought it was a cool name. Me, not so much, and I shortened it."

"I'm glad you decided to take me up on my offer," Madison said. "And Dani will be too. But why didn't you ring the doorbell? Why sleep in the car?"

"I didn't want to be a bother. How is Dani?"

"She's improving." But she'd gained a stalker, all because of Madison. "I plan to bring her here as soon as she's released."

"Sweet."

Madison opened the refrigerator. "Let's see what's in here that we can have for breakfast."

Nadine shooed her away from the door. "I remember the last time you made breakfast—I'll make it."

"I was twelve years old," she said with a laugh. Madison refused to budge and found a pound of bacon and a can of biscuits in the refrigerator. After she put the biscuits in the oven, she laid several slices of the bacon on a microwave rack and eyed Bri. "Cheese omelet?"

"Sounds good."

"How about you, Nadine?"

"Yes. This I must see."

Twenty minutes later, Madison set plates in front of Bri and Nadine and then one on the other side of Bri for herself. She waited anxiously for Nadine to taste her omelet.

"Why, this is good," the older woman said. "When did you learn to cook?"

"When I moved out on my own. It was that or starve."

When they finished, she showed Bri to another guest bedroom on the second floor. "You're about my size—I'll loan you a pair of jeans and a T-shirt. When we go to see Dani, we'll pick you up some clothes."

Bri's eyes teared up. "Why are you doing this?"

"Doing what?"

"Helping me."

"Because it's the right thing to do."

"But I've been involved with some bad people and did things you don't want to know about."

"What happened to you wasn't your fault, Bri. How old were you when you were first trafficked?"

She glanced down at the floor. "Fifteen," she whispered. "They said it was my fault. That I was a bad person."

"Who said that?"

"The people at the foster home they put me in after I was rescued the first time. I figured life on the street was better than living there, and I ran away."

"Dani was taking you to a place in Jackson, right?"

"Wings of Hope. And they were going to help me to get into nursing school. I don't know what will happen now, since I didn't show up."

"Dani called them, but if it'll make you feel better, I'll call them again and see if anything has changed." Madison didn't remember Dani giving her a phone number. "Do you have a number?"

"I think there's a folder in Dani's car. But if it's okay with you, I'd like to stay here long enough to make sure Dani is going to be okay."

"I'll ask, but first a shower and clean clothes."

In the kitchen an hour later, Madison reached the contact person in Bri's file and discussed her case, asking if the organization could wait until the first of the week to pick Bri up. She gave Bri a reassuring smile as she disconnected. "Someone will pick you up here at the house around noon Tuesday. And the person I talked to said your scholarship isn't in jeopardy."

Bri brushed tears from her cheeks. "Thank you! I was sure everything was messed up."

"Nope." Madison hugged the young woman. "Just keep on believing in yourself."

"I will. And Jesus."

"And Jesus," Madison echoed. Her cell phone rang and she checked the ID. Clayton. "I need to get this."

"I'll go upstairs," Bri said.

"No need. It might be about Dani."

Bri settled on a stool at the island and scrolled through her phone while Madison answered.

"Good morning," she said, putting an upbeat spin in her voice.

"Good morning." He sounded a little surprised. "You sound as though you may have gotten a good night's sleep."

"I did. Even slept until eight." She refused to think about Emerald Mound. "I haven't talked to Hugh this morning. Have you?"

"Just got off the phone with him."

"Did he say whether the neighbors saw anyone here at the house yesterday around noon?"

"Unfortunately, most of the neighbors were at work or shopping. And he didn't find any new prints in the judge's study."

That didn't surprise her. Whoever broke in and trashed the study would have worn gloves. "How did they get past the alarm?"

"It hadn't been tampered with, so either the intruder knew the code or it wasn't set. Do you remember setting it?"

She let out a slow breath. "I can't tell you that I specifically remember doing that, but I'm thinking Nadine and Dad were in the house when I left, so I may not have. I'll check with her and see if she set it."

"I wish the judge had installed cameras when he put in the security system," Clayton said. "Have you talked to Dani?"

"No, she was in the shower when I called. Bri and I plan to go see her around noon."

"Bri? Have you heard from her?"

"She's here, actually spent the night in the back seat of Dani's Civic in the drive."

"Would you object to me picking you two up and driving you to the hospital?"

Madison hesitated, but safety won out. "Sure. You want to pick us up in about an hour?"

She ended the call and turned to Bri, startled by the frightened expression on the girl's face. "You know Clayton. He won't hurt you."

"It's not that." She chewed her fingernail. "I heard you ask if your neighbors saw anyone at this house yesterday."

"And?"

"I came by here. Your car was here, and a woman was walking up the drive. It looked like she went to the back door. You didn't talk to her?"

"No. What time?"

"Around lunchtime, 'cause I thought I might get something to eat here. But when the woman didn't come back, I figured she was a friend, and I didn't want to bother you, so I went to McDonald's."

"I was with Clayton at the hospital. Can you describe her?"

"I didn't see her real good—I was on the street and she was near the back of the house . . . but I do remember she had dark hair and wore some kind of exercise clothes and tennis shoes. If it hadn't been the middle of the day and so hot, I would've thought she'd jogged here."

"You didn't see a man with her?"

"No, but if there was one, he could've already gone around to the back."

How Madison wished her grandfather had installed those cameras. That way she wouldn't be wondering who the intruder was.

57

Eight o'clock Monday morning, Madison's cell phone rang as she unlocked her Impala to drive to the lawyer's office. Hugh Cortland showed up on the caller ID.

She answered, and after they exchanged greetings, she asked, "Have you found anything that points to who might have killed my grandfather?"

"I'm afraid not," he said. "We're looking into each of his judgeships, but he had a long career and it'll take a while to go through them."

That wasn't a surprise. "How about Aaron Corbett? How solid is his alibi?"

"I'll find out today—I'm bringing him in to Chief Nelson's office for questioning."

"Anything on who trashed his study?"

"No. Whoever it was wore gloves, so no prints."

"Whatever happened to Locard's Exchange Principle? Surely they left something behind."

Dr. Edmond Locard had determined that an offender always left something behind at the crime scene and took something from the scene with him.

"We did find a dark hair in the office closet, but it's from a cheap wig you can buy at Walmart or Amazon. We've requested a list of orders for this area, but that could take weeks," he said.

"That tracks with what Bri said."

"Who's Bri?"

"The girl with my sister when she was shot. She drove by the house and saw someone with dark hair entering the house."

"Can she make an ID or give a description?"

"No. She only noticed the hair and that the woman wore exercise clothes."

Hugh was briefly quiet. "I know you have your grandfather's funeral, but what does the rest of your day look like?"

"I'm hoping to access my case files today. There was a glitch in the website this weekend, and I couldn't get into my files."

"Have you had a chance to look at the files for the kickback and theft ring?"

"I finished going through what I had yesterday. Several of the invoices from one particular company have inflated prices, and the amount delivered to the National Park Service was less than what was listed on the invoice while the payment was the same. Same thing with the county. I've pulled the files for you to look at. And I have two employees that I need warrants for their bank accounts—brothers. One works for the county, the other for the park service."

"You've been busy. Get me their names and I'll get those warrants."

"It was work or go crazy. I'll call you back in a minute."

Madison turned around and went back inside to get the names. She'd worked on the case Saturday afternoon and Sunday. She hadn't even returned to visit Dani after the Saturday morning visit, talking to her on the phone instead. It'd been worth it, though. The evidence she'd found should be enough to wrap up the case, and as soon as they found the person after Dani, she could return to Hot Springs.

In her bedroom, she found the file and called Hugh and read off the names.

"Good. Oh, and I received a call from Paul Davidson a few minutes ago, and he has a few more files for you to go through."

"I think I have enough evidence now."

"He seemed to think they were important. His secretary is supposed to bring them by your house."

"Vivian Hawkins?"

"Yes. Evidently, she went to church with your grandfather. She indicated she was bringing a dish by and would drop the files off then."

Madison groaned. More food. Even though they'd given the mission a lot of the food that had been brought, more kept coming and she didn't know what they were going to do with it all. The back doorbell rang. "Someone's here—probably her. I'll call you back if I need to."

"I'll see you at the funeral."

"Okay. With so many people expected, I'll be at the church by noon. Thanks."

She pocketed her phone and hurried to the back. "Ms. Hawkins, Agent Cortland said you were coming by. Won't you come in?" Perhaps if she was nice to her, Madison might find out why Vivian disliked her.

"If you'll take the files, I'll go back after the brownies I brought."

"You shouldn't have gone to the trouble to make brownies." Madison took the box of files and set them on the floor beside the entryway. "I'm sure you're quite busy."

"The judge was a special person. Making a few brownies is the least I can do."

"Are you feeling better?"

Vivian's brow wrinkled. "Feeling better?"

"Paul said Friday you were out sick."

"Oh yes. I feel much better. Let me get those brownies."

When Vivian returned with the food, Madison held the door open for her. "Just set them on the island, and I'll get something to put them in and you can take your platter back."

"I'll pick it up later." Once Vivian set the plate down, she turned to Madison and gave her a hesitant smile. "I want to apologize to you. I think I've been rather rude."

You think? But instead of voicing the question, Madison gave her a tentative smile. "I wondered what I'd done."

"I thought you were investigating Paul, but when he gave me these files, he explained what was going on. Have you discovered who's stealing money?"

The question caught her by surprise even more than the fact that Davidson had revealed the investigation to Vivian Hawkins. And Madison certainly wasn't going to reveal details to his personal assistant before briefing the supervisor.

"It's still an ongoing investigation." Madison studied Vivian. Once again, she was struck with the sense that she'd met her somewhere before. "Did you know my grandfather long?"

Vivian blinked. "I remember him from when I was a little girl. He always gave me a sucker."

"Have you lived in Natchez all your life?"

"Most of it. Lived in Dallas a while."

"Really? I did too." Her first white-collar investigations were in Dallas. "Why did you come back?"

For the briefest second, her eyes narrowed and then she tossed her head back slightly. "After the man I was going to marry died in an auto accident, there was nothing to keep me in Dallas. My family was here in Natchez."

"I'm sorry about your fiancé," Madison said.

Vivian's fingers shook as she fished a tissue from her pocket and dabbed her eyes. After a minute she put away the tissue. "I'm sorry. I didn't mean to get emotional. You'd think after three and a half years, I'd be able to talk about it without crying."

"I'm sure it's very hard," Madison said.

"How about you—are you moving to Natchez now?"

"I doubt it." Madison had no reason to move here. The memory of Clayton taking her in his arms blindsided her, and her stomach did a backflip. Which was precisely why she would not move here. Love hurt too much to expose your heart. When things went wrong, the pain lingered—Vivian Hawkins was a perfect example.

Madison looked around as Bri wandered into the kitchen. "Hello, sleepyhead," she said with a smile, then she introduced the two. "There's cereal in the cabinet and milk in the fridge. Or you can make yourself bacon and eggs."

"Cereal is fine." Bri studied Vivian for a minute. "You look familiar."

"I don't think I've ever met you before."

Her tone said that she would have remembered the thin girl with the spiky hair and silver balls lining her ears.

Bri's brows lowered in concentration, then she held up her finger. "You were at that restaurant, reading a book."

"Excuse me?"

"Last week. A friend and I stopped to eat. Downtown. Don't remember the name of the place, but you were there."

Vivian palmed her hand. "You must have me mistaken for someone else. I rarely eat out."

Bri frowned. "I don't think so . . ." Then she shrugged. "But who knows, maybe you're like Madison here with a twin sister you didn't know about."

A dazed look crossed the woman's face. "I'm not sure . . ."

"It's nothing," Madison said as the alarm on her phone buzzed. "I'm sorry, but that was the reminder that I have an appointment. Thank you so much for bringing the brownies and the files."

"Anything I can do to help—just let me know."

"Thank you," she repeated and grabbed her purse before turning to Bri. "I should be back by ten to get ready, and then I'm going by to see Dani before the funeral if I have time."

"Can I go with you to see Dani?"

Madison hesitated. It would push her to come back to the house, but she understood Bri's need to see Dani. "Sure."

The girl was still staring at Vivian Hawkins as they walked out together. Madison understood Bri's feelings—there was something off about Vivian. Or maybe it was the sadness that emanated from her . . . with good reason. It was plain she still grieved for the man she was supposed to marry.

Vivian stopped at her RAV4. "I wasn't at whatever restaurant the young lady thought she saw me, but I do eat out occasionally, especially lunch. Perhaps we can get together for a sandwich sometime before you leave town. I could even give you a tour of the Old Jail."

"Perhaps we can." Maybe the woman was just lonely.

A text chimed on her phone, and she checked it. Clayton. Why was he coming to the house? She hadn't seen him since he drove them to the hospital to see Dani Saturday morning. And she wasn't sure she wanted to see him now. Cancel that. She was sure she didn't want to see him. She'd spent way too much time every night remembering his kisses instead of sleeping.

58

Clayton pulled into Judge Anderson's drive, blocking Madison's Impala just as a RAV4 drove away. She climbed out of her car, and he met her halfway.

"Why are you blocking me?"

"How are you?"

They'd both spoken at the same time. "You go first," he said.

"I need you to let me out. I have an appointment with Grandfather's lawyer and I'm running behind."

"I'll take you."

"Do you really think that's necessary?"

"Whoever wrote the note left at the hospital is not stable." Surely she hadn't forgotten what the note said. "*Revenge is mine, not the Lord's.*" "The person could change their focus from your family to you at any time. You are wearing body armor?"

"It's become a second skin," she said dryly.

Clayton opened the passenger door of his SUV. "Your carriage awaits, milady."

"Oh, all right."

After he climbed in on the driver's side and fastened his seat belt, she gave him the lawyer's address that turned out to be right downtown. He parked out front and turned to her. "Are you okay? I know this isn't easy."

"I'm fine."

She didn't sound fine.

Madison took a deep breath and blew it out. "Growing up with a bipolar mother taught me how to compartmentalize, put my emotions on ice, at least until I get everything taken care of."

"I don't know if that's healthy."

"Healthy or not, it's the way I deal with things." She opened her door.

"Hold up."

"You're not going in with me."

"Just to the waiting area."

An hour later, Madison returned to the lobby, and he escorted her to the SUV. "How'd it go?" he asked once he pulled away from the office.

"All right, I suppose. Grandfather made me executor of his will, which was no surprise. That means I'll be in and out of Natchez for the next few months taking care of everything."

He couldn't stop the smile that spread across his face or the way the news lifted his heart. "Where to now?"

"Back to the house to get dressed, then Bri and I are going to check on Dani. After that, I'll drop her off before I drive to the church by twelve."

He checked his watch. "That's a lot to cram into two hours. Why do you have to be there at noon?"

The look she gave him indicated the reason should be obvious. "This is the only visitation and there will be a lot of people coming to pay their respects. Nadine isn't coming until one, so that leaves me to be there early to greet them."

Clayton shook his head. "Can I at least help by chauffeuring you to the hospital and back?"

She hesitated, then gave him a warm smile. "That would be nice."

A few minutes later he pulled into the judge's driveway. As they walked to the front door, Clayton asked, "What will you do with the house?"

"Nothing for a while. Grandfather left Nadine the apartment as a lifetime dowry. I can't very well sell the house with that kind of string attached."

Again, he wasn't sorry. The house would keep her tied to Natchez.

"There is a problem, though. The attorney has an unsigned copy of the will, and he has to have the signed one. I don't have a clue where it is."

Clayton considered where the will might be. "If Hugh had found it in his study, he would've given it to you. Do you know if the judge had a safe?"

"I've never seen one if he did." She unlocked the door, and they entered the hallway. "I hate that I'm wondering if that's what Dad was looking for instead of the Hargrove file."

"Why would he want it?"

"He may have thought the will was written before Mom's death and that he would receive her part of Grandfather's estate. He would have if Grandfather hadn't updated his will a month ago." She massaged her temples. "Sometimes I wish my job didn't make me think the worst in people. Since reading the will, I've even wondered if Buddy and Joe hired someone to find and destroy it. Grandfather left them a generous bequest, but if there's no will, they'll receive a third of the estate, which is considerably more."

"I don't think whoever was here found what they were looking for," he said.

"Why do you say that?"

"All the files had been emptied from the cabinet. I doubt that the very last file in the drawer would've been what they were looking for, so it stands to reason, if they'd found their prize, they would've stopped searching, and there would have been files left in the drawers."

She turned to face him, and a smile tugged at her lips. "Anyone ever tell you that you have a convoluted way of looking at things?"

"A few times." He thought a minute. "Did the judge have a safe-deposit box?"

She tapped her forehead with her open palm. "I can't believe I hadn't thought of that. Yes, he has one, and a few years ago he added me to the account."

"Then that's probably where the will is. Do you have a key and know which bank?"

"First Natchez was the bank, and I'm sure he gave me a key, but it was right after what happened in Texas. I don't remember a lot from that time, and I certainly don't remember what I did with the safe-deposit key."

"Your grandfather would've had one, and it's probably in the house. You want to look for it now?"

"I've seen a silver box on his dresser with all kinds of keys. Maybe it's there." She was already walking to her grandfather's bedroom. "I'll call Dani and tell her we'll be a few minutes late," she said over her shoulder.

"I'll call her—you go look for the key."

When he made the call, Dani told him she was going down to radiology for a CT scan in the next hour. If nothing showed up, she'd be discharged midafternoon, and she suggested they come then so they could pick her up from the hospital.

After Clayton hung up, he joined Madison in the judge's bedroom. "Find the key?"

"No, and if we're going to the hospital, I'll have to wait until after the funeral to look for it," she said.

"Oh, Dani said not to come this morning, that the doctor is discharging her this afternoon."

"Good! That'll give me more time to look for the key." Then she scanned the bedroom and frowned. "Oh dear. I should have stripped the bed yesterday."

"Maybe Bri could do it?"

"I hate to ask her . . ."

"I'll check, and tell her you're not going to the hospital now."

He found the girl in the kitchen with Nadine, and she readily agreed to help.

"Tell Madison not to worry. We will take care of it." Nadine turned to Bri. "Come, I will show you where the linens are."

He returned to the bedroom and relayed Nadine's message. "Will you need rooms for Buddy and his family?"

"No." She opened the bottom dresser drawer and rifled through the items in it. "He called yesterday to tell me he wouldn't be here. Seems he fell off a ladder and broke his leg and can't travel." She scanned the room again. "Where could that key be?"

"I keep mine on my key ring," Clayton said.

Madison snapped her fingers. "Of course." Then she frowned. "What did I do with my grandfather's keys that Pete Nelson gave me?"

"You put them in your bag." He picked up the purse she'd dropped near the door and handed it to her.

"You're a lifesaver."

If only she really believed that. Clayton was afraid he'd blown it with her at Emerald Mound. But he couldn't take his actions back. Remembering the way she returned his kiss, he didn't want to. He squared his shoulders. If God wanted them to be together, he'd work this out.

She pawed through the bag and held up a set of keys. "Here it is."

"Why don't you get dressed for the funeral, and we'll stop off at the bank on the way?"

The look on her face said she hadn't considered him going with her.

"What are you going to do with the papers you find in the judge's safe-deposit box while you're at the church? The gun safe in my SUV would be more secure than your purse."

When she agreed, he hurried home to dress for the funeral. Forty-five minutes later, Clayton followed Madison into the vault that held the bank's safe-deposit boxes. After she dated and signed the form, the bank clerk compared her signature to the one on file, then found the box that matched the number on the key.

"Here we go." She inserted the bank's key, then Madison's, and pulled the box out before she pointed to the corner. "You can go through the box at that table. And once again, I'm very sorry about your grandfather."

"Thank you."

Clayton carried the box to the table. Madison sat at one of the chairs and he took the other. Her hand shook as she reached to open the lid. "I don't know why I'm so nervous."

"With all that's happened lately, being anxious is understandable. You want me to open it and look inside?"

Madison hesitated. "No. It's just that when Grandfather added my name to the account, I didn't expect to be doing this so soon." She took a breath and opened the box and peered inside. "Thank goodness—there's the will."

She laid it aside. A velvet jewelers bag came next, and she looked inside. "Grandmother's pearls." She smiled softly. "He always said they would be handed down to me."

Madison laid the velvet bag aside as well, then took out a collapsible cloth bag that she'd brought. "I think I'll just put everything in here to look at after the funeral."

She scooped up the envelopes from the box and stuffed them in the bag. One envelope slipped out of her hand and landed on the table. He caught his breath at the same time that Madison gasped and her fingers gripped the edge of the table.

"Madison's Adoption Papers" was printed in bold letters.

59

Madison stared at the envelope. "I wasn't expecting this."

Even though the dizziness she'd experienced when she saw the wording on the envelope had faded, Madison's face still felt icy. She loosened the death grip she had on the table edge and picked up the envelope that held answers to questions she'd had all her life.

"You want to wait and deal with this after the funeral when Dani will be with you?"

Madison had forgotten for a minute that she didn't have just herself to consider. Would it be better to wait? "No. I want to open it now and at least skim over the papers. Then when Dani and I are together, we'll examine what's here in depth."

She took the pocketknife he handed her and slit the envelope that contained a thick sheaf of typed papers and one handwritten letter. Madison immediately recognized her grandfather's handwriting. She folded it and placed it in her bag to read later.

There were several sets of papers clipped together, and Madison picked up the top set. It appeared to be an agreement of some sort. The last page was her original birth certificate, and she found the space with the birth mother and father names. Teresa Winslow. The name she'd wondered about for so many years. Teresa had a nice ring to it. Did Madison have any other siblings?

She showed Clayton the line with their birth mother's age. "Dani was right when she said she was only fifteen."

"Does it give your father's name?"

"Jimmy Cassidy, but beside his name, it says deceased." Their birth mother had found herself pregnant and alone. No wonder she'd given them up for adoption.

"Wonder what happened to him?" Clayton said.

"Maybe we'll find out once we find our birth mother. Why is her name so familiar?"

"Last name's the same as Judith Winslow's."

Madison flipped the sheets back to the beginning and scanned through them, her breath catching at the mention of fifty thousand dollars to cover the cost of the pregnancy. By the time she reached the last page where William Samuel Anderson and Judith Winslow had signed the document, Madison was glad she was sitting—if she'd been standing, her legs would've given way. No matter how they framed the wording, her birth grandmother had sold Madison to her grandfather.

She raised her gaze to Clayton's. "Was this even legal?"

"I don't know. I do know this has to be a terrible blow."

A terrible blow didn't even begin to describe how Madison felt. The one man she thought she could depend on had bought her like she was a piece of property. She pressed her fingers to her temples.

The alarm she'd set for eleven forty-five buzzed. Madison stared at her watch. And now she had to attend a funeral that would honor his exemplary career as a judge and human being. And not just attend but eulogize him.

"I'll be praying for you this afternoon," Clayton said.

"Don't bother. I doubt God's listening." Madison stood and stuffed the papers in the bag with the others. When it came down to it, she only had herself to depend on.

"You've been mostly happy, haven't you? I mean, with your parents, growing up in Memphis . . ." Was this what her grandfather wanted to

talk to her about Wednesday night? If it was, no wonder he'd been relieved when she was called out.

Madison closed the now-empty box and shoved it back in the vault before removing her key. "Do you think my parents knew about this?"

"You could ask your dad."

"I'm sure he'd deny it."

"Then you have no way of knowing, unless there's something in the files we missed, or in the handwritten note."

Ah yes. The note. Well, she wasn't ready to read it. Didn't know if she ever would be. Like a robot, Madison grabbed the bag she'd put the papers in and handed it to Clayton to store in his gun safe until after the funeral. She didn't even want to touch it. With her back ramrod straight, she walked out of the vault. *Don't think. Don't feel.* It was the only way she could get through the funeral.

For the next two hours, Madison accepted condolences from the stream of people coming to pay their respects, most she didn't know from Adam. She had no idea what she said to any of them. Hopefully she thanked them for coming.

Once she saw Judith Winslow but then lost sight of her. Madison had a few questions for the woman. At times her father stood nearby, giving her support, and that surprised her. Even more surprising—he'd left Margo at the Burn.

But most of all, she drew strength from the way Clayton rarely left her side, his hand often resting on the small of her back, telling her she could do this. When her voice cracked, he brought her a bottle of water, and when she thought her legs wouldn't hold her up another moment, he appeared with a stool for her to sit on.

If circumstances had been different . . . if she didn't have so much baggage . . . But she did. After the way her grandfather had betrayed her, Madison didn't think she could ever trust another living soul.

Just before the service was to start, she escaped to the restroom to freshen up a bit. She wet a paper towel and blotted her face, then freshened up her lipstick. Another hour and a half to put on an act. She wished she hadn't gone to the bank before the funeral.

The door opened and Madison froze as Judith Winslow walked into the small room.

"Hello, dear. I'm glad I caught you—the line has been so long that I simply avoided it, hoping I might see you later."

"How could you sell your own grandchildren?" The words were out of Madison's mouth before she could stop them.

The color fled from the older woman's face. "Excuse me? I don't think I understood you."

Judith Winslow didn't even have the decency to admit what she'd done. "You understood me all right. I found my adoption papers."

Judith stood statue still. "I don't have a clue what you're talking about." She turned on her heel and walked out of the restroom.

"I think the FBI will be interested in what I found in my grandfather's safe-deposit box," Madison called after her.

The woman kept walking as though Madison hadn't spoken. She wanted to kick herself. Why had she said anything? But the words had popped out before she could stop them. And telling the FBI hadn't been an idle threat. She was pretty sure Hugh would be interested in what she'd found. He was here at the church and had told her he'd come by later. She would show him the papers.

There was a knock on the restroom door. "Madison?" Clayton called. "The service is starting."

"I'll be right out." She smoothed her skirt and straightened her shoulders. She had a eulogy to deliver.

Forty-five minutes later, Madison concluded her words at the end of the service. "William Samuel Anderson served his country, his state, his district, and his county well. He will not soon be forgotten."

When she'd composed the speech, she'd meant every word, and several times the memories of the man she thought he was had overridden what she'd learned today.

She stepped away from the microphone and stood as the bugler stepped forward to play "Taps." Madison glanced at the sea of faces and shivered as unease rippled through her. It was almost as if she'd felt a wave of hatred directed toward her, and she scanned the crowd, seeking the few people she actually knew.

To her right, Judith Winslow dabbed her eyes . . . crocodile tears, Madison was certain. Nadine smiled through real ones. Clayton's smile was warm, encouraging. Hugh gave her a thumbs-up.

She was surprised to see Steven Turner and Terri Davis in the church. She hadn't realized they'd come to the funeral. Both were somber. Terri stared off to her right, her eyes narrowed, while Steven stared straight ahead, his lips pressed in a thin line. Maybe he was remembering his brother's funeral.

As the bugler lifted the horn to his lips, her gaze shifted, and she saw Vivian Hawkins furiously dabbing at her eyes. Probably remembering her fiancé's death. Tears burned the back of Madison's eyes as the lonely notes filled the church, and she turned her attention to the casket in front of her.

She choked down the lump in her throat. *Oh, Grandfather, why?*

Clayton escorted Madison and Nadine from the sanctuary since it had been decided before the service that it was too dangerous for them to go to the cemetery. There were too many places for a sniper to hide.

Madison gripped his arm. Her heart had to be breaking. In spite of that, she'd done an amazing job eulogizing Judge Anderson. He squeezed her hand. "I was praying for you."

"It must have helped—I got through it."

"Are you ready to leave?"

"Not quite. The church ladies have prepared a meal, and while I don't think I can eat one bite, they went to a lot of trouble. I want to go by and thank them and everyone who stayed behind for being here."

Before they reached the dining hall, Gregory Thorn approached. "You did an amazing job today," he said.

"Thank you." She gave her father a who-are-you look.

"I'm not staying for the meal, and I won't come by the house tonight . . . but I'd like to see you tomorrow before I leave for Memphis."

Madison still wore a dazed expression, but she nodded. "Just give me a call before you come."

Then she turned and followed Nadine to the fellowship hall. Clayton stood near the doorway as Madison made the rounds.

As she tried to make her exit, another of the ladies hugged her, then thrust several to-go boxes in her hands. She thanked her, then turned and walked toward him. "Sorry—I didn't know how to say no to the food. I'm ready to leave now."

Clayton pulled his SUV to the back of the church and helped Nadine into the front seat while Madison climbed in the back and set the boxes beside her. Once they pulled away from the church, the housekeeper turned to Madison.

"What you said at the funeral was beautiful."

"Yes," Clayton added. Only he knew how hard it had been for her. "You did a great job."

"Thanks," Madison murmured and then leaned forward toward Nadine. "How much do you know about Judith Winslow?"

Nadine was quiet for a moment. "I haven't always approved of her tactics, but you have to give credit where it's due—she has made a better life for so many babies."

"Did you know she's my grandmother?"

The older woman turned toward Madison and clasped her hand. "I have never seen it in black and white, but in here"—she tapped her heart—"I knew."

"How close was she to Grandfather?"

Nadine hesitated.

"Was she his friend?"

"More like a business partner. I . . . always felt she held something over him."

Clayton knew what that was now. His cell phone rang and he checked the ID. "It's Dani. You want to answer it?" He handed the phone over his shoulder, and she took it from him.

"She probably called my phone, but I forgot to turn it back on." She punched the answer button. "Hello?" She listened for a minute, then said, "We'll pick you up in half an hour. Is that okay?"

He took the phone when she handed it back. "I take it we're picking Dani up at the hospital?" He looked in the rearview mirror. Judging from the slump of her shoulders, the events of the day were wearing on her.

She nodded. "The doctor just came in and discharged her. I thought we'd drop Nadine off and then go to the hospital," she said, her voice flat, unemotional.

He hated seeing her hurt so badly and not being able to make things better.

Once they reached the house, he walked Nadine to her apartment, and Madison waited until he cleared it before they checked to make sure Bri was okay. Then he turned to Madison, who had set the food on the island for the girl to put away. "Ready?"

She nodded and followed him out the door. Clayton wanted to reach for her hand—do something to take the haunted look from her eyes. What if he only made matters worse? What if she rebuffed him?

He took her hand anyway, and his heart kicked up a notch when she squeezed his fingers. "What you did today had to be hard," he said gently as they approached his SUV.

For a minute she didn't respond but instead looked back toward the house, her profile granite. "It's like I'm free-falling without a parachute. Grandfather is the only person I trusted, and it hurts, but the pain is nothing compared to what it'll be when what he did sinks in. It'll be like hitting the ground full force."

Clayton cupped her chin and turned her face to him. A strand of her blond hair had worked loose from the messy bun, and he brushed it back behind her ear. "I'd like to be there to catch you."

Her face softened, and she leaned into his touch as her eyes filled with tears and spilled down her cheeks. "I trusted him so much."

Clayton pulled her to him, gently stroking her back as she laid her head on his chest, and let her cry. More than anything in the world, he wanted to protect her from being hurt again. When the sobs subsided, he lifted her chin. "It's going to be okay."

"I wish I believed that."

"I'm not saying it'll be easy, but in time, you'll get past this. Maybe when you read that letter he wrote you, you'll understand why he did it."

"The letter. I'd forgotten about it. And the will. I need to take it to the lawyer's office."

"I have it in the gun safe, and since the lawyer's office is on the way to the hospital, why don't we drop it off?"

"That would be one thing off my to-do list for tomorrow."

When they dropped off the will, Madison agreed to the time the secretary gave her for the formal reading on Wednesday. An hour later, Clayton pulled around to the back of the judge's house with Dani in the back seat and helped her out of the SUV. He couldn't wait to see Nadine's reaction to Madison's twin. Now that she wasn't lying in a hospital bed, she looked so much like Madison, he might have trouble telling them apart. "We'll go in through the mudroom—there aren't any steps."

"Oh wow. This is nice," Dani said, looking up at the two-story antebellum. "Did you grow up here?"

Madison shook her head. "I grew up in Memphis, but I spent summers here when I was a kid—that's when I met Clayton for the first time."

"She was a determined little booger," he joked.

"I wish I'd known back then that you made my cousins leave me alone—at least when you were around." Madison patted him on the hand. "How did you do that?"

"I threatened to give them a knuckle sandwich. And I might've threatened tell the other boys we hung around that they were sissies for picking on a defenseless little kid. Then you made a liar out of me when you laid Buddy on the ground."

Madison laughed, and he knew she was remembering that hot summer day. At least he'd lightened the weight of her grandfather's betrayal that she carried on her shoulders. He hoped he was right, that time would ease the burden. If he got the opportunity, he would remind her only one person would never betray her. Everyone else had the potential, even him.

Bri met them at the back door and gently hugged Dani. "I'm so glad you're here!"

Once they were in the kitchen, Madison guided Dani to a chair. "Why don't you rest here a minute. I have someone else I want you to meet."

She disappeared out the back and was back in less than two minutes. "Close your eyes." Madison led Nadine inside the kitchen and stopped right in front of Dani. "Now you can open them."

Nadine blinked, then her eyes widened as she took in both women. "Oh, chère . . ." She examined Dani's face, then turned to Madison. "I know you told me . . . but I didn't think it was possible she looked so much like you!"

"Who sent the flowers?" Clayton nodded to a vase of almost-black roses sitting on the island. As he came nearer, he could see they weren't true black but dark burgundy. Either way it seemed an odd color to choose.

Bri slapped her palm to her head. "I forgot to tell you—they came while you were at the funeral."

Madison jerked her head toward the island and gaped. "How did we miss those when we came in?"

"I think you were a little busy planning a surprise for Nadine." Clayton approached the vase. A small card was tucked in the middle of the arrangement. "Did you see who delivered them?"

Bri shook her head. "The back doorbell rang, and when I answered, the flowers were there."

Clayton felt his belt for his latex gloves, but he wasn't wearing his uniform. "Be right back."

As he jogged to his SUV, he texted the police chief requesting someone be posted at the judge's house, then he unlocked the door and took his P229 from the gun safe and strapped it around his waist. Clayton didn't like it that someone had been bold enough to walk right to the back door and leave the roses.

Once he grabbed the papers from the bank and a couple of pairs of gloves, he returned to the house. Madison took the bank papers, and he pulled on the gloves and carefully took the card out by its edges. It wasn't sealed, and he flipped the envelope open and pulled out the card.

"God says an eye for an eye. You destroyed my family, so you and yours for mine."

The color drained from Madison's face. "Why? Who is doing this?"

Clayton and Madison's cell phones both alerted to a text.

"It's from Chief Nelson," Clayton said. "He can't put a guard here, but he'll send patrol cars by more often." He dialed the chief's number. "Maybe this will change his mind."

Nelson answered on the first ring. "I wish I had the manpower, but I don't," he said before Clayton could question him. "Besides, that place is like a fortress if you arm the security system."

"I'm calling because Madison just received another threatening note."

"I'll be right there."

The chief arrived in ten minutes with a CSI tech in tow to examine the vase and card. "Have you gone through your case files to see who might have it in for you?"

"Our server has been down, and I only got the electronic files today," Madison said. "I'll start on them tonight."

"And Brooke Danvers is going to help," Clayton added.

"I'll take these with me." Nelson nodded toward the vase and card. "I really wish I could put an officer here, but—"

"I'll check and see if Hargrove can send someone over," Clayton said. He'd been counting on an officer being stationed outside. "I'm staying tonight, anyway."

"Good idea." He turned to Madison. "We'll get this sorted out. Whoever is doing this is getting cocky. He or she will make a mistake and then we'll have them."

"I hope so." After the chief left, she turned to Clayton. "Thank you for offering to stay, but I hate to take your time. Maybe Hargrove can send someone over."

"I'm already involved," he said, squeezing her hand. With a start, he realized he meant that in more than one way. He dialed the private investigator's number and learned that all of his operatives were tied up with other cases. They'd only gotten the operatives at the hospital because someone postponed a trip for a couple of days. "Hargrove is out."

Madison turned to Nadine. "Can Nanette pick you up?"

"No, chère." She raised herself up to her full height, but Madison still had to look down at her. "I will not be run out of my home. Besides, there is strength in numbers."

"But it could be dangerous for you to stay, and we should get Bri out of here. Dani too."

"I'm not leaving." Bri fisted her hands on her hips.

"You'll be much safer in Jackson," Clayton said. "I'll call Brooke and see if she can run you and Dani up there."

"Good idea!" Madison shot him a look of appreciation.

Dani shook her head. "I'm not up to a two-hour drive."

"And it'll be dark before we get there—what if someone follows us and runs us off the road?" Bri jutted her jaw. "I'm staying here—I figure you two will keep us safe."

Clayton chewed his bottom lip. It might be better to stay together. "Then Nadine needs to stay in one of the guest bedrooms."

Nadine reluctantly agreed to stay in an upstairs bedroom. He couldn't shake his uneasiness. He didn't like was that the house sat at the edge of town in the middle of five acres with a privacy hedge all around, and no entrance gate that could be locked, and no cameras. He texted the chief and reminded him to send officers by as often as he could.

Clayton's sixth sense was screaming that things were about to pop.

61

Madison picked up the cloth bag with the bank papers. "I'll take these to my room."

Clayton followed her out of the kitchen. "I could help you go through them after dinner, if you'd like."

"Thanks, but I think I'll put off looking through them until tomorrow. I honestly don't think I can absorb one more shock today."

He grimaced. "I shouldn't have brought it up."

"Nothing to worry about," she said. "I am going to get started on my files once we eat. Brooke texted me earlier that she'd already started combing through them."

"I can help, if you'd like."

"Let me see what I can get done tonight." She stopped and impulsively hugged him, breathing in the light woodsy cologne he wore. Clayton wasn't like any man she'd ever known. "Thank you for being here for me."

"No problem."

She grinned at him, then started for the stairs and stopped. "If you'd like to help Dani to Grandfather's bedroom, I'll be right back to help her get settled in."

"Aye, aye," he said, saluting.

Madison hummed as she climbed the stairs.

Once she got to her room, she placed the cloth bag on the

bed and then decided to put the items in her briefcase. Madison hesitated when she came to the handwritten letter, then put it with the other papers. She couldn't read it tonight. If she did anything, she would boot up her computer and start on her case files like she'd told Clayton.

Who was threatening her? And why? If she was honest with herself, several cases she'd investigated qualified, especially from her violent-crime days. There would probably even be people she'd put away for theft and kickbacks who wanted to see her dead.

One white-collar investigation popped into her mind. Not her best investigation, but it'd been her first. In stomach-turning detail, she recalled the case, another collaboration with the FBI. A realty firm was selling oil rights they didn't own, and she'd painted every employee with the same guilty brush.

One man, Howard Douglas, swore he knew nothing about the scam, but she'd ignored his claim until the owner cleared him. Her accusations could have very easily ruined his career, but he'd died in an auto accident. That case had taught her so much and was the last time she accused anyone of a crime until she had all the facts. Madison wished she'd gotten the opportunity to apologize to him for the anxiety she put him through.

There were other cases where she'd been threatened with retaliation, but they were years in the past. Why now? What was the trigger?

Hopefully after a good night's sleep, something would come to her.

A spicy Italian aroma wafted up the stairs, making her stomach growl. Nadine must be making Madison's favorite comfort food—lasagna. She checked her watch. But why was she so hungry? It was only a little after five, then she realized once again she hadn't eaten since breakfast.

Dani was in her grandfather's recliner when Madison walked into the bedroom. "How are you feeling?"

"Tired . . . and that aroma is making me hungry."

Madison had a lot to tell her, but not tonight. "Tomorrow, we'll talk," she said to her sister. "But right now, we need to eat. Are you up for lasagna?"

"It's one of my favorites."

"Sounds like we may have more than looks in common—it's mine too," Madison said with a chuckle.

After dinner Madison made sure everyone was settled in before she ascended the stairs and booted up her computer. Maybe she should ask Clayton to help her with the files . . . but his definite masculine presence in her bedroom would be a distraction.

The park service had given her access to a Dropbox where she could view the files, and she'd passed on the login details to Brooke. Madison planned to start with the latest cases while the ranger would start with the older ones. The first three Madison read through involved meth labs and marijuana growers, but the people involved in those cases were in jail and not one of them possessed the wherewithal to track her down.

Pain radiated through her shoulders, and Madison rubbed her tight muscles. She closed the laptop and stretched. It might only be a little before eight, but there was simply no way she could concentrate on these cases tonight.

Steven wrapped the C-4 together and attached the timer to it. He would have preferred to use a cell phone and detonate the bomb from a distance, but to get in the house he would have to render the security system useless with a jammer.

No phone calls would go out and none would come in as long as the jammer was in place. His cell phone rang, and he jerked, almost dropping the bomb. When his heart calmed down enough to look at his phone, his dad's ID showed up. "Are you all right?"

"Don't worry about how I feel. Have you done it?" He stopped for a breath. "Is she dead?"

His dad sounded so much weaker. Steven was tempted to lie, but his father would hear it in his voice. The scars on his back had taught him early on to never lie to him. "Not yet, but she will be before the night is over."

"You have to do it tonight. She killed your brother, and she has to pay before I die."

All his life, his dad had drummed it in their heads that no one harmed a Turner and got away with it.

"What if she had no choice?"

"She had a choice. Chad's FBI friends told me she could have taken him in without killing him."

Part of Steven's mind questioned that. Everything in Madison's report had turned out to be true. Chad's ex-wife had been found murdered in Seattle; the pilot of the plane had confirmed they were picking Chad up and taking him and Noah to a small town in Mexico. Chad would've killed Madison rather than let her arrest him. But none of that mattered. For four years, Chad's death had eaten at his father's mind the same way the cancer ate at his body.

"Madison Thorn has to pay for what she did."

"There are others in the house."

"I'm sorry about that, but it changes nothing." He stopped to breathe. "Just make sure you let her know why"—another breath—"she and the others in the house have to die."

"It's too risky."

"You've been in riskier situations and took care of it. She's not smarter than the Taliban, is she?" His voice was stronger, but he still had to stop and breathe in oxygen. "I'll be waiting to hear from you that the job is finished."

Steven stared at the dead cell phone. He would never be able to live with himself if he didn't do what his father asked.

He picked up the bomb and slipped it into a backpack just as someone knocked at his hotel room. Automatically he pulled the Glock from the holster against the small of his back. "Just a sec," he said.

"It's me, Terri."

He holstered his gun. What was she doing here? What if she suspected . . . ?

Steven sucked in a quick, uneasy breath and grabbed the backpack and crossed the room with the bomb, then gently set it beside his suitcase near the door. He swiped his clammy hands on his pants before he opened the door. "I thought you'd left."

"No, I decided to stay a day or two longer." When he didn't ask her inside, she gave him an odd look. "Can I come in?" He hesitated and she added, "Just for a minute."

"Sure." Steven watched her face for signs of deception but saw none as she stepped inside the room and looked around.

"You're leaving?"

He shifted his gaze briefly to the backpack and suitcase. "Yeah. Got a call about my dad. He's taken a turn for the worse, and I need to get back to Texas pronto."

"I'm sorry." She reached down to pick up the backpack. "I'll help you take your stuff down."

"No!"

Terri stopped with her hand on the bag. "What's wrong?"

"I, ah, I'm not leaving right this minute."

She straightened, and he flinched under her unwavering gaze. "I know you, Steven. Something is wrong."

"I don't know what you're talking about." If she kept pushing, she must know what he had planned. But how? He hadn't told anyone. Sweat beaded his forehead, and he swiped it away. "I think I'm coming down with a bug. And then my mom calls and tells me Dad is weaker. Couldn't happen at a worse time."

"Okay, I'll buy that." She chewed her bottom lip. "But if something's bugging you, you'd tell me, right?"

"You know I would. Even though you're a woman, we're still brothers-in-arms." He quirked his mouth in a grin. "You'd help me with anything."

"You know it."

"Uh, I thought I'd drop by Madison's house and tell her goodbye."

"After burying her grandfather, she may not be up for company. Could even be in bed."

"At eight o'clock? I doubt it, but I'll call her." He quickly dialed her number, and when she answered, he explained why he was leaving and asked about coming by.

"I'm sorry about your dad," Madison said, "but maybe we better say goodbye over the phone. It's been a hard day—"

"But I have something I want to give you, a reminder of Noah, and Terri's with me—I'm sure she'd like to see you." He ignored the puzzled look his friend shot him.

Madison hesitated. “Okay. Come to the back door.”

“See you in a minute.” Then he turned to Terri. “She’s good with it.”

“Yes, but why did you tell her—”

“I don’t know. Maybe to seal the deal. Ready?”

“Uh, sure.” She dropped her gaze to the backpack once more, then looked at him with narrowed eyes. “That the present?”

“Yeah. I’ll get it, and you can bring the suitcase down.” He’d caught the tremor in her voice. Undoubtedly, she was remembering the backpacks with IEDs in them in Afghanistan.

Terri Davis had to die now. He knew this with a certainty he couldn’t think away or dismiss. Even if she had saved his life in the Middle East.

63

Clayton buckled his smaller Sig around his ankle. His gut told him something was happening tonight, and he wanted to be ready for it.

It was still early, just a little after eight thirty, but it'd been a long day and everyone had retired to their bedrooms. He walked through the first floor of the house, rechecking the windows and doorways and that the alarm was set. There was no way an intruder could get inside without warning him.

Madison was coming down the stairs, still dressed in the jeans and T-shirt she'd changed into after coming home from the funeral. "I thought you were resting."

"I was, but Steven called. His father has taken a turn for the worse and he's leaving and wants to stop by a minute. He has a present he wants to give me. Terri is coming with him." She turned toward the kitchen. "Where is everyone?"

"In their rooms." Headlights flashed in the window. "I guess he's here. I'll leave so you can have privacy."

"I'd really rather you stayed."

Clayton eyed her. "So, something about them bothers you too?"

"Yeah. Steven had said his father sent him here to give me photos of Chad's son, Noah, but the thing is, I never thought his father liked me."

Both Steven and Terri triggered his radar—something was

off about both of them, but he couldn't pinpoint what it was. "What's with the two of them? Are they a couple?"

"I don't think so. Just really close friends—being in Delta Force and Afghanistan together does that, I understand."

There was a light rap on the door, and Madison hurried to let them in.

"I tried to talk him out of coming by here," Terri said as they entered the kitchen.

"I wanted to say goodbye," Steven said. "And give you this." He placed the backpack on the island.

Clayton tensed. Steven's voice was as hard and cold as the granite countertop he set the backpack on, and his body was like a too-tight spring ready to uncoil.

"May I open it?" Madison asked.

"Oh, definitely. Here, let me take it out for you." He unzipped the backpack and pulled a square-looking box from it.

Deathly quiet settled in the room. Clayton swallowed hard. He hadn't seen many bombs, but he'd seen enough to know this one was for real.

"Steven." Terri's cautious voice broke the hushed silence.

He whirled around, a gun in his hand. "Shut up."

"No!" She walked toward him.

"Stop or I'll shoot."

"You're not doing this." Terri kept walking.

"Do what he says." Clayton reached for her, but she shook him off.

The gun did not waver in Steven's hand. "I don't want to kill you, Terri, but I will."

She ignored his command. Clayton couldn't let him shoot her. He lunged for the man, jerking Steven's arm up just as he pulled the trigger.

It wasn't enough, and the bullet slammed into Terri's shoulder. She stumbled and collapsed just as Steven rammed his knee in Clayton's stomach, doubling him over.

Clayton clutched his middle as Madison jumped up to help Terri. Steven pointed his gun at her. "Stay where you are."

"She's bleeding. You'll have to shoot me too." When Steven hesitated, Madison grabbed a hand towel hanging from the back of a chair and pressed it to Terri's shoulder.

With Steven's attention diverted, Clayton grabbed for his Sig, but he wasn't fast enough. Steven kicked it out of his hand. "I ought to kill you right now. Where's your backup?"

When he didn't answer fast enough, Steven pointed his gun at Madison. "I'm not asking again."

Clayton clenched his jaw and flipped the strap on his ankle holster and handed over his smaller pistol, ignoring the smirk on Steven's face as he took out a small box and pressed a button.

"What're you doing?" Clayton demanded. It couldn't be the timer for the bomb unless it was set far enough out for Steven to get away.

"This little baby will jam your phone signals so no one can call out." Steven turned slightly toward the hall doorway. "Everyone in the hall, come in here." When no one entered the kitchen, he said, "Now! Or I'll shoot Clayton."

"Don't listen to him," Clayton yelled. "Get out of the house."

"You do and he'll die, and it'll be your fault."

"Don't shoot anyone," Dani said as she hobbled into the room.

Steven's eyes widened. "You really do look like Madison." Then he looked past her. "Where are the others? The girl and the old woman?"

"They're not here," Clayton said. He was hoping and praying Bri had climbed out a window and had gone for help.

Steven turned to Dani. "Is that true?"

She nodded.

"I don't believe you." He jerked her to his side and dragged her to the kitchen drawers. "You know what they do to liars in the Middle East, don't you? They cut their fingers off."

He opened and closed several drawers until he found the one

with knives in it. "Now," he said, holding up a butcher knife. "We'll start with the thumb."

"Stop!" Madison cried. "Why are you doing this?"

He held the knife in midair. "You killed my brother. You have to pay. You and everyone you care about."

"You?" Madison stared at him. "You killed my grandfather? And shot Dani?"

He frowned. "I'm not answering your questions."

"Why did you shoot Dani and then try to kill Madison at the hospital?" Clayton asked. If he could keep him talking, maybe Bri could escape and get help.

Steven ignored him. "I'm giving the two in the hall to the count of three to get in here, or I'll take her fingers off, one at a time. One. Two. Three—"

"Don't do it. We're coming."

"That's more like it," Steven said as Bri stomped into the room with Nadine behind her. He shoved Dani into a chair and waved his gun. "Have a seat, everyone."

Clayton took the stool nearest Steven. He couldn't let the others die, and if he could get close enough, maybe he could tackle him successfully this time. Steven took zip ties from the backpack and tossed them to him. "Tie them up. Hands behind their backs."

"No." If Steven had to tie them himself, Clayton might get the drop on him.

"Then I'll kill them now." He put a gun to Dani's head.

"All right. Just move the gun away from her."

"When you finish. And tie them to the chair as well."

Clayton started with Bri.

"I tried to call 911, but my phone wouldn't work," she said, her voice low.

"No talking, you two! And move on."

Clayton put the tie loosely around Dani's hands and then secured them to the chair. Last of all, he bound Nadine's hands, being as gentle as he could. "I'm sorry."

"It's not your fault, chère."

But he felt like it was. He should have listened to his gut about Steven.

64

Steven nudged Terri with his foot, and she didn't respond. Madison hoped that she'd just passed out and wasn't dead. Clayton's service gun lay just out of reach. They had to do something. Once he had them all secured, he'd set the bomb and leave.

"Get up," Steven said. When Madison didn't move fast enough, he jerked her to her feet.

She used the momentum to throw her weight into his shoulder and knock him off balance. Clayton must have been watching him, because he dove for his gun.

Steven aimed his gun at Clayton. Madison grabbed his hand just as it went off. The bullet grazed Clayton's head, and he fell to the floor. Steven backhanded her with the gun, hitting the side of her face. She fought to stay conscious, but when he hit her again, darkness closed in.

When she came to, the room whirled around her. Madison shook off the dizziness and got to her feet.

"I thought he killed you," Dani said.

"Where is he?"

"He left while you were unconscious. Right after he set the timer for three minutes. There are only two minutes left."

Madison stumbled to the counter and grabbed the butcher knife he'd threatened to use on Dani. Seconds later she cut Dani's ties. "Cut the others loose and then get out of here!"

"We can't—he said if somehow we managed to get loose, he'd be waiting to kill us as we came out. Said he rigged the front door with another bomb as well. It'll go off if we open the door."

Madison pressed her hands to her head. "Cut their ties and get everyone out the window in your bedroom—you'll have to use the key to open the bars on the window. It's on the windowsill."

Dani cut the bindings on Nadine's and Bri's hands, then she herded them to the hallway. Seconds later Bri ran back. "The key isn't there."

An iron fist gripped Madison's stomach. Steven had covered all his bases. He'd pick them off if they tried to go out the back. The windows on the second floor had no bars—but there was no way to get Terri or Nadine to the ground.

She turned to the timer. Ninety seconds. Her mouth dried. Somehow they had to defuse the bomb.

Clayton groaned, and Madison dropped beside him. Blood ran down the side of his head where he'd been grazed. "You know how to disarm a bomb?"

"Took a class . . . a long time ago. Help me up." She helped him to sit up. "Where is Steven?"

"He's gone. And there's no way out of the house."

65

Madison's face was the color of chalk. His heart almost stopped when she quickly filled him in. She was right. They had to defuse the bomb. "Help me to stand."

Once he was on his feet, he lurched to the counter. Sixty-five seconds. Sweat popped out on his face as he studied the small, square box with C-4 attached to an electronic timer that relentlessly counted down. Fifty-five seconds.

Madison stood beside him. "If it's electronic, will the jammer keep it from going off?"

"No. It's battery operated. And I don't know which wire to cut. We have to get out."

"Not without Terri."

Forty seconds. "Help me to get her to her feet. Maybe I can carry her fireman style."

"Our only way out is through one of the upstairs windows, and you'll never get her up the steps."

They'd never make it. "I have to try. The rest—go! Tie sheets together, anything, but get out of this house!"

"I can help."

He turned as Terri tried to roll over on her side. Blood soaked the front of her shirt. She struggled to sit up but fell back. The circle of blood on her shirt turned darker with fresh blood. "I didn't know Steven—" She closed her eyes. "And I didn't see the bomb. Describe it."

He described it down to the four wires attached from the C-4 to the timer.

"What color?"

"Red, yellow, white, and black." Clayton wiped blood from the side of his face. "And we have thirty seconds."

"Got to see it."

If he moved her, the bleeding would get worse. If he didn't, they'd all die. He slipped his arms under her body and lifted her. His head swam and he focused on a spot on the wall until it stopped.

"Seven seconds," Madison said.

Clayton staggered to the counter and set Terri on her feet. She leaned in to examine the bomb. "Cut the black one."

Madison slapped a pair of scissors into his hands. He bent over the timer. Sweat ran down into his eyes as he isolated the black wire. "You sure?"

"Four seconds." Madison's voice shook.

"Yes," Terri whispered.

Still, he hesitated. What if she was wrong? They'd all die. If he didn't try—they'd die for sure. His hand shook as he snipped the black wire.

66

Madison stared at the timer. It had stopped at two seconds. Her legs turned to jelly, and she sagged against Clayton. "You did it."

"No. Terri did it." He wrapped his arms around her and pulled her to his chest. For a second she didn't know which one was holding the other up. Behind them the others murmured their thanks to God, and she lifted up her own prayer of thanks before she stepped back. Madison knelt beside Terri. It looked as though the bleeding had stopped. She took her hand. "Thank you. We would have died if it hadn't been for you."

"You would've figured it out."

"Not in time. Lie still until we can get you help."

Terri nodded. "I'm so cold."

"I'll get a blanket," Nadine said.

Clayton knelt beside them. "We're not out of the woods yet. When the bomb doesn't go off, he'll either run or come see why. Where're your guns?"

"Upstairs. I'll go get them, but we need to move everyone except Terri out of the kitchen—it's the first place he'll look if he comes back. And lock the back door."

She took the stairs two at a time and retrieved her service pistol and a smaller backup semiautomatic along with two loaded magazines. Then she grabbed her phone on the dresser. No signal. But maybe that would change once they got out of the house.

Clayton met her on the stairs, and she gave him the Sig and an extra clip for the magazine. "You want to climb out my window?"

Clayton shook his head. "I figure he's in the grove of trees near the back of the property—it has a direct view of your bedroom. We'll have to climb out a window on the front side."

Madison led the way to Nadine's room that had a veranda, but it would be at least a ten-foot drop. She grabbed the sheet from the king-sized bed. They could tie it to the railings and shorten the drop.

Outside the moon was still full enough to give off low lighting as Clayton tied the sheet to one of the rails. "I figure he's standing behind that big oak at the back of the property—it's the best vantage point."

What if Clayton was wrong? She waited to follow him. "When we get on the ground, I'll go to the right, you go to the left."

"You sure you want to split up?"

"Yes. If he gets the drop on one of us, the other can go for help."

Clayton nodded and went over the balcony. Once he dropped to the ground, Madison followed. She crept from the front of the house and eased around to the other side until the big oak that she'd played under when she was a child came into view. It was hard to see in the shadows, and she wished for night vision goggles. No sign of movement, but from what she remembered Chad saying, Steven had been a sniper at one time—he could sit for hours without moving. Or he could back then. Her impression of him now made her believe he was too nervous to be still for very long. His car was still in the drive, though, so he hadn't left.

What if he'd gotten inside the house? No. The back door was locked. She remembered her phone and tried it again. Still too close to the jammer.

Voices came from the back of the house, and she died a little inside. Steven had gotten the drop on Clayton.

"Olly olly oxen free." Steven's voice singsonged the kid's phrase. "If you don't show yourself, I'll kill him."

"Don't listen to him, Madison!"

It sounded like they were on the other side of Nadine's apartment. Maybe the patio. He wouldn't expect her to come from inside the apartment, and she tried the door. Locked. She felt along the top edge of the door—sometimes Nadine left a key there. Her fingers closed on the piece of metal. *Yes!*

The click when the deadbolt slid open sounded like a gunshot. She waited, listening. Nothing. She proceeded inside the apartment, carefully dodging Nadine's furniture. Gauzy curtains covered the patio door, but she made out the forms of two men. But which one was Clayton?

She eased to the door and barely moved the curtain. Relief flowed through her when Clayton faced her, but it was short lived—the way they were standing, Steven could see her from his peripheral vision if she opened the door. At least he stood close to it. She'd give anything for a flash-bang.

"Come on, Madison," Steven shouted. "Counting to ten. You don't show yourself, he's dead. One, two . . ."

She crouched and waited until he reached nine and raised his gun. Madison flipped the overhead floodlight on as she burst through the door, screaming like a howler monkey on steroids.

Judging from the stunned look on his face, the bright light and screaming was almost as good as a flash-bang. The door slammed into his arm, but he held on to the gun as he stumbled forward. He quickly found his footing and swung his pistol toward her, firing.

The bullet whizzed past her ear as she dropped to the patio and rolled. Madison brought her gun up and fired, hitting Steven in the chest. He took a step toward her, emptying his semiautomatic in her direction.

Clayton tackled him from behind, and they both went down. Steven's gun fell from his hand. Madison kicked it across the patio as Clayton rolled off him. Steven's breathing became shallow, and she knelt beside him. "Why, Steven?"

"Had to. Dad . . . You hurt . . . a Turner . . . you pay."

"But why shoot Dani and my grandfather?"

His brows lowered, maybe from pain. "Dad . . ." Air gurgled in his chest. The frown lines in his face relaxed as the life in his eyes faded.

"He's gone." Clayton lifted Madison to her feet.

"No! I need answers." She stared at Steven's body. "I killed him." First Chad, now his brother. Madison sagged against Clayton and he wrapped his arms around her.

"It was self-defense."

That didn't help.

"Listen to me. He would have killed us both—everyone, even his friend."

Terri. She needed an ambulance. "See if you can find the jammer."

He searched Steven's pockets and held up a small black box that he tossed to her. "Here you go."

She turned the jammer off and took out her cell phone. Finally, she had a signal and dialed Chief Nelson's number.

Soon sirens split the night air as police cars and an ambulance converged on the property.

Once Terri was loaded onto a gurney, Madison took her hand. "You saved our lives."

"So did you and Clayton. If you hadn't stopped him, he would've come back for us."

Madison shrugged off the praise. "You're welcome here once they release you."

"We'll see."

Dani approached and squeezed Terri's other hand. "Thank you for what you did. We'll come see you in the hospital."

"I hope so," Terri said as they loaded her into the ambulance.

The paramedic slammed the bay doors, and they drove away, red-and-white lights flashing.

"She seems so sad," Dani said.

Madison slipped her arm around her sister's waist. "Maybe she doesn't have anyone."

"You talked to her more than I did. Did you ask?"

"I didn't think of it. We'll go see her tomorrow. Find out who her family is."

Habit and the aroma of coffee woke Clayton early Tuesday morning after only four hours of sleep. Four hours that only brought nightmares of timers and bombs along with a pounding headache. And with it a nagging concern that Steven hadn't confirmed that he'd shot Judge Anderson and Dani. But if not him, who?

The thought stayed with him while he dressed and went downstairs for a cup of Nadine's strong coffee. Madison sat at the island in her robe, staring at the cup in her hands . . . at least he thought it was her. "I didn't expect to see you up."

She raised her gaze and smiled. "Couldn't sleep."

No, it was Dani, which was confirmed when the back door opened and Madison entered the room with a newspaper in her hand and dressed in her ranger uniform.

"Don't you two ever dress alike. Please." He poured a cup of coffee. "Anyone need a refill? And where's Nadine?"

Both shook their heads no. "Nadine's in her apartment." Madison tossed the newspaper on the table.

Clayton took his coffee to the island and sat down, glancing at the headlines. The events of last night happened too late to get in the news. "Can't quit thinking about how Steven never answered about shooting Dani or killing the judge."

"I don't think he broke in here and shot my grandfather."

"Any thoughts on who did?"

"I still believe it's the brother of the man who died," Madison said. "Aaron Corbett."

"I don't know. He has a strong alibi. Have you had time to go through the papers you found at the bank?"

"Oh my goodness!" Madison pinched the bridge of her nose. "I can't believe I forgot about the adoption papers. I need to show them to Dani and then examine the papers we took from the vault before I do anything else."

"Adoption papers?" Dani leaned forward. "What adoption papers?"

"Mine." Madison stood. "I'll go get them, and we'll look at them now."

"We need fuel while we go over them—I'm going to scramble a few eggs," Clayton said. "And toast some bread."

By the time he had the eggs and toast ready, Madison had returned and spread the papers on the island. He noticed that the handwritten letter from her grandfather was missing.

"Eat." Clayton set the eggs and toast down, and the other two moved to the other end of the counter and did as he ordered. As soon as they finished, Madison handed Dani the contract with her birth certificate attached while Clayton sorted through the other papers.

As Dani read, a frown creased her brow. "This is so hard to believe. Our grandmother essentially sold you to William Anderson. I wonder if . . ." She pressed her hand to her mouth. "Are there any other contracts?"

"I don't know," Madison said. "I haven't looked through them."

Clayton read the first set of papers he'd picked up, his stomach turning sour. The date was the same as the contract for Madison's adoption. He quickly flipped through the other bound pages. "These are all contracts." He handed Dani the top set. "I believe this is what you're looking for."

She quickly flipped through the pages and dropped them on the counter. “I can’t believe it.” Dani leaned back in the chair. “I knew my parents were fairly wealthy, but I had no idea they’d paid $50,000 to adopt me.”

Clayton picked them up and scanned to the last page. Judith Winslow had arranged the adoption. “The judge met with Judith last Wednesday at Coffee and More. The judge didn’t seem too happy to see her, and thinking back, they could’ve been arguing . . . and then he was shot that night.”

“What!” Madison said. “You’re just now telling me?”

“But I did tell you, and Chief Nelson—the night the judge was shot.”

Madison stood and started for the door. “I’m going to see her. Now. And then I’m going to the district attorney. She needs to pay for what she’s done.”

Clayton stood and checked his watch. “I’ll go with you. She’s probably at Bright Horizons.”

“I’d like to go as well,” Dani said.

“You sure? You’re still recuperating.”

“I’ll be fine.”

Madison gathered the papers. “We’ll need these when we confront her.”

“We don’t want to take the originals. Let’s make a copy,” he said. “Do you want to call Chief Nelson?”

Madison shook her head. “Not yet. Let’s see what she has to say—if he’s there she might clam up.”

The drive to the pregnancy center was quiet. As soon as Clayton parked, Madison climbed out and marched to the door.

“Wait up.” He’d stayed behind to help Dani.

“Sorry. I’m just so angry.”

“I know,” Dani said. “But we won’t get anything out of her if we try to bulldoze her.”

“She’s right,” he said. “Judith Winslow has a reputation for being a tough lady. You’re not going to outshout her.”

Madison palmed her hands. “Okay. I get it.” She turned to Clayton. “Why don’t you do the talking . . . at least initially.”

He agreed and held the door for Madison and Dani. Inside the center, soft music played overhead. Photos of babies lined the walls. Two young, very pregnant girls sat in the lobby. Clayton approached the window and showed his credentials. “I’d like to speak with Mrs. Winslow.”

“Do you have an appointment?”

“No, but tell her Judge Anderson’s granddaughter is here to see her.”

She gave him a curious look. “I will. Have a seat and I’ll let her know you’re here.”

Five minutes passed. “She’s not going to talk to us,” Madison muttered.

Clayton held up his hand. “Let’s give it a few more minutes, and then I’ll play the Chief Nelson card.”

The side door opened and the girl from the window motioned for them to come. She led them to an office at the back of the center and knocked softly.

“Come in.” There was a finality in the tone of voice.

The girl opened the door and ushered them inside with Madison going in first, then Clayton, and Dani bringing up the rear. He turned his attention to Judith Winslow, who sat behind a massive cherry desk, her blood-red lipstick standing out against her pale face.

“I’ve been expecting you.” She extended her hands to the chairs in the room. “Have a seat.”

“This isn’t a social call,” Madison said, her voice tight.

“I’m aware that it isn’t, but there’s no reason we can’t be civil.”

Dani stepped from behind Clayton, and Judith caught her breath and pressed her hand to her chest. He hadn’t thought her face could get any paler, but it did.

68

Judith Winslow straightened her shoulders and turned to Madison. "I assume you found the papers."

She hadn't been expecting the woman to be so direct. Madison simply could not think of her as her grandmother. "I did. Contracts, actually, between you and my grandfather and scores of adoptive parents."

Madison tilted her head. "It was you who trashed Grandfather's office and locked Nadine in the closet."

Judith shrugged but didn't look away. "Did you have a good life?"

Madison narrowed her eyes. "I suppose so, on the days my mother wasn't in the depressive stage of her bipolar disorder. Then all bets were off."

"That's still better than your life would've been with a fifteen-year-old with no future." She tented her fingers. "You see, your mother lived that life. I had her when I was fifteen. Her father never contributed a dime to us. But then, it would be hard for a sixteen-year-old boy to provide for a family. There were many nights we went to bed hungry. I was determined that history would not repeat itself."

"But did you have to sell us?" Dani asked softly.

"I did not sell you." Judith Winslow's eyes were steely. "There are legitimate costs to a pregnancy. Part of the money went to a trust for my daughter and the rest helped start this pregnancy center. Your parents didn't think it was too much money." She turned to Madison. "Or your grandfather."

"You argued with him Wednesday morning at the coffee shop." Madison leaned forward. "Did you go to the house that night and kill him?"

Judith jumped to her feet. "Get out of my office."

Suddenly, pain flashed across her face, and she pressed her hand against her chest again. Judith swayed, then sank to the chair and jerked the desk drawer open. Seconds later she pulled out a small amber bottle, shook a tablet into her hand, and popped it under her tongue.

"Are you all right?" Clayton asked. "Can we call someone?"

For a few seconds she sat very still with her eyes closed, then she winced and popped another pill. "I think you better call an ambulance. I'm having a heart—" She pitched forward on the desk.

Dani called 911 and then went to the front to get help while Madison and Clayton jumped to get Judith out of the chair and onto the floor. Once they had her resting on her back with a pillow from the sofa under her head, Madison felt for a pulse. "It's irregular."

Judith's eyes fluttered open, and Madison was looking at the same eyes she saw every morning when she looked in the mirror.

"So . . . sorry."

"Shh." Guilt pressed into Madison. She shouldn't have pushed her so hard. "Don't try to talk."

"Might not make it . . . got to tell you."

Her voice was low, and Madison leaned closer to hear her words.

"William. I . . . killed him, may God . . . forgive me."

She rocked back on her heels.

Judith Winslow killed her grandfather.

Not Steven. Not Aaron Corbett. But someone she would never have suspected. "Why?"

"Couldn't let him tell . . ."

Sirens wailed to a stop outside the building. Judith gripped Madison's wrist. "Tell . . . Teresa . . . I'm proud of her."

"How? Where is she?"

"Your friend . . . Terri Davis . . . my daughter . . . your mother."

Madison heard the words, but they made no sense. Terri? The woman who saved their lives? She was their birth mother? Her mind would not wrap around the concept.

Suddenly the room swarmed with paramedics. Someone pried Judith's hands from Madison's wrist and helped Madison to her feet.

"We need to move out into the hall." Clayton tugged her out of the room.

From her vantage point, Madison watched as the paramedics worked on Judith. She was barely aware when Dani joined them in their vigil.

"Stand clear!"

Judith must have coded. *Judith.* If she lived, would Madison ever think of her as her grandmother? She doubted it. From what she could tell, Judith Winslow wasn't grandmother material.

"We have a heartbeat." A different voice.

Her heart was still beating when the medics transported her to a waiting ambulance. Madison and Dani walked out into the sunlight while Clayton stayed behind to talk to Chief Nelson, who had arrived with the ambulance.

When they reached his SUV, they waited for him to come with the keys. Madison was still trying to process what she'd learned when Dani leaned into her. Madison wrapped her arms around her sister, drawing strength from her twin. She'd never be alone again.

They'd been through so much, but they'd both refused to let adversity break them. If anything, they were stronger. Strong enough to weather this new revelation about Terri. At least she hoped they were.

"You okay?"

Madison leaned against the fender of the SUV. "I don't know. I feel responsible. I should've realized she was sick. If I hadn't—"

"Don't do that to yourself."

The door locks clicked open as Clayton approached. "Do you want to follow the ambulance to the hospital?"

Dani blew her nose and stepped away from the SUV. "We probably should."

"I'm so angry, I don't know if I can." Madison crossed her arms. Then she sagged against the vehicle. "But it probably was my fault this happened, so I agree, we should go. And we have to tell Hugh and Chief Nelson about her confession."

"Even if she doesn't make it, Hugh needs to close the case."

Madison agreed. He opened the door and Madison hopped in the front seat, then he helped Dani into the back seat.

He got in and started the SUV. "How about Terri? Do you want to go see her?"

"I do." Madison took a deep breath and released it. "But how much do we tell her? She may not know who we are—we didn't know she was our mother until an hour ago."

Dani shook her head. "I don't think we need to bring up what we know. Let her bring it up if she's aware we're her daughters. If she doesn't, we can tell her after she's released from the hospital." Then she frowned. "But how will we tell her about Judith? She needs to know how serious it is with her mother."

Clayton looked over his shoulder. "Why don't I tell her? I can talk to Terri while you two check on Judith."

"I like it. How about you, Madison?"

"It's a good idea." She chewed her bottom lip and turned to face Dani. "Do you think Terri knows who we are?"

"I don't know. She did submit her DNA to Ancestry.com. If she checked her account, she should've seen our names."

"Then why didn't she tell us who she is?"

Clayton stopped for a traffic light. "Maybe because she doesn't know how you'd react, and she's afraid. Don't forget there hasn't been a good time to bring it up." He tapped his fingers on the steering wheel. "She, ah, met with the judge last Wednesday a little earlier than Judith did."

"What?" Madison jerked straight up. "Why haven't you told me before?"

"I didn't know she was your mother or Judith Winslow's daughter until you did." The light changed and he accelerated. "After she explained why she met the judge at the coffee shop, she wasn't on my radar as a possible suspect in his shooting."

"Why did she meet with him?"

"To offer her condolences in the death of his daughter. Turns out your adoptive mother was Terri's fifth-grade teacher, and she made a real difference in Terri's life."

"I wonder if that was the only reason?" Madison turned and stared out the window. Was it possible she'd been trying to get information on her twin daughters?

69

Hugh believed that with Judith's confession and Steven's death, all the shootings were wrapped up, but Clayton still pulled under the pull-thru to let the two sisters out. Dani was too weak to walk from the parking lot to the hospital entrance anyway, and he hurried around to help her out.

"Do you want me to get a wheelchair?" Madison asked.

Dani shook her head. "I need to walk—it's the only way I'll get my strength back."

Both women amazed him with their inner strength and determination. "I'll text you after I talk to Terri."

They inquired at the front desk about Judith and learned she'd been rushed to the cath lab and would be returning to ICU unless she went straight into surgery. He left them in the waiting room and walked up to the third floor to Terri's room. Clayton stopped outside her room and gathered his thoughts, then he took a deep breath and knocked on the door.

"Come in." The voice was weak.

He pushed the door open and entered the room. Terri was sitting on the bed, fully dressed with her arm in a sling.

"Are you going somewhere?" he asked.

"The doctors are releasing me."

"Voluntarily or did you threaten to walk out?"

She grinned. "The bullet went through without hitting anything major. There was no need for me to stay."

He knew at least one of her daughters was just like her. "Where are you going?"

"Back to the hotel for tonight, then I guess I'll return to Ocean Springs." She looked at him curiously. "I'm surprised to see you here by yourself."

"Dani and Madison are downstairs in the ICU waiting room."

"Why?"

Clayton slipped his hand in his pocket and jingled his change. "I'm not quite sure how to tell you this . . ."

"How about straight up?"

He wasn't sure he should just blurt out what shape her mother was in. "When I left them, your mother, Judith Winslow, was having a heart cath."

"My mother? She doesn't have a heart."

He could see how she might feel that way. "I'm afraid she had a major heart attack about an hour ago."

Terri pressed her hand against her chest and dropped her gaze to the bed. "Is . . ." She sucked in a breath. "Is she going to be all right?"

"I don't know. Madison and Dani went to find out, and I haven't heard from them."

Her head shot up and she stared at him, searching his face. "Do they know that I'm . . ."

Clayton nodded. "Just found out." He could almost see the wheels turning in her mind. "They didn't know if you were aware of who they are. They wanted me to talk to you first."

Air whooshed from her lungs as tension left her shoulders. She blinked back tears that suddenly appeared in her eyes.

"After what happened with Judith, they were afraid to spring something like that on you."

A frown creased her brow. "What do you mean?"

He explained what happened at the pregnancy center. "Madison blames herself—she thinks if she hadn't accused Judith of killing Judge Anderson, she wouldn't have had a heart attack."

"Oh, what a tangled web we weave . . ." Terri said softly. "My mother's life has been one lie after another."

"She's done a lot of good."

"But how many girls has she destroyed by taking their babies? And separating Madison and Dani . . ." Terri swallowed hard. "If she lives, will she be prosecuted?"

Clayton looked away.

"You're not telling me something."

"I'm afraid Judith confessed to killing Judge Anderson. So, yes, if she survives, she will go to jail." He cocked his head. "But that's down the road. Right now, Dani and Madison want to see you—if you're up to it and want to see them."

Terri wiped away tears with the back of her hand. Then she smiled. "More than anything in the world."

70

Madison stared at the text from Clayton and then lifted her gaze to Dani's. "She wants to see us."

"Really?"

Madison nodded. "Are you ready?"

"Yes, I've been ready, but how about you? This is all new to you."

It might be new, but all her life she'd wondered about the woman who'd birthed her. For years she'd been angry about how she could have just given her away. And now, not just her but Dani as well. But after learning how old Terri had been when they were born and how Judith manipulated the situation, her anger had dissipated—toward Terri anyway. Not so much toward Judith.

She looked up and smiled at her sister. "New or not, I want to get to know her, especially after she saved our lives last night."

They paused outside the door. Dani's eyes were closed. Praying, probably. She had a better relationship with God than Madison. With a quick breath, she tapped on the door, and seconds later it swung open.

"Good," Clayton said. "I was getting uneasy when you didn't text me back."

Madison winced. "I didn't think to."

"That's okay. Come on in. I'm going after coffee."

He squeezed Madison's shoulder when she brushed past him, and she thanked him with her eyes. Once they were in the room, an awkward silence fell until Madison noticed Terri was dressed in street clothes. "Are you leaving?"

"The doctor discharged me. I plan to return to the Hampton Inn, at least until tomorrow."

"No, come to my grandfather's house . . ." She owed Terri that much after she'd helped them defuse the bomb.

"We'll see." More silence followed.

Surreal. That was the feeling Madison experienced as she studied the woman sitting on the side of the hospital bed. It wasn't that she didn't know what Terri looked like—she'd talked to her at least three or four times since meeting her last week. But it was the first time seeing her, knowing she was their mother.

At least now she knew where they got their blue eyes and heart-shaped face. Not the blond hair, though. Had that come from their father's side? There would be time to ask questions about him later.

What did she even call her? Mom? No. That's what she'd called her adoptive mother. Terri? That sounded so . . . what? Not quite right. Madison glanced at Dani. From her expression, she was having the same thoughts.

Madison didn't have to figure that out yet, not when she had so many other questions. Like why?

"Why?" Terri asked, her voice cracking.

Heat infused Madison's cheeks as she looked up at her birth mother. "I'm sorry. I didn't know I said that out loud."

"It's okay. It was the same question I asked for years. But you have to understand I didn't have any choice. I never wanted to give you up."

"Then . . ."

"I was in the ninth grade and barely fifteen when you were born. My mother didn't tell me, but she'd arranged for your and Dani's adoption well before your birth. I had no say-so in the matter."

Dani blotted her eyes with a tissue. "Did you get to see us at all?"

Terri nodded. "I refused to let them put me to sleep, like my mother wanted," she said with a wry smile. "Thank goodness the doctor was sympathetic to me and allowed me to have a spinal block. I'll never forget when he laid you both on my chest, and I felt your heartbeats.

"Mother never intended for a bond to be formed, and if there'd been any way I could have kept you, I would have. But know this—as soon as I turned eighteen, I started looking for you. That's when I discovered Mother had the records sealed."

"I found a copy of the adoption papers in Grandfather's safe-deposit box." Madison flexed her fingers. She hated to ask about the money, but she had to know the answer. "Did you know your mother got fifty thousand dollars from each of our adoptive parents?"

"Fifty thousand dollars? I don't understand."

"Grandfather had contracts in his safe-deposit box, and that was the figure on the papers."

Terri's shoulders sagged. "I should have known it was more than the ten thousand she gave me when I turned twenty-one." She turned and looked first at Dani then at Madison. "I haven't touched it . . . been saving it to give you if I ever found you."

Terri wiped a tear away. "But the worst part is you two were separated. I'm so sorry."

Madison would never forgive Judith and her grandfather for that. Tears sprang to her eyes, and Madison pressed her lips together to keep her chin from quivering. Saving the money for them erased any doubt she might have had that Terri was telling them the truth. Impulsively she wrapped her mother in her arms and found that Dani had the same thought.

Sometimes crying was good for the soul, and this was one of those times. When their tears dried, Madison squeezed Terri's hand. "Let's go get your things from the hotel."

There was a knock at the door and Clayton entered the room. Immediately his face alerted her to bad news. Before she could ask, he said, "I'm afraid Judith didn't make it. They had to take her to surgery, and her heart stopped on the table."

"No." Terri closed her eyes, and pain filled her face. After a minute she opened them and turned to him. "Do you think they would let me see her?"

"Are you sure you want to do that?" Dani said. "You're still shaky."

"Yes. It's something I need to do."

"Why?" Madison asked.

"She was my mother." The words were simple but heartfelt. "I forgave her a long time ago for what she did. That doesn't mean I didn't get angry about it sometimes, or approved of it, or that I had to be around her, but I do believe she loved me in her own way. She thought she was doing what was best for me when she made me give you up for adoption."

Madison didn't agree. "I—"

"Hear me out. She was fifteen when I was born, and while her parents allowed her to marry my father, it didn't work out. He disappeared before I was born, and she didn't want you to go through what I went through—being hungry, living in bug-infested apartments, never enough heat or air.

"She could have taken the money and lived off of it, but instead she created a safe place for unmarried, pregnant women." Terri held up her hand. "I know she profited from it, but still, she could have taken it all."

"I understand." Clayton walked to the door. "I'll ask if you can have a few minutes with her."

"I understand too," Dani said and put her arms around Terri again.

Well, Madison didn't, and she didn't understand the peace on Dani's and Terri's faces. What was she missing?

71

Clayton climbed the steps to the gazebo with Madison. It'd been a week since Judith Winslow's death, and the funeral earlier today had been a private affair with only Terri, Dani, Madison, and Clayton in attendance.

He hadn't been certain Madison would go, but in the end, she went to support Terri. It had cost her a lot emotionally, and that was why he'd brought her downtown to Bluff Park overlooking the Mississippi. He'd felt it was safe enough since all the law enforcement officers involved in the case believed Steven had been the one who'd shot Dani and then fired on them in the hospital parking lot. On the off chance everyone was wrong, Clayton had Brooke Danvers still combing through Madison's cases when she had time.

She turned to him. "How can Dani and Terri forgive Judith Winslow?"

It was a difficult question to answer. He turned, and a cool breeze from the west brushed his face. At four in the afternoon, the sun was still fairly high. Storms were forecasted for later, but for now, cumulus clouds dotted the sky. One blocked the direct rays of the sun with beams shooting out the top and bottom. Below, the great river silently flowed toward New Orleans as he thought about Madison's question.

Forgiveness required giving up her right to resentment and

revenge. Instinctively he knew that would be the wrong thing to say. Clayton took a breath and sent a prayer heavenward for words that wouldn't make matters worse. "Have you asked Dani and Terri?"

She shook her head and turned back to face the river as a barge came into view.

"Maybe that would be a starting place." Cop-out. He braced his hands on the railing. "Can I ask you something?"

Madison dipped her head, and he took that for a yes. "Have you forgiven Chad Turner for trying to kill you?" He was taking a risk in case she hadn't.

"I didn't have any choice—I killed him."

She was also dealing with guilt. "You've released your resentment and wanting to get revenge to God?"

"He's dead. That was more than enough revenge."

"But what if he were alive?"

Her face reddened. "I don't know. It would be difficult. Have you forgiven everyone who ever wronged you?"

"As far as I know, I have."

"Even your brother-in-law who deserted your sister and niece?"

"Even him."

"How could you do that? He turned his back on them."

Clayton didn't answer right away, trying to choose his words. "Because God forgave me for all the ways I've hurt others. Was it easy? One of the hardest thing I've ever done."

Madison pressed her lips together, and the muscle in her jaw worked furiously. Then she stilled. "How did you do it?" she whispered.

"I didn't. God did it in me. But I had to give up my right to be angry and resentful. And sometimes forgiveness isn't a one-and-done deal. A few days out of his Word and I find myself slipping back into pointing a self-righteous finger at Jake. That's when God finds a way to remind me of my gambling addiction."

"It doesn't sound easy."

"Didn't say it was. But I found forgiveness freed me. Anger and resentment no longer hold me prisoner."

"But Judith Winslow not only sold us, she separated us. And sold other babies too. To fund a pregnancy center of all things."

"I'm not saying you gloss over what she did, but you don't have to focus on it until it makes you bitter."

"Just how do I keep from focusing on it?"

He chewed the inside of his cheek. Explaining how he'd gotten to the place where he could forgive when someone hurt him was hard. "Let's say you have two puppies from a litter. Both born at the same time, both the same size, but one grows to be much bigger than the other. How could that happen?"

She thought a minute. "Maybe he was fed more."

"Bingo." Then he smiled at her. "You can focus on the bad things like what Judith did, or you can focus on the good things—you have a twin sister and you've found your birth mother. But you have to make a choice."

Minutes passed as Madison turned and stared down at the Mississippi. Then she looked around at him. "I'll think about what you've said." She took his hand. "Thank you for caring."

Madison didn't know the half of it. He held her gaze, losing himself in her intense blue eyes. More than anything, he wanted to take her in his arms and kiss her hurts away.

She touched his jaw, setting off a fire inside him. "How's that vow of restraint holding up?"

"At this minute, not very well," he said, his voice husky.

Madison's cell phone rang, jarring the air, and she dropped her hand. With a sigh, she looked at the caller ID and frowned. "Dani."

"You better answer it."

She slid the button. "Is everything okay?" Then her face flushed and she checked her watch. "I totally forgot. I'll be home soon."

When she disconnected, he queried her with raised eyebrows.

"When Vivian Hawkins stopped by the house to pick up her platter, she offered to give me a tour of the Old Jail after five—Paul Davidson had told her I'd expressed an interest in seeing it. She called this morning with a tour all arranged, even invited Dani, who's really excited."

He remembered Madison expressing an interest in exploring the historic building. "Is Terri going?"

"No. She's not into history, said it sounded gruesome to her."

Clayton agreed with Terri. "Guess I better get you home."

He held her hand as they descended the steps.

"Thank you for this, Clayton. And I promise, I'll think about what you said."

72

Madison hurried in through the back door of her grandfather's house. Clayton had given her a lot to think about. He'd taken her by the lawyer's office and then brought her home after he'd gotten a phone call from his brother-in-law in a panic because he couldn't get ahold of his sponsor. Evidently, he was in danger of relapsing.

If Clayton was half as good with Jake as he'd been with her today, everything would be all right. She blushed at the memory of touching his face. She'd never thought it possible to be drawn to another man after what Chad had done. But Clayton had proven he was not Chad.

A box of files sat on the floor near the door. She'd set them there after they decided to take Vivian up on her offer of showing them the Old Jail. "I'm back," she yelled.

"Oh, good." Dani walked slowly into the kitchen.

Her sister still wasn't 100 percent healed. "Are you sure you're up to walking the stairs at the jail?"

"I'll make it—may be slow, though."

"Let me grab these boxes and we'll head out." She and Hugh were trying to wrap up the case that had brought her to Natchez, and she was returning some of the files to the supervisor's office.

Madison picked up the box of files, and the body armor that Clayton and Hugh insisted she still wear pinched her side. No one had threatened them in over a week, and she was tempted to remove it, but a quick check of her watch let her know it was almost five. As soon as she returned home, though, it was coming off and not going back on without good reason.

Dark clouds were rolling in as she held the passenger door for Dani. "Are you sure you feel up to this? It looks like it might rain."

"Definitely. The research I did said it was worth seeing. As for the rain, we'll be inside."

"Good. I've wanted to tour it ever since I first saw it."

They both turned as Terri pulled in and parked on the other side of Madison's Impala. She was glad Terri had agreed to stay with them at the judge's house while she recovered, giving the three of them time to get to know one another.

Terri had led a fascinating life in the Army as a Delta Force G operator, and she kept them amazed at her exploits. And Dani had been incredible in her crusade to stop human trafficking. Madison didn't know that she would have continued after having to fake her death.

"You want to come with us?" Dani asked.

"No thank you! Even if it were somewhere other than a jail, the funeral and then going through Mother's things has been tiring. And I've been looking at an apartment near here."

"Awesome!" Madison and Dani said at the same time. They'd discovered they were alike in a lot of ways, including the way they expressed themselves.

"Did you rent it?" Dani asked.

"I'm thinking about it." She raised her eyebrows. "Any chance either of you might relocate to Natchez?"

Dani grinned. "I'm thinking seriously about it . . . if you and Madison relocate here."

Madison had actually been giving it some thought. Hot Springs was five hours away whether driving or flying—not conducive to building relationships with her mother and sister. Or Clayton. Immediately she brushed that thought away—even though he'd kissed her, he hadn't said he was interested in anything other than friendship. "Since I travel so much, I could be based almost anywhere to do my job."

Dani's phone dinged with a text. "It's Vivian Hawkins checking to make sure we're still coming."

"Let's talk about this when you get back," Terri said.

Less than ten minutes later, they pulled into the deserted parking area beside the Old Jail, and Madison climbed out of the car, glancing toward the west as she grabbed the box of files. An angry, dark bank of clouds with lightning arcing from it hovered over Vidalia, Louisiana, across the river. "We better hurry if we don't want to get wet."

73

Clayton called Brooke Danvers as he raced south on Highway 61 with his eye to the west. A dark cloud inched toward them. He'd spent the last half hour with Jen trying to track down her husband. "Jake just called. He's sitting in the parking lot of the Blues Lounge. I'm going to try and talk him down. Don't call me unless it's an emergency."

"I thought they shut that place down when the sheriff arrested the owner for selling drugs."

"Evidently it's opened back up."

"I've found something interesting in Madison's first white-collar investigation."

"Go on."

"Seems a victim in the case was engaged to someone who grew up in Natchez. I found a note from one of the detectives in the case that she'd lost it when her fiancé died and made threats against Madison."

"Who is it?"

"I'm still looking for her name."

"Let me know if you discover anything." He turned into the parking lot of the Blues Lounge. "Jake's still here. I'll call you later."

Clayton disconnected and used his watch to turn his phone on Do Not Disturb before slipping it in his back pocket. Only people in his Favorites could reach him, which included Brooke. He pulled in beside where Jake sat white-knuckling the steering wheel of his pickup.

Clayton needed to stay in his SUV in case an emergency occurred. He lowered his window, and Jake did the same. "Get in with me."

His brother-in-law hesitated.

"Dispatch needs to be able to reach me." Fat drops of rain splatted the windshield, and a cold wind blew from the north. Clayton let his engine idle.

Jake climbed out of his truck and crawled into Clayton's SUV as the storm hit. He sat rock-still, staring out the window at the rain.

"What's going on?" Clayton kept his tone even.

"I can't do it." Jake's voice cracked.

"Yes, you can. Just take a deep breath and tell me what happened."

He kept staring out the windshield, his shoulders tense. Clayton waited. "The dentist gave me oxycodone for a toothache . . ."

Clayton winced. A free relapse. That's what addicts called being given legally prescribed drugs.

"I wasn't going to take one, but the pain got so bad I had to do something. And now I want more."

Clayton knew what it was like to be blindsided, and he drew on that. "I understand. Been there with the gambling. How long have you been drug free?"

"Ten months. Nine of it at a rehab."

"It's easier to stay clean when you're in a safe place."

Jake swallowed hard. "I know—it's the only way I got clean in the first place."

"Now you think you can do this on your own."

Jake gave him a shrug. "Who else is going to do it?"

"You need to lean into God on this." He scraped his hand over his jaw. "He'll guide you, but you have to trust him to do it."

Slowly Jake turned to Clayton. “You really believe that?”

“I know it’s true, or I’d be down at the casino right now. No one can do it for you. You have to trust that he’ll do what he says he’ll do—he won’t leave you.”

His phone buzzed in his back pocket, and Clayton glanced at his watch showing the incoming call. *Brooke?*

“I need to answer this.” He yanked his phone from his back pocket.

“Yeah, sure.”

He tapped the answer button. “What’s going on?”

“The fiancée’s name is Vivian Hawkins.”

No. “Madison and Dani are with her at the Old Jail now. Let me call Madison.”

“I’ve already tried. It goes to voicemail.”

He tried anyway and got the same result and redialed Brooke. His stomach churned. He should have known the threat wasn’t over—Steven hadn’t admitted to shooting Dani or being at the hospital. Vivian had been biding her time. “Meet me at the Old Jail.” He turned to Jake. “I’m not going to leave you by yourself, but I have an emergency so I’m taking you with me.”

They were a good fifteen minutes from the Old Jail. Clayton flipped on his siren and wipers before he threw the SUV into drive and punched the gas pedal. The Interceptor shot out of the parking lot with rain pounding the SUV.

He tossed his phone to Jake. “Call Chief Nelson’s cell phone and put him on speaker.” Nelson was soon on the line. “I believe Vivian Hawkins is holding Dani and Madison hostage at the Old Jail.”

The bottom fell out just as Dani and Madison reached the small porch, and Vivian Hawkins had the front door open, waiting for them. "I'm glad you made it before the storm hit."

Thunder rattled the windows, and Madison glanced behind her. Rain was coming down in sheets. "I didn't think it was supposed to storm until later."

"Thunderstorms can pop up anytime around here in the spring. Come on in and look around." She flinched when thunder boomed again. "I can't get over how much you two look alike."

They exchanged glances. "We hear that a lot lately," Dani said.

Madison smiled her agreement and closed the door behind them. "Thank you for offering to show us around. I hope we aren't inconveniencing you or anyone else."

"You're not." Vivian walked around them to the door. "I hope you don't mind, but this late in the day I usually keep the door locked. Anyone could walk off the street into here."

A shiver went down Madison's back as the lock clicked in place. She doubted anyone would venture out in this weather. She wouldn't have if she'd checked the radar, but the storm had moved in so quickly.

"I'm glad you're here. As for this building, often towns tear down their old structures, but the architecture and history on this one are so interesting they decided to renovate it. Don't you love the Wedgwood blue in this room? It's very soothing."

Madison had loved the blue walls the first time she was here. "Clayton said something about it being haunted. Something about moaning and groaning."

"It's an old building. Of course it's going to make noises." Vivian shook her head as she grabbed a handful of paper towels from her desk and stuck them in her pocket. "Some of these rooms are dirty. And I wish townspeople would stop propagating that ridiculous rumor. Half the officers refuse to do a security check after dark. Follow me and I'll show you the rest of this floor."

They trailed after her as she walked through the downstairs rooms. "Where you came in is where the jailer and his family lived, and through here are the cells that were on this floor." She led the way to an iron doorway.

"You mean there were actual cells on this floor?" Dani hesitated at the doorway. "With the jailer and his family?"

"Oh yes. We use the space for storage now."

A dank, oily odor came from the room as Madison peered through the metal doorway at the dungeon-like cells. She'd seen all she wanted to of the jail on this dark and gloomy day. "Why don't we save this for another visit when the sun's shining."

"I agree." Dani turned to Vivian. "Thanks so much for showing us around. Your offices were beautiful, but the cells—they creep me out."

"But it's raining so hard. You can't leave."

The strident tone in Vivian's voice was almost lost in a pop of lightning and the instant boom that followed. Madison had heard enough to trigger a memory in the back of her brain. Beside her Dani gasped.

Madison jerked her head toward their tour guide. Her face reflected a murderous rage. But it was the gun in Vivian's hand that had Madison's attention.

"What's going on?" Madison kept her voice calm.

"You are so stupid. What does it look like?"

It was coming back to her now. Something about Dallas. Vivian had lived there. Was engaged. Her heart dropped to her knees.

"You were engaged to Howard Douglas."

"Yes. And you killed him."

"I didn't have anything to do with his death. It was a car accident."

"It was no accident. He purposely drove into the bridge abutment because you hounded him until he couldn't take it any longer. I heard how the FBI wanted to drop the investigation into him, but the big important ISB ranger wouldn't let it go." Her face hardened. "You killed an innocent man. And now you'll pay."

Was she responsible for Douglas's death? It'd been her first white-collar crime. She'd been so certain he was selling oil rights he didn't own until his boss confessed after Douglas's death. "Let Dani go."

"Sorry. She dies first so you can see how it feels to lose someone you love."

"You shot Dani at Coles Creek." The clues were there all along. The dead fiancé, Vivian was a crack shot . . . "And you were the shooter at the hospital."

"Enough talk." Vivian motioned with the gun toward the iron door. "Get inside the cellblock."

Madison planted her feet. "You won't get away with this."

Vivian's lip curled. "Oh, but I will. An unfortunate accident. You two were trapped in the house when a fire broke out. This place will go up like a tinderbox."

"No one will believe you." Dani's voice cracked.

"Yes, they will. Now get inside the cellblock."

The woman was crazy. There was no reasoning with her. Madison's cell phone rang, and she checked the ID on her watch. Brooke Danvers.

Vivian leveled the gun at Dani. "You answer it, and I'll kill your sister."

She hesitated, fearing if she pulled the phone from her pocket, Vivian would shoot.

"Give me your phone. And your watch. Both of you."

Dani's eyes widened. "You're the one who came into my hospital room! Did you follow me to Coles Creek?"

"Gee, your sister is almost as bright as you are."

Vivian's sarcasm ratcheted Madison's pulse. Somehow she had to get Dani out of here.

"I really thought you were Madison at Coles Creek." She waved the gun. "Now hand them over."

Dani complied, but as Madison pulled her phone from her pocket, it rang again. Clayton. Somehow she had to let him know what was going on. She unfastened her watch, pressing the answer button as she did. "If you shoot one of us, they'll know our death was no accident," she said before Clayton had a chance to say anything.

Someone pounded the outside door. "Police. Open up!"

"It's over," Madison said.

"No." Vivian took a lighter from her pocket as a thud sounded at the front door. "It's just beginning."

She stepped to the door leading to the front. "You come in here and they're dead," she yelled.

The thudding stopped.

She backed up to the corner of the room and kept the pistol pointed at them as she leaned down and picked up a can. After switching the gun to her other hand, she splashed liquid on one of the wooden desks before she placed the paper towels she'd grabbed earlier on the corner.

Madison's heart jumped into her throat. Vivian planned to burn the building down.

Using one hand, she flicked the lighter. A flame immediately appeared. "Move toward the cellblock." Vivian motioned with the gun.

Madison palmed her hands up, waiting for an opportunity to make a move. "Let's talk about this."

"Shut up." The flame went out, and she flicked the lighter again. When it flamed up, she glanced down at the paper towels and lit them.

Madison lunged for the gun, grabbing Vivian's wrist.

75

Clayton careened around the corner of State Street and floored the gas pedal again. A block later, he slammed on the brakes in front of the police car barricading the street. He turned toward Jake. "Stay here!"

He jumped out of his SUV and ran to the front of the Old Jail, where a police officer leaned a battering ram against the house. "Where are they?" he asked another officer.

Chief Nelson turned. "Inside. Hawkins is threatening to shoot them if we don't back off."

Suddenly a gunshot rang out from within the house. The officers grabbed the battering ram and knocked the door open. Clayton rushed through the door. The front room was empty, then Dani stumbled through the doorway. "Hurry! She's on fire!"

"Where?" They could be in any number of rooms.

"Next to the cellblock."

Clayton raced to the back of the jail.

76

Drop and roll!" Madison screamed.

Vivian must have gotten kerosene on her clothes. When Madison attacked her, she'd dropped the flaming paper towels and her shirt had ignited.

Instead of doing what Madison said, Vivian grabbed for the gun Madison had wrested from her hand. They struggled and the gun went off. Vivian's grasp loosened and she fell to the floor, her clothes still on fire.

Madison beat at the flames on her shirt, and then snatched a curtain from the window. She smothered the flames just as Clayton rushed into the room. He grabbed Madison. "Are you okay?"

As the police spilled into the room, she leaned against him and nodded as he wrapped his arms around her. "I think it's finally over."

EPILOGUE

My Dearest Madison,

From the day you came into our lives, you captured my heart. Your laughter, your stubborn determination, your unconditional love for me—you were a gift from God. I love you from the bottom of my heart. Please always remember that when you learn of my shortcomings.

And you will learn of them, I'm sure.

First of all, I'm sorry for separating you from your twin sister. You will find paperwork that should help you to find her and your birth mother. I pray you are able to find them both and only regret that I didn't give you this information sooner.

I hope you will find it in your heart to forgive not just me but your grandmother Judith. Neither of us deserve it, but forgive for your sake, not ours. To hold on to unforgiveness is like a cancer to your soul.

You brought sunshine and love into my life, and for that I will always be thankful.

With love,
Grandfather

She would not cry. Madison pressed her quivering mouth tight. She would not. Tears came anyway, and at first, she tried to knuckle them away, then she simply let them fall as memories of her grandfather washed over her.

Gradually the tears softened the hardness in her heart. He'd loved her. Madison never doubted that, and she wouldn't now. Judith was another matter . . . but both Dani and Terri had forgiven her. When Madison asked how, both had responded the same way—God had forgiven them.

Madison smiled through her tears. She'd wrestled with that a few days and Clayton's story of the two dogs, and she'd finally understood the message. Who was she to judge her grandmother?

Her cell phone dinged with a text. Clayton.

Want to take a ride?

It's 9 o'clock at night.

Perfect time for where I want to go.

Madison bit her bottom lip, her fingers hovering over her phone.

Sure.

Forty-five minutes later, she leaned back in Clayton's arms at the top of Emerald Mound, staring at the clear night sky.

"Sorry there's only a crescent moon tonight," he murmured against her hair.

Madison scanned the sky, looking for . . . "There's my shooting star!" she cried as a light streaked across the heavens.

"Making a wish?"

She nodded. Tonight's wish was for the peace in her heart to never end. But she knew it wouldn't be a shooting star that granted that wish.

Clayton turned her to face him. "You have a new beginning with Terri and Dani, and I hope you'll include me in it."

She brushed her fingertips along his jaw. “Does that mean you’ve given up the vow?”

For an answer he pulled her closer, his lips claiming hers. She slipped her arms around his neck and gave herself fully to his kiss. When they broke apart, he murmured, “Does that answer your question?”

Wow did it. “You are definitely in my future,” she said as he claimed her lips once more.

ACKNOWLEDGMENTS

The past two years have been difficult, and the prayers and encouragement from my family and friends have kept me going. Thank you.

To my editors, Rachel McRae and Kristin Kornoelje, thank you for making my stories so much better.

To the art, editorial, marketing, and sales team at Revell, especially Michele Misiak and Karen Steele, who have to deal with me directly—thank you for all your hard work. And to the ones behind the scenes, you're awesome!

To Julie Gwinn, thank you for your direction and for working so tirelessly with me and for being my friend.

I've enjoyed my time in Natchez, and a heartfelt thank-you to the rangers who have patiently answered my questions! Any mistakes are totally on me.

To my readers . . . you are awesome! Thank you for reading my stories. Without you, my books wouldn't exist.

As always, to Jesus, who gives me the words.

TURN THE PAGE
TO READ AN EXCERPT OF
JUSTICE DELIVERED . . .

The nip in the air invigorated Carly as she cantered the Arabian mare on the smooth lane. Getting up an hour early to ride Angel had been so worth it. The horses at Tabula Rasa had been a deciding factor in accepting the recovery center's job offer.

Carly's earliest memories had involved horses, and after her parents died, her mare, Candy, had been her biggest comfort. She'd like to know if the horse was still alive . . . horses lived thirty years sometimes. But to see her would mean revealing who she was to the world. What if Blade tracked her down?

No. For now she'd have to settle for the horses at the center. She brought the mare down to a trot then to a walk, and then she leaned over and patted the horse's neck. "Good girl. Are you ready to go back to the barn?"

Carly didn't know what she'd do if the mare answered her with more than the toss of her head.

She reined Angel around and nudged her into a trot, rising out of the saddle to match the one-two beat of Angel's rhythm. Her mind turned to the counseling sessions for later in the morning. Over the weekend a new girl had arrived at the center, and Carly was anxious to meet her. No one had said exactly what her problem was . . . probably drugs. That was the majority of the girls' problems here.

An hour and a half later, Carly lit a lavender candle, then turned as the door opened and girls filed in for their session. She made eye contact with each girl as they handed her a sheet of paper that listed their name and what they wanted to discuss. Most smiled and nodded, but not the new girl. Carly had learned from one of the other counselors that her name was Jenna Carson.

After she collected the last sheet, Carly scanned the room, searching until she found Jenna sitting in a rocker with her knees pulled close to her chest, ignoring the activity around her. Brassy blond hair almost covered a pixie face. Carly hadn't had an opportunity to look over the girl's paperwork, so she knew nothing other than her name. By noon, that would change when she plowed through the stack of folders on her desk.

She nodded to the two assistants who would sit in on today's session and then turned to study the other girls in the group. All recovering addicts, and all still in their teens. She skimmed the papers the girls had handed her. Jenna had written only her first name and age, seventeen, on the sheet. Evidently there was nothing she wanted to talk about.

Typical of a new girl who was still hiding from her past. After eight years, Carly understood that better than anyone. But it was her job to get Jenna to realize the past did not define her. Here at Tabula Rasa she had a clean slate. That's what *tabula rasa* meant in Latin. Carly had to remind herself daily that she had a clean slate because not a day went by that she didn't struggle with her past, and especially with her sister's death.

She hadn't discovered Lia was dead until almost six months after they'd met at the state park. When a week went by and her sister hadn't contacted Carly again, she figured once Lia had time to think about what she'd learned, she'd decided Carly had too much baggage. And Carly didn't blame her, but she wasn't about to contact Lia again and suffer more rejection.

It had been Jamie who had tracked down Lia's unsolved murder case that the police termed a random act of violence. Hers was similar to three other unsolved shootings on the 385 bypass.

"Ms. Carly, when we getting started?"

"Shortly," she said, blocking the memories. She turned to Trinity. The eighteen-year-old would graduate from the program in two weeks, an accomplishment that had been hard to envision five months ago. Surly and uncooperative, she'd only been there because the alternative was prison. But somewhere around two months into the program, Carly had broken through the hard shell encasing the girl and helped her see her worth, freeing the prisoner inside. Breakthroughs like she'd had with Trinity kept her going.

Carly scanned the room again. Jenna now stood facing the window with her arms wrapped around her thin body. Carly stepped closer to Trinity and lowered her voice. "Could you try and engage Jenna? Let her know she's in a safe place?"

Trinity glanced toward the other girl. "She's been through a lot. Not going to be easy for her to trust."

Carly queried her with her eyes.

"She's been trafficked."

The bottom dropped out of Carly's stomach and her knees threatened to buckle. Instinctively, she fingered the chain around her wrist. Why had Jenna been put in her group? The director knew she didn't counsel victims of human trafficking. "How do you know?"

Even as she asked, she recognized the symptoms in Jenna—avoiding eye contact, isolating herself, like now at the window, arms crossed over her body for protection. She'd heard the facility planned to take in rescued women who had drug and alcohol problems, but she thought they'd be in their own group. Trafficked girls dealt with more than addiction and would need specialized treatment.

The director didn't know Carly's history, only that she wanted to focus on counseling victims of substance abuse. No one knew her story except her psychiatrist, Laura Abernathy, and her friend, Jamie Parker. Carly rubbed the scar below her left elbow, feeling the ridge that surgery had not been able to completely erase. Her first impulse was to call Dr. Abernathy or maybe Jamie.

No. Both women would only tell Carly to face this challenge head-on, even though she didn't want to. Not right now.

She had two weeks of vacation coming. Maybe now was the time to take it. But what if it was too short notice? She wouldn't know unless she tried, and as soon as this session ended, she'd put in for her leave.

But there was nothing to be done for this session except see it through. She turned to Trinity. "Call the girls together," she said, her voice cracking. "I'm going to grab a water bottle and my pen and pad."

The teenager shot an odd glance toward her, then arranged the chairs in a circle and announced the start of the meeting.

One by one the girls took a chair while Carly sipped her water. It did little to relax her throat. *Focus on getting the meeting started and then let the girls take over.* Maybe she could plead a sore throat . . . No, she could do this.

Jenna was the last to take a seat at the far side of the circle. Carly scanned the waiting faces, stopping at a girl who'd been at the facility two months. Taylor was inches from a breakthrough. Could be today. Her gaze finally rested on the new girl. Jenna never looked up from studying her fingers.

"Good morning," she said and received mostly mumbles from the girls. It was going to be a long day. "Tell me how you feel today. What are your P.I.E.S.?"

Each session started with the patients telling where they stood physically, intellectually, emotionally, and spiritually. No one spoke up. Carly waited. Finally, Trinity nodded toward the girl sitting next to her with her head ducked. "Birdie's upset."

The girl elbowed Trinity. "My name's not Birdie. It's Holly."

The girls had nicknamed her Birdie because of her small frame and quick movements. "But are you upset?" Carly asked.

Holly lifted her shoulder in a shrug.

Carly waited again.

Huffing a breath, Holly said, "My mama came to see me Sunday afternoon."

That explained a lot. Her mother's visits usually left the girl angry for days. "You want to talk about it?"

"Not really." She picked at her thumb. "When she left I was wiped. She told me if I wasn't so dumb, I'd already be out of here."

Carly's jaw tightened. She'd counseled with the woman, asking her to be positive when she came to see her daughter. Maybe it was time to let the director deal with her. Before she could encourage her, Trinity spoke up.

"You're not dumb."

"She said I had to get new friends when I got out too."

"She's right about that," another of the girls said.

Holly pressed her lips together. "I know it's what I have to do, but I don't have to like it."

"You'll be right back here if you don't find new friends," Trinity said.

Carly nodded. "That's right. Who can tell me why?"

"Because they'll want you to party with them," Trinity said. "They'll tell you that one drink or a snort won't hurt you."

Another girl agreed. Jenna never spoke up as the group batted the question around, and Carly directed the discussion back to their P.I.E.S., asking each girl to talk about how they were feeling. She kept an eye on Jenna, noticing her agitation when the discussion turned to God.

"God is my best friend," Trinity said. "He had a good plan for my life, and I messed it up, but he's gonna take my mistakes and make something good from them."

"Oh, give me a break! What if you didn't make a mistake and

you were just at the wrong place at the wrong time!" Jenna stood and palmed her hands toward the group. "Y'all can sit here and listen to this baloney, but I'm out of here."

She turned and bolted from the room.

Carly took a deep breath. Everything in her wanted to let the girl go.

Patricia Bradley is the author of *Standoff*, *Obsession*, and *Crosshairs*, as well as the Memphis Cold Case novels and the Logan Point series. Bradley won an Inspirational Reader's Choice Award in Romantic Suspense, a Daphne du Maurier Award, and a Touched by Love Award; she was a Carol Award finalist; and three of her books were included in anthologies that debuted on the *USA Today* bestseller list. She is cofounder of Aiming for Healthy Families, Inc., and she is a member of American Christian Fiction Writers and Sisters in Crime. Bradley makes her home in Mississippi. Learn more at www.ptbradley.com.

Also by
PATRICIA BRADLEY . . .

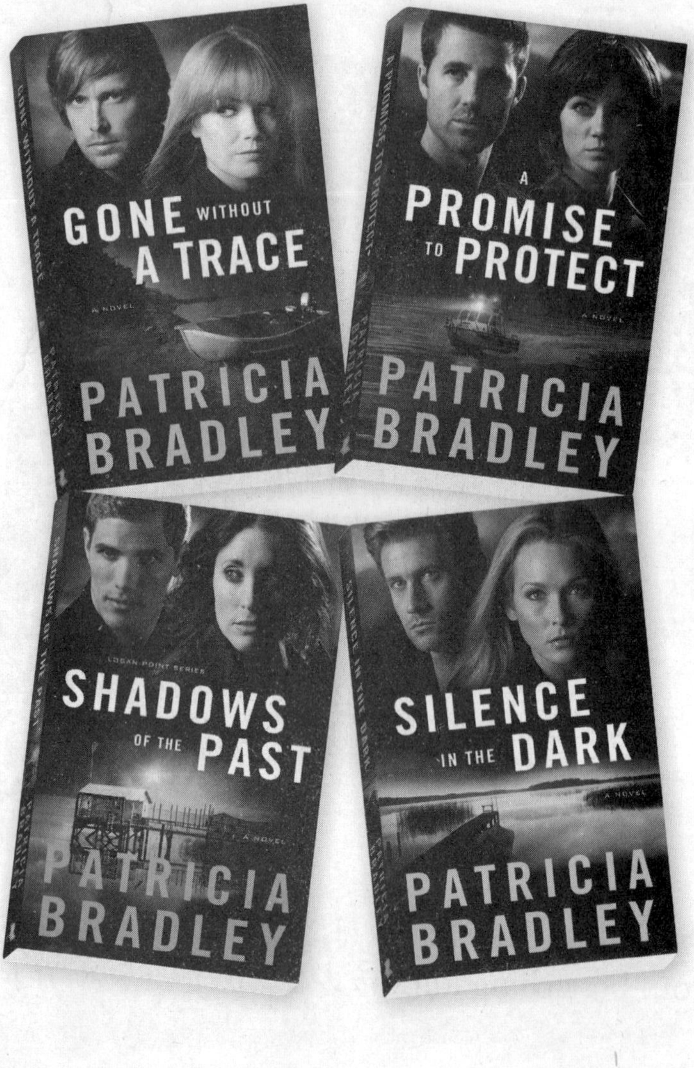

Revell
a division of Baker Publishing Group
www.RevellBooks.com

Available wherever books and ebooks are sold.

Meet

Patricia BRADLEY

www.ptbradley.com

 PTBradley1

 Patricia Bradley Author

- Share or mention the book on your social media platforms. Use the hashtag #Crosshairs. Write a book review on your blog or on a retailer site.
- Pick up a copy for friends, family, or anyone who you think would enjoy and be challenged by its message!
- Share this message on Twitter, Facebook, or Instagram: **I loved #Crosshairs @PatriciaBradley // @RevellBooks**
- Recommend this book for your church, workplace, book club, or small group.
- Follow Revell on social media and tell us what you like.

RevellBooks

RevellBooks

RevellBooks

Pinterest.com/RevellBooks